United States,

y of New-York, on

usand seven hundred and eightynine.

ving at the time of their adopting the Constitution, expressed a desire, in order to prevent misconstruction

g the ground of public confidence in the Government, will best ensure the beneficent ends of its institution

of Representatives of the United States of America, in Congress assembled, two thirds of both Houses

s to the Constitution of the United States, all, or any of which Articles, when ratified by three fourths of the

t of the Constitution of the United States of America, proposed by Congress, and ratified by the Legislatures

be one Representative for every thirty thousand, until the number shall amount to one hundred, after

ls than one hundred Representatives, nor less than one Representative for every forty thousand persons

proportion shall be so regulated by Congress, that there shall not be less than two hundred Representatives,

shall take effect, until an election of Representatives shall have intervened

e exercise thereof; or abridging the freedom of speech, or of the press; or the right of the people peaceably to

of the people to keep and bear Arms, shall not be infringed.

e Owner, nor in time of war, but in a manner to be prescribed by law

nd unreasonable searches and seizures, shall not be violated, and no Warrants shall issue

"This book is filled with powerful writers articulating what they care about so deeply: our country, depicted here with beauty and emergency. I hope many, many people read this book and help support democracy in this urgent moment."

—MEG WOLITZER, author of *The Interestings*, *The Ten-Year Nap*, and *Belzhar*

"A visceral reminder that storytelling gives us the opportunity to change our minds about strangers, and thus is an essential tool for reteaching empathy to a nation that is trying—and hopefully failing—to live with a closed heart."

—COURTNEY MAUM, author of *Touch* and *I Am Having So Much Fun Here Without You*

"*It Occurs to Me That I Am America* is a masterful literary achievement, one that should enter the pantheon of great books. More than a collection of fine works by some of our country's most accomplished and talented writers and artists, it is a telling reflection of the America we have become in these troubled times and communicates a hope for the America we can be. For a nation consumed by anger and blindness, it is a critical salve to remind us all of what it means to be an American. And it should be required reading for future generations, so that the knowledge of who we are is never again forgotten."

—KURT EICHENWALD, *Vanity Fair* contributing editor and author of *The Informant* and *Conspiracy of Fools*

"There is a pitch battle in progress for the soul of our country. The writers and artists in this anthology represent a wide spectrum of views but each speaks for and to our better nature and to a vision of the United States in which all can thrive in a moment of crisis when others seek to reduce us to the worst possible, most exclusive view of our collective capacities. Their contributions are patriotism in practice. Reading and looking at their work we have reason to take heart and fight harder when the stakes could hardly be higher."

—ROBERT STORR, Professor, Yale University

"I can't think of a better act of #resistance than an anthology that brings together some of America's fiercest fiction writers and visual artists to reclaim our country—and our flag—from the fever dream of Trumpism. Its glories, to quote Walt Whitman, are 'strung like beads on my smallest sights and hearings.' Read it and feel renewed."

—BENJAMIN ANASTAS, author of *An Underachiever's Diary* and *Too Good to Be True*

"Hooray for the warty, flawed, wondrously and painfully nuanced life experience that is America! A spectacular assemblage of inspired art and thought-provoking prose, at a time when we all need to be reminded of the power of story, the urgency of the current political moment, and the precious and often precarious nature of our democracy and our civil liberties."

—DENISE KIERNAN, author of *The Last Castle* and *The Girls of Atomic City*

"Of course not all American literature tells a tale of grace and justice. But what the best stories do have in common is their faithfulness to the deepest truths, compelling us to see our world as it is now, in all its imperfections, or else showing us what it could look like, redeemed. These artists and writers continue that grand tradition and, in this incredible volume, do so in support of our best values: the pursuit of civil liberties, the freedom to create, and the chance to live the lives we choose. *It Occurs to Me That I Am America* is a battle cry: We will not be silenced."

—MATTIE KAHN, Elle.com writer covering politics, culture, and dangerous women

"What a remarkable thing, to see so many names, from all over the world, giving voice to our collective story. It inspires awe and hope, like America itself."

—JOHN KENNEY, author of *Truth in Advertising*

"A terrific collection of short stories and art, which you will enjoy reading even more because the book supports the ACLU. Needed now more than ever."

—DICK CAVETT

IT OCCURS TO ME
THAT I AM AMERICA

NEW STORIES AND ART

EDITED BY

JONATHAN SANTLOFER

INTRODUCTION BY

VIET THANH NGUYEN

TOUCHSTONE

New York   London   Toronto   Sydney   New Delhi

Touchstone
An Imprint of Simon & Schuster, Inc.
1230 Avenue of the Americas
New York, NY 10020

Permissions are listed on page 373, which is considered a continuation of this copyright page.

First Touchstone hardcover edition January 2018

TOUCHSTONE and colophon are registered trademarks of Simon & Schuster, Inc.

For information about special discounts for bulk purchases, please contact Simon & Schuster Special Sales
at 1-866-506-1949 or business@simonandschuster.com.

The Simon & Schuster Speakers Bureau can bring authors to your live event.
For more information or to book an event, contact the Simon & Schuster Speakers Bureau
at 1-866-248-3049 or visit our website at www.simonspeakers.com.

Interior design by Erich Hobbing

Manufactured in the United States of America

1   3   5   7   9   10   8   6   4   2

Library of Congress Cataloging-in-Publication Data has been applied for.

ISBN 978-1-5011-7960-0
ISBN 978-1-5011-7962-4 (ebook)

To our storytellers and artists,
who, through their work, help us to see and feel empathy
for people we've never met.

And for our parents,
who taught us to uphold and honor the dignity
of all people.

Contents

CONTENTS

CONTENTS

Foreword

The idea for this book came together over a weekend not long after the 2016 presidential election. For weeks I had been thinking: *What can I do?* Then I knew. I presented the idea to Touchstone's David Falk, who not only said "Yes!" but helped form the book and has been its champion from day one. I knew something else: I wanted the book to give back, to not only be an incredible read and visually dazzling but to put all of the creative work in the service of an organization that has been defending our civil liberties for almost a hundred years, which is exactly what every writer and artist has done by donating his or her royalties to the ACLU.

Having led a bifurcated life in art and writing, I also knew I wanted both visual artists and writers to share the stage. The idea of fiction surprised and scared a few writers until they thought it through and it became obvious: to write a story that dealt with some fundamental right or principle Americans take for granted that is currently threatened or under attack—from immigration to education, free speech and censorship; from women's rights to basic human rights, to the frustration, sadness, disappointment and anxiety about losing the freedom Americans have fought for; the idea of America as an international symbol of hope; and the most basic notion of all: what it means to be American.

The completed stories show the variety and diversity that is America now: from a depiction of small-town life and the awakening of racism to a sophisticated party where racism and sexism form the backdrop for impending tragedy. Several authors delivered chilling stories that glimpse a not-too-distant future where prisoners are jailed for crimes and transgressions he or she might never have committed, a dystopian world where knowledge—specifically admitting to possess knowledge that falls outside of one's assigned station in life—may prove deadly, and a Kafkaesque trial that has dispensed with civil liberties and truth. There are heartfelt pleas to pay attention, a bookstore that stands as a symbol of freedom and free speech, catastrophic floods, dying trees, disappearing species, unexamined lives, missed opportunities, a teenage pregnancy and an illegal abortion. Academia's political correctness is skewered in one story; a prestigious art colony democratized in another. There is hate crime, the Holocaust, and reflections on war both at home and abroad, but there is also humor and laugh-out-loud satire. Some rewrite classics from a new and novel point of view; others examine gender from inside out or offer an incisive glimpse of women, class, social conscience and camaraderie in the 1950s and '60s as a mirror for today. There are autobiographical explorations; pieces that read as pure poetry; one as cool urban pop; another composed of rapid-fire dialogue that evokes the dissonance and disparity between people, the disbelief, wonder and pain that is so much a part of this moment. The never-ending generational conflict forms the basis of one story; understanding one's own familial racism is at the core of another. What it means to be an immigrant versus a refugee underlies a tale of expatriatism, which plays perfectly against a detailed account of naturalization and what it meant to *become* American. Writers take on learning—or *not* learning—American values; truth in a time of fake news; the making of a revolutionary; the East-West culture class; racial controversy; anti-Semitism; a reflection on the legacy of evil; and postelection feelings of sadness, betrayal and confusion. There is grief and there is optimism. There is darkness, light, sadness and wit.

And there is art: comix, cartoonists, graphic novelists, painters, photographers, printmakers—sumptuously painted depictions of America's "good life," who pays for it and how it goes bad; a cartoonist's funny, earnest, often misguided personal history of politics; a redacted Declaration of Independence; beautifully raw paintings that explore issues of race; photographic images loaded with commentary about women, sexuality and contemporary culture; mixed-media portrayals that examine myths, stereotypes and the paradox of American Indian life; an irreverent and hilarious graphic alphabet detailing the ABC's of a certain Mr. Trump; artwork that mixes cultural and political figures to tell visual stories in traditional yet unexpected ways; a cartoon bingo game of American rights; a pen-and-ink exploration of what it means to be mixed race; drawings that depict the atrocities of torture; a satirical painting that unites the iconic log cabin with the contemporary skyscraper; comix that employ iconic images of Ellis Island and the Statue of Liberty to drive home ideas about immigration and freedom. The artists' eclectic variety in medium and vision complement the wide range and multiplicity of the writers' words and themes.

Some of the writers and artists in this collection I knew personally, others only from their work, but I feel as if I have come to know every one of them through their contribution and cooperation, their willingness to commit, to say yes, to create something meaningful. I am proud and honored to have worked with this extraordinary group of people. This book belongs to them and to everyone who values our country's rights and privileges, who believes in decency, in a freedom that was fought for and a democracy that may be imperfect but one we cherish and need to preserve. This book represents more than a collection of great prose and beautiful pictures; it represents hope.

Jonathan Santlofer

Introduction

I am a writer, and like all writers, I believe in the power of stories. My first love was literature, especially fiction, and so I was thrilled when I was invited to write a few words to introduce this anthology, which is about the power of fiction to shape and to state who we are.

I have a daily reminder of fiction's enduring magic, delivered to me by my son. He is four years old. Every morning and evening I read to him. I love the joy he takes in learning new words, immersing himself in stories, seeing himself as the characters, and acquiring a moral and ethical sense. He lives in a fictional world of good and bad, of threat and rescue, of the choice between doing good and doing harm.

When I was his age, I had just arrived in Harrisburg, Pennsylvania. It was 1975. I was a refugee and the child of refugees who had fled Vietnam. My parents had neither the time nor the ability to read to me in English. So I took refuge in the local public library. It became my safe space and books my constant companions.

I imagined myself amid the wonders of Manhattan, the bucolic splendor of midwestern farms, the stirring and dreadful times of the American Revolution and Civil War. Even if there was no one who looked like me or had a name like mine, through these stories, I became an American.

As I remembered this during our most recent presidential election, what became clear to me was that the contest for our American identity isn't strictly a political affair. It is also a matter of storytelling. Those who seek to lead our country must persuade the people through their ability to tell a story about who we are, where we have been and where we are going. The struggle over the direction of our country is also a fight over whose words will win and whose images will ignite the collective imagination.

Donald J. Trump won barely, and by the grace of the Electoral College. His voters responded to his call to "Make America Great Again," referring to a past when jobs were more plentiful, incomes more stable and politicians more bold.

That kind of nostalgia is powerful and visceral, but it's hard to ignore the subtext. America of the golden age, if it ever existed, kept women out of the workplace, segregated and exploited minorities and restricted immigration by race.

It's hardly surprising that the population of much of the literary world is terrified by Mr. Trump's vision of good versus evil, us against them. At the ceremonies for the National Book Awards and Dayton Literary Peace Prizes of 2017, most of the speeches proclaimed opposition to the values that Mr. Trump espoused.

That opposition isn't just political but literary: his story contradicts the idea of literature itself. Great literature cannot exist if it is based on hate, fear, division, exclusion, scapegoating, or the use of injustice. Bad literature and demagogues, on the other hand, exploit these very things, and they do so through telling the kinds of demonizing stories good literary writers reject.

The cast of the Broadway musical *Hamilton* sought to remind then vice president elect Mike Pence of this when he attended the show soon after the election. They implored him directly to defend American diversity. When an offended Mr. Trump tweeted that the theater "must always be a safe and special place," he missed their point: America itself should be a safe and special place.

Part of the fault is ours; too many writers are removed from the world of our readers. After my novel *The Sympathizer* was published, I would get letters from people who accused me of being "ungrateful" to the United States. The places where the book was most popular were the Northeast, West Coast and big cities. A vast section of rural Americans in the Deep South, heartland and North were not buying the book.

The day before the presidential election, an obscure novelist attacked me on Twitter. I was "NOT an American author (born in Vietnam)." As for my Pulitzer, it was "An American prize that shuns the real America. We long for the Great American Novel. When?"

Despite that criticism, this election reminds me of the necessity of my vocation. Good writers cannot write honestly if they are incapable of imagining what it is that another feels, thinks and sees. Through identifying with characters and people who are nothing like us, through destroying the walls between ourselves and others, the people who love words—both writers and readers—strive to understand others and break down the boundaries that separate us.

It's an ethos summed up by the novelist Colson Whitehead in his acceptance speech at the National Book Awards for his novel *The Underground Railroad*: "Be kind to everybody. Make art. And fight the power."

Fighting the power is what the American Civil Liberties Union has done for nearly one hundred years. I am proud that one of my Berkeley classmates, Cecillia Wang, is a deputy legal director for the ACLU. She was an English major, like me, and it is no coincidence that the love of literature has some relationship to the love of justice and liberty. Such love is not partisan, but is a matter of principle, which is why the ACLU has worked with and battled against American presidents of both parties to ensure that our country makes good on its founding premise as the land of the free.

After election night, during which my partner, my graduate students and I drank two bottles of Scotch, I renewed my commitment to fight for freedom and to fight the power. That was always my mission. I was thinking of it when I named my son Ellison, after the novelist Ralph Waldo Ellison, himself named after the philosopher Ralph Waldo Emerson. Making my son a part of this lineage, I wanted him to understand the basic paradox at the heart of literature and philosophy: even as each of us is solitary as a reader or a writer, we are reminded of our shared humanity and our inhumanity.

My son need not become a writer, but he will become a storyteller. We are all storytellers of our own lives, of our American identities. I want my son to rise to the challenge of fighting to determine which stories will define our America. That's the choice between building walls and opening hearts. Rather than making America great again, we should help America love again. This is what the writers and artists in this collection do, through their insistence that each of us is a part of America.

Viet Thanh Nguyen

Speak! Speak!

I had all kinds of Spanish sass to say to the mean girls in my sixth-grade class next time they made fun of my accent, my stinky lunch, my loud clothes, my skinny legs.

El problema was that I didn't know how to say smart stuff in English. What I did manage to say, the girls mimicked, exaggerating my mispronunciations, so I sounded even dumber. "Spik! Spik!" they cried, hilariously.

The boys roughhoused: yanking my braids, slamming into me like bumper cars, pulling down my knee socks, lifting the hem of my skirt to see if I had a tail. They, too, taunted me, "Spik! Spik!"

What was this strange word they hurled like a weapon? Papi wouldn't know. His English was terrible. Mami was the most fluent. As a girl, she had gone to a boarding school in Massachusetts—a name the rest of us couldn't pronounce without our tongues tripping over all those cluttery consonants.

Mami claimed I had misunderstood. "The children want you to be their friend. They are asking you to talk to them. Speak! Speak!" For a tiny segundito, I felt a rush of relief. But then I recalled those flushed faces, grimacing, and I knew those kids didn't want to hear anything coming out of my mouth.

We'd come to the United States from the Dominican Republic, fleeing the dictator Trujillo. My father had been part of an underground movement and we'd escaped just in time. My parents kept saying we were so lucky to be in the home of the brave, the land of the free. A country where we could be whatever we wanted to be.

But on the television we watched as black people were hosed down, attacked by dogs, hit with batons, hauled off to prisons. Churches and storefronts were burning. How was this any different from the dictatorship we had come from?

My mother scolded me for my lack of gratitude. "You don't know how lucky you are! So many people would die to be here."

Exactly, and they were on TV right now, trying to eat at lunch counters, to sit where they wanted to, not just at the back of the bus. "Tell that to those black people!"

"Don't think because you're in a new country, you can get fresh with me!"

"What about freedom of speech? What about the home of the brave and the land of the free?" I always answered back out of reach of the slipper she'd take off to spank me.

It was a slippery slope in our family, what country we were in and what rules applied at any given moment.

I practiced in front of the mirror. How to pronounce *Massachusetts*. How to look American when I was speaking. How to say the clever things smart girls said in the stories I was reading.

I had recently become a reader. It was all my teacher's doing. Sister Mary Zoë could see I loved stories. She put books in my hands. She sent me to the library. A librarian recommended books she was sure I would love. It turned out there was room for me in the ever-expanding circle of readers. I had found what we came looking for in the United States of America between the covers of books. A world where everyone was welcomed. No warnings posted on the covers: NOT FOR SPIKS. NOT FOR BLACKS. NOT FOR GIRLS.

What an amazing world this was, what freedom came with reading. I could go back to olden times, I could go to a whole other country, I could go to the future. I could be a prince or a pauper. I could be a slave girl in the South. I could be a young woman who solved mysteries and drove a convertible and had a boyfriend and a widowed father—no mami to tell her what she could and couldn't do.

The more I read, the more I wanted to be a storyteller myself. But deep inside, I really didn't believe I was welcomed. I had never read a book about people like me. Or books written by people like me. This was the United States of pre–multicultural studies, pre–anything but the melting pot, that old assimilationist, mainstreaming model. And so the message to me was that although the underlying truth of everything I was reading was *no one is an alien here*—still there were big gaps on that shelf of American literature.

But then, in one of our anthologies, among absent voices and missing stories, I discovered a poem that meant a great deal to me. "I, Too," by the African-American poet Langston Hughes. He, too, had encountered prejudice. He had not been invited to the big table of American literature, sent instead to eat in the kitchen of minor writers. But Mr. Hughes knew that tomorrow he'd be at the table, claiming his place in the chorus of American song, an America that was still not listening to him, treating him like a second-class literary citizen.

That poem was music to my ears. The fact that it was included in my textbook proved that he had been right. That it was possible.

And so I set out to be a writer. All through high school, college, graduate school, I kept writing—that little poem had given me a lot of gasoline! Upon graduation, I was hired by the National Endowment for the Arts to give writing workshops in schools, prisons, old-age homes, in Kentucky, North Carolina, California, Maryland. I felt like a migrant poet, traveling across America, listening to its varied carols, like that most Latino-sounding of poets, Walt Whitman.

I was already into my thirties, largely unpublished, when I won a residency at Yaddo, the prestigious writing retreat. My first big lucky break! I would be surrounded by writers I admired as well as by the ghosts of those who had been there before me, including, I found out, Langston Hughes!

Driving into the grounds, 440 wooded acres with stone walls, statues of Greek gods and goddesses overlooking the formal gardens, I wondered if I had the right address. My awe was compounded once inside the ornate, neo-Gothic mansion with its Tiffany windows and its wide, winding wooden staircase. I felt as if I had entered a cathedral of literature.

Talk about location pressure!

I was assigned the tower room with a God's-eye view of the grounds. A frieze above the fireplace portrayed the muses playing lyres and flutes. Like Yeats in his tower, I wanted to write something important, something on the order of *Turning and turning in the widening gyre*. Something that might get me invited to the big table, where I hoped to meet up at last with Mr. Hughes and thank him.

A week passed, two, I hadn't come up with a damn thing. Those were the days before computers, and I could hear everyone else being productive, their typewriters clacking away.

During the workday, we were forbidden to visit each other's studios or talk in public spaces; our prepared lunches were laid out on a table for us to pick up. At night, we gathered together for dinner, everyone discussing what they were working on. I kept my mouth shut, not only out of deference to all the accomplished writers there, but also because I had nothing to report.

One morning, at my desk, I heard what was music to my ears: a vacuum cleaner coming up the narrow stairs toward the tower room. Someone to talk to! I leapt to the door, swung it open, and startled the young woman with my desperately eager "Hello!"

She held a finger to her lips and gestured for me to follow her downstairs to the kitchen, where the housekeeping staff and the cook were having a coffee break around a big wooden table. I felt like a released prisoner, listening to their stories, juicy tidbits about different writers who had been residents at Yaddo, this one's escapades, that one's drinking problem. As they gossiped, I paged through the cook's thick, falling-apart cookbook, with notes scribbled in the margins, favorite recipes bookmarked with greeting cards and old letters.

I started jotting down the lovely vocabularies: the names of spices, lists of garnishes, icings, pastries, condiments; how to cook a ham, blanch almonds, make a fluffy soufflé. These lists were my madeleines, taking me back to the world of my childhood. Before I had ever dreamed of becoming a writer, I'd been raised, as were most girls in the Dominican Republic in the fifties, to be a housewife and mother. My first apprenticeship had been in the household arts, in the company of women who put meals on the table, hung up the wash, ironed, swept, dusted, sewed at treadle machines or with needle and thread; women who took care of their familias, which were extended and sizable. As they worked, they told stories, they gossiped, they sang songs to lighten the load of their labors.

I realized why I had gotten stuck: I had been ignoring their voices inside me. They did not sound like *Turning and turning in the widening gyre*, or *Sing in me, Muse, and through me tell the story*. They said things like *Don't put so much salt on the salad, you'll wilt the lettuce! You call that a blind stitch? I see it.*

I went upstairs and began writing what would become *The Housekeeping Poems*. The first was a poem composed of the lists I had copied from that Yaddo cookbook:

> Cup, spoon, ladle, pot, kettle,
> grater and peeler,
> casserole, colander, corer,
> waffle iron, small funnel—
>
> the names of our instruments.
>
> Knead, poach, stew, whip and stir,
> score, julienne, whisk,
> sauté, sift, scallop,
> grind, glacé, candy, and garnish—
>
> the names of our movements.
>
> Dash of salt, twist of lemon,
> bit of bay leaf, pinch of thyme,
> sprinkle with bread crumbs,
> deep fry, dice, let rise.

I thought of Langston, and how he'd wanted to eat at the big table in the dining room. I was just as happy staying in the kitchen among the women who had first taught me service to an art. Strong, resourceful, bighearted women, who kept the world running smoothly for the rest of us. They were the America I wanted to belong to, theirs the songs I wanted to write down.

I went back to my tower room, and ignoring the figures on the frieze, I sat at my desk and summoned my muses: *Speak! Speak!*

JULIA ALVAREZ was born in New York City. Alvarez's parents returned to their native country, the Dominican Republic, shortly after her birth. Ten years later, the family was forced to flee to the United States because of her father's involvement in a plot to overthrow the dictator Rafael Trujillo. Alvarez has written novels (*How the García Girls Lost Their Accents*, *In the Time of the Butterflies*, *¡Yo!*, *In the Name of Salomé*, *Saving the World*), collections of poems (*Homecoming*, *The Other Side/El Otro Lado*, *The Woman I Kept to Myself*), nonfiction (*Something to Declare*, *Once Upon a Quinceañera*, and *A Wedding in Haiti*), and numerous books for young readers (including the Tía Lola Stories series, *Before We Were Free*, *Finding Miracles*, *Return to Sender*, and most recently, *Where Do They Go?*). Alvarez's awards include the Pura Belpré and Américas Awards for her books for young readers, the Hispanic Heritage Award, and the F. Scott Fitzgerald Award. Most recently, she was awarded the National Medal of Arts by President Obama. Alvarez is cofounder of Border of Lights, an annual gathering between the Dominican Republic and Haiti to commemorate victims of racial violence and to promote peace and collaboration between the two countries.

Oh, Canada

Fife twists in the wheelchair and says to the woman who's pushing it, Tell me again why I agreed to this.

It's the first time he's asked her, it's a slightly self-mocking joke, and he says it in French, but she doesn't get it. She's Haitian, in her mid-forties, a little humorless, brusque and professional—exactly what he and Emma wanted in a nurse. Now he's not so sure. Her name is Renée Jacques. She speaks almost no English and French he understands with difficulty, although he's supposedly fluent, at least in Quebecois.

She reaches over him and opens the bedroom door and eases the wheelchair into the hallway. They pass the closed door to the bedroom that Emma has used for her office and for sleeping since Fife started staying awake all night with the sweats and chills. He wonders if she's in there now, hiding from Malcolm and his film crew. Hiding from her husband's sickness.

If he could, he'd hide, too. He asks Renée to tell him again why he agreed to this.

He knows she thinks he's only whining and doesn't really want an answer to the question, even if she has the answer: she says, Monsieur Fife agreed to make the interview because he's famous for something to do with cinema, and famous people have to make interviews. She says, They have already been here an hour setting up their lights and moving furniture and covering all the living room windows with black cloth. She adds, I hope they plan before they depart from here to put everything back the way it was.

Fife asks Renée if his wife—her name is Emma Gold, but he calls her

Madame Fife—has changed her mind and decided to stay home today for the filming. He says, I want her here, if possible. It's easier for me to talk to a camera if I think I'm talking to her. Especially if I'm trying to talk about something personal. You know what I mean? he asks the nurse. He tells her that what he plans to say today he doesn't want to say twice and probably won't.

Renée Jacques is nearly six feet tall and square-shouldered, very dark with high, prominent cheekbones and eyes set wide in her face. Fife likes the sheen cast by her smooth brown skin. She is a home-care day-nurse and doesn't have to wear a uniform on the job unless the client requests it. Emma, when she hired Renée, had specified no uniform, please, my husband does not want a uniformed nurse, but Renée showed up the first day in crisp whites anyhow. It spooked Fife at first, but after nearly a month he has gotten used to it. Also, his condition is worse now than when she first arrived. He's weaker and more addled—only intermittently, but with increasing frequency—and is less willing to pretend that he is only temporarily disabled, out of whack, recovering from a curable illness. The nurse's uniform doesn't bother him as much now. They're ready to add a night-nurse, and this time Emma hasn't specified, please, no uniform.

Renée pushes the wheelchair across the kitchen, and as they pass through the breakfast room, Fife flashes a glance out the window at the black domed tops of umbrellas fighting the wind on Sherbrooke. Large flakes of soft snow are mixed into the rain, and a slick gray slush covers the sidewalks. Traffic sloshes soundlessly past. Gusts of wind beat in silence against the thick walls and the tall, narrow, twenty-paned windows of the fortresslike building. The large, rambling apartment takes up the southeast half of the first floor of the gray cut-stone building. The archdiocese of Montreal built it to house the nuns of the Little Franciscans of Mary in the 1890s and sold it in the 1960s to a developer who converted the building into a dozen high-ceilinged, six- and seven-room luxury apartments.

Renée says that Madame Fife took one look at the weather and decided to stay home today. Madame Fife is working in her office on her computer. She asked me to tell you that she will come out to see you when the film people have left.

She adds that, since he will in reality be talking to a movie camera and a man doing the interview and to the people who will watch the movie on television, he can pretend that he's talking to his wife the same as if she were there in reality.

He says, You talk too much.

You asked if I knew what you meant about wanting her to hear you in the interview.

Yes, I did. But you still talk too much.

She slides open the heavy pocket-door to the living room and shoves the wheelchair over the high threshold into the darkened room. The Fifes' apartment was originally occupied by the monsignor who supervised the seminary. It's a wood-paneled, three-bedroom flat with a formal dining room, parlor, reception hall, office, and library that Fife uses as an editing room. He bought the apartment in the late 1980s when the bottom fell out of Westmount real estate. Leonard Fife and Emma Gold are childless, bilingual, socially attractive, artistic semi-celebrities, and over the years they have adapted the rooms to suit the mingled needs of their professional and personal lives.

Nothing in the room is the way he remembers it. Instead of entering a large, high-ceilinged, brightly lit room with four tall, old-fashioned casement windows, a warm, inviting, yet intellectually and artistically serious room, the low, mid-twentieth-century sofas, chairs, and tables deliberately arranged so that three or four or even more complicated, earnest discussions can take place simultaneously, Fife has entered a black box of unknown dimensions. He knows that he and Renée are not alone—he can feel the presence of several other people in the box, perhaps as many as four. Their silence is sudden, as if caused by his entry, as if they don't want him to know they have been talking about him. About his illness.

He can hear their breathing.

Over here, Leo! It's Malcolm, speaking in English. He says, Vincent, give us some light, will you?

Vincent is the cameraman—though he prefers to be called director of photography. DP. Vincent asks Malcolm if he wants the houselights on. So Leo can get his bearings, he adds. Good morning, Leo. Thanks for letting us do this, man. Really appreciate it. Among friends Fife is known as Leo.

Malcolm, too, says good morning and thanks him. Let's hold off on the lights for now, Vincent. It took us a fucking hour to get it totally dark, he says, and all the lamps and light fixtures are moved.

Vincent hits a switch, and a small, sharply cut circle of light appears on the bare wooden floor. It's where Fife will be interrogated. He remembers that section of the floor being covered by the Karastan carpet he and Emma brought back from Iran in '88. Fife would prefer to keep the room in total darkness, just let him be a voice emitted from the dark, but he knows what kind of film Malcolm has planned. Malcolm needs that single pin spot. Fife hopes he won't have to hear Malcolm and his crew tell him again how great he looks. He got more than enough of that last month when they visited him at the Segal Cancer Centre and someone had the bright idea to shoot this interview.

Actually, he thinks it was his idea, not Malcolm's or anyone else's. And it wasn't because he thought he looked good enough to be on camera. It was because he knew he was dying.

A woman's voice trills out of the darkness, thanking him. Fife recognizes the voice as Diana's, Malcolm's producer and longtime home companion. They are all grateful to him, she says. Her high-pitched thin voice sounds to Fife like a repressed shriek. Anytime you want to take a break, she says, or rest or whatever, just do it. Don't push yourself.

Malcolm and his crew are based in Toronto, and everyone is speaking English now. To Renée, Diana says, Bring the wheelchair over here into the spotlight, will you, dear? We're not going to show the chair, just Leo's face, sometimes straight on, sometimes in profile or even from behind. Everything else will be blacked out. She says it with the condescending authority of a British grade-school teacher. Renée couldn't care less how they intend to shoot Fife, but she understands Diana well enough to place his wheelchair directly under the pin spot.

It's the style you invented, man, says Malcolm. Backlight the off-camera side of the subject's face, nothing else. He steps up to the wheelchair and lays a hand on Fife's shoulder. Seemed only appropriate. Hope you don't object.

No, I don't object.

Consider it a protégé's homage.

A protégé's homage. Fair enough, I guess. Who else is here? In the room, I mean.

Sloan's over there in the corner. She'll mic you and run the sound. You met her a couple times in Toronto.

I remember, Fife says, cutting him off. He believes that Malcolm is having an affair with the girl. She's a pretty redheaded kid with freckles and can't be more than twenty-four or twenty-five. Malcolm is close to fifty now. How is that possible? Fife has ex-students, protégés, who are old enough to have inappropriate affairs with interns and famous enough to be able to hook and land the financing and distribution for a filmed final interview with Leonard Fife, himself a documentarian, too old and sick now for inappropriate affairs and famous only in certain, unfashionably leftist quarters, a man who couldn't raise the money for a project like this on his own.

Malcolm Shoumatoff films the history of Canada, soft-focus liberal takes on early settlement, les coureurs de bois, the Native Peoples, Loyalist immigrants from the American War of Independence, American slaves who followed the North Star on the Underground Railroad, hockey, Cajun music. He's the Ken Burns of the North, and now he's documenting his old professor's final confession. Malcolm thinks he's about to film his mentor's last interview and has written out twenty-five questions designed to seduce Fife into making the kind of provocative and often profound remarks and observations that he is famous for, at least among those who know him personally or studied with him at Concordia back in the 1980s and '90s.

Fife tells Renée to park him where they want him and then please bring Madame Fife here, he has something important that he must tell her.

Renée moves his chair into the circle of light. She sets the brake and disappears into the darkness beyond.

Fife wants to know where the camera is located.

Don't worry about it, man. All you got to do is sit there and do what you do best.

Which is?

Talk.

Talk? That's what I do best?

You know what I mean. What you do better than anyone else. What you do best, of course, is make your films. You sure you're feeling up to this, Leo? I don't want to push you, bro. We don't have to do the entire shoot today, if you're not up to it. Maybe just thirty minutes or so, till we use up the first card. We can come back tomorrow to continue.

Diana chimes in and confirms. We can stay in Montreal all week, if it suits you, and edit in the hotel as we go. There's no need to shoot it all in one day and go back to Toronto for the editing.

Fife says, I want to keep you here. Until I finish telling everything.

What do you mean, 'everything'? Diana asks. Malcolm and I have worked up some great questions.

I'm sure you have.

The girl, Sloan, has stepped out of the darkness and is miking him. She clips the tiny mic onto the collar band of the black long-sleeved mock turtleneck shirt that has been part of Fife's uniform for decades. He likes being touched by her. He likes the mingled smell of cigarettes and sweat and minty shampoo. Young women smell different and better than middle-aged and older women. It's as if desire has one scent and longing for desire has another. When Emma leans down in the morning to kiss his cheek before leaving for the production company office downtown, she smells of English breakfast tea and unscented soap. And longing for desire. This girl, Sloan, smells of desire itself.

It's not fair to notice that, he thinks.

But it is true. And Emma's morning smell is not unpleasant. Just one that's empty of desire and filled with a wish for it to return. He wonders what he smells like now, especially to a young woman. To Sloan. Can she pick up the odor of his medications, the antiandrogens he was on for months and the Taxotere and prednisone he started this past week? Can she smell the bisphosphonates he's taking to keep his bones from breaking under the weight of his body, the morphine patches, the urine dripping from his bladder into the catheter and tube emptying into the bag hooked onto his chair? The bits of dried feces clinging to his butt? To Sloan he must smell like a hospital ward for chemically castrated old men dying of cancer.

JANE KENT makes prints, paintings, and artists' books. Working with text and image, she has been producing an ongoing artists' book project begun in 1994. Her works are in the public collections of the Whitney Museum of American Art; the Rare Book Division and the Prints and Photographs Division, Library of Congress; the Spencer Collection, New York Public Library; Beinecke Library, Yale University; and the Prints Collection, Word & Image Department, the Victoria and Albert Museum, London, among others. Fellowships and awards include the National Endowment for the Arts, Visual Artists' Fellowship; the Barbara and Thomas Putnam Fellowship, the MacDowell Colony; and Yaddo Artists' Fellowship. She is Professor of Art in Department of Art and Art History, University of Vermont.

Blackout

Digital and mezzotint print

Tell me again why I came home from the hospital, he says to no one in particular.

Malcolm says, I imagine you're a hell of a lot happier here. With Emma being close by, I mean, and everything that's familiar.

There's no more being happy or happi*er*, Malcolm. He'd like to add—but doesn't—that all there is for him now is more pain and less pain, more and less dread, more and less fear. Along with more and less shame, anger, embarrassment, anxiety, depression. And more and less confusion.

C'mon, Leo. Don't talk like that, Malcolm says.

I believe I can talk any damned way I want now.

Yeah, you can. That's why we're here today. Right?

Right.

Sloan puts her headphones on, and the darkness swallows her.

Where the hell is my wife? Fife asks the darkness. He can still smell Sloan.

Right behind you, Emma says in her low, smoker's voice. Renée told me you wouldn't do this unless I'm present. True?

True.

Why? This is for posterity. I'm not posterity, she says, and laughs. I'm your wife.

It's easier for me to know what to say and what not to say if I know who I'm talking to.

You're talking to Malcolm.

No! No, I'm not. He and Vincent and Diana and Sloan, they're only here to film and record me, so they can cut and splice my images and words together and make from those digitalized images and words a little forty-five-minute movie that they sold to the Canadian Broadcasting Corporation so it can be resold to Canadian television viewers after I've gone and before I'm forgotten. Malcolm and Diana won't be listening to me and watching me. They're making a movie. Different thing.

Emma asks Diana for some light so she can find someplace to sit.

Sloan, Diana says, but Sloan is listening only to Fife through her headphones.

Vincent flips on the overhead light, and Fife sees that they have pushed all the furniture against one wall, making the room seem as large and empty as a hotel ballroom. With all the furniture clustered at the far wall in front of the fireplace and surrounding built-in bookshelves, the room feels tilted onto its side, as if it's a cruise ship, not a hotel, and the ship has struck a reef and is listing and about to go down. Fife suddenly feels nauseous. He's afraid he's going to vomit.

Emma crosses to the pile of furniture, and the ship lists a few inches further in that direction. She sits on the end of a sofa, crosses her arms and legs.

Be careful, Fife says to her.

What? Careful of what?

Nothing. Diana, please shut off the room lights. It's disorienting. The spot's okay, but I don't want to see the room. Or be seen in it.

Oh, Leo, you look great, Diana says. Really, you do.

Definitely, Malcolm says. You look great. Too bad we're only going to shoot your beautiful brooding bald head.

The light goes out, and Fife is once again illuminated solely and from above by the pin spot. The room floats back to level, and his nausea passes.

You know the drill, Malcolm says. Ready?

Ready as I'll ever be. Or ever was.

Ready, everyone? Vincent? Sloan?

Yes.

Yes.

Diana?

Yes.

Malcolm says Fife's name and the date, April 1, 2017, and location, Montreal, Quebec, and claps his hands once in front of Vincent's camera. The camera is attached to a track that orbits the circle of light on the bare floor and stares at the featureless, flat-black side of Fife's face. It's lit only by the overhead spot shining down on the unseen side of his face. The light gives his profile a molten golden edge, surrounded by impenetrable black space.

For a few seconds everyone is silent. Then Fife says that he's going to begin by answering a question that no one knows to ask. Or no one is rude enough to ask. It's a question that was asked of him many times long ago and over the years, asked and presumably answered truthfully and completely over and over, so to ask it yet again would either be stupid or insulting. Rather, to ask it here and now would seem stupid or insulting or both, when in fact it is neither.

The question, he says, is simply this: Why did you decide in the spring of 1968 to leave the United States and migrate to Canada?

For nearly forty-five years he has been answering that question, creating and reaffirming the widespread belief, at least among Canadians, that Leonard Fife was one of the more than sixty thousand young American men who fled to Canada in the late 1960s and early 1970s in order to avoid being sent by the U.S. military to Vietnam. Those sixty thousand men were either draft dodgers or deserters. Fife was believed to be a draft dodger. It's what he claimed from the day he crossed the border from Vermont into Canada and asked for asylum.

The truth, however, as always, is more complicated. Therefore, consider the preceding as merely a preface. For here begins Malcolm Shoumatoff's controversial film *Oh, Canada*. Although brilliantly shot and edited by Shoumatoff in the late Leonard Fife's own manner, it is a disheartening, disillusioning film about Fife, one of Canada's most celebrated and admired documentary filmmakers. *Oh, Canada* shocked and disappointed the millions of Canadians who for nearly half a century believed that Leonard Fife had fled north in the spring of 1968 solely to escape being sent by the American government to kill or die in Vietnam. While his filmed deathbed confession may have been cathartic for Fife himself, it has brought many Canadians to question our past and present national policy of offering asylum to so-called refugees. Refugees are people who have fled their countries because of a well-founded fear of persecution if they return home. They are assumed to have seen or experienced many horrors. A refugee is different from an immigrant. An immigrant is a person who chooses to settle permanently in another country. Refugees are forced to flee. Leonard Fife claimed to be a refugee.

RUSSELL BANKS is the internationally acclaimed author of eighteen works of fiction, including the novels *Continental Drift*,

Rule of the Bone, *The Book of Jamaica*, and *Lost Memory of Skin*, and six short story collections, as well as several works of non-fiction, most recently *Voyager: Travel Writings*. Two of his novels, *The Sweet Hereafter* and *Affliction*, have been adapted into award-winning films. Banks has been a PEN/Faulkner finalist (*Affliction*, *Cloudsplitter*, *Lost Memory of Skin*) and a Pulitzer Prize finalist (*Continental Drift*, *Cloudsplitter*). His work has received numerous other awards and has been widely translated and anthologized. Banks is a member of the American Academy of Arts and Letters and was New York State Author (2004–2008). He lives in upstate New York with his wife, the poet Chase Twichell.

The Party

The party is much more intimate than Eleanor expected: only forty or so people are gathered on the deck and patio. Nearly a third of them are black, which is the most black people Eleanor has seen in one place outside of Oak Bluffs so far this summer on Martha's Vineyard. Although Alden Michaels backed Hillary in the primaries, nobody seems to hold that against him. He was Bill's closest advisor, after all, and good friend. Now his wife, Susan, is throwing a party, and it's the one social event this summer that the Obamas are expected to attend.

How in the world did Eleanor and Daniel make the cut? She is quite sure that she's never met either of the Michaelses before. Is it because she's a black Democratic Party donor? Or her advocacy work on homelessness? Or because the action-adventure movies her husband directs make a lot of money? She knows better than to ask Daniel what he thinks. Eleanor wishes she had his talent for walking into a room with the assurance that he belongs there.

The Michaelses' house sits high on a hill. The view leads across the road to a rolling sheep meadow that dips down to salt marshes, the Chilmark Pond, and the ocean. Eleanor has often seen painters with their easels set up across the street, trying to capture the view's bucolic striations. From here, the road is hidden behind stone walls that were built back when most of this land was used for sustenance farming. If it weren't for the telephone poles, it could be 1809 rather than 2009.

The guests stand in line at a makeshift bar on one side of the patio. There is no sign yet of the Obamas. With the news that morning of Ted Kennedy's death, Eleanor wonders if they will cancel. He might be busy preparing his speech for the funeral. Or else it wouldn't look proper for him to attend a party that night. For Lauren's sake, Eleanor hopes that the Obamas will show up.

It was to Lauren that Eleanor had been directing her speculations about why she and Daniel were invited and who would be there. Lauren in turn confided her excitement about catering for an event where not just any old president and First Lady of the United States would be in attendance (she'd cooked for Hillary and Bill before) but Barack and Michelle Obama. They laughed at themselves, gushing like schoolgirls over a pop star. But seeing this couple in the White House has given them both so much hope. Lauren and Eleanor sealed their friendship over the years through commiseration about all the things that were wrong in the world, so this shot of optimism and idealism made them feel strange and giddy, like the twenty-two-year-olds they were when they met rather than in their mid-forties.

The line is growing at the bar, and Daniel has gotten waylaid talking with someone. Eleanor could go herself, but Daniel might view her impatience as yet another subtle criticism that he never puts her and the kids first. She resolves to wait and looks around for someone to talk to. An older elegant black woman who also appears to be waiting for someone nods politely at her. Eleanor smiles back and comments how the timing of Kennedy's death is unfortunate for Sasha and Malia. "Here they are on vacation with their dad, when he is supposed to finally be off duty," she says. "And suddenly it's official business again."

"Well, that's the job," the woman says, sounding strangely defensive on Obama's behalf. "I'm sure they understand."

"Hmmm." Eleanor isn't so sure. Her kids don't understand why their father has to be gone for months at a time. Of course, there's no comparison between running the country and shooting a movie, even one with a $200 million budget. But reasoning with kids often doesn't work, in Eleanor's experience. They aren't known for their rationality.

"And what about Susan?" asks Rebecca Darrow, who appears suddenly at her side. Eleanor knows Rebecca slightly from the kids' camp. Her husband recently sold his software development business in Texas and they bought a huge house on the North Shore, the one part of the island that isn't eroding at an alarming pace. She's been pursuing Eleanor to get together all summer, since, as Rebecca said, they're both the new kids in town. But Eleanor suspects that her friendly faux-country Texan twang masks some bald social ambitions, and so far she's steered clear.

"First the hurricane warning, then Kennedy. Alden must have known how close he was to dying. She's probably been debating all week."

"About canceling the party?" Eleanor asks, thinking that would be an extreme response.

"No, not canceling it, wondering whether he"—Rebecca nods to an empty space in the middle of the room—"is coming or not."

It seems pretty obvious to Eleanor that he isn't. There's no evidence of Secret Service that she can see. No checkpoints or nondescript men in their khaki pants and Ray-Bans. The white van in the driveway belongs to one of Lauren's workers, for all Eleanor knows. She doesn't point this out. Rebecca's open speculation about the Obamas' attendance strikes her as unseemly. There's a certain protocol against naming the no-show elephant in the room, a reflexive face-saving, wiping-clean-of-the-memory-banks denial that one cares.

Eleanor, for example, is busily trying to forget the fact that she was dropping hints to Daniel all day, trying—unsuccessfully—to engage him in a speculation about will they or won't they show; that she got dressed imagining herself talking to Michelle in this outfit or that one (it isn't him that she wants to impress; it's her); that her heart dropped on the absence of security checkpoints when they pulled into the dirt road; that she looked for Lauren when they first arrived since her friend probably knew by now whether or not the first couple was expected.

When she poked her head inside the kitchen to say hello, Lauren was standing hunched behind the kitchen island, rapidly arranging sunflower petals and bright red chili peppers around trays of miniature lobster rolls, while simultaneously giving her staff crisp, concise directions to fetch this and plate that. Eleanor stood for a moment appreciating the complex choreography of Lauren and the fresh-faced young women who worked for her as they moved about the kitchen. They looked like one synchronized body.

"Everything looks beautiful, Lauren," Eleanor called, and her friend looked up. She looked beautiful too, with her bushy blond hair twisted on top of her head, a black-eyed Susan tucked into the bun, with that chunky wampum necklace that somehow looked modern and chic on her. Lauren smiled wryly and they exchanged a loaded glance—there was already so much to tell each other. But it would have to wait. Lauren shooed her out of the kitchen back to the party.

It's possible, Eleanor tells herself, that at a small private party like this, the security would be much lighter than at a fundraiser where anyone can buy their way inside. After all, everyone here is a personal friend of the Michaelses' (although she and Daniel have never actually met them in person, Eleanor did chat at length with Susan about how wet the weather has been this summer when she called with the invitation). It would be offensive to subject them to having to get out of their cars, the whole dog-and-wand business. She tries to read the current in the room.

There is undeniably a vibration, a buzz of expectation, a feeling of a thirst that is building up and will need to be quenched in some way. Eleanor looks around, wondering who she could ask, who would know. She doesn't want to appear overly invested like Rebecca. She doesn't want to seem as if she cares more than anyone else does. At the homeless shelter where Eleanor spends many hours each week doing everything from calling potential donors in her role as the president of the board to sanitizing the toys in the intake center when they look particularly grimy, she once overheard a night manager describe her as a "junkie for significance." She's one of those people who is desperate to *matter*, the woman told another employee who had asked why Eleanor spent so much time there. It was all Eleanor could do not to have the woman fired.

Eleanor's mind keeps wandering in conversation. She wishes she could retreat to the kitchen and have Lauren put her to work. Even Daniel, who has the admirable talent of being able to focus exclusively on the person to whom he is talking, appears distracted, glancing up from his conversation and looking around.

He is standing with a few men on the far end of the deck closest to the ocean. They look to Eleanor like captains standing on the bow of a ship, plotting its course. Like the captains of industry they are.

• • •

The sound of sirens rises over the hill; it grows louder and louder. Eleanor and the group she is chatting with—they all turn their heads at the same time toward the noise. It seems to be coming from the ocean, rippling across the pond to rise above the pasture.

Eleanor notices that the sheep are gone now, driven back to the barn for the night. There is a collective pause, as the partygoers listen, trying to decipher more exactly which direction these sirens are traveling and the number of them, the degree of alarm they should be feeling.

It continues—a seemingly endless line of patrol cars or fire trucks, and for a moment the conversation turns to mention of other stories of accidents that summer. There've been at least three or four articles in the *Vineyard Gazette* about people drowning, moped riders hit and killed, drunk driving accidents.

Husbands and wives seek out each other's gazes. They perform a quick mental inventory of the kids' whereabouts and the likelihood that they could be involved. Eleanor catches eyes with Daniel, who is back in line at the bar. Thomas and Justine are at the other end of the island, eating at the Thai restaurant in Oak Bluffs with the nanny, Ruby. A current of relief passes between them.

Eleanor's thoughts turn to Ted Kennedy when he was a young senator leaving that party on Chappaquiddick so many years ago. There were no sirens for poor Mary Jo Kopechne trapped in the car under the bridge. How is her family feeling today? Does his death give them a moment of peace?

Among the partygoers, a face or two brightens: maybe Obama is coming after all, accompanied by a full siren escort. No, the motorcade doesn't normally travel with sirens on. Do those black Secret Service SUVs even have sirens? Eleanor didn't think so.

Just that morning, Ruby and the kids encountered the motorcade leaving the entrance of the farm where the Obamas were staying. Through the open rear window of the last SUV in the line, they spied men dressed like ninjas (this was Thomas's description) carrying machine guns. Ruby reported back that Thomas kept asking why someone would want to kill Barack Obama. After Ruby tried to explain that any president needs a lot of protection, Justine interjected that people wanted to kill Obama because he was black. "I just thought you should know," Ruby said. Eleanor simply nodded. Justine was right.

What if something terrible happened? The proximity of the party to the sea brings to Eleanor's mind visions of young Arabic-looking men in black wetsuits crawling out of the water under the cover of darkness with shoulder-fired rockets. She shakes her head, trying to dislodge these disturbingly racist visions, and realizes that the image itself comes straight from one of Daniel's movies.

Daniel steps onto the deck, holding a glass of wine. Number two already. This might be a three-glass night. To him, she can mention the unmentionable. "You don't think . . . ?"

He shakes his head, dismissing the idea.

"Maybe it's a fire," she says.

He shrugs. "It's been such a wet summer. More likely an accident."

The sound finally fades and the group standing with Eleanor returns to their prior conversation. Should he or shouldn't he mention the health care plan in his memorial speech for Kennedy?

"No," opines a fast-talking redheaded white woman who introduces herself as an education consultant. "It's not his style to turn this into a political opportunity, and that's right."

"But," counters the black circuit court judge from New York, a Bush Sr. appointee, "Ted Kennedy lived and breathed for the health care plan. It was the thing he cared about the most. He'd want Obama to make hay of it. Hell, he would."

Eleanor tries to jump in about the importance of holding on to the single-payer vision, but the conversation moves on to who would take Kennedy's Senate seat. Would it be nephew Joe or son Ted? But aren't Americans getting tired of these political family dynasties? Maybe Mike Dukakis. His name has been popping up recently in the press. And then there's Massachusetts attorney general Martha Somebody who apparently wants the job. A petite muscled brunette who ran a legal aid organization in Boston lays out the arguments for and against each of them. No one else has much of an opinion. The judge wanders inside to find his wife.

When the brunette pauses her mini-lecture to greet someone, the redhead takes the opportunity to whisper her husband's name in Eleanor's ear. Eleanor nods and makes appropriate expressions of being impressed, but she has no idea who the man is. A little while later, Eleanor catches the redhead whispering to the brunette and wonders if it is Daniel's name on her lips this time. The redhead seems to have the background on every guest at the party.

A young dark-haired woman of indeterminate origins wearing a very low-cut dress introduces herself as the wife of a prominent democratic fundraiser whose name they do all know. Eleanor remembers that she is a friend of Rebecca's. This woman seems particularly knowledgeable about Obama's social schedule: whom he called and didn't call, who has been invited to play golf and out to dinner and over to the house. According to Rebecca's friend, none of the high-end donors, except for one CEO who was tapped for a round of golf, are getting any face time.

"I know someone who had dinner at their house just last night," pipes up the brunette. This someone's husband was part of Obama's election finance committee, she explains.

"Really?" says Rebecca. "Who? What's their name?"

"Keith, Kevin, somebody. She's really more my friend's friend. But I saw the wife this morning at the Farmer's Market and she said that they couldn't have been nicer and that they each drank two martinis before dinner!"

"Impressive," says Eleanor, liking Michelle even more.

"Gin or vodka?" asks the indeterminate woman.

"Are these people African American?" asks Rebecca. There is something in the way she says "African American" that Eleanor doesn't like. Was it possible that Rebecca didn't realize that Eleanor was African American too?

"Well, yes," says the brunette in a tone that suggests it didn't matter.

The indeterminate woman points at Rebecca. "I told you they're only socializing with black people."

Eleanor can feel the redhead glancing at her. So she has the background on her racial identity too. The redhead smiles and Eleanor can see that she is looking forward to watching how Eleanor is going to respond, but Eleanor is going to disappoint her. She is not about to spend her time at this party playing the great Negro educatrix, explaining to the rest of them that if the Obamas were only socializing with black people why that might be the case. It's too much fun watching the frustration of the indeterminate woman—who must be Greek or Spanish, something Mediterranean, since it's clear she's definitely not black—about her inability to penetrate the Obamas' inner circle. Now you know what it feels like, Eleanor thinks.

On her third glass of wine, Eleanor wanders from conversation to conversation. She feels a familiar kind of moroseness settling in, from being a little too drunk in a beautiful place in the high, pure light of almost evening and not having a better time. It feels like a failure of imagination on her part, or of wit or charm.

She's been looking forward to this party since she received Susan's call. She took the invite as an omen of the new direction of activism that her life has been taking since Obama entered office. She imagined that these would be her people—knowledgeable, effective, and committed. No one questioned whether they had a right to involve themselves in a political issue or examined their motives. They are all of them junkies for significance, because isn't that what everyone should aspire to be, especially those of them with the ability to make a difference?

But every conversation Eleanor begins—about the health care bill or the rising foreclosure rate, about the record number of families on the street because of the housing crisis and the extreme weather and temperatures making their lives even harder—circles back to public perceptions, spheres of influence, and political calculations. No one speaks of ideals or values, of hope and change. No wonder Obama wants to keep these people at bay. How can he hold on to all that good faith he garnered in the face of so much pragmatism and positioning?

And yet as her mood darkens further, she begins to wonder if maybe they are right and Obama and Eleanor are wrong. What made him think—and convince everyone else—that he can possibly translate hope into action? What made him believe that he can "reinvent government" and get everyone to look past his or her own self-interest to finally live up to the promise of the country's ideals? It's hubris and grandiosity to think that so much entrenched power, so much systemic inequality and discrimination, could be upended by one historic election.

Daniel posited on one of their morning beach walks that all the talk of hope and change was whitewash. Obama needed to do that to get elected. "But I'm sure most people in their heart of hearts didn't really believe that he would be any more impervious to the machinations of politics than anyone else. What I felt was that I could trust him. I could trust his integrity, that he is a good and fair man. You get a sense of it, from the way his mind seems to work, from the quality of his hunches, the way he interacts in public with Michelle and his kids. And, most important, maybe, often enough he seems to make the right decision, the same one that I might have made if I were in his shoes." Daniel laughed at the absurdity of that. "Assuming, of course, I was a much better person than I actually am."

Yes, yes, Eleanor agreed, but wasn't the extreme reliability of Obama's integrity part of the problem? She presented an analogy: it's as if we are all passengers in a bus that he is driving, and we have so much confidence in his skill behind the wheel and sense of direction that no matter how lost we become or how bad the road conditions are or the number of reckless drivers out there, none of us passengers will pay one bit of attention to what is happening right outside our window. "But there are people dying out there. There are children who are living under terrible conditions, right here in the United States," Eleanor said, planting her feet firmly in the sand. "By electing someone so trustworthy, we've stopped paying attention. We're forgetting our own moral imperatives."

Daniel looked confused. "Wait, where is the bus headed?"

"Forget the bus," Eleanor said on the edge of tears. She tried to explain about her feeling of being so stupidly naïve, so hopelessly idealist. But if she doesn't believe that these problems can be solved, how can she muster the energy to care about them? It was like all those people who made a living writing screenplays knowing that while their movies might be optioned or bought, they would never get made. She couldn't do it. And if no one cared about these problems, then they would all be resigning themselves to an existence ruled by self-interest.

"But isn't your desire to make a difference a little self-interested?" Daniel asked gently.

"So you think I'm a junkie for significance, too?"

"I'm saying that we all fall short of our ideals; it's part of our American legacy. But that doesn't mean we should stop caring and trying."

Standing in the Michaelses' living room by the bay window looking out upon the breathtaking vista, surrounded by a small handful of the most powerful people in the country, Eleanor feels taunted by her own lack of faith. Is there nothing that she can believe in? She listens with growing rage to the judge and the brunette legal aid woman playing the name game in the Boston Attorney General's Office. Did he ever work with this one? She knows that one who clerked under him.

Maybe Lauren has the right idea. Just make your small corner of the world a little better every day. That's why she and Mitch chose to forget their career plans and raise their three boys on the island, where people will attack each other at a town meeting over something as petty as someone's fence being a foot over a property line and then hand over their last dollar the minute someone is sick or her house catches on fire. There was the feeling that all of them were in this together, for better or worse. As Lauren liked to say, no man (or woman) is an island, entire of itself, especially on an island. Eleanor couldn't say the same about her life in Los Angeles, where her friends, while generous and civic-minded, had little to do with people outside their immediate circle.

Eleanor puts her hand to her purse. Her evening bag is vibrating. She pulls out her cell phone, grateful for the interruption. It's the local exchange. After the call goes to voice mail, she sees that this is the second call that she has missed from this number. She steps outside onto the deck and returns the call. "This is Eleanor Temple," she says, hoping whoever it was can't hear the faint slosh of wine in her voice. "I just missed—"

"Eleanor, it's Mitch."

She puts a finger to her ear. "I'm sorry, who?"

"Mitch. It's Mitch. Lauren's husband?"

"Mitch, hey. What's up?"

"I got your cell from the fridge. I mean the number is written on the fridge."

The people next to her burst into laughter at something Alden has said. Eleanor glances over; she hasn't had a chance to talk to him or Susan yet.

Over the din, she can just make out Mitch's voice asking if she could go somewhere more quiet.

She walks onto the lawn past the line of tiki torches. "Mitch. Hi. Sorry. It's so loud here. The food is great. Everyone's been—"

"Listen, Eleanor," Mitch cuts her off. "I need you to listen," he says again in a forceful voice that scares her.

"Sure," she says. "Is everything okay?"

"Is everything okay? No, no. It's not."

Eleanor, listening very intently now, notices that his voice is shaking. "There's been an accident. Jamie. He, he, he was on his bike. I don't know what happened, a car was passing a moped, that guy's dead, there was sand on the road."

Eleanor puts her hand to her mouth. "Those sirens."

"Yeah." He breathes in the word, like the Swedes do.

"Is he . . . ?" She is about to say "all right," but that is clearly not the case, yet she can't bring herself to say "dead." "Is he . . . ?" she begins again.

"He's alive."

"Oh my God. Thank God."

"But they said he was hit pretty hard, and—"

Eleanor can hear the violent effort he is making to control his voice.

"And the stupid little shit wasn't wearing his helmet." He starts to sob, which makes Eleanor start to cry too.

"None of them want to wear their helmets," she says. "None of them."

"He's unconscious but he's alive," Mitch says when he has himself under control again. "They're going to medevac him to Boston as soon as possible. I'm going to the hospital now to see if I can ride with him, but you need to get Lauren to the hospital as quickly as you can. She'll want to go too if she can make it there in time."

"Okay."

"I tried calling but she didn't pick up, and . . ." His voice starts to break again. "I can't tell her on the phone. I can't fall apart right now. Just say that there's been an accident. And then drive her to the hospital as quickly as you can."

The way that he keeps repeating the phrase "there's been an accident" makes Eleanor realize that someone—the police—must have used it with him.

The accident. Life will forever become the before and after.

"Eleanor, can you do this?"

"Yes, of course. I'll do it, and we'll get her to the hospital. We'll meet you there as soon as we can.

"Wait, Mitch?" she calls just as he's about to hang up. "Should I tell her how bad it is?"

"Umm." Her question seems to paralyze him and she immediately regrets asking it. "I don't know. Umm."

"I think I shouldn't," she says quickly, wanting to spare him in some way. "I'll just say that we don't know. Better for her to be hopeful right now."

She turns back toward the house in a kind of delirium of grief and rage. All the people talking so intensely with each other—about tennis games and political appointments, about abstract notions of how to make the world a better place. What does it matter? Her friend's son has just been hit by a car. He might die or never be able to walk again. Feisty Jamie, with his unruly hair and skinny torso, his fingers that are as delicate as a woman's.

Jamie might die. That is real.

But it isn't real. Eleanor can't begin to feel the depths of this anguish. She can't foresee how she will upend her own life and marriage over the next year to see her best friend through the worst imaginable thing anyone should have to go through. She strides across the deck to find Daniel before heading to the kitchen's back door.

When people at the party tell the story later, they will search for how to describe the sound that Lauren makes on seeing Eleanor's face, connecting the echo of those sirens with the realization that they came for her own flesh and blood. The partygoers will start by explaining that they were at the Michaelses' place, standing in the living room or on the deck—the Obamas are supposed to come, but then Ted Kennedy died and they don't make it; the party is still very nice until . . . There are these sirens, I remember, that go on forever, and everyone seems to have the same thought at once: Has something terrible happened to the president? The sirens pass and the party resumes, until about forty-five minutes or so later, another sound comes from the kitchen. It's like a sharp cry—like a bird that's been shot. Or a keening—isn't that the word? It's the sound of someone's heart just being ripped right out and it cuts through all the political talk. The caterer's ten-year-old son. Traumatic brain injury. There was a moped involved, the rider died. Apparently the boy wasn't wearing a helmet. So incredibly sad. Maybe you saw the posters for the fundraiser to cover his medical expenses, since their insurance didn't. Hillary Clinton went, which was nice of her.

Eleanor stands outside the kitchen door, invisible in the darkness on the deck, looking in on her friend, seated now on a stool at the kitchen island, a little juice glass of red wine at her side, chatting with one of her staff, soaking up the relief of a big night that has come off well. And it has, Eleanor thinks. The food was delicious; everyone kept saying so. And her trays, with their petals and peppers, looked so beautiful.

BLISS BROYARD is the author of the bestselling story collection *My Father, Dancing*, which was a *New York Times* Notable Book, and the award-winning memoir *One Drop: My Father's Hidden Life—A Story of Race and Family Secrets*, which was named a best book of the year by the *Chicago Tribune*. Her stories and essays have been anthologized in *Best American Short Stories*, *The Pushcart Prize*, and *The Art of the Essay*, among others, and she has written for many publications, including the *New York Times*, newyorker.com, and *Elle*. She is at work on a novel set on Martha's Vineyard called *Happy House*.

Compline

(1)

In the attic room with its lunette windows of stained glass covering three points of the compass, the man they call the Lecturer writes and writes and writes as he waits for the pigs to come and kill him. The autumn afternoon is crisp and bright. The attic is cool. The daylight prisms through the windows and shimmies on the ancient carpet in a slow promenade of color. He is alone in the cavernous Harlem town house. Junie and Sharon were the last to depart, and they begged him to join them. The Lecturer refused. He no longer believes in God but he still believes in fate. He is where he is supposed to be. An old Ruger .22 and an Iver Johnson Cadet .38 lie side by side on the table near his yellow pad, and a Walther snuggles in the brown leather holster looped around the back of his hard wooden chair. On the floor within easy reach is a 12-gauge shotgun, broken open because he is nervous about the shells. Beneath the front window an M1 carbine leans against the wall, but he mistrusts the M1, which has a tendency to jam. Beside it is a Remington Gamemaster, a hunting gun that doubles as a sniper rifle. Other weapons are scattered here and there, but the Lecturer prefers to rely on explosives. Hand grenades are wired to the front and back doors, and he has played a little game with Semtex beneath the stairs. He is perfectly aware that the other comrades are afraid of him. They also suspect he might be crazy, but what they see as madness he sees as dedication. Sharon tried to tell him where the group was heading, in the hope that they might rendezvous later, but the Lecturer would not listen. He has been tortured before and has the misshapen fingertips to prove it. Should he be taken alive, he has no illusion that he could long resist drugs or electrodes or whatever else J. Edgar and his gray men might pull out of their bag of tricks. With Nixon in the White House, anything is possible.

The Lecturer is writing with a Flair, the felt-tip pen that has lately become all the rage. Another in the series of pointless toys developed by the capitalists to enthrall the masses. He has finished three pages. He puts down the pen and stretches his fingers. Agony is done. That is the name by which the public knows the terror cell that over the past week has all but disbanded: Agony. Just last month they were still eight. Two days ago they were four. Wayne, the youngest, fled this morning. Sharon and Junie were the last two. Except for Frederick, the Lecturer reminds himself, unconsciously balling his fists. Frederick, he of the mysterious sources. Frederick, not a member of Agony but somehow always in touch. Surely Frederick was lurking somewhere nearby: Frederick, who called just past midnight to say that the Federal Bureau of Investigation knew they were in Harlem and would soon find their hideout. Frederick, who, as the Lecturer told the others yesterday, himself bore all the marks of playing both sides of the street. It must have been Frederick, he said, who sold them out to the FBI. Sharon, the drug-addled blonde who had seized command of Agony three years ago, insisted that the idea was ridiculous, but Sharon was besotted with Frederick. Junie, too, came to Frederick's defense, most likely because she did not want to think ill of a man she had known since they were children.

It makes no difference now, the Lecturer tells himself grimly.

The Lecturer. All the comrades call him by that name except Junie, who still calls him Jeremy, the nom de guerre under which he traveled on the occasion of their second meeting, in the safe house down in Charleston in 1966, where he had been sent to investigate the murder of the elderly Klansman who was locked in the basement, the only key to which she wore around her neck. She swore that she had not let it out of her sight, and yet it was impossible that she could be the killer. That was why they needed an expert. And that was when they became bitter enemies.

The pen scratches across the page. The Lecturer pretends that he is writing to his mother, who still lives in New Haven in the house where her boy was raised. He has not seen her since he left graduate school five years ago, during the Mississippi Freedom Summer of 1964, in which he did not participate because he was overseas. Then he decides that he is writing to his father, who died at the hands of the police while his boy was in college. No, that is a lie. He is writing for posterity. The FBI will surely seize the letter, and the pigs never throw anything away. The pages will sit in a file in a vault in a storeroom for years or decades. And one day someone will find them, read them, maybe publish them.

For posterity.

(2)

When the man whose name is not Jeremy was a small boy, his father used to take him to baseball games at the Polo Grounds to see the New York Cubans, owned by the colorful numbers runner Alex Pompez, and later, as the Negro leagues faded, to see the New York Giants with their colored stars: first Monte Irvin, and then, in 1951, Ray Noble and Artie Wilson, who was soon sent back to the minor leagues in exchange for an unknown rookie named Willie Mays. The boy loved these excursions with his father. They would take the streetcar to Union Station, not far from Yale, where they would board the trim, modern cars of the New York, New Haven and Hartford Railroad for the air-conditioned ride into the city. At Pennsylvania Station they would board the Eighth Avenue line of the IND for the ride to Upper Manhattan. The boy valued these hours alone with his father. His father was a big, bluff man, with a stern mien that scared the toughest kids in the neighborhood halfway to the grave. He worked in New Haven as a hotel doorman. He was the senior deacon of the church. He loved to read. Their house was full of books. As they walked from the subway to the ballpark, he would tell his son stories from Shakespeare and Aeschylus and William Wells Brown.

Outside the Polo Grounds the throng would jostle and push, but the boy's father managed somehow to create an island of peace around the two of them. Perhaps it was the stories. He would keep talking right up until they were inside the gates, where he would buy a program and a pencil because he was teaching the boy to keep score. But what the Lecturer remembered best was how just before they ducked beneath the wall, his father liked to point to the tall apartment buildings on the bluff overlooking the stadium. That's where the rich Negroes live, his father would say. The crest of Harlem. Sugar Hill, it's called. The boy would stare, goggle-eyed. Sugar Hill. Even the name was magic. True, he did not entirely believe that such things as rich Negroes existed, but he would never dream of disputing his father. Sometimes he wondered whether he might live in one of those grand apartments one day. Sometimes he hated himself for coveting that life and wondered whether he might be headed to hell. But as he grew older, he came to despise the people who lived in those elegant apartments more than he despised the white people who made the rules that confined them there. They were the most talented members of what his father called the darker nation, and should therefore have been leading the revolutionary cadres. Instead they spent their lives eagerly gathering the crumbs that fell from the capitalist table. That, at least, was what Kimberly always said, back in the days when he still believed that Kimberly was always right.

(3)

The light has changed. He crosses to the southwest window, sweeping up the .38 in one smooth motion. He stands on a chair and peers down into the alley. The house fronts on Edgecombe Avenue, at one time the smartest address in Sugar Hill. For a moment his vision clouds as he remembers his mother's tales of dinner tables laid for twenty or more, of Duke Ellington on the piano, of antique furnishings imported from Italy and France, of the Negro society weddings where one might find Frank Sinatra among the guests. In his mind's eye, black men and women dressed to the nines promenade through glittering hotel ballrooms as the band plays. Then, with an effort of will, the Lecturer wipes the images from his mind. It is all nonsense. This is 1969, not

1949. They were enemies to the revolution and traitors to the race. In any case, they long ago fled Harlem, leaving their less fortunate brethren behind. The very town house Agony is renting—the group was far too savvy to risk being caught by playing the role of squatters—is owned by a woman named Veazie, who according to Frederick once presided over Harlem society, deciding who would be invited to the best parties and who would be frozen out.

"What nonsense," the Lecturer repeats aloud.

He is still at the window. He is watching a blue appliance repair van that has been parked across the street for at least two hours now. Maybe. Maybe not. On the stoop of an apartment building, three men are passing a bottle back and forth. They could be the neighborhood drunks; or they could be watching the house.

He will know soon enough.

He abandons the window, returns to the table, and once more takes up his pen. He has decided that he is actually writing for the eager, frightened kids he has instructed in training camps in Cuba and Algeria and Syria, the youngsters whom he helped transform from callow, disillusioned children of the West into cadres prepared to do whatever is necessary to advance the revolution. His legacy.

He wonders, briefly, how many fascist provocateurs his protégés have eliminated, and tries not to think about how many innocents have died alongside them. There are slogans and arguments to justify those deaths, and he has led the chants, but at the moment he finds himself not quite able to remember them.

Junie's influence, he suspects.

(4)

Around age thirteen, the Lecturer joined what the members called a gang, although by then he was perfectly aware of the real gangs that were starting to battle for New Haven street corners. The boy's gang numbered five or six, together with a scattering of hangers-on. None of them were considered the toughest kids in the neighborhood, but banding together made them feel as if they were. They did no violence. They extorted no money. They climbed on the girders at construction sites and snuck into Yale buildings after dark. The oldest boy, Charles, whom everyone called Sug, would swipe candy bars and gum from stores. Sometimes Sug would post one of the others as lookout, but the boy who would grow into the Lecturer refused. He also would not take the candy. But he was usually the leader on the expeditions through the steam tunnels connecting the various university structures. He loved the close ceiling, the gurgling water, the heat, and the darkness. The pudgy Sug could barely keep up and half the time found an excuse not to go. So the Lecturer's main companions were Rhoden, a dark, skinny youth with bright, scary eyes, and the Packer twins, Mark and Marvin, who both wore glasses and were always getting into fights with each other. There were Sunday afternoons when the group would sneak around the campus for hours. They were never caught.

The Lecturer took a secret pride in these expeditions, not so much because the tunnels were scary but because Yale was. Yale dominated New Haven, but apart from a handful of students, no Negro dared step onto the campus except in service. That was what his father always said. His mother cleaned the offices at Yale and his father greeted the returning alumni when they came to the hotel where he worked, but otherwise his parents avoided the university grounds with an almost superstitious awe. All of New Haven's Negroes did. There were stories of a colored student spotted here or there, but none of the gang was quite sure if the stories were true. The students whom they encountered were big and white and resplendent in their Yale sweaters and scarves and seemed to float above the concerns of real people. His father used to say that Harvard trained its men to run the country and Yale trained its men to run the world. And already at age thirteen, the boy understood that he would never be part of either group. And so he settled instead for leading his gang through the steam tunnels, peeking into the hidden corners of the campus, enjoying the sense that he could, quite invisibly, infiltrate this citadel of which New Haven's whites were so proud.

On a rainy evening in July 1953, the Lecturer and his gang found their way into the blocky granite fortress housing one of what Yale called senior societies and most of the world called secret societies. The place was like a mausoleum, marble and cold. These societies, his father had taught him, were the places where they chose the men who would run the future. The boys were agog. The exterior was so bland but the inside was so opulent. There were chandeliers. There were paintings and tapestries. Display cases lined the walls. One case held carvings of animals and monsters from around the world. He stared. Most were labeled with the names of their countries of origin, but the card on one shelf read simply *Africa*. Even at thirteen he understood the discrimination. Africa was a European invention. That was what his father always told him. The rest of the world America saw as countries—Germany, France, India, China, Argentina, Peru—but Africa was just Africa, an agglomeration of separate tribes and nations for the convenience of the West. The Lecturer stood there staring, and eventually the other boys, who had been running raucously up and down the stairs and trying to make the elevator work, came and stood beside him. The Packer twins asked him what was wrong. He said nothing. But Rhoden had a sixth sense. He was holding a shiny gold tankard with an engraved inscription that he evidently intended to take as booty. Now Rhoden swung the tankard hard at the case with the little carved animals and monsters. The glass shattered. He dropped the tankard, which bounced loudly and, now dented, rolled along the slate floor. Help yourself, he said. The Packer twins hesitated. The Lecturer did not. He gathered as many of the "Africa" carvings as he could. The twins got the message and swept up the rest. The Lecturer led them downstairs to the grand hall with its long wooden banquet table. He placed the carvings on the table, one in front of each chair. The other boys followed his example. There were thirty chairs, and they did not quite have enough carvings to put one at each place, but it was close enough. Are we done? asked one of the Packer twins, trembling with excitement and fear. The Lecturer was perfectly calm. I believe we are, yes, he said, in the strange cadences he had learned from his father. It's just a joke, he told them. They left the way they had come in, through the steam tunnels in the basement, and they did no more damage, although Rhoden turned out to have stuffed four silver place settings into his jacket. For my ma, he said.

Not long after that their little gang disbanded. The twins discovered girls,

Sug got expelled, and Rhoden went out for football. For a while the Lecturer explored the campus still, and every now and then he was joined by Mark or Marvin, but for the rest of school he was mainly a loner. By the time he started college, he had largely lost track of the gang, except that Sug had joined a real gang and dropped out. When the Lecturer returned to New Haven for his father's funeral, his mother told him that Rhoden was in medical school down south somewhere. The Packer family had moved to Brooklyn. She had no idea what had happened to the children. Sug was dead.

In May of 1969, the Lecturer returned to New Haven for the last time, recruited to serve on the jury that tried Alex Rackley at the Black Panther headquarters on Orchard Street. He traveled clandestinely. He was careful to avoid places where his mother or family friends might show up. Later, when the police and the FBI were busy scouring the entire Northeast for Rackley's accused killers, the Lecturer was concealing two of the suspects almost in plain sight—underneath the Yale campus. He led them down into the tunnels he had learned so well as a boy, showed them the corners where no maintenance man ever trod, and left them to their own devices. Their occasional forays upward to find a bathroom led to rumors about homeless men living in the dormitory basements.

Junie accompanied him on this trip. She was just back from Chicago, where she had attended the convention of the Students for a Democratic Society. The Lecturer had been present only for a day, but he had heard reports. Junie had made a nuisance of herself by buttonholing fellow radicals in coffeehouses and safe houses to suggest that the time had come to renounce violence as an instrument of social change. She preached the same sermon to the Lecturer as they drove up to New Haven, where, masquerading as husband and wife, they stayed in a motel out on the Long Wharf. Even as they lay in their separate twin beds she would not leave the subject alone. He was not at all surprised when Junie turned out to be the only member of the jury who voted to spare Rackley's life. She had once been a law student, and was a demon for due process and proper burdens of proof.

(5)

That was four months ago. Since then the remnants of Agony have begun to scatter. The handful who holed up in this once-elegant Harlem town house were the last. The Lecturer stands at the front window once more, squinting at Edgecombe Avenue through the sniper sight mounted atop the Remington Gamemaster. The sharp little circle dances along the block, pausing here and there to pick out details in the gathering dusk as he tries to decide whether he is watching the random Brownian motion of life or the carefully scripted changing of the guard. The blue van has finally moved on, as have the men on the front stoop of the aging low-rise apartment building across the way who looked a little too alert to be passing a bottle back and forth. A Con Ed truck has broken down. The driver is cursing as he hunts around beneath the hood. The Lecturer sees nobody else in the cab, but he is willing to bet that a repair crew will be along soon, and FBI agents love to play repair crews. Lights have come on in a few windows across the street, and any one of them might mark a static observation post. The stalled truck looks like a good place to conceal heavy weapons. He watches the scene for a few more minutes, then shrugs. Either the pigs are here or they are not. There is nothing he can do. He sets the Gamemaster back in its place, checks the booby traps on the attic door, and returns to his desk. As he picks up the Flair, his eye falls once more on the Gamemaster. The rifle is mostly for show. Frederick procured it for him. Frederick can procure most things, and enjoys being secretive about how he does what he does. Sharon, rather smarmily, accused the Lecturer of bourgeois sentimentality for wanting a Gamemaster in the first place. But Frederick in his strange, shadowy way understood. So did Junie. Like the others, she did not much care for the symbolism, but she understood. A year and a half ago, a Remington Gamemaster was used to murder Martin Luther King, Jr.

The Lecturer catches himself wondering what Kimberly would have thought, but it's too late to ask.

(6)

The boy turned out to have a flair for mathematics, and when he finished high school he won a scholarship to Cornell to study physics. His parents could scarcely contain their pride. The church gave a party. People came up to the boy and shook his hand and tucked envelopes in his jacket: a quarter here, a dollar or two there, it all began to add up. He was saving to buy a car and he thought the gifts from the party might put him over the top, but his mother kissed him and took the money away and put it in the savings account she had opened for him when he was born. Be patient, she told him. Let it grow. His father beamed, and told the boy how wise his mother was. The boy believed every word. Years later he would marvel at how his parents lived in such utter thrall to the property trap.

Ithaca, New York, was another world. Compared to his hometown, it was almost rural. Unlike New Haven, a Democratic stronghold with an uneasy balance of power among the Negroes, the Irish, and the Italians, all of them in turn subject to the hegemony of Yale, Ithaca was white and Republican, a town whose tiny colored population was seen but never heard. At Cornell, he performed respectably but not sensationally in his science classes. In the fall of his sophomore year, he enrolled in a seminar on cultural anthropology taught by a youngish professor named Tris Hadley. The Lecturer knew nothing about the field, but the course sounded interesting. As it turned out there were only five students. The class was being boycotted because the House Un-American Activities Committee had labeled Hadley a Communist. The professor heat-edly denied the charge, and the university stood tepidly beside him, but the students had taken protective action on their own. Nobody wanted to explain to a potential employer or graduate school why Professor Tristan Hadley was on his résumé. In the classroom, Hadley did what any good seminar leader does: nudged them toward his point of view without ever quite saying what it was. He did not assign Marx but he did urge them to consider whether the culture of democracy and markets that the West was slowly imposing upon the rest of the world produced any significant good other than profits for the capitalist. He gave them the Opium Wars, he gave them the settlement of the Americas, he gave them the colonization of Africa. In which of these circumstances, he asked, was the West truly driven by any motive but the motive to profit off the labor and resources of others? In which of these circumstances, he asked, are the indigenous people made better off through the hegemony of the West? One young woman, an economics major named Bernstein, had the temerity to suggest that a rising tide lifted all boats. Hadley was scathing. Even if you're right, he said, it's interesting how it's always the man in the fifty-foot yacht who tells the family in the leaky canoe that they're better off at sea. As for the Lecturer, he at this time was still dimly in touch with the church of his childhood. Terrible things might have happened, he told the class, but at least people came to Christ. Jesus loves everyone. There were a few snickers. Hadley gave him a carefully measured look, less than scornful but more than pedagogical, a look the young sophomore was already coming to know, a look that says: I will let you off the hook this time because you are a Negro and I am a liberal, but sooner or later you will have to concede that I am right and you are wrong. What Hadley said was: If your Christ loves everyone, it's an interesting coincidence that He always grants victory to the colonizer.

Two weeks later, the Lecturer went to his adviser and switched his major from physics to philosophy.

The following spring the Lecturer was part of a reading group that met twice a month at Hadley's house well out in Cayuga Heights. The reading was heavy and radical, ranging from Lenin to Fanon at the hard end, and from Jean-Paul Sartre to Alphaeus Hunton at the soft. Over the course of the term, Hadley slowly weeded out those he considered less dedicated. By spring there were only two, and when the other young man took a position at his family firm on Wall Street for the summer, there was only the Lecturer. It was 1961, and Professor Hadley was headed south to do voter registration work. Why don't you join us? he suggested. The Lecturer never hesitated. He told his parents that he would not be coming home to help in the church as he had promised. But at the last minute, the professor announced that he wouldn't be going. So the Lecturer drove south instead with Hadley's girlfriend, a colored graduate student named Kimberly Elden, who told him that the professor had stayed in Ithaca because, number one, he was a coward, and number two, he had run out of excuses to give his fiancée.

Kimberly was tall and dark and wise and reminded him of Miss Deveaux, who long ago had been his Sunday school teacher. She told him that Tristan had her cast as his Iseult, but without any of the messy dying-of-grief business. Kimberly was from a grand Negro family that was on the verge of disowning her, not because of her left politics but because she seemed to have no interest in marriage. During the drive she told him that her great-grandfather had been in the construction business in New Haven until the whites drove him out. Kimberly herself had grown up in Harlem, on 162nd Street, in one of those apartments overlooking the Polo Grounds that his father was always pointing out. You could use a pair of binoculars to watch the games through the window, she said. At this bit of intelligence, the Lecturer's chest pulsed with hot resentment.

They did voter registration work together in Sunflower County, and spent their days raising great clouds of dust as they motored up and down the hardpan, usually with a white student or two along for what Kimberly liked to call coloration, by which she meant camouflage. A local activist was always in the car, someone who knew the lanes and the farms and the people. Not one of the thousands of Negroes in Sunflower County was registered to vote. The citizens' council told the press that the Negroes simply were not interested. When the students knocked on doors, they found many of the stone-faced sharecroppers openly hostile toward the outsiders who brought such suffering upon their heads. All of them had friends who had tried to register and been thrown off land their families had farmed for a century. Even the middle class was uneasy. A doctor who had tried to organize a local chapter of the NAACP had been driven from town. The police chief of Indianola, the county seat, was said to be keeping lists of local Negroes who were considered unreliable, to be dealt with after the students and the press went home.

In the evenings at the boardinghouse on the edge of town, Kimberly would kick off her shoes and close her eyes and mutter that the work they were doing was pointless. Instead of helping the sharecroppers to form a revolutionary consciousness, they were urging them to participate in an illegitimate system that guaranteed their continued serfdom. The Lecturer was torn. He saw her point but also experienced a tug. He liked these people and wanted to help them free themselves. In bed, Kimberly told him he was a fool. Negroes could be lumpen, she said, or they could be petit bourgeois. The one thing they could never be was free. Freedom would require the elimination of racism, the elimination of racism would require the taming of the ego, and the taming of the ego would require the regimentation that only the Party could provide. He stared for a long moment, then cursed himself for his naiveté. It was the first time he had realized that Kimberly was a Communist.

She was his first lover, but grew bored of the way he constantly tortured himself with guilt for what he called their sin. After their third week together in Mississippi, Kimberly told him that she'd gotten a letter from Tris, who had invited her to join him in Mexico, where he was doing fieldwork in the mountains of Guanajuato. Packing her things in the car, she told him to try to grow up. A few days later, the Lecturer hitched a ride north with a couple of journalists. A part of him was distressed in turns by what had happened with Kimberly and by what had not, but the rest of him took pleasure in regaling the journalists with the tale of his three nights in jail, because the day after Kimberly's departure, he and another student had been arrested while distributing flyers on the sidewalk outside the county clerk's office in Indianola and charged with loitering and disorderly conduct. Although they unfortunately had not been beaten, he had remained behind bars until his proud parents were able to wire his bail money. He looked forward to telling Kimberly the story in the fall, but she did not return to school. Tris Hadley told him that she had moved to California to become a labor organizer. Five years later, the Lecturer would be called upon to decide whether to put a bullet in her head.

(7)

A faint creak shakes him once more from his reverie. In a single compact motion he slips from the chair and spins toward the door, the Ruger already in his hand. He flattens himself against the southeast wall, the only one with no window, and stretches his perception. That was what they called it in the camps. He shuts his eyes and listens until he hears the creak again. Not in the stairwell. Not on the landing. Above him. Either the house is settling or they are on the roof. He waits. Does his sums. Suppose they are on the roof. They will set charges in two or three separate spots, blow them all at once, figuring that the blast will disable him, maybe kill him; but if it doesn't, there will suddenly be three different points of entry, and he cannot cover all of them at once, even with a machine gun, which in any case he does not have. Will they give him the chance to surrender or immediately shoot to kill? He guesses the latter. Prosecutions of radicals are nowadays occasions for big speeches in the courthouse and street fighting outside.

He gives them five minutes. Ten. Fifteen, all of which he spends crouching along the wall. He watches a beetle crawling across the floorboards. *Prionus laticollis* is his tentative identification, but he is guessing, because he knows only about a dozen names. Dark wings flutter and buzz but the creature never leaves the ground. It just goes on crawling. Still he waits. Nothing else happens. False alarm. The house is settling after all. The Lecturer straightens. He marches back to the table, returns the gun to its place. Just panic. At the camps they would have been laughing their heads off. His parents raised him to value dignity, and if he has shed most of their teachings over the past decade, he has never managed to surrender his pride.

Perhaps that is why he had the argument with Frederick. The big one, just last week. Frederick, the man of shadows. Frederick, who has been hanging around Agony from the beginning but is always magically absent when trouble rears its head.

The argument arose at the dinner table. Wayne, barely out of college, was declaiming about how much the black community had accomplished in the face of racism, and how important it was that everyone know the history, the great men and women the race had produced. Sharon or somebody asked him what accomplishments he meant. Wayne told her to look out the window, to consider the grand society that had once occupied these favored blocks. Sharon, who was quite high and not quite thinking, pointed out that the great buildings out there had been constructed when the neighborhood was white.

ERIC FISCHL is an internationally acclaimed American painter and sculptor. His artwork is represented in many distinguished museums throughout the world as well as prestigious private and corporate collections, including the Metropolitan Museum of Art, the Whitney Museum of American Art, the Museum of Modern Art in New York City, the Museum of Contemporary Art in Los Angeles, the Saint Louis Art Museum, the Louisiana Museum of Modern Art in Denmark, the Musée Beaubourg in Paris, the PaineWebber Collection, and many others. Fischl has collaborated with other artists and authors, including E. L. Doctorow, Allen Ginsberg, Jamaica Kincaid, Jerry Saltz, and Frederic Tuten. His extraordinary achievements throughout his career have made him one of the most influential figurative painters of the late twentieth and early twenty-first centuries. He is a Fellow at both the American Academy of Arts and Letters and the American Academy of Arts and Science, and a Senior Critic and board member at the New York Academy of Art. He lives and works in Sag Harbor, New York, with his wife, the painter April Gornik.

Scenes from Late Paradise: Stupidity

Late America

Oil on linen (both)

Then, realizing her faux pas, she changed tactics slightly. Whatever they had built, they had built through the sufferance of their white masters.

Wayne's smooth brown face trembled. He had just been slapped down by his commander. He was new to this life, too green to understand that he was free to argue back until a decision was made. But Frederick rode to the rescue. Wayne was right, he said. What had been built here was a remarkable thing. To succeed so in the face of such implacable hatred was a miracle that should be trumpeted.

The Lecturer felt the anger rise. But Frederick was constantly sticking up for those traitors to the proletariat. Of course he was. Most probably he was one of them. The Lecturer began to speak. He carefully reminded the group of how the petite bourgeoisie, clinging to their bits of property, constitute the greatest enemies of the revolution, more dangerous than the capitalists themselves. Frederick told him that he did not know what he was talking about. A silence fell. Nobody interrupted the Lecturer in full cry; well, Junie sometimes, but nobody else, and Junie was away tonight. The Lecturer stared at Frederick, so small and clever with his sepia skin and burning eyes and his air of being a person who has been places and seen things that others can only imagine. Of the handful of comrades who had been in and out of the town house over the past few months, he was the only one—apart from Junie—by whom the Lecturer was even slightly impressed. The others were afraid of him. More afraid, maybe, than they were of the Lecturer.

Calm as always, the Lecturer asked exactly what part of his analysis Frederick found flawed.

"I didn't say it was flawed. I said it was wrong." As the others stared, Frederick went over to the attack. He said that those who once lived here had done the best they could with what they had. He said they should be admired for defying the expectations of a racist society by building a world in which it was possible for their families to thrive. The Lecturer hid his panic behind a supercilious smile. When he was certain that Frederick was done, he proceeded to instruct him. He reminded him of Trotsky on the role of the bourgeoisie in maintaining order with the complicity of the petite bourgeoisie who secretly hated them. He pointed to the promise of reform as the key element in maintaining order among both petite bourgeoisie and proletariat within the capitalist order.

Of course, Frederick knew all this, but the condescension was intentional. The Lecturer expected the older man to explode. Instead, he shrugged. "Well, you're entitled to your view," he said smoothly. "You know what they say. Differences of opinion make horse races."

The Lecturer kept his face placid but inwardly he seethed. The temerity! Differences of opinion! No wonder the pigs were winning the war in the streets. Even the most radical Americans had no discipline. They did not understand that a revolution held no room for disagreement. The Party took a position and it became everyone's position. There were no exceptions. The toleration of dissent was a sign of weakness. Those who were wrong should be shouted down and disciplined. They should lose their places in the movement, which would proceed to roll right over them.

Violently if necessary.

Nodding in firm agreement with his own exposition, the Lecturer goes back to his writing.

(8)

In the summer of 1962, at the conclusion of the Lecturer's junior year at Cornell, Professor Hadley invited him to Mexico, just as he had Kimberly the summer before. The young man never hesitated. By this time the serious turn of their conversations had led him to suspect that what his mentor was grooming him for had little to do with his academy. His suspicion turned out to be right. The six weeks of fieldwork in the uplands of Guanajuato, out of contact with the world, turned out to be six weeks of training in Cuba, mostly by East German teachers: ideological instruction in the mornings, and after lunch what was known as technical work—how to shoot, how to fight, how to guard a prisoner, how to send secret messages, how to blow things up. The course was intense and scary. Only four of the twelve who began were able to finish, and he was one of the four. It was at the training camp that he got his name, for he spoke excellent Spanish and passable French, and in the evenings would present long, passionate arguments accompanied by copious spoken citations. The instructors were amused, and called him *prepodavatel*—a Russian word that can be translated as "teacher" . . . or "lecturer." Nobody at the camp quite liked him, but nobody liked him at Cornell either. Nobody had liked him even in high school, and it had been some while since he actually cared. He had decided back when he was sneaking into buildings at Yale that being liked was an unimportant part of life. Machiavelli was right. Being respected and feared mattered more.

After the Lecturer returned to Mexico with top marks, Hadley told him that his job now was to continue his education. The young man was surprised. He had expected an assignment. He pointed out that Kimberly had not stayed in school. She had been sent to California. The professor shrugged. Kimberly, he said, possessed a different set of skills. In time you will have a great deal of work to do, but for now you will go back to school. Those are the orders. But by now the Lecturer was beginning to get Hadley's measure. Maybe there were orders, maybe there weren't. Either way, nobody was going to trust Tris Hadley with any secrets. The professor loved to play the clandestine revolutionary, but in truth he was more like a travel agent, making sure the people who mattered got to where they were supposed to be. And the Lecturer, a college junior all of twenty-one years old, realized that he was one of the people who mattered—and Tristan Hadley was not.

Nevertheless, the Lecturer went back to Cornell, where that fall the whole campus, like the whole of America, was terrified over the possibility that the Soviet Union, by smuggling missiles into Cuba, had brought the globe to the precipice of nuclear war. The Lecturer found himself for the most part untroubled. Everything would be fine, he insisted in seminar rooms and coffeehouses. The capitalists were too greedy to blow up the globe; the Communists were too patient. When the crisis was settled, others pointed to the decisive action and wise statecraft of the youthful American president they so admired, but the Lecturer knew that it was only the inevitable turn of the wheel of history. A few months later he finished his philosophy degree with honors. He spent two vacations and half the summer back in Cuba, and one night in July engaged in ferocious argument with a black woman who had delivered a controversial talk that morning on the appropriate uses of nonviolent resistance. Her nom de guerre was Miranda, but she was notorious across America as Commander M, leader of the terror group known only as Agony, which had carried out several actions across the South.

She was accompanied by her second-in-command, a sandy-haired Southerner in overalls who nodded at her every sentence. His name was Paul, and he seemed to be in love with her. The Lecturer could not tell whether she reciprocated. Later that evening, he took Paul aside and reminded him that in a revolutionary movement, bourgeois sentimentality about romantic attachment was a vice. But the fool professed to have no idea what he was talking about. The Lecturer decided not to worry about it. This was his first meeting with elements of Agony, which had always struck him as a rather amateurish lot; he assumed that it would be his last.

Back in the States, the Lecturer entered graduate school in New York City, where he kept arguing political theory in coffeehouses and across chess tables and kept writing his increasingly ferocious articles. More than one of his professors urged him to calm down. But he was always calm; always in control. They simply did not like what he was saying and, in his judgment, were unable to refute it.

Two days before Christmas of 1963, the Lecturer packed his bags to head home for a few days to visit his mother. He was on a wooden bench at Grand Central, waiting for the train to New Haven, when two men in overcoats plopped down beside him, one on each side. The one on his left was a Negro. Even before they flashed their identification wallets, he knew that they were J. Edgar's boys.

"My name is Special Agent Stilwell," said the one on the right. "This is Agent Barron. We're with the Federal Bureau of Investigation. We'd like a brief word with you if it's not too much trouble."

"It's too much trouble," the Lecturer assured him. "Go away."

"All we want is a little information," Stilwell continued in a murmur. The *Daily News* covered his face. No one else would know that he was saying a word. "A little help, to keep things from getting too violent."

"Leave me alone."

"You've gotten yourself involved with some very nasty people," said Barron, the black agent, from his left. "The game is about to get very rough. Very scary. You might want to start with an ace in the hole. A way out."

"That's us," added Stilwell.

"I told you to leave me alone. I know my rights."

"Keep your voice down. Don't look at us. Just sort of whisper without moving your lips. Didn't they teach you that in Cuba?"

"I don't have anything to say to you," said the Lecturer, unable to hide the tremor of surprise.

"We don't care about what you might do overseas," Stilwell purred. "That's not our purview. We care about what happens here. Who gets blown up or shot to pieces. That's what Agony does. They're dangerous people."

"Anything you can tell us," said Barron. "Whatever she may have let slip. We're just trying to keep people alive here. That's all."

The Lecturer stared at Barron. Then he stared at Stilwell. He felt his control return. "Even if I knew what you were talking about, I would have nothing to say. You are the satraps of false authority." The Lecturer got to his feet. So did the FBI agents. "Now, if you'll excuse me, I have a train to catch."

"Think about it," said Stilwell, and slipped a business card into the Lecturer's pocket. "Track eighteen," he added.

The Lecturer strode angrily away. Now he was shaking. He headed toward the washroom. For the first time since the beginning of his mad odyssey, he understood that this was all real. That he had made choices and left other possibilities behind. He glared at his face in the mirror. He washed his hands. He had felt so superior to Tristan Hadley, but the professor had trapped him quite neatly. Now two roads loomed before him, and two only. He washed his face. He pulled out the agent's card, studied it briefly, then shook his head, tore it to pieces, and threw them in the overflowing waste can.

Christmas with his mother was grim. They both knew that her boy had come home to say goodbye, but neither of them could find the words.

(9)

The Lecturer puts down the Flair and closes his eyes. Thinking back, he realizes that he had been scared only of what he had gotten himself into. Never of the agents. They were not supermen. They were flesh and blood like everybody else. In a camp he had worked at in Algeria, the targets were gussied up to look like soldiers—French soldiers, American soldiers—and the students shot them full of holes without so much as flinching. That scared him sometimes. That scared him a lot. The fact that they didn't flinch. The Lecturer had been in the car with Huey Newton and Bobby Seale in Oakland in 1967 on the fateful night when a cop pulled them over and Huey sparked a movement when he climbed out of the car carrying his gun, told the cop he was exercising his constitutional rights, and warned him that if he tried to take the gun away he would get shot. That night and the nights of armed black patrols that followed put the Black Panthers on the map. The Lecturer had been sent to California to bring back a report on their ideology, but the truth was he did not entirely believe that they had one. They had discipline, though, and they had commitment, and he admired both. Despite their public image, the Panthers were not true revolutionaries. Their manifesto, when stripped of the rhetoric, was largely reformist. Well, except for that nice business about holding a plebiscite in which Negroes would get to vote on whether or not to remain part of the nation. The Communist Party had supported self-determination for America's black population since the 1920s, and the Lecturer supposes that as a formal matter, it supports it still.

He opens his eyes and, without rising, looks up through the stained glass at the house across the street. Once more he imagines old Harlem. Frederick's Harlem. Kimberly's Harlem. The black bourgeoisie. They would never vote to leave. He thinks about the tens and hundreds of thousands who volunteered to fight in the nation's wars—his own father among them. They fought and often died. They, too, would never vote to leave. That they risked their lives for a country that hated them implied that they loved that country even more than the Caucasians did.

The Lecturer shudders. The weight of that realization is, for a mad instant, all but unbearable. How will the revolution ever reach those who take such pride in their patriotic fervor? Maybe Lenin was wrong.

He shakes off the mood and once more lifts his pen.

Time to admit the truth.

He is not writing to his mother, or to his father. He is not writing for posterity, or for those he sent out to kill. The truth is that he is writing to Junie, writing in the shameful desperate hope that whether by the will of God or through some random act of governmental incompetence, his letter will find its way into her hands. He wants her to understand that he is sorry for what he did to her, and why, if he could go back and do it again, he would have done things exactly the same.

(10)

He had his second encounter with the notorious Commander M in the summer of 1966, when he was sent home to solve the murder of a Klansman. By this time he had left graduate school, and indeed left America. During spring break of 1964, he had traveled to Algeria for a conference on revolutionary theory and never returned. By this time he had several hardline essays in fringe publications to his credit. One of the pieces, written shortly before independence, had extolled Ahmed Ben Bella, leader of the *Front de Libération Nationale*, which most of the West considered terrorist thugs. Ben Bella was now president of Algeria, and the essay had come to his attention through the efforts of Tris Hadley, who continued to take an interest in his protégé and had connections everywhere. After the conference, the Lecturer was asked to remain in Algiers for a few days. A week later he was asked if he was willing to undertake a special action—

(Sitting at his attic desk, he hesitates, then decides not to describe either the action or who asked him to do it.)

—and when he had performed the task, he was asked whether he would be willing to do ideological training more frequently. There would be risks, he was assured, but the work was important to the revolution, and there were few who were good at it. The way they were buttering him up, the Lecturer was sure that the risks were even greater than the recruiters were describing, and he turned out to be right. Nevertheless, he persevered in his calm, orderly way. He trained cadres in walled compounds in North Africa where guards and dogs protected the perimeter and in dank shuttered basements in Latin America where every shuffle in the street outside might be a prelude to a raid by the security services and an introduction to the delights of interrogation. Conferring with a revolutionary cell in the back room of a beer hall in Munich, he marveled that nobody sees the unhappy symmetry. Meeting American students who had traveled to Hanoi to protest the war, he is struck by both their appealing naiveté and the dangerous simplicity of their view of the world. In between he found time to give papers at conferences, including the second Afro-Asian Conference, held in Algeria in February of 1965, where he was part of the audience that wildly applauded Che Guevara's speech on why the socialist countries had an obligation to afford financial and other support for all anticolonialist and anti-imperialist movements, whether they were socialist or not.

At the time of the summons to return to America, the Lecturer was at a camp in Syria, brushing up what his kind called technical skills and lecturing on the ideology of revolution to volunteers who only gradually, now that it was too late to back out, had started to understand just what they had joined. Months earlier he had been in graduate school, but in this business every month was an eternity. One day after the usual lunch of lamb stew with rice, the camp commandant called him in and told him that he had an assignment back in the States. The air was stifling. The electricity was out, so the fan on the desk was useless junk. The Lecturer pointed out that he was now a wanted man at home. That would not be a problem, the commandant assured him. Documents had been prepared. The Lecturer asked what the task was. When he had heard the commandant out, he erupted in fury—which is to say that he raised an eyebrow and frowned. Why do we care about the death of a Klansman? he asked. Surely his execution serves to advance the cause.

I have your orders here, the commandant replied.

And so of course the Lecturer packed his bag. He had no idea at what level the decision had been made, or why the duty devolved on him rather than on someone else. But he was a soldier, and he would go where he was sent.

On a sultry, lazy afternoon two days later he rang the rear bell of a lovely Victorian house in what must have been the whitest neighborhood of America's most segregated city, Charleston, South Carolina. To avoid worrying whoever might be peering from the windows next door, he arrived in a plumber's van and wore dirty overalls. Through the screen, a uniformed Negro maid asked whether she could help him.

"Somebody called for a plumber," he said. "I'm Jeremy."

The maid opened the screen door. "You'd better come in," she said.

They stood together in the kitchen. The maid looked him over. He returned her scrutiny. She was small and dark and appropriately somber, but something in the wide brown eyes announced that she was playacting every bit as much as he was. And no wonder, given that the woman standing before him was Commander M.

"I thought you'd be older," she finally said. "I can't believe they sent me an expert ten years younger than I am." She offered her hand. "I'm Junie," she said.

"We met in Cuba," he reminded her. "And my instructions are that I am to call you—"

"Call me Junie."

He finally shook. Her hand was warm and firm. "A pleasure to meet you, Comrade Junie."

"Just Junie, please."

She smiled then, a quick mischievous flicker, before undoing her apron and tugging a small handgun from her waistband. She laid it on the table. She whistled twice, and a thickset black man in a threadbare blue suit stepped from the hallway. A shotgun rested in the crook of his heavy arm. "This man-mountain is Hammie," she said. "And you are?"

"I told you. Jeremy."

"We use real names here. We don't keep secrets."

"I do." He realized that the time had come to assert himself. "Who else is in the house?"

"One upstairs, watching the street, and two out running errands." Again she gave him that searching look. Then she moved toward the counter. "I just brewed some coffee."

He allowed her to pour him a cup. They sat at the table. Hammie had vanished, leaving them alone to talk.

"Would you like to see the basement?" she asked. "The scene of the crime, so to speak?"

"Yes, please, in a moment. First I would like to understand your living arrangements."

Junie explained. The fiction was simple and clever: Sharon and Paul, the two Caucasians in the group, played the part of a happily married white couple (more coloration). Paul was from Tennessee, and put it about that he had inherited a small sum and had settled in South Carolina to write the great Southern novel everyone had been waiting for since Faulkner. His "wife" got to know every merchant in town. The couple had a lot of money to spend, and because it was inherited money it was respectable. Also living in the house were three Negroes: a maid, a cook, and Hammie, who doubled as chauffeur and yard man. Junie was the cook. Kimberly was the maid—

The Lecturer interrupted. "Kimberly Elden?"

"That's right. Why do you ask? Do you know her?"

"Never mind. Please continue."

Junie sipped her coffee. Anyway, she said, that was the public profile: a white couple and three colored servants. Privately, however, the cadre remained under her command. Paul ranked just beneath her. The others did as they were told. The other thing nobody in Charleston knew was that the house was an arsenal, packed with enough weapons to hold off the state militia for a week.

That was the profile, she repeated.

Then she told him about the crime.

(11)

Two weeks ago (said Junie) Paul had returned to the house in a frothing fury. At a local country club, he and his "wife" had been introduced to an elderly man whose name was familiar. At the public library Paul had discovered that the man had once been a leader of the local Klan, and although his night-riding days were long behind him, some fifteen years ago he had been suspected but never indicted in the disappearance of the plaintiff in a desegregation case in Clarendon County. Junie warned her cadre that they were not there to seek revenge. They had a mission, which she declined to discuss with the Lecturer. He approved of her discretion: he was an outsider, after all.

Despite Junie's order, a few days later Paul, Sharon, and Kimberly arrived back at the safe house with the retired Klansman in the trunk of their car.

"How had the abduction been accomplished?" he asked.

"He has a house down by the river. They drove right up to his door. A white couple and their maid wouldn't raise an eyebrow. As soon as they were sure he was alone, they pulled their guns."

"Someone could have seen the car."

"I know. I told you, it was stupid."

"*Did* anyone see the car?"

"I have no idea. I'm trying to find out."

"I see." The Lecturer did not disguise his unhappiness with this answer. "Please continue."

Junie gave him a look but went on with the story. When her three subordinates arrived with the Klansman, she was flabbergasted—and, for once, indecisive. She told them to keep him bound and blindfolded and to lock him in the basement. The only entrance was through the kitchen. She ordered that food and water be sent down, then padlocked the door and put the key around her neck. He was not to be bothered, she said. Nobody was to do anything until she'd had a chance to think. She sensed their sullen resentment, but she was the commander, and they had other work to do.

"You should have killed him at once," said the Lecturer. "Then you would not be in this mess."

"That's certainly what my cadre thought," Junie conceded. She and Sharon had to go out that night to a meeting about which she would say no more. There was no way to avoid it. She left Paul in charge. She told him that she was trusting him to see that no harm came to the prisoner. She told him to stand guard in the kitchen until she and Sharon returned. When they got back a few hours later, Junie undid the padlock and went downstairs to check on the prisoner. He was alive. She was sure of that. She came back up and relocked the door. Paul and Hammie were to take turns guarding the kitchen. Then she went upstairs to the room she shared with Kimberly, her fellow colored servant. In the morning the prisoner was dead. Strangled.

Hammie had stood watch most of the night, but he freely admitted that he had left his post when he heard a trash can fall over outside. He had hurried into the yard. A raccoon, he thought. He swept up the garbage, reclosed the can, and returned to the kitchen. The padlock, he swore, was still in place.

"The trash can was a diversion," said the Lecturer.

"I know that," said Junie. "I just don't know who did the diverting." She fingered her necklace. "Or how the killer got into the basement if I had the key."

"You were asleep."

"The key was still around my neck."

"Is there a second key?"

"No. This is the only one."

"How do you know?"

His browbeating was starting to annoy her, which they both knew was his intention. "I bought the padlock myself. I threw the other key in the river."

"Why?"

"Because if I ever needed to lock anything up, I wanted to be sure I could control who got at it."

The Lecturer pondered. He did his sums. He knew that his sudden silence was irritating her but he wanted to check the addition.

"That's your third cup of coffee since I arrived," he said.

She looked at her cup. "I suppose. It could be."

"Do you drink a lot of it?"

"Yes."

"Even at night?"

"Sometimes."

"On the night in question?"

"Probably."

"Your coffee was drugged."

Junie gasped. Then laughed. "That's crazy. Who would drug my coffee? That's nuts." She grew serious again. "Besides, drugging me wouldn't do them any good. Even if I was asleep upstairs, the key would still be around my neck. They couldn't get it without waking Kimberly. Or did they drug her, too? I don't— Oh."

"Yes. Oh." The Lecturer looked at her closely. "You are not truly surprised. You are pretending."

"That's not true."

He ignored this. "You've known all along who it was. I'm not here to solve the murder. I'm here to confirm your diagnosis and help you decide what to do about the disease."

"The disease?"

"When a comrade does not follow orders, Commander, there is a disease. A serious one. Undiscipline. Nothing is more threatening to the revolution."

"But—"

"There are only two possible killers. Kimberly or yourself. And ever since your Cuba speech, your commitment to nonviolence is legendary."

She was angry at last. "If it was Kimberly, who created the diversion?"

"I do not know. But surely you have studied methods of compulsory interrogation."

"You're not going to torture one of my comrades."

"I'm not going to do anything, Commander. The question is what you're going to do." He was packing his bag. "You have the killer. She must be punished severely. Not for killing the Klansman, for he was a monster and deserved his horrible death. But you must establish discipline, swift and clear discipline. Your comrades should know that they dare not disobey you."

"Nobody deserves to die."

"This is a revolution, Commander. Not a Broadway musical."

"The Klansman was a human being. Kimberly is a human being." She shook her head decisively. "I won't do it. I won't torture a member of my cadre. And I certainly won't kill her."

"It will make no difference what you decide. Hesitate in this matter, and your subordinates will take command and carry out the punishment anyway.

A commander unwilling to act when the situation demands it can be no commander."

"I can live with that."

"Perhaps you can. But even that will no longer be your decision, will it?"

Her eyes widened. She said nothing.

"I have been here too long already," said the Lecturer. "I must be out of the country tonight."

"What about Kimberly?"

"What about her?"

"Shouldn't you see her? Talk to her?"

"She is your problem now, Commander. Not mine. Excuse me."

He let himself out, walked around the front of the house. He knew she was watching from the window, and therefore he was careful not to look up. He climbed back into his truck and drove off.

(12)

The Lecturer went first to Canada, then to Paris for a conference of socialist comrades, before finally returning to Algeria, which had become his home. Time passed. Rumors were everywhere. Commander M had refused to punish Kimberly Elden, and, just as the Lecturer predicted, she had lost her command. A show trial had been held. She had been demoted to the lowest level, taking orders from everyone in the group. Eventually she disappeared. One report said she was dead. Another had it that she had abandoned radical activism to go in search of the child—children, plural, said some—whom she had borne while underground and put up for adoption.

Kimberly Elden surfaced in New York late in 1966 and was promptly arrested. Her wealthy family hired the finest lawyers. The government, whatever its suspicions, was unable to prove that she had committed any crimes of violence. She pled guilty to a weapons charge and spent a year and a half in prison. Upon her release at the end of 1968, she was hired as an instructor at a private college in the Midwest.

In early May of 1969, the Lecturer returned to the States, tasked with helping Agony wind down its operations. He would rather have avoided the job, but his superiors were adamant. He was familiar with Agony, they said. The work had to be done. His instructions were to make contact with elements of Weatherman and explore the possibility of a merger. The negotiations were to take place in Chicago, during the convention of the Students for a Democratic Society. At a barricaded apartment on the South Side, the Lecturer met a couple of people who might or might not have been part of Weatherman. Afterward he went to a bar in Lincoln Park to confer with the representatives of Agony. Sharon he had of course expected. Paul's presence, too, made sense. Junie was a surprise. The Lecturer prepared himself for enmity. But she was surprisingly friendly and even charming. The negotiations looked unpromising, but Sharon said she would take Weatherman's terms back to her people.

Her people. The Lecturer reminded himself to use that one.

Afterward, Sharon and Paul left. Junie finished her scotch, and the Lecturer his club soda. They went for a walk along the lake. The water was heavy and invisible in the quiet darkness. They talked a bit about old times—Cuba and Algeria but not Charleston—and about radicals who were mutual acquaintances, most of them in prison or in hiding or in the ground. Then they lapsed into a companionable silence as the waves whispered their slow messages along the shore.

"You're really not part of it anymore, are you?" he asked after a bit. "Agony. You've left all of that behind."

"I'm not sure if I'm part of it or not. I come and I go."

"And Sharon allows this? It seems undisciplined. Also bad security."

"That's your big thing, isn't it? Discipline." Her smile was wan. "Not mine. My dad was a preacher, but I was always the rebel in the family. My brother, my sister—they argued some, sure, but basically they did as they were told. They were good kids. I wasn't."

Unsure how to respond, he decided to say nothing.

"You're a revolutionary. It's different for you." She spread her palms. "Anyway, as you might have noticed, Sharon's not all that big on discipline either. She thinks she is, but she's not. She's not that big on anything just now."

"The drugs," he intoned.

"And other things. She's happy to let me come and go."

"She apprises you of her whereabouts?"

"I know. Bad security, right?"

She laughed.

They strolled for another hour. They talked about the prospects for a merger they both knew would not be happening. They talked about the decision of an American publisher to bring out Marighella next year, in English: would that be good or bad for the revolution? They agreed that it was a shame about Kimberly Elden. He wanted to ask Junie whether it was true that she had children, and if she had found them, but found himself unexpectedly shy. He walked her back to the apartment building where she was crashing and stood for a few minutes on the step. Before he quite knew what was happening, the Lecturer heard himself agreeing to meet the group next month back at the safe house in New York.

"I have to go to New Haven first," he said, a complete and entirely unprecedented breach of security.

"Come to Harlem on the way," said Junie. "Pick me up. I'll go with you."

(13)

He puts down his pen. He has no more to say. He folds the letter and slides it into an envelope. He writes nothing on the outside. He stands up and stretches, and it occurs to him that this would be the perfect moment for a sniper to catch him from across the street, but no shot is fired. He sits on the sofa with two guns in his lap and lets his eyelids droop.

Nothing to do now but wait.

He remembers a small boy who loved his gentle mother and stern father more than anything in the world. He remembers how wounded he was after he watched both being humiliated by the university that then as now dominated New Haven. Because they were colored. Because it was the way things were. People said things were changing, but he knew it was all on the surface, the superstructure of capitalism. All the colleges were promising to admit more black students. Nobody seemed able to see the contradiction. If capitalism was the enemy, then turning more black people into little capitalists would only serve to strengthen the very system that oppressed the working class. The darker nation was excited at the changes in the wind, but deep down the ruling class was laughing at—

(14)

This time the footfall on the stair is unmistakable. The pigs have arrived at last. The Lecturer hears a fumbling at the door. He throws himself onto the floor on the far side of the desk. If the knob is turned the wrong way the grenade will go off. He has the Walther in hand. He has pulled the Ruger to the floor with him. He duck-walks backward and grabs the M1, then changes his mind and takes the Gamemaster instead. He kneels. Adjusts the sight. Focuses on the door.

Which swings half-open.

No explosion.

"It's me," says Junie. "Don't shoot."

(15)

They are sitting on the sofa together, underneath a side window, out of line of sight from the door. They are armed to the teeth.

"You shouldn't have come back," he says. They have been sitting in silence for almost an hour. Outside it is full dark.

"I know."

"We're going to die here."

She considers. "Maybe," she says. "I hope not."

He looks at her. "You're not staying."

"No. You shouldn't either. There's still time to get away."

"Let me guess. You're not going to the alternate safe house."

She shakes her head. "I went to Chicago for Sharon's sake. I guess that's why I stayed here, too. But it's over for me. I'm out of it. I can't do this anymore."

And you found your babies, he thinks but does not say. Perhaps the rumor is true. But he knows she will never tell him.

"And you're not here, I suspect, to save my hide."

"I know your mind is made up. That's not why I'm here."

"Why, then?"

"I wanted to thank you," she says.

"For what?"

"For forcing me to admit the truth."

"What truth?"

"That I should never have joined Agony. I should never have been the commander."

"I've wondered about that," he says after a bit. "I've gone over every one of Agony's actions, all the way back to 1958. I've found an interesting pattern."

"What pattern is that?"

"You were violent without being violent." He smiles at her evident puzzlement, which he is certain is feigned. "Agony blew things up. You shot up the car of a sheriff who'd beaten demonstrators, or the home of a deputy who'd let the mob have its way with his prisoner. You carried out exactly twenty-two actions during the period when you were commander. And in those twenty-two actions, only one person was killed, probably by accident. Besides, that was at the very end, when others were calling the shots."

"You're forgetting the Klansman."

"No, I'm not. I'll come to him in a moment." He yawns. The work of waiting has worn him out. He wishes they would come. "I think this pattern was intentional. You never wanted to kill anyone. How Agony was formed—where the money came from—who placed you in command—these are mysteries the answers to which I will never know. I have my suspicions, but I will never know. Still, whoever it was who chose you did so precisely because you would keep the violence under control. Scare people without killing people. It's actually rather clever."

"It's not clever at all, and I'm not as pacifistic as you think."

"From my point of view as a revolutionary, no. It is not clever. It is remarkably stupid. A waste of resources. Nonviolent actions will rarely suffice to awaken the sleeping conscience of the proletariat." He holds up a palm to forestall her response. "I know. I know. But listen to me. If your goal is not revolution but reform, then Agony is the perfect vehicle. You scare people but never hurt anyone. If you had your way, nobody would even be scratched. This is not a compliment. You should never have been the commander."

"But I was."

"Yes. You were the commander. And when you refused to punish Kimberly Elden for disobeying your orders and killing the Klansman, everything was clear."

"That I would be deposed, you mean. That Sharon and Paul would take over, and Agony would turn violent."

"No, Junie. What was clear was that you were the killer."

(16)

"Look at it from my point of view. I am called to America to solve a murder that is already solved. I am asked how to deal with a comrade who has disobeyed your orders, even though you know my views on the revolution well enough to know what I will say. And then you refuse to carry out the only true option you have."

"From which you conclude what?"

"From which I conclude that you never intended to discipline Kimberly Elden. You needed me to find her guilty, but that was only to divert the suspicion from yourself."

She is staring at him now, beautiful brown eyes wide in the gray darkness. She says nothing.

"You accepted the story about the drugged coffee too easily. But you know as well as I do that drugging people with any certainty is no easy task. If they used enough to make sure you wouldn't wake up, you would have tasted the difference. Or, even if you didn't, you'd have been knocked out before you could climb two flights of stairs."

Junie is fingering the trigger of the Walther. The Lecturer watches her do it, and knows she knows he is watching.

"You can relax," he says. "There's nobody here but us."

"How did I do it?" she asks. "When? The diversion—the trash can being knocked over—I was upstairs asleep when that happened. And if Kimberly didn't do it, then Kimberly can vouch for me." She considers. "And before that, I was miles away. Sharon can vouch for me."

"I thought about that. And at first I reasoned that the two of you were working together. If you and Sharon snuck back to the house, naturally she would vouch for you. But then I decided the idea was ridiculous. Sharon was after your job. She would have no reason to cooperate. As for Kimberly, she was little more than a hanger-on. She would have betrayed you in a second, and you know it."

"From which you conclude—"

"That you acted alone."

"But how? When could I have done it? Before we left, the prisoner was guarded. After we got back, the prisoner was guarded. When could I possibly have killed him?"

"You told me yourself. When you got back with Sharon. Just before you told Hammie and Paul to guard the basement all night. Remember? You told me that you unlocked the door and went downstairs to make sure he was all right. You came back up and told the group that he was. But that was a lie. You had killed him, right under their noses. And you knew you would get away with it, your reputation for nonviolence unsullied."

They lapse into silence again, almost as companionable as by the lake that night in Chicago.

"Wow," she finally says.

"Wow indeed."

"So what happens now?"

"Nothing. You go off to find your children, and I sit here and wait for the feds."

"You mean the pigs."

He smiles. "Sorry."

"You're getting soft in your old age."

"All the more reason."

They stand. Face each other. Hug. Briefly, then fiercely.

"What's your real name?" she asks. "I'm tired of calling you Jeremy."

"It's just a name," he says. "It doesn't mean anything."

"Tell me anyway."

He tells her. There is no reason not to tell her. In a day or two she will read it in the papers anyway.

"That's a nice name," she says.

"My parents thought so."

"I bet they were great people."

"Quite excellent, in fact."

For some reason they both laugh.

"Come with me," she says again.

"I can't do that."

"You can. Everything's arranged. Transport out of here. We'll be gone before the FBI gets here. I can promise you that."

Frederick again, he is thinking. But maybe not. Maybe this strange, brilliant woman has contacts of which he knows nothing.

"I have to stay," says the Lecturer. "I've done terrible things. I have to pay for my sins."

"I've done terrible things, too."

"They don't compare. Not even close."

"I killed a helpless old man."

"You executed a vicious, murdering Klansman. A man for whom you actually had compassion. I imagine that you stood there, you took the tape off his mouth to ask if he needed anything, and he said something foul. You lost control for an instant. That's all."

"That's what you imagine."

"Yes, Junie. That's what I imagine."

"You didn't say 'Commander.'"

"You're not the commander anymore."

They have drawn apart now but their hands are still linked.

"He was still a human being," she says.

"I know."

"He didn't deserve . . ."

She trails off. At first the Lecturer thinks that she has tired of her own argument. Then he realizes that she has heard something that he missed.

"It's time to go," she says. "Right now."

"Goodbye, Junie."

"Are you sure?"

"It's the best thing," he says, "for the revolution."

She smiles at that, gets up on her toes, kisses him lightly. Then, without a look back, she slips out the door and is gone.

The Lecturer remains in exactly the same spot, unmoving, hands outstretched as if reaching for hers. He is still standing there, unarmed, when they blow three holes in the roof and come pouring in.

STEPHEN L. CARTER is the William Nelson Cromwell Professor of Law at Yale, where he has taught for more than thirty-five years. He is the author of six bestselling novels, including *The Emperor of Ocean Park*, *New England White*, and *The Impeachment of Abraham Lincoln*. He has published dozens of articles in law reviews and many hundreds of op-eds, as well as eight acclaimed works of nonfiction, including *The Culture of Disbelief* and *The Violence of Peace: America's Wars in the Age of Obama*. His next book is a biography of the first black woman prosecutor in New York, who battled the Mob in the 1930s.

New Blank Document

This all was about ten years ago, back when I didn't get many cold calls at all. Maybe I would get two in a month. Sometimes three. Random assignments, because I was cheap, and I was always available. I was a new freelancer making his name, fully aware that for a long time pickings would be slim, so I was also always willing. I was happy to go anywhere and do anything. A couple thousand words here or there would pay my rent. Another couple thousand would put food on my table.

My phone rang and I answered it and heard faint whistling and scratching. Not a local number. Turned out to be a magazine editor in Paris, France. A transatlantic call. The first I ever got. The guy's English was accented but fluent. He said he had gotten my name from a bureau. The place he mentioned was one we all signed up for, in the hopes of getting a little local legwork for a foreign publication. Turned out my hopes had come true that day. The guy in Paris said he wanted to send me on just such an assignment. He said his magazine was the biggest this and the biggest that, but in the end what it boiled down to for me was he wanted sidebar coverage about some guy's brother.

"Cuthbert Jackson's brother," he said, reverently, like he was awarding me the Nobel Prize for Literature.

I didn't answer. I pecked out *Cuthbert Jackson* one-handed on my keyboard, and the search engine came back with an obscure American jazz pianist, an old black guy, born in Florida but for a long time permanently resident in France.

I said, "Cuthbert Jackson the piano player?"

"And so much more," the Paris guy said. "You know him, of course. My magazine is attempting a full-scale biography. We plan to serialize it over thirteen weeks. Recently, for the first time ever, Monsieur Jackson revealed he has a living relative. A brother, still in Florida. Naturally we need to include his point of view in our story. You must go see him at once. Am I correct you live near Florida?"

As a matter of fact he was correct, which I guess explained how he picked me out of the bureau's list. Simple geography. Less mileage.

I said, "Florida is a big state, but yes, I live right next to it."

"Ideally you should obtain biographical detail about their family situation. That would be excellent. But don't worry. Worst case, we can use anything you get, as purely sidebar coverage if necessary, as if to say, by the way, Monsieur Jackson has a brother, and this is where he's living, and this is what he's doing."

"I understand," I said.

"This is very important."

"I understand," I said again.

Ten years ago the net was not what it is today. But it was far enough along to give me what I needed. There were message boards and fan forums, and websites with old photographs, and jazz history sites, and some political stuff, mostly in French. Long story short, Cuthbert Jackson was born in 1925 in a no-account shit hole in the Florida Panhandle. There was one piano in town and he played it all the time. He was such a prodigy that by the time he was four people were so used to it they stopped mentioning it. At the age of eighteen he was drafted by the U.S. Army and trained up as a support engineer. He was sent to Europe with the D-Day invasion. He was sent to Paris to march in the GI parade after liberation. He never left. At first he was listed as AWOL, and then he was forgotten about.

He played the piano in Paris, all through the grim postwar years, sweating in tiny downstairs clubs, for people desperate for something new to believe in, who found part of it in American music played by an exiled black man. He would have said he was evolving the music, not just playing it, perhaps faster and more radically because of his isolation. He wasn't in L.A. or Greenwich Village. He wasn't really hearing anyone else's stuff. Which made some folks call his direction a school or a movement, which led to existential disputes with devotees of other schools and movements. Which led to growing fame, which in an adopted French way made him more and more reclusive, which made him more and more famous. What little he said, he considered plain common sense, but when translated into French he sounded like Socrates. His record sales went through the roof. In France. Nowhere else. It was a thing back then. There were black writers and poets and painters, all Americans, all living in Paris, all doing well. News weeklies did a couple of stories. Cuthbert Jackson's name came up.

Because of the political stuff. France was moving right along. It had aerospace and automobiles and nuclear bombs. Everyone was doing pretty well. Except Americans were doing better. Which led to a heady mixture of disdain and envy. Which led to criticism. Which led to a question: Why do your black people do better when they come over here?

Which was kind of smug, and totally circular, because it wasn't really a question, but a move in the game. Either way it was buried by the gigantic storms already brewing at home. By contrast it seemed quaint and civilized. People agreed a movie could be made. People wondered if a State Department memo could be optioned.

Cuthbert Jackson himself generally ignored the issue, but if asked a direct question, he would answer, with what he considered plain common sense, though as he got older and terser the French translations came out more and more weird and philosophical. One guy wrote a whole book about Jackson's five-word answer to a question about the likely future of mankind.

His most recent CD was with his regular trio, and it had sold pretty well.

His most recent public statement was that he had a brother.

On my map the address everyone seemed to agree on looked to be in hardscrabble country, most of a day's drive away, so I left early. I was sure there would be no motels. I figured I would sleep in the car. Anything and anywhere. I had rent to pay.

The town was as bad as I had expected. Maybe a little meaner. It was all low houses, grouped tight around what looked like the archeological ruins of a previous civilization. Some kind of an old factory, maybe sugar, and the stores and the banks that followed, some in decent buildings, even handsome, in a modest, three-story kind of way, all abandoned decades ago, now overgrown and falling down. I got out of the car where I saw a group of men gathered. They were all waiting for something. There was a mixture of impatience for it and certainty it would arrive.

I asked a guy, "What's coming?"

He said, "The pizza truck."

It showed up right on time and turned out to be their new version of a bar, since their last real bar fell down. The pizza guy had cans of beer in a cooler, which might or might not have complied with county ordinances, but which either way turned eating pizza into a standing-around event, like the best kind of place, with the beer playing the role of the beer, and the pizza standing in for the potato chips and the salted peanuts. I counted twenty people. I told one of them I was looking for Cuthbert Jackson's brother.

He said, "Who?"

"Cuthbert Jackson. He played the piano. He had a brother."

Another guy said, "Who?"

And then another. They all seemed interested. Maybe they ran out of things to say about pizza.

I said, "He's famous in France."

No reaction.

I asked, "Who is the oldest person here?"

Turned out to be a guy aged eighty, eating a pepperoni pie and drinking a High Life.

I asked him, "Do you remember World War Two?"

He said, "Sure I do."

"Cuthbert Jackson went in the army when he was eighteen, which would make you sixteen at the time. Prior to that he could play the piano real well. You probably heard him."

"That kid never came back."

"Because he stayed in France."

"We thought he was killed."

"He wasn't. Now he says he has a brother."

"Is he still a musician?"

"Very much so."

"Then maybe it's a metaphor. You know what it's like, with artistic people. Maybe he had some kind of spiritual epiphany. All about the brotherhood of man."

"Suppose he didn't?"

"Are you a reporter?"

"Proud to be," I said, like I always planned to.

"Who do you work for?"

"Anyone prepared to pay me. Right now a magazine in France."

The guy said, "We thought he was killed. Why would he stay in France? I don't see how that's natural."

I said, "Do you know his brother?"

"Sure," he said, and he walked me a couple of steps, and waved the pointed end of his pepperoni pie at the last house on the next street.

I knocked on the door, and it was opened by another guy who looked about eighty. Which was about right. Cuthbert himself was eighty-two. His long-lost brother would be plus or minus. The old guy said his name was Albert Jackson. I told him a guy from these parts named Cuthbert Jackson had become very famous in France. Recently he had added to his bio that he had a brother.

"Why would he say that?" Albert asked.

"Is it not true?"

"On the television shows they want the truth, the whole truth, and nothing but the truth."

"I'm just a reporter asking a question."

"What was the question?"

"Are you Cuthbert Jackson's brother?"

Albert Jackson said, "Yes, I am."

"That's good."

"Is it?"

"In the sense that the new bio is proved correct. Future historians will not be misled. In France, I mean. A guy wrote a whole book about five words he said."

"I haven't seen him for more than sixty years."

"What do you remember of him?"

"He could play the piano."

"Did you think he was killed in the war?"

Albert shook his head. "He told me many times. He was going to let them take him all over, and he was going to pick out the best place he saw, and he was going to stay there. He said if the war lasted long enough for me to get drafted, I should do the same thing."

"Because it would be better somewhere else for a black man?"

"Who plays the piano, I guess. Although plenty of piano-playing folk are doing pretty good right here."

"Did you ever hear from him?"

"One time. I wrote him about something, and he wrote me back."

"Were you surprised he never came home?"

"I guess a little at first. But later, not so much."

"Would you help me out with background information about your family situation?"

"I guess someone needs to."

"Why's that?"

"You think the bio is correct, but it ain't. Historians will be wrong. I don't know why he said what he said, that he had a brother. I'm not sure what he meant. I might want some time to figure it out."

"I don't understand. You just told me you and he are brothers."

"We are."

"Then what's the problem?"

"The bio should say he had two brothers."

We sat down and I took out my computer, and Albert started to tell me the story, but as soon as I saw where it was going I paused him momentarily, and saved the French file, and opened a new blank document, for what I felt was going to be the real story. I remember the moment. It felt like journalists ought to feel.

A black farmer named Bertrand Jackson had three sons and three daughters, all thirty months apart, all perfectly interlaced in terms of gender, Cuthbert first, the eldest boy, who grew up playing the piano, then went to war, then stayed overseas. The middle boy was Albert, sitting right there telling me the story, and the youngest boy was Robert. The girls in between were delightful. Their mother was happy. The land was producing. Things were pretty good for the farmer. He felt like a man of substance. Altogether a success. He had only one problem. His youngest son, Robert, was slow in the head. He was always smiling, always amiable, but farm work was beyond him. Which was okay. The others could carry him.

Then the farmer made a mistake. Because he felt like a man of substance, he tried to register to vote in the presidential election. He felt it was his civic duty. He kept on going a good long time before he gave up. Afterward a county guy told him never to try again. Things got chilly. They were jealous, he figured. Because his farm was doing well. Maybe a little disconcerted. November rolled into December.

Meanwhile the farmer had gotten Robert a job sweeping up in the dry goods store where he bought his seed. The owner was a white guy. Sometimes his daughter worked the register. Christmas was coming, so Robert made her a card. He labored over the writing. He put, *I hope you send me a card too.* Her daddy saw it, and he showed it to his friends, and pretty soon a lynch mob was coming for Robert, because of his lewd interracial suggestion. He was made to stand on a riverbank, tied hand and foot. His daddy, the farmer, was made to watch. Robert was told he had a choice. He could fall off the riverbank by himself, or they could shoot him off. Either way he was going in the water. He was going to drown. Nothing could be done about that part. Robert said, Daddy, help me, and the farmer said, I'm sorry, son, I can't, because I have four more at home, and a farm, and your mother. Robert fell in by himself. Afterward the same county guy came by and said, now you see what happens. He said, voting ain't for you.

Albert said he told Cuthbert all about it, in great detail, in a long letter. About how it didn't even make the local paper. How the county police wrote it up as a disobedient child warned not to swim. Cuthbert wrote back from Paris, depressed but resigned. And impatient. They had fought in the war. How much longer? After that Albert stopped being surprised his brother didn't come home.

I drove two hundred miles back the way I had come, and took a nap in the passenger seat when I got tired, and then I carried on again. I wanted to get to work. But when I did, I couldn't. I felt ethically the story belonged to the French magazine. But it was a story I didn't want them to have. Or any other nation. I wasn't sure exactly why. Not washing dirty laundry in public, I guessed. United we stand, divided we fall. Clichés were clichés for a reason. I felt like a bad journalist.

Then I realized Cuthbert Jackson had made the same choice. All through the political years. He was Socrates. He could have told a devastating tale. He could have leveraged his exile sky high. But he didn't. He never said a word about Robert. I wondered if he knew exactly why. I wanted to ask him. For a minute I wondered if the magazine would fly me to Paris.

In the end, I stayed home and wrote it up purely as a sidebar. I put, in effect, by the way, Monsieur Jackson has a brother, and this is where he's living, and this is what he's doing. I got paid enough to buy dinner for my friends. We talked about Cuthbert's silence all night long, but we came to no conclusions.

LEE CHILD, previously a television director, union organizer, theater technician, and law student, was fired and on the dole when he hatched a harebrained scheme to write a bestselling novel, thus saving his family from ruin. *Killing Floor* went on to win worldwide acclaim. His most recent novel is *The Midnight Line*, the twenty-second Reacher novel. The hero of his series, Jack Reacher, besides being fictional, is a kindhearted soul who allows Lee lots of spare time for reading, listening to music, and watching Yankees and Aston Villa games. Lee was born in England but now lives in New York City and leaves the island of Manhattan only when required to by forces beyond his control. Visit Lee online at LeeChild.com for more information about the novels, short stories, and the movies *Jack Reacher* and *Jack Reacher: Never Go Back*, starring Tom Cruise. Lee can also be found on Facebook: LeeChildOfficial, Twitter: @LeeChild Reacher, and YouTube: leechildjackreacher.

BRIDGET HAWKINS is a New Jersey native currently living in Bedford-Stuyvesant, Brooklyn. She was born in Philadelphia in 1996 and spent most of her childhood in the North Jersey community of South Orange. As a biracial black woman living in America, issues of race and gender are never far from her mind or her work. She's interested in using graphic memoir to explore both the personal and political, making annotated storytelling from a variety of perspectives possible. Bridget is currently at Pratt Institute, earning a BFA in Writing and specializing in short fiction and poetry. She earned an Honorable Mention in the Academy of American Poets Prize.

Tell Her Anyway

Pencil and pen

I'VE BEEN THINKING ABOUT HOW HE ONLY CAME TO THE NORTH BECAUSE A WHITE MAN TOLD HIM ON NO UNCERTAIN TERMS HE WOULD BE JUST ANOTHER DEAD NIGGER IF HE SAW ANOTHER NORTH CAROLINA MORNING. ABOUT HOW MOST...

OR MAYBE I'M STILL THINKING ABOUT IRENE.

MY GRANDMOTHER. HOW SHE BUST ASS FOR FORTY YEARS AT A JOB ONLY SENDING HER RETIREMENT CHECKS 20 YEARS AFTER SHE'S DEAD.

DON'T GET WARNINGS.

I'VE BEEN THINKING ABOUT MY GREAT AUNT FRANNY. HOW SHE TOLD ME AT A CRAB BOIL WHEN I WAS 8 TH AT THERE WEREN'T NO MORE LYNCHINGS IN THE SOUTH LIKE WHEN SHE WAS YOUNG. HOW SHE TOLD ME WE WERE SAFE UP HERE, THAT THINGS HAD CHANGED.

—at night, some-times. But you don't worry about that now, babygirl...

BUT I COULD SEE THE LIE IN HER ONE GOOD EYE.

ABOUT ALL THOSE YEARS ON HER OWN, SWALLOWING PRIDE WITH A GLASS OF BOOZE, TRYING TO MAKE FUTURES FOR HER SONS. ABOUT HOW SHE DIED FROM AN INFECTION THEY COULD HAVE TREATED. ABOUT HOW SHE'S JUST A PHOTO NOW, COLLECTING DUST...

OR ABOUT HER SON, MY FATHER, HOW HE WAS TOLD BLACKS LIKE HIM COULD NEVER MAKE IT IN HIS FIELD.

AND ABOUT HOW PROVING SOMEONE WRONG EVERYDAY WEARS AWAY YOUR SMILE.

MAKES YOU INTO SMOKE.

LATELY... I'VE BEEN THINKING ABOUT FENCES.

That's it, Bridie! Come to Mommy!

LIKE THE ONE BETWEEN ME AND MY WHITE MOM.

—immerman has been acquitted of second degree murder tonight as—

I'VE BEEN REMEMBERING HOW CLEAR THIS COUNTRY ALWAYS IS ABOUT HOW MUCH BROWN SKIN IS WORTH.

BUT NO ONE CARES ABOUT THE COST. THE LOSS. NO ONE CARES ABOUT IRENE'S LAUGH OR PUNCHY'S WINNING SMILE. THEY BURIED HER IN SOME CEMETERY IN CAMDEN, ERASED HER. THEY LEFT HIM BEHIND IN A BAD PHOTOGRAPH. AND THEY DO IT ALWAYS.

AND NO ONE CARES...

NO ONE CARES ABOUT MY DAD'S CHILDHOOD DREAM TO BE A VET.

NO ONE CARES GREAT AUNT FRANNY PLAYS TRICKS WITH HER GLASS EYE.

NO ONE CARES THIS COUNTRY IS BUILT UP AROUND THEFT. THAT IT HAS LOST A THOUSAND LITTLE BLACK GIRLS + BOYS, THAT IT BOXES THEM INTO DEAD ENDS.

I'D LIKE TO LIVE IN A WORLD WHERE MY EXISTENCE DOESN'T HAVE TO BE JUSTIFIED.

I'D LIKE TO LIVE IN A WORLD WHERE STRANGERS DON'T CUSS AT ME ON THE STREET AND BURN CROSSES AND HOLD OFFICE.

I'D LIKE TO LIVE AS A PART OF THIS COUNTRY. STARES GONE. SENSELESS DEAD RESTORED. I'D LIKE TO PUT TO REST—

I'D LIKE TO HOLD MY CHILD ONE DAY, TELL HER THE FENCES ARE GONE. TELL HER SHE DOESN'T HAVE TO TWIST HERSELF. THAT SHE CAN'T BE ERASED

...

People like you have no right to call yourself American.

—ALL THE GHOSTS MY SKIN IS MADE OF.

I THINK I'LL TELL HER ANYWAY.

Veterans Day

It's a shame the weather is so bad for the Veterans Day Parade, Jack Kearns thought, as he settled in his chair. Because he didn't march any longer, he was grateful that from the window of their third-floor apartment on Fifth Avenue, he wouldn't miss a minute of it.

"Are you all right?" Valerie asked as she walked into the living room. "Anything you want—coffee, water, a Scotch?"

"No thanks to all three, and I'm absolutely fine," Jack said cheerfully.

"I know you're disappointed not to be marching today, but at ninety-two, it was time to give it up."

Jack smiled as his wife dropped a kiss on the top of his thinning hair. "Just because you're only eighty-five doesn't mean you can start treating me like an invalid," he warned. "In fact, you're nearer to eighty-six than eighty-five."

"And you're nearer to ninety-three than ninety-two," Valerie retorted. "All right, I'm off to the hairdresser. Enjoy the parade."

Jack heard the click of the door closing, then gave his full attention to the scene in front of him. It sure does look pretty miserable outside, he observed again, as he watched the remaining World War II veterans waving gamely through the rain that was pelting down on the floats they were riding.

As always, his thoughts turned to his twin brother. "We're missing marching in this one, Tim," he said aloud. "But you can't blame me. Val always was the boss in this house." He was sure from the affectionate tone in his voice that Tim knew he was only kidding.

And then his mind went back to that terrible day when the Japanese attacked Pearl Harbor. The words of President Roosevelt rang through his mind. "A date which will live in infamy . . . a state of war exists . . ."

Tim, you and I were high school students. We couldn't wait until we had our diplomas in our hands before we could enlist and be on our way. You in the army and me in the navy. I sang "Anchors Aweigh" and you tried to drown me out by bellowing "You're in the Army Now." And then we were off to war. A couple of kids who couldn't even imagine what it would be like. You landed at Normandy and my ship got hit by a bomb in the Pacific. It was several long years before it was over. And then the whole country was jumping with joy.

We had always planned that we would go to Fordham together. It was there that I met Valerie. Of course, you always had eyes for only one girl. You met Jenny in kindergarten, and there was never anyone else for you.

And after that there was never a time when you weren't nearby. You were there the day I graduated from Fordham, and you were there again when I got my law degree. The days when Timmy and Rob and Johnny were born. You were always there.

Jack raised his hand and spontaneously waved to one of the oldest veterans in the parade. That poor guy better have a good stiff drink when he gets out of the rain, he thought. Oh, Tim, I wish we were watching this together. I can imagine the stories we would be telling.

But of course it wasn't to be. I came home from service, and you didn't. I remember the first time I went to Normandy and visited your grave. Sergeant Timothy Michael Kearns. You were lying between a captain on one side and a lieutenant colonel on the other. Right where you should be.

• • •

But you've always been with me. Every day of my life. Jenny waited ten years before she married. I know you would have wanted her to have a husband and children. But she told me long ago that a piece of her heart will always belong to you.

Jack stood up and reached his hand to touch the Gold Star in the window, the symbol of a serviceman who gave his life for his country. "You were proud to do it, Tim," he said. And then as he looked down, he saw what seemed like a battalion of veterans looking up at the window and saluting Tim's Gold Star.

MARY HIGGINS CLARK's books are worldwide bestsellers. In the United States alone, her books have sold over 100 million copies. Her most recent suspense novel, *All By Myself, Alone*, was published by Simon & Schuster in April 2017. She also published a collaborative novel in November 2014 with Alafair Burke, *The Cinderella Murder*, *All Dressed in White* in November 2015, and *The Sleeping Beauty Killer* in 2016. She is the author of thirty-seven previous bestselling suspense novels, four collections of short stories (the most recent, *Death Wears a Beauty Mask*), a historical novel, a memoir, and two children's books. She is coauthor, with her daughter Carol Higgins Clark, of five suspense novels. Two of her novels were made into feature films and many of her other works into television films.

Atonement

Yes, I've committed some of the crimes. The little crimes. Sure I have. Who hasn't?

Have I lied about love?

Have I allowed others to believe that it was all their fault?

Have I flattered fools, pretended to have read certain books, claimed never to have received your messages?

Yes, yes, yes, yes, and yes.

Who hasn't? Not those exact transgressions, of course, but others, we all have our litanies, some of which we talk about and some of which we don't.

I've learned to talk about mine, if only to myself. If only because no one else seems to be listening.

The tricky part is determining which of the crimes was the one that mattered. Because (as I've learned, being here) almost all criminals, the people I once thought of as *real* criminals, consider their deeds justifiable, or inevitable, or, at the outer edges of the extreme, punch lines to long, bad jokes about childhood deprivation and abuse; about the eagerness of their victims to *be* victims (in the common area, a sultry-voiced man said, just recently, *I made those people famous by killing them, they were nobody before I came along, and then they were in* People *magazine*); about the smashup of civilization or the chip implanted in a molar by that emergency-room dentist in late-night Indianapolis.

It's one of the surprises. Nobody, no one I've met, looks into a mirror and thinks, *Here stands a criminal.* Not seriously. We've only committed the little crimes.

The jacket you never returned, the falsified résumé, the affair with the kid who was really too young to know better. The rape, the bludgeon, the slit throat.

We had our reasons, pretty much every time.

Which means that all crimes are little crimes, or that no crimes are little crimes. Or that there's not much difference between the two.

But which of my own crimes was the one that mattered?

We spend most of our time in our rooms, pondering that question. We call them our rooms. If we call them by any other name when we speak to one of the guards, we're corrected. "You're asking to leave the common area and go back to your *room*, is that what you're asking?"

It is. I tend to prefer my room to the common area, where people say things I don't always like to hear.

Once I get out of this place I'm going to slice up all her babies, right there in front of her.

I just want to know where my husband is, I don't understand why no one will tell me that.

No other country'd have you, even if you could get there, asshole.

I've finally begun my metamorphosis, wait until you see what I'm becoming.

We're here because we're peculiar, they're quarantining peculiar people, don't you understand that?

I don't spend a lot of time in the common area partly because I dislike so much of what the others say and partly because I'm here to contemplate my crime, which is easier to do in the silence and solitude of my room. My room is immaculate, perfectly white, and devoid of everything I don't need, everything that could divert me from concentration. Those are my instructions, those are everyone's instructions. We live in our rooms, where we contemplate our crime. Those are our only instructions.

I did, however, take note of the use of the singular, when I was brought here. Contemplate our *crime.*

There was one, then. One that mattered.

I've run through the obvious candidates. Who wouldn't? My voting record, of course. Those posts online. The demonstrations (three of them), the words printed on that T-shirt (though I only wore it once), the tipsy argument I had at some after-hours party, with the stern woman in the green blouse.

But some of the others here voted differently, or didn't vote at all. One of them thinks private property should be confiscated, and redistributed across the population. Another believes that everyone with cancer, in any form, should be executed, because the only cure for cancer is the elimination of all the people who have it.

We can't be here for our opinions, then. Not when one of us insists that only black people should be elected to public office because only black people know what the world truly intends, and another maintains, with equal conviction, that black people have been praying collectively, for years, to melt the polar ice caps.

Go to your rooms, all of you, and contemplate your crime.

I'm always cheerful and obedient. Unlike some. One of the guards smiled at me once, I swear it—the quickest knick of a smile, an idea of a smile that passed across his face like a rampant, forbidden thought.

Go to your room and contemplate your crime.

I don't ask questions. I occupy my situation. I think of myself as a member of the team. It's easier that way. And I keep thinking about how, and when, and if, the guard might smile at me again.

I contemplate my crime. I eagerly await confession. But first I have to remember what, exactly, it is that I've done.

Some act or idea that had been legal must have been found to be illegal after all, and none of us knew about it. Laws change, what we mean by *evidence* changes, it's hard to keep up. If you can't believe what you see or hear, you really can't believe what you don't see or hear.

Or should you be able to? Are we guilty of failing to know what we shouldn't do?

It's a game I play, sometimes, with myself. A private quiz show. Okay, now, for the championship: What single, common act might have been committed by:

a stocky, smiling man who killed seven college girls, all of them named Ashley;

a wistful clairvoyant with an artificial hand; and
a tattooed teenage boy who never stops laughing?

What could these people possibly have in common, beyond the most rudimentary bodily functions? What could I have in common with them?

I've been asking that question for months now. It must be months, though it's hard to tell time here, even day from night. The lights are always on. The lights aren't harsh, and the food isn't bad. We're not being punished, not exactly. We're being held. We're being held until . . .

Here's the funny part. I call it the funny part. I'm not sure what else to call it.

I haven't been asked to confess. As far as I can tell, no one has. We simply remain, contemplating. We can seem, sometimes, like monks and nuns, cloistered, living lives of atonement, meditating on a central mystery we're meant to ponder but never, actually, to solve.

That can't be true, though. Not for us. Not for citizens of a country founded on all that can be discovered, all that can be forgiven, and all that can be repaired.

Sometimes one of us tells a guard that we know what we did, that we're prepared to admit to it, and suffer the consequences. The answer is always the same, though. *Stay in your room and contemplate your crime.*

We feel confident—I do, anyway—that our confession day will come. Why would we be here if we weren't working toward redemption, or punishment? Think of what it costs the taxpayers, just to feed and shelter us.

When the guards come to take me out of my room and march me to . . . wherever it is they take us . . . I've decided that I'm going to confess everything. Everything I've ever done. I don't mind about how long it'll take, and—I feel sure about this—that the guards won't, either. The guards will listen, their faces grave and forbearing as painted gods looking down on the faithful from a domed ceiling. And when I find my way to my crime they will hold me, they will welcome me back, they will stroke my hair as I soak their suit jackets with my tears. I will be forgiven. And I'll travel on from there.

• • •

MICHAEL CUNNINGHAM is the author of six novels: *A Home at the End of the World, Flesh and Blood, The Hours, Specimen Days, By Nightfall,* and *The Snow Queen,* as well as a story collection, *A Wild Swan and Other Tales,* and a nonfiction book, *Land's End: A Walk in Provincetown. The Hours* received the Pulitzer Prize and the PEN/Faulkner Award in 1999, and was made into a film in 2002, featuring Meryl Streep, Julianne Moore, and Nicole Kidman. Cunningham's fiction has appeared in the *New Yorker,* the *Atlantic,* and the *Paris Review,* among other publications. He is a Senior Lecturer in English at Yale University.

Intersections

Nothing but green lights. Six city blocks' worth, on a straight, empty, six-lane road at 3:33 in the morning.

This is what my client saw when, tired from a long day, he came to the crest of a broad, main street that cuts through Newark, New Jersey, on his way home from late-shift work at a metal fabricating plant.

I went to the site of the accident in the early-morning hours the day after I was retained by my client's family. I had to see what he saw at the exact time the accident occurred. And I had to imagine what he didn't see: a petite young woman, dressed in black from a night out, running across the street against a red light and outside the crosswalk.

There were no skid marks before the point of impact. Only after. Thirty-two feet of them, indicating excessive speed for a 25 mph zone but nothing out of the ordinary.

And then he drove away.

It was 3:33 a.m. exactly when I parked at the hillcrest near the intersection where Francisco Duarte hit Megan O'Hara. All those green lights, a wide-open alley, beckoning him to move ahead.

"He should have stopped," I said to myself, then wrote it down on a legal pad, knowing it would be my opening before the jury when the case went to trial.

"He should have stopped to help." Sentence number two.

A good criminal attorney goes to the scene to see what their client saw. A very good one crawls around in their client's brain and tries to make reason out of the unreasonable, find the thinking behind the unthinkable. Francisco Duarte knew he should have stopped; he confirmed as much by turning himself in less than an hour after the accident, just as Megan O'Hara was being pronounced dead at University Hospital.

When the family came to retain me, I saw who he came from. Good people, humble and now shamed, embarrassed that their son took a life and ran. They sat in front of me, the father in a forest-green janitor's uniform from a local Catholic school, the mother in the smock of a neighborhood day care center. Their hands were clutched, their heads bowed. I was a man in a suit. An authority. An educated person. Someone to respect. The mother and father, unable to pronounce my Italian surname, respectfully called me "Mr. Mike." Their daughter, who spoke English as well as my own sons, got "Mr. Tricarico" right on the first try.

My first question to his family was whether Francisco felt remorse, my mind already racing ahead to possible mitigating circumstances. "After all," I said, leading them, "*the young woman shouldn't have been in the intersection.*" I wanted to gauge their son's sense of fault and responsibility.

His parents nodded, understanding the question.

"*Sí*, Mr. Mike. *Se siente terrible. Nunca duerme, llora toda la noche,*" his mother, Consuelo, answered, looking at me through teary eyes as if I understood.

I turned to the daughter, Maria, for help.

"My mother says, 'He feels terrible. He never sleeps, he cries all night,'" she said.

"*Nunca dormimos tampoco, sabiendo que está en ese lugar,* Mr. Mike," the mother added as the father, Enrico, nodded in agreement.

"We never sleep, either, knowing he's in that place," Maria said. "When Frank turned himself in, the police called ICE and they came and got him."

"Frank? He goes by Frank?" I asked.

"Yes," Maria said. "To everybody but my parents."

As I momentarily processed this Americanization of Francisco to Frank, Maria cut the thought short.

"There's a problem, Mr. Tricarico," she said. "A big problem."

"You have no papers," I said.

"*Sí, sí*, Mr. Mike," the parents said in unison.

"We are undocumented," Maria said. "Except for my younger brother and sister. They were born here."

Several years ago I visited Ellis Island with my boys. We found my grandfather's name inscribed on the wall, paid for by a donation from my uncle.

But what moved me more were the grainy black-and-white photographs inside the museum. There were no smiles on the old immigrant faces; just shock and exhaustion. If they were at all optimistic, it was masked by a grim countenance, as if they knew the task of building a new life here was going to be laborious and joyless.

I saw this look now on the faces of the Duarte family as I explained to them that my job was to try to keep Frank Duarte out of jail. There was nothing I could do to keep him in the country. They needed an immigration lawyer for that.

"We have one," Maria said. "There's nothing she can do. Frank has already confessed."

Sometimes a defense attorney's task is not about raising questions or offering theories that make intellectual room for reasonable doubt. It's about finding room for mitigation. That's the legal term. In the old days, they called it "the mercy of the court." I would have to find it for Frank Duarte to keep him out of prison for a significant term, because the facts were not in dispute. Yes, he confessed to the police, in the most Catholic sense, after he turned himself in—a full, tearful admission, a recorded account of the events, with painstaking accuracy. He did this without an attorney present, knowing he risked prison, and knowing he would never absolve *himself*, whether he came forward or not. He would live with what he'd done, either way.

Frank was charged, at first, with leaving the scene of an accident after giving the police his statement. The most incriminating detail was that he thought he had hit a large black dog, until he saw the lifeless form of a woman in his rearview mirror and heard the screams of her friend, who ran back to the curb. Then he panicked and took off.

According to New Jersey statute 39:4-129, leaving the scene of an accident where bodily harm may have occurred is an indictable offense, known in the common legal lexicon as a felony. Under President Obama's "Immigration Accountability" executive order, local police had no choice but to call federal immigration officials, even before word of Ms. O'Hara's death came and "vehicular homicide" was added. Frank would be detained by immigration officials until trial. If found guilty, he would be deported. This was a moot point; he had confessed. I would have to try to undo the confession.

"Where is he?" I asked Maria. "Please don't tell me Essex."

"Yes," she said. "The county jail."

And with those words, his mother began to weep as only grieving mothers can.

There are two federal immigration detention centers in the Newark area. One is in Elizabeth, which borders Newark and is 60 percent Hispanic. The other is the leased wing of the Essex County jail.

While county inmates and federal detainees are generally separated, it's still a prison. The cell doors slam shut, yard time is restricted, and the ominous security checkpoints, which require government photo IDs of some type, keep immigrant families away.

"County jail" is a soft description. It conjures up an image of the town drunk sleeping it off under the care of a local deputy. *Mayberry, R.F.D.*, for my generation.

Essex County jail is no sweet vanilla sitcom. It's a dark, roiling sea of anger and hatred, frightening in ways only the men incarcerated there can understand. Street gangs war inside; lineal derivatives of blues and reds battle in orange jumpsuits. In Newark, they have names like Grape Street (Crips) and Red Breed Gorillas (Bloods). The Southside Cartel (Bloods) supplanted Sex,

Money, and Murder (also Bloods) as the city's most vicious gang after a pro-
longed street war. The Latin Kings brawl with the blacks and MS-13, a gang
with Central American drug cartel beginnings. Men are beaten and stabbed
in this prison. Some commit suicide. Drugs feed the hostility of sociopaths.
Men who have murdered have no compunctions about murdering again, nor
do rapists about raping. It is not a place for a young man like Frank Duarte,
who left the scene of a tragic accident. *If he had only stopped.*

And the more I learned about Megan O'Hara, the more I feared for Frank
Duarte. I had to be ready with a narrative to defuse the media's fixation on
the heightened Trump Era rage against "illegals." I didn't want Frank's face on
FOX News. I didn't want some inmate sticking him.

"If I had a daughter, I would want her to be like Megan O'Hara." I wrote this
down to use at some point in court—opening or closing, or sentencing—after
researching the young woman.

It was, at first, a defensive move. If I got press inquiries about Frank, I
would switch the focus to Megan O'Hara. The real story, I would say, is the loss
of this very special young woman. And very special she was. She was a leader.
A high school class president, a field hockey team captain, then on to Vassar,
where she was majoring in nonprofit management, of the humanitarian sort.
She did internships and volunteer work at Church World Service in Pough-
keepsie, an agency devoted to helping refugees and immigrants find their foot-
ing in their new American home. She marshaled the student volunteer force
for the Dutchess County Community Action Agency and learned Spanish to
better communicate with the clients.

I learned this from her obituary and Facebook page, which contained
more than five hundred messages of heartfelt condolences. I read every one,
and realized this young woman impacted every life she touched. And now
mine.

She came from an affluent family in Short Hills, one of the wealthiest
suburbs in New Jersey, and one evening at twilight, I drove by her house for
only one reason: to look for a dark room and connect to her parents' grief and

anguish. The whole house was warmly lit except for a black corner over the attached garage.

I parked and sat for a moment. She was twenty-two, in her senior year at Vassar, home for the weekend when she was hit. Her parents had raised her to be brilliant and sent her into the world to share her gifts, only to have her die in the most rudimentary way, not heeding the advice every child has drummed into their heads: *look both ways.*

From the winding road on the eastern slope of the Watchung Mountains where she lived, there are views of the Manhattan skyline and the industrial basin of New Jersey, the turnpike corridor of power plants and shipping ports. Smokestacks and container cranes rise from landscape like skeletal skyscrapers. At Ports Newark and Elizabeth, the freight landing for the entire New York metropolitan area, the cranes are painted in red-and-white horizontal stripes. Against the backdrop of a clear blue September sky, they stand like an American welcome to merchant seamen from all over the world, not unlike the Statue of Liberty and Ellis Island, a scant four miles away.

I mention September because that's when the accident occurred—September of 2016, during the full-throated build-a-wall rhetoric of the election campaign. In Megan O'Hara's neighborhood, political signs were all but absent. The wealthy abstain. They maintain decorum. They speak with their wallets.

The panoramic view from Megan O'Hara's bedroom window included not only the distant neighborhood where Frank Duarte lived but also the detention center where he was now housed in the industrial port section, surrounded by storage yards, where shipping containers were stacked like great pyramids, and towing companies, where acres of junked cars came to rust.

The early history of human settlement is shaped by the earth's geology, geography, and climate. Once survival was conquered, only the man-made forces of politics and economy made habitable places inhospitable.

I am, by ancestry, a southern Italian. Man's presence on the land is as ancient as war itself; the boot has been the crossroads of civilizations since the

Paleolithic Age. It was conquered by invading armies of Greeks and Romans and Lombards and Normans, right through to the British and Americans in the Second World War.

As such, southern Italians are, by nature, distrustful and resistant to authority, be it a king, a landowner (including the church), or an elected government.

Somewhere in my DNA, there lies the reason I am a defense attorney.

It's also why my grandfather came to the United States as an illegal immigrant in 1916.

When Italy declared war on Austria-Hungary in 1915, my grandfather could have been forgiven for thinking it was a northern Italian border land-grab that southern Italians shouldn't die for. Italy was unified just forty years before his birth, so allegiance to the new country was in its infancy.

The family stories about him were colorful and comic, but there was a dark hue to them, an undercoat of shame.

He grew up in a Basilicata farm town called Brienza, and his family worked olive groves on land owned by the Catholic Church. My grandmother's family lived nearby, and they courted as teenagers. Her uncles were among the first wave of the great southern Italian migration that emptied out half the boot from the 1880s until after the Second World War. My grandmother came to the United States with her parents in 1914, and she left her childhood sweetheart behind.

When Italy went to war on its northern border, my grandfather ignored his draft notice. Two army officers were dispatched to get him, but he jumped out the back window of the family farmhouse with a dress belonging to one of his sisters. He threw it on, rolled up his pant legs, and headed for the olive grove. When the officers checked the property, they saw only a woman working in the field. This went on for weeks, prior to the Isonzo Offensive, when one hundred thousand farm boys like my grandfather were sent with little training to the mountains of present-day Slovenia. Sixty thousand were slaughtered. My grandfather was determined not to be one of them.

He wrote to my grandmother, offering a marriage proposal. She conspired to send him the identification papers of one of her uncles. That man was twenty years his senior, so my grandfather grayed his hair by rubbing talcum powder in it and boarded steerage on the *Mauretania*. Two weeks later he walked, unaccosted, into America, smelling like diesel oil and a fresh haircut.

They married, and almost thirty years later their oldest son was awarded two Silver Stars, a Bronze Star, and a Purple Heart during the invasion of Sicily as part of General Patton's Seventh Army. He lost part of his trigger hand at Mount Etna but continued on to the mainland, valuable because he spoke the language.

My uncle's heroic actions helped fast-track his father's citizenship two years later, no questions asked.

Two men, a father and a son, on different sides of history. The fate of individuals cannot be divorced from their times.

The Duarte family landed at Newark airport in 1999 with tourist visas to visit Consuelo's green card–holding cousin. They never left. Instead, they found menial jobs and an apartment in Newark's Ironbound section, a Portuguese area of squat wood-frame working-class houses set off from the rest of the town by railroad lines and the ports. The Portuguese came after World War I, supplanting the Germans, Lithuanians, Poles, and Italians who had all labored in the tanneries and other dirty factories of the city's industrial center.

When the Portuguese migration ended, Brazilians and other South Americans followed, mostly to work as laborers in mom-and-pop construction companies started by Portuguese who themselves began as laborers. That is the American way, the promise of this country since the *Mayflower*.

Francisco Duarte started kindergarten in 1999 at the Ann Street School, where he became Frank. It was the beginning of his Americanization. By second grade he was fluent in English; by sixth all trace of his accent was gone unless he purposely affected it. Also by then, his two younger siblings had been born, both in the emergency room of Beth Israel Medical Center under charity care. Both were American citizens as a birthright.

By the time big brother Frank entered high school, he forwent his native soccer to play American football and was a wide receiver at East Side High.

I thought of how much had changed since 1999. The terror attacks of 9/11; the wars in Iraq and Afghanistan; the mass shootings that came with greater frequency; the economic recession; the sport of political divisiveness, led by media and party operatives who exploit our differences rather than explore our similarities. Through all this turmoil, immigration was either at the center or on the periphery of American discontent, depending on what other pressing issue consumed the public's attention at the moment.

In 2012, Obama's Deferred Action for Childhood Arrivals executive order shielded kids brought into the country illegally from deportation. He did this because a warring Congress couldn't pass a law.

But in 2014, under growing anti-immigrant sentiment, Obama signed the "Immigration Accountability" order. It carried the slogan *Deporting Felons, Not Families.*

Not quite.

Not for Frank Duarte.

In September 2016, with chants of "Build a wall" cascading around Donald Trump like victory confetti, Frank Duarte could not escape his times. Not when his life tragically intersected with Megan O'Hara's.

Behind the thick glass windows of Essex County jail, the Latino men in the booths had the same look on their faces as the people in the old photos at Ellis Island: stunned indifference, eyes and thoughts worlds away. Most were silent on their end of the intercom phones, quiet as a still picture. The intake and outtake of American history, 140 years apart.

On my side, hushed Spanish chattering from wives, parents, and lawyers broke the void of silence.

At booth 48, Frank Duarte waited. I sat down, and he picked up the intercom phone on the other side of the glass. My first thought, honestly, was that Frank Duarte was every bit as Caucasian as Megan O'Hara. My own olive skin was darker than his. Somewhere hidden in his family tree must have been

Germans or Poles who immigrated to Paraguay from as far back as the 1880s. America, we're led to believe, has a lock on immigration. It does not.

Frank was no more than a boy, only a man by legal definition. His jail beard growth was scattered and soft, so light in color that the circles under his eyes were darker than his hair. After some small talk about his conditions and the food, tears came to his eyes.

"Mr. Tricarico?"

"Yes?"

"I'm sorry. So sorry. How do I tell her parents I'm sorry? That's something I have to do."

"I don't recommend that, son," I said. "I'm exploring ways to make your confession inadmissible—to get it thrown out—because you didn't have an attorney present. Writing a letter to her parents would be another form of admissible evidence, like a second confession."

"Father Ramon said contrition is the only way I'll get God's forgiveness."

"Son, with all due respect, God's forgiveness may keep you out of hell, but it won't keep you out of prison," I said. "Do you want to spend ten to fifteen years in a place like this?"

"I did something horrible," he said.

"It was an accident."

"Not the part about running away." He looked down. "I was a coward."

Many times in my line of work, I'm asked how I can defend killers, sexual predators, lowlifes, and skels with a clear conscience. My stock reply is, "I don't defend the person, I defend the system."

But Frank Duarte was on the unforgiving side of the system, the shit end of the stick. As a person, he needed defending.

"Why did you run away?" I asked.

"I was scared. All this talk about illegals," he said. "I was afraid of exactly this. Ending up here. Getting deported."

"You're going to be deported unless we go to trial and a jury finds you innocent."

"I'm not innocent," he said.

"I misspoke. I meant 'not guilty.' There's a difference."

"But I am guilty."

I changed tactics.

"Son, do you have any family left in Paraguay?"

"One uncle."

"You realize that if you get deported, you can never return to the United States. And if your parents and Maria visit you in Paraguay, they risk not being allowed back in."

"Yes."

"You understand all that?"

"Yes."

"You understand you may never see them again, or at least not for a very, very long time, until the laws change."

"Yes."

"And this is still what you want to do?"

"Yes."

I knew then the guilt he felt over Megan O'Hara's death was asphyxiating. The obsessive images of the horrific impact and his panicked flight sucked the air out of all his thoughts. They filled his brain like a poisonous black cloud. He would never live again—no matter where—if he didn't apologize. Deeply and sorrowfully.

"Write the letter, then. I'll give it to the prosecutor to give to her family. I can't guarantee they'll accept it. But I'll try."

In my car I wrote down the words "This is the collateral consequence of the immigration debate. This is a real kid, a real family being broken up, not some abstract, shadowy menace." I would use those words at his sentencing.

My grandfather was the oldest of eight siblings in Italy. He never returned for fear of being arrested. He never saw any of them again. I had never even considered the magnitude of that separation until I sat for a moment in the parking lot after leaving Frank Duarte.

• • •

I began to collect mitigating factors, preparing for either trial or sentencing. Frank, at twenty-two, the same age as Megan O'Hara, had been an altar boy and was now a youth minister in his church. He had no criminal record, not even a speeding ticket. He was in technical school to get a certificate in metal fabrication and welding, while already employed in the field. He had been steadily employed since age fourteen, the legal age for working papers in New Jersey, bussing tables and dishwashing in Ironbound restaurants.

Though on different ends of the economic spectrum, he was filled with the same hopes and ambitions as Megan O'Hara.

As I gathered more information, I pressed the state to drop the vehicular manslaughter charge. Frank told me he called 911 seconds after the accident. His phone records and county dispatch tapes proved it. Her friend also called. The prosecution narrative that "he left her there to die" wasn't exactly true. The medical reports stated that her head injuries were so extensive and severe because she fell in front of his bumper. That's why he thought he'd hit a dog. And then came the toxicology report.

"I don't want to make this ugly," I told the prosecutors during a discovery conference. "Her family has suffered enough. But I'll use it if I have to."

Even now, I'll leave it at that, except to say that she did not make the decision to bolt across the street against a red light with a clear mind.

The statement of her friend corroborated Frank's account. He had the green light, and when his headlights appeared at the crest of the hill, she turned back to the curb. She tried to pull Megan with her, but Megan went forward. That's when she stumbled. She admitted that both were intoxicated, clubbing in Manhattan until closing time.

The lead prosecutor, Jack Hurley, had been a friend and respected adversary for twenty years.

"Can we make 'vehicular homicide' go away?" I asked. "Otherwise the victim gets excoriated in court. Nobody wants that, Jack. It doesn't bring her back. Neither does him sitting in prison for fifteen years."

"I'll take it upstairs. And to the family," he said. "But the kid is getting deported. Nothing I can do about it. ICE is breaking my balls on this. They want him gone. Like now."

"He's prepared for that," I said. "He knows what it means. He thinks it's a punishment that fits the crime. I don't agree, but what I think doesn't matter."

"That's the world we live in," he said.

I handed him Frank's letter.

"The kid wants to apologize. I read it. He begs for their forgiveness. It's heartfelt. Unbelievably so," I said. "I got choked up reading it."

"There are two empty bedrooms, twelve miles apart. One is in Short Hills, where Megan O'Hara grew up before following the dreams that led her to Vassar and a life filled with determination to help the needy.

"The other is in Newark's Ironbound, where Frank Duarte lived with his family, pursuing the same American dream as all our ancestors.

"One of the tragic ironies of this case is that Megan O'Hara was working to help people like Frank Duarte assimilate into our country.

"But now their empty rooms are vaults of grief for two families. They are places of profound sorrow, filled with the memories, the love, the laughter, and the voices of two young people who are never coming home.

"Your Honor, what follows is not an attempt to equate the losses suffered by the O'Haras and the Duartes. There is no comparison. Megan is dead, and Frank is not."

This was how I opened my statement to the court at Frank's sentencing.

A deal was struck, with the O'Haras' permission. Frank would plead guilty to "leaving the scene" and receive a five-year suspended sentence. He would be deported, and if he tried to come back, the sentence would be imposed. And now he sat in court at the defense table in his orange prison jumpsuit with his family directly behind him and the O'Hara family across the gallery aisle. He had the right to have his handcuffs removed but refused.

"She was taken away in the most cruel and inexplicable way—the way parents dread when their children are little and impulsive and so admonish them repeatedly to 'look both ways' before crossing a street.

"To say what happened that night is 'every parent's nightmare' seems inadequate and cliché. It does not capture the anger, the depth of sadness, the imbedded memory loop, the sleepless nights and the restless days.

"The O'Hara family lives with that every day—every second, every minute of every day. Frank Duarte understands this all too well. He lives with it, too. As you will hear from him in a few moments, he will serve a life sentence of guilt and shame and isolation—for what he didn't do.

"Your Honor, Frank Duarte panicked. He should have stopped. He should have stopped to help, even if to hold Megan O'Hara's hand while her life slipped away. To bring her the comfort of a stranger. But he kept going. This is his cross to bear. This is his prison."

I detailed the good works done by both Megan and Frank. I did my best to bring her to life, and him, too, as a "real kid, with a real family." I chose the words "collateral consequence of the immigration debate" rather than "victim" to not offend her family. There was only one victim here.

Maria took the stand to testify on Frank's behalf, and offered the O'Hara family "my family's most sincere condolences and prayers that God gives you strength."

It was the first of many references to God, by both families, and truth be told, a believer could feel His presence in that courtroom, where so much loss, grief, and, eventually, forgiveness and mercy would come to bear.

Father Ramon Suarez was next, and echoed Maria's sincerity. He spoke of Frank's remorse and contrition, as well as his service to the church.

When it was Frank's turn to speak, I instructed him to address only the judge. Instead, he turned to Megan's family. With a trembling voice and tears streaming down his face, he said, "I took a life that was valuable to God. I ended the life of a very good person. Please know I, too, think of her every second of every day. Please know I have no life left in me because of this. I am hollowed out, and all I want now in my life is your forgiveness. I beg God for forgiveness. I beg you for your forgiveness."

At the moment he said the word "forgiveness," James O'Hara, Megan's father, gave him a slight, almost imperceptible nod.

There were tears on both sides of the courtroom aisle already when Julie O'Hara, Megan's mother, came forward to read the victim impact statement.

She spoke of how their family "was as close as family could be" and how Megan was the center. She used words like "incalculable loss." She mourned not only her daughter but the grandchildren she and her husband would never have. She spoke of phoning their other daughter to tell her that her only sister was gone. Of how "the shattering wails of grief" that followed haunt them still.

And then she addressed Frank, whose head was bowed as he cried.

"The God I believe in forgives you," she said. "The God I believe in loves you. I am so sorry this has happened to us, and I'm sorry it has happened to you. But the God I believe in has a plan for us—and for you. We, and you, will be okay. We forgive you."

The magnitude and humanity of those words continue to resonate with me. They were equally stunning in their simplicity and kindness. There is hope for this world with people like the O'Haras in it. Compassion and empathy, if given a chance, can overpower all the noise of political posturing.

When the sentencing was over, Frank was led out of court to be processed for an immediate deportation flight to South America. He looked over his shoulder at his family as sheriff's officers held him by each arm and escorted him out of the courtroom to the holding cell. The door shut behind them. That's how they said good-bye. Eyes locked. Silent. Without so much as a touch.

The O'Haras, too, watched him leave. I thought it was strange until the families began to file out. It was then that the mothers and fathers of the two lost children embraced one another. The O'Haras and Duartes held each other, sharing loss and grief, before going their separate ways, inextricably linked forever.

MARK DI IONNO is a lifelong journalist and a Pulitzer Prize finalist in news commentary for his work on the aftermath of Hurricane Sandy. His front-page columns regularly appear in the *Star-Ledger*, and its online partner, NJ.com. He began his career covering sports with the *New York Post*, where he helped break many significant stories, including baseball's case against Pete Rose and the undoing of Mike Tyson. He is the author of several works of nonfiction and the debut novel *The Last Newspaperman*. His forthcoming novel, *Gods of Wood and Stone*, will be published by Touchstone/Simon & Schuster in July 2018. He is an adjunct professor of journalism at Rutgers University and a father of six children. He lives in New Jersey.

The Third Twin

For as long as you can remember you have loved looking into shimmering surfaces. The tremble of juice in the glass clutched in Henry's hand as your father ambled past you through the kitchen; the glassy look of love from the dog when tossed a bone; the waver of horizon as lightning touched down at the center of the pond. Tonight, it's the spin of square light across the walls of a dance floor that has you dizzy. You've left the trappings of your body, your lonely brain dislocating with the gentle guidance of drugs and the possibility of touch.

There is a woman dancing across from you. She leans toward you, through the fog, the one that's emanating from the machine in the corner as well as the one that has taken up residency in your mind, and says her name is Lacuna. That it means *lake, a chapter of a book never written, the hollow part of a bone.* You move closer until your knuckles brush against each other's.

When the music stops you wander into the bathroom alone, peer at yourself in the smudged glass of the mirror, study the line of your chin, the way a soft blond mustache has appeared above your lip. Some mornings you pluck it, but secretly you feel proud of it. It makes you think how you have always been molting, attempting to cast off some part of yourself, your body, to transform into something other. Maybe not just one, maybe several others. There is a plurality deep inside you. You are, and in other ways you are not. You are beside your self. You have been trying to explain this to people but they don't understand.

. . .

You walk out into the night for a cigarette you will regret. Not because of the molten damage to your lungs but because smoking guarantees a throbbing migraine in the morning. But you need to fumble with something, to do something with your hands, so you strike a match and take a sharp inhale. There are clouds over Central Square and the air has that clean cold smell to it and then the sky opens and you are standing under a streetlamp in the falling snow.

You already are another, your mother says when you try to explain it. *You are a twin.*

You have a real live double on the outside of your body; for most of your life he was there across the room from you, reflecting you, his very existence a taunt you had to learn to love. Even now, Henry is reflected in every mirror you look into. What you share and what you own: a forever-moving target. Henry hardly considers it; you can hardly bear it. You'll be seeing Henry tomorrow; he's asked you to help him knock on doors for one of his causes. This week it's cystic fibrosis, last week it was fracking, next week polar bears or melting ice caps or Lou Gehrig's disease, any incurable catastrophe. Sometimes it feels as though your brother was born guilty and running with every hopeless cause is his attempt to circumvent his pain. You agree to help him simply because, well, you're used to doing things with him. What your mother doesn't know and what you'll never really say to her is that you have *another* double. You are not just the masculine woman people see when they look at you, the one who looks like Henry, but there is another brother, inside of you, a third twin.

You think about returning to the dance floor but it's late and the snow is piling up and your heart is drumming from the nicotine, and if you're going to be honest your anxiety is also drumming from being close to someone else. Drinking helped, but walking is better, so you set off into the night, fast, over the river, up the hill until you are at the steps of your apartment. You take the dog out. She tries to bite the snow as it falls. In bed you open a book and close it. Turn the lights off. You think about how most nights feel like a kind of eclipse. You close your eyes and move into intervals of darkness, your sense of self a fracturing of form so that when you dream, you dream in pieces. You wake up late with nothing but the coming and going of night to ponder, get into your car, and go. The migraine is like an earth quaking inside your head. You knew better than to smoke that cigarette, but a little brain damage can also be a welcome distraction.

The coffee at the union office has the taste of wet cardboard. The volunteer explains Henry is already out, knocking on doors, that he couldn't wait for you but has picked a packet of houses for you.

The first door you knock on: blinds flip open, a ghost-white naked torso leans against the windowpane. Opens the door. The man has a shaved head. Says he hasn't been well. You try to maintain eye contact while also trying to make out if that is a swastika tattoo on his biceps. He doesn't seem to register that you are a woman or a man, or at least that's how you perceive his indifference. That's as good as it gets these days. He says he won't be donating. He's been sick with . . . something else.

The next address is at the end of a cul-de-sac off the main road. As you approach you notice a MAKE AMERICA GREAT AGAIN bumper sticker on a Crown Vic parked in the driveway. Next to the door there is a wooden sign that reads: ERIC'S WAY. You glance at your sheet and notice the names don't match—you are looking for someone named Daniel.

You are about to knock on the door when you remember an old English fairy tale that was once read to you and Henry on a school outing. The story was of a woman engaged to a murderous man named Mr. Fox. Through every door of his house the woman passed there was this warning: BE BOLD, BE BOLD, BUT NOT TOO BOLD. LEST THAT YOUR HEART'S BLOOD SHOULD RUN COLD. You had closed your eyes to listen and while you did a photographer snapped your picture for a local paper. You were in a red-and-white-striped shirt, your long hair twisted into braids. In the picture it looks like you are dreaming. You thought that with your eyes closed you looked more like a boy. You thought maybe if you were a boy you'd be safe. But then maybe you'd be vicious like the man in the story named Fox.

You knock on the door and this time a small man answers, says, *Hello*. He reminds you of Rumpelstiltskin, like he'd be good at stomping around. He takes one look at you and asks you if you are looking for Henry. For some reason this worries you but you say, *Yes*. The man invites you in and there is your brother, Henry, sitting on the couch. He doesn't seem glad to see you. There is sadness and an uncertainty in his eyes. He grips the clipboard on his lap. You look around the room. There is one black sneaker on a shelf beneath the television, on one of the walls several paintings of a thin young man with dark hair and doe-like eyes. A chessboard, mid-game, sits on the table but has the feeling of having never been touched. There is a woman in a rocking chair in a corner of the room, her plump hands rest over a pile of drab-colored yarn she has been knitting. You sit next to her and notice there are tears in her eyes. Eric, you learn, was the couple's son, who died in a motorcycle accident years ago. This house was his and his parents now live here. The woman asks you if you'd like some sweet bread as her husband shows your brother posters for the benefit they hold for local schoolchildren in her dead son's name. *He told me he was too tired to play chess that day*, the man says. *I just don't know what he was doing out on that road.*

You watch Henry out of the corner of your eye, the way you have since you were born, just minutes before him. He seems defeated. For all of his charitable work you're not sure your brother has ever really listened to the stories people carry with them and tell him and here he is in a mausoleum of grief.

When you get home that evening you walk the dog along the Charles River and notice that the dog's hair, once white at her chest, is turning orange, almost red. At the grocery store you see the woman from the dance floor the night before. Lacuna. She tells you she has just come from yoga class and you start rambling on about mandalas and how at the four gates there are eight different graveyards and in the graveyards are jackals and crows and sometimes zombies but also sometimes something called *clear understanding* and they are supposed to represent individuation and how your mother took you and Henry to graveyards as children and you are starting to feel like you are having an out-of-body experience when she puts her hand on your wrist and asks you if you want to come over for dinner. You let out a breath and in the same moment you get a text that your friend across town has gone into labor. You drop your phone and when you pick it up there is a crack across the frame that you study for a moment then realize Lacuna is still looking at you waiting on an answer, and that you like it when she looks at you and you say, *Dinner, yes.*

After she leaves you buy wine and a chicken and you walk slowly to the address Lacuna gave you. When you reach it you walk around the block again and again in a circle which is actually a square and it feels as if you are walking a labyrinth, and you do this until you understand that your circumambulating is in direct conflict with time and the minutes passing, which crush down on your shoulders until you finally stop in front of her house and press the buzzer.

Inside, Lacuna shows you a drawing her father made. It is blue and compass-shaped and you immediately feel affection for it. You and Lacuna grill vinegar chicken on the fire escape even though it is very cold outside. Later, she invites you into her bed. She sleeps and you stay awake. Her apartment is level with the elevated trains that run late into the evening. There is something about the train that reminds you of high school, the feeling of being awake forever, of always trying to undo some puzzle inside while your brother slept soundly on the bunk bed above your head. And there is something about Lacuna's hesitation, and yours, that puzzles you. Hesitation, you think, is intimate because its origin is fear and that makes you think you may never be here with her again so you try to imprint the night onto your mind: the feel of her fingertips tracing your ear as she drifts into sleep; the way, in her sleep, she shakes her fist in the air as if angry at someone you hope is not you. When you gently press your nose into the soft place at the back of her neck her body moves into you. You think of your friend giving birth, air flooding the baby's tiny lungs for the first time. Across from the bed is a Langston Hughes poem tacked on the wall and you read it over and over again by the streetlamp's light until it feels like a kind of mantra. When you finally close your eyes you dream of the sun's corona, of garlands, of heat and boundlessness.

The next morning you are still high from holding her as you walk home to find Henry on your stoop holding a cat. He shoves it into your arms and says, *Here. I found it in a dumpster. I'll die if something happens to it.* You are about to ask him in for coffee when he gets back into his car and drives away. The cat licks your shoulder and tries to bite at your ear. Inside, the red dog seems taken with this new creature. You think about Henry's growing attachment to the wounded. You pour some milk in a bowl and add cat food to the list on the refrigerator that reads: *spatula, paint for the living room, box grater, call the electrician about the fixture in the hallway, find a surgeon who takes your insurance, milk*, and now *cat food*. You cross off a few things; ones you think about every day and never do. Last time Henry had been over for dinner he had scrawled at the bottom of the page in red ink: *Having a list is almost as good as having*.

At the supermarket to buy cat food you stop in the cafeteria to eat lunch and catch up on reading. You are at the corner of a long table sitting beside a quiet Middle Eastern family. There are four of them, father, teenage boy, a slightly younger girl, and a young boy who seems perhaps seven or eight. You watch as the younger boy reaches for his father's food, the old man slapping his slender fingers away from the cardboard box of tabouli. When the boy hangs his head in shame the father beckons him back, fills a spoon, and hands it to him. None of them have said a word, which makes you curious about them, but to learn anything you would have to look directly at them and that feels strange, invasive. Still, you glance at them from time to time.

The young boy is now playing with his plastic spoon, his older sister obviously annoyed, and then he loses control of it and the spoon slingshots through the air and lands, lentils splattering, in the center of your book. You pause, knowing he is watching, wondering how you will react, and you slowly reach down, pick up the spoon, and raise it to your lips as though you are going to eat the lentils and you and the boy both start laughing almost uncontrollably and the laughter breaks the silence and words come tumbling out of the boy, racing out of his mouth, his body shifting with each one as though words themselves were at the very heart of what animates him. He wants to know, *Do you like movies? Have you seen any scary ones? Do you know about Chucky?* He asks you if you are a boy or a girl and you shrug and he teaches you an elaborate handshake ritual that ends with the two of you pulling on each other's earlobes. The girl tells you how much she loves Michael Jackson, gets up, and does a pretty good moonwalk, her slight form gliding across the cafeteria floor, sneakers squeaking on the tile. The teenage boy leans in and asks you what you are read-

POLITICS

ROZ CHAST has established herself as one of our greatest artistic chroniclers of the anxieties, superstitions, furies, insecurities, and surreal imaginings of modern life. She is the author of more than a dozen books for adults, including *Can't We Talk About Something More Pleasant?*, a *New York Times* 2014 Best Book of the Year, a National Book Award Finalist, winner of the 2014 Kirkus Prize, and a winner of the National Book Critics Circle Award, the first time a graphic novel received the prize for autobiography. Chast is also the author of numerous books for children, including *Around the Clock*, *Too Busy Marco*, and its sequel, *Marco Goes to School*. When she was twenty-four, *The New Yorker* added her to their roster and has published her work continuously ever since. Chast has provided cartoons and illustrations for nearly fifty magazines and journals and has received numerous awards, including honorary degrees from Pratt Institute and the Art Institute of Boston; was inducted into the American Academy of Arts and Sciences in 2013; and has received the Reuben Award from the National Cartoon Society in 2015 as well as the Heinz Award for her body of work. Her new book is *Going into Town: A Love Letter to New York.*

Politics

Pen and ink

ing. You look down at the books; there are always two, as though your brain needs to be able to move in two divergent directions at all times. One is *The Melodious Plot: Negative Capability, Keats, Axis Mundi, and Learning to Love Beyond Logic*; the other is a dog-eared copy of *Self-Esteem for Dummies* that you picked up at a tag sale last summer. You can't help but blush as you read the latter title out loud but when you look up the family is nodding thoughtfully. It occurs to you then that the father may be mute, that until you interrupted the family had been communicating in his language, a language made of gesture. For a moment you feel bad, as though you have inadvertently created a situation in which he might feel excluded. But when you nod back at him the father smiles and silently offers you a box of cookies.

That night you are in Jamaica Plain for the monthly queer hip-hop dance party. You meet a trans man tattoo artist and he shows you his scars from top surgery, thin reminders of where his breasts used to be. He gives you a number for a surgeon and as you fold it and slip it into your wallet you stop and think again about hesitation.

You think of you and Henry racing through a field of sweetgrass when you were children, your shirts off, your bodies nearly indistinguishable save for the long braids your mother made you wear; you think about last night in bed and how you didn't want to take the binder off your breasts and how you don't often wear a binder because your breasts are too large and it hurts your chest and feels even less natural, but that afternoon you had felt especially loose and chaotic in your body so you had put it on; you think about how, when your breasts are bound, you breathe differently; you think how fight-or-flight roils constantly inside your body and you think about how, when you were small, you were afraid of houses and how you hid in the field, stayed in the lake, and how it must have been hard for Henry, the way you were always missing.

Was there some kind of monster inside of every house? Perhaps it was the feeling that there was a monster inside of *you*. But you don't feel monstrous. You feel like part of a lineage that has never been recorded. You feel like . . . an interval.

It begins to snow again as you walk to the store to buy bread and salad greens for dinner and another tin of food for the cat. In the bakery you run into Lacuna. You see a nervousness wash across her face. She tells you of the dream she had while you were holding her. She dreamt that she had found you at the end of a road that disappeared into brambles, that you were obsessively digging into the dirt at the end of that road and that you were muttering something about omens, and that she was trying to reason with you, and shaking her fist in the air because in her dream she was afraid you would dig so far that you would fall through the earth and never stop falling and nothing would ever contain you again and when she said this you stopped digging and she thought she had finally reached you but instead you had found what you were looking for: a tiny perfect blue cube. It was mesmerizing, she said, and it glowed from the inside and just when she was reaching out to touch it you threw it into the air and the cube turned the world of the dream into night and then all the stars started to shift around in the sky and from your pocket you produced a dried flower for her, one you said you had carried across the ocean.

You tell her how you used to stuff flowers into the books you read as a child and how they were always falling out, and that you were disappointed as it wasn't the form but the fragrance and the color, the grace you wanted to preserve, and about the letter your father has just sent you about physics and the imagination, which has sent you into a minor fugue state. And you say when you used to study music you became obsessed with fugues because you wanted to know more about imitation within variation. You tell her that you love the dream because you're not sure you've ever come across a problem that you could resolve.

You think about finding your brother Henry in the stranger's house and how you thought you had just witnessed him becoming a man and the strangeness of that phrase because you have never felt as though you were becoming more or less of a woman or man, and you realize that what you saw was Henry becoming more *human*, you saw your brother finally taking in and holding some of the trouble in the world, and you remember your father when he was a postman, coming home from work in the middle of a storm, carrying three kittens he'd found in a snowbank on the side of the road, two orange and white and one calico, and how suddenly everything ceased to exist as you and Henry sat on the rug watching the kittens rumble and scratch, shaking off the snow.

ANNA DUNN was born in Western Massachusetts and greatly appreciates Bruce Springsteen, rescue pups, mezcal, and *Murder, She Wrote*. Early on, her mother threw the television out when Anna let it slip that she aspired to be Magnum P.I. when she grew up. She is the coauthor of two cookbooks, *Dinner at the Long Table* and *Saltie: A Cookbook*, and served as editor in chief of *Diner Journal*, an independent food, art, and literature magazine, for a decade. Most nights you can find her mixing cocktails at Roman's in Fort Greene, Brooklyn, or tucked away above Marlow & Sons collecting recipes and artwork for a forthcoming cookbook. She won the Dirt Press Poetry Award and has been published by Brooklyn Based, the Center for Fiction, *FAQNP*, and *Famous* magazine. For at least twenty minutes every day she is hard at work on her first crime fiction novel and/or concentrating on her breathing.

LOUISE ERDRICH

Balancing Acts

In 2001, I decided to open a small bookstore. Birchbark Books. We've gone through rough times, but we have survived. Democracy evolved along with the printing press. In fact, I think that democracy is made of books of all kinds, but as poetry expresses the ineffability of freedom best, I think the strongest link is there. A well-functioning democracy reminds me of a Leonard Cohen quote: If your life is burning well, poetry is just the ash. When democracy is burning well, poetry and literature and independent bookstores are the ash. We are beautifully there but not desperately there. We get taken for granted. People love us, but don't seek us out with the sort of intensity that occurs when democracy is visibly, viscerally faltering. When democracy is not burning well, poetry burns harder. Literature becomes dangerous, independent bookstores are bonfires that light the mind. (Or we are democracy cells, an Amy Goodman phrase.) In recent times, underground bookstores, writers, presses, have set flares for people's revolutions. But the horsemen of the apocalypse have ridden through the flames in China, Egypt, Libya, Hong Kong, Turkey. When that happens, when autocracy or fascism descends, literature and bookstores and booksellers are the first to go.

Maintaining a healthy flow of information, nurturing the brilliance of the individual, the iconoclast, the eccentric, the ever-fragile status of those who use words to illuminate human truths, is a bookstore's job. It is always important; it is always a labor of love. Selling books is less a business and more a way of life. Large online or big-box retailers like Amazon, Walmart, and Target have undercut the relationship between people and what they read by making books into loss leaders, that is, by cynically using the fair price of a book against the book itself. The loss leader is basically a fishing lure to obtain consumer information or to sell other stuff. Truly caring about books, choosing them thoughtfully, selling books to people who are hungry for books, is joy to me and to other booksellers. Among other things, democracy is about respect for joy, and books are joy. They are satisfying objects. As well as selling books, we give away a lot of books. Yesterday I gave a book to someone, and the first thing he did was breathe in the scent of the book. I loved that moment. It was like seeing a hungry person bend over a plate of delicious food to get the fragrance before eating. The smile on his face was like that too. Rapt with anticipation. Of course, he was going to read the book, not eat it.

But then again, maybe it's the same thing.

Here is a story about what a book can do to center a heart.

People surprise me by making our bookstore a destination stop when they come here—sometimes from faraway cities and countries. Maybe they see pictures of the birchbark trunks that make up our loft, or like the birchbark baskets on the shelves, or the rows of notes our staff fixes to the shelves to recommend books. Sometimes, maybe, they like my books. Other times they hope to make a connection with the Native world because our bookstore focuses on Indigenous literature in every genre. One day I blundered into the bookstore, dressed in saggy sweats, weary. I was slipping in to do some chores back in the office, when I overheard a woman talking to a book. She was holding Colum McCann's *Let the Great World Spin*, a novel of magnificent humanity.

Thank you, she murmured to the book. You taught me how to balance.

Let the Great World Spin centers on the story of a French man, Philippe Petit, who walked a tightrope between the Twin Towers at the World Trade Center in 1974. The art of his balancing walk resonates down the years, casts a strangely beautiful and painful shadow on 9/11, and is the subject of other books and movies. McCann's stories, reeling off the day of Petit's transcendent performance, are filled with emotional truth and a stark sense of what the city was like in those years.

I like people who unbalance me, says one of McCann's characters.

In an afterword to the book, the author says that when telling stories we are engaged in a democracy like no other.

After 9/11 and after the last election, people came to the bookstore for solace, calm, and balance.

We are a still new country coming to grips with a bloody and divided history. Falling is part of balancing. Books are where we learn to do both of these things.

LOUISE ERDRICH owns Birchbark Books, in Minneapolis, and Birchbark Branch, an online bookstore. Her latest novel is *Future Home of the Living God*, a science fiction novel in which pregnant women are hunted down and incarcerated. Her other books include *Love Medicine* and *LaRose*, both winners of the National Book Critics Circle Award, and *The Round House*, winner of the National Book Award. Her favorite flower is monarda, also known as bee balm. One of her all-time favorite books is *Let the Great World Spin* by Colum McCann.

ANGELA FLOURNOY

The Miss April Houses

After a survey of University trustees, experts, faculty and community members, the Committee puts forth the following recommendations:

In literature associated with the property, prior occupants of the "Miss April Houses" should be referred to as "people" or "inhabitants." In special circumstances approved by the Committee they may be referred to as "workers." Under no circumstances should they be referred to in any other fashion.

The committee lacked a librarian, they explained. I was new to campus. So new that my badge wasn't programmed yet. For the first month, I had to stand out front of the Jefferson Building in the humidity before each meeting (twice weekly, at lunch) and wait for another committee member to swipe me in. It was usually Becca Samuels, from University Counseling Services, with her enamel pins and cat's-eye glasses and shaved side making me feel like I hadn't moved to a new place at all. Then we'd sit around a conference table in the Office of the General Counsel. My job at these meetings, as it was explained to me, was to vote when called, but mostly to listen to the proceedings and at the very end consider how the library might set up a web page with links to supplemental information and research suggestions for interested students and visitors. That wasn't the only reason I was there, I suspected, but it was a fancier job than I'd had before and fancy jobs always have their particular requirements.

Nobody wants to be stuck in meetings during their lunch break after just having moved a thousand miles and not even having time to get the lay of the land, or buy a microwave or figure out where to get decent towels, but I figured it could have been worse. We could have used parliamentary procedure and meetings could have gone on forever. Instead Dr. Gander, the co-chair, kept the meetings under an hour each time, no matter what.

The Committee endorses the Board of Trustees' proposal to continue calling the structures in question the Miss April Houses, and approves the following language for a commemorative plaque at the site:

Miss April Lee-June Walters (1902–1974) was born in House #2 and lived in both houses with her two sons and first husband, John Binker Walters (1897?–1955), then with her second husband, Woodrow Gendry II (1920–1981). Miss April was a cherished part of the University community and a longtime member of the hospitality and dining services staff. During the Great Depression vegetables generously shared from her small farming plots were often the sole source of fresh produce that students and faculty ate. Following campus expansion in 1963, when the houses were moved from the southeast to northwest corner of campus, independent community members replanted Miss April's garden, ensuring that she enjoyed sustainable, locally grown produce for the rest of her life.

It was right around the time that my badge started working that Nnamdi Watson, PhD, joined the committee. A visiting lecturer in African American history with a five-year appointment that had been renewed once, putting him on year eight. The week prior, Lyle Sanders, the professor of rhetoric and oldest black tenured faculty member, had quit the committee, citing health concerns, which was just as well. He mostly slept through the meetings, his head dropping suddenly and freaking everybody out. Nnamdi was there to keep our number at a respectable two, we both figured. Solid build, neat, shoulder-length locs. Short, but cute. Horn-rimmed glasses, bow ties or tweed vests over crisp, long-sleeved oxfords every day. A Kappa, I could tell before he told me so. Friendly enough. He said he liked my twist-out, called it glossy. I laughed, said thank you. He called me "sista" and I did not roll my eyes. By this time I'd also finally bought a microwave.

The following informational display has been approved:

A mounted poster highlighting the furniture and tools in the houses, including one kitchen table, one bed with a quilt similar in style to those sewn by Miss April during her tenure, one washing board, an embroidery hoop and one broom.

Items currently in the houses but hereafter prohibited from display:

A hatchet, found hanging near the fireplace of House #1.
Seventeen handmade dolls that comprised Miss April's collection (some inherited from her mother), donated to the University by her sons.
The 6-inch by 12-inch wooden box with a cross carved into its top, found buried behind House #2 in 1983.
All contents of this box.

In consideration of the preservation of the approved objects for display, the Committee recommends that access to the interior of the houses be limited to scholars with written permission from the University's Department of Special Collections, and various special persons as designated by the Board of Trustees. Visitors from the general population should view the interior of the houses from the front and back porches via the double-paned, shatterproof windows.

A typical committee meeting went like this: We were all given a proposal for an element to be included in the restoration of the houses, then thirty minutes would be devoted to presentations regarding the merit of the proposal, sometimes made by the authors themselves, but more often from third-party experts. Then we'd deliberate for twenty minutes or so (usually less) and issue our recommendation. Patricia Dwyer, the head of the Office of the General Counsel, would then run the recommendation through whatever sort of legal analysis was necessary, and return at the next meeting with the proper wording for us to adopt. Pretty efficient, I thought. The catered lunch varied from sandwiches to Italian to Chinese.

The Committee acknowledges receipt of a petition presented by community member Shaw Hammers proposing that the site include literature about the transatlantic slave trade, including the amount paid for original inhabitants as listed in University archives.

Finding: Committee finds such literature to be outside the scope of the goals of the restoration project.

From the outset, Nnamdi had taken issue with the omission of the word *slave* and the use of *houses* over *quarters* or *cabins*. I was with him at first. I mean, if you don't use it, that's erasure, right? But then Becca Samuels from University Counseling—the woman who swiped me in in the early days—finally stopped speaking in slogans and said something that made a little sense on the day we discussed the petition (it had two hundred signees, but only about eighty from people affiliated with the university, and most of those were classified staff). Becca asked: Would the relatively small population of students of color find comfort in these houses, or would they become fodder for ridicule used against them? She presented research about young people and constant proximity to sites of past trauma. "It can feel like stepping on the same land mine day after day just to get from one class to the next," she concluded. This was more flourish than reality because the houses, being tucked up in the corner of campus like they were, weren't on the way to anyone's class.

Predictably, Patricia Dwyer rattled off a bunch of legalese that suggested the proposal could one day bankrupt the university. I didn't care about Dwyer's point, but Becca's—it was worth mulling over, her land mine analogy notwithstanding. Who am I to say what causes another person trauma? In the end I decided to show solidarity and vote with Nnamdi. We lost 2–6.

In accordance with a recommendation from expert linguists, the following language and accompanying illustrations* have been accepted by the Committee:

"Lenny Roberts used the phrase "lee little" to mean very small. "Lee" is similar to a WOLOF word that means small."

"One of the inhabitants of this House was named Esther Malink. MALINKE is the name of an ethnic group, also known as the Mandinka, the Mandinko, the Mandingo or the Manding."

"To express amazement, inhabitant Buster Griggs would exclaim, "Great Da!" The FON people (also known as the Fon nu, the Agadja or the Dahomey) worship a god named Da."

"Miss April referred to peanuts as "pindas." Pinda is the KONGO word for peanut. The Kongo people are the largest ethnic group in the Democratic Republic of Congo.

*Illustrations should show a map of West Africa with corresponding geographic regions of each ethnic group highlighted in either of the University's official colors.

This linguist (there was only just the one—not plural), Dr. Nichole Valdes-James, made a very compelling argument. Even Nnamdi, who hated us all by now, had to admit it. Gander, the co-chair, looked charmed in spite of himself. Who can argue with enduring language? Who would see a posting like that and not be impressed, intrigued? Apparently Nnamdi had expected plenty of people to be offended. After the meeting he walked me back to the library. "A decade ago you hardly ever heard the word *Africa* on this campus if not in the pejorative," he said. I said, "Well, Africa's pretty trendy up north these days." He looked at me like I was an idiot, muttered, "This isn't up north." But then he invited me to get a drink with him.

The Committee recommends the following permanent information placards be added to the façade of the Miss April Houses wherever the restorers find aesthetically pleasing:

A display highlighting the restoration efforts of University researchers, with attending photographs of the process of transporting the cabins to their current location.

A display with the names of members of this Committee.

I left Brooklyn because I was at the point where just walking to the post office made me want to reach out for the nearest stranger's neck and squeeze it, and I'm not a particularly violent person. All of these forever-children in wrinkled clothes with make-believe jobs and very real bank accounts looking down their noses at *me*, as if the sight of me made the neighborhood bad? I know, I know. But just because it's happening all over the place doesn't make it any easier to stomach. Plus, I was single again. Plus, all my friends were having kids and moving away, or just moving away because things had gotten so unbearable in Brooklyn. I was sitting at my desk at my branch library one day, with a stack of books to weed, and thought: "You know what? They can have this place." I went online, applied for this job, and got it, even though I don't have any university experience. The air is much, much cleaner down here.

The Committee acknowledges receipt of a petition presented by community member Shaw Hammers, submitted on behalf of Dr. Nnamdi Watson, Visiting Lecturer in African-American Studies (and member of this same Committee, hereby recused from this vote), proposing an informational placard featuring scholarship speculating on how and against what odds particular words and phrases might have lasted in the inhabitants' lexicon over the generations.

Finding: Committee finds that such a placard would be outside the scope of the goals of the restoration project.

It was stupid of the committee to accept proposals on a rolling basis. This was a policy established before I arrived. Of course Nnamdi would try to take the one thing everyone was enthusiastic about and flip it on them. I told him the night before to just leave it alone, be happy they don't just bulldoze the houses altogether, but he said, "It's the principle of the matter." And I said, "That's usually what someone says before they do something dumb," and he shook his head and threatened to leave my apartment. But he didn't. He didn't leave the committee either. He came twice a week, ate heartily and smiled too much at everyone there.

The following permanent placard must be affixed within twenty feet of the entrance of both Miss April Houses:

A display thanking the individual and corporate donors that made the restoration project possible. Language on this display is up to the donor's discretion, granted such language meets the guidelines outlined above.

The semester was nearly over by the time we worked our way through all of the proposals. No, I didn't let them put my name on the official committee placard; I was new and maybe I didn't quite understand the stakes, but I knew better than to put my name on either one of those houses. They didn't even ask me to explain why I abstained. No, I did not join Nnamdi, Shaw Hammers and the seven others who staged a sit-in for three days on the porch of House #1. That doesn't mean I didn't care.

If you focus on what we did accomplish as a committee, versus what was left out, we communicated two important truths: the past inhabitants made do with what they had—a few pieces of furniture, a humble kitchen—and they found ingenious, albeit small ways to make their language endure. That's not nothing. That's huge, I think.

And maybe a later committee can add more information.

ANGELA FLOURNOY is the author of *The Turner House*, which was a finalist for the National Book Award and a *New York Times* Notable Book of 2015. The novel was also a finalist for the Center for Fiction First Novel Prize, the PEN/Robert W. Bingham Prize for Debut Fiction, and an NAACP Image Award. She is a National Book Foundation "5 Under 35" Honoree for 2015. Her fiction has appeared in the *Paris Review*, and she has written for the *New York Times*, the *Nation*, the *Los Angeles Times*, and elsewhere. Flournoy was the 2016–17 Rona Jaffe Foundation Fellow at the New York Public Library's Dorothy and Lewis B. Cullman Center for Scholars and Writers. A graduate of the Iowa Writers' Workshop, she received her undergraduate degree from the University of Southern California. She has taught at the University of Iowa, Columbia University, and the New School. She is currently a Lecturer in Creative Writing at Princeton University.

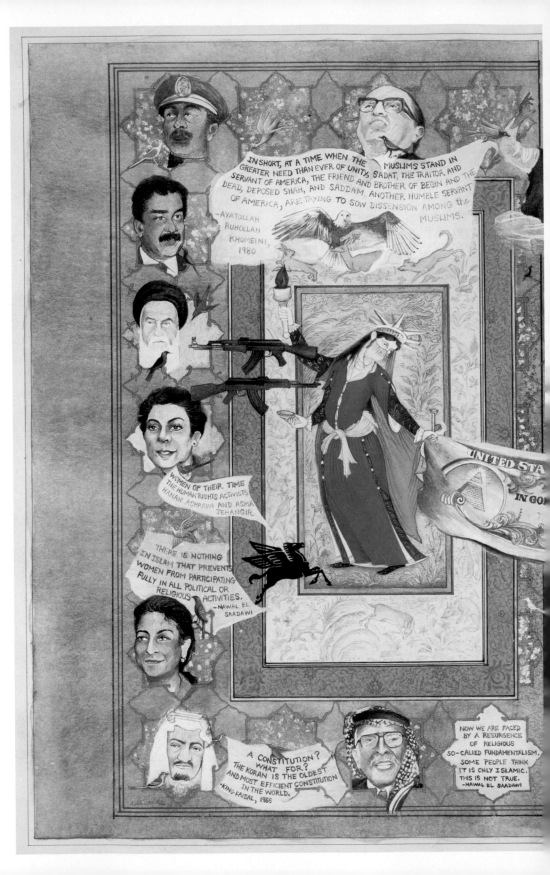

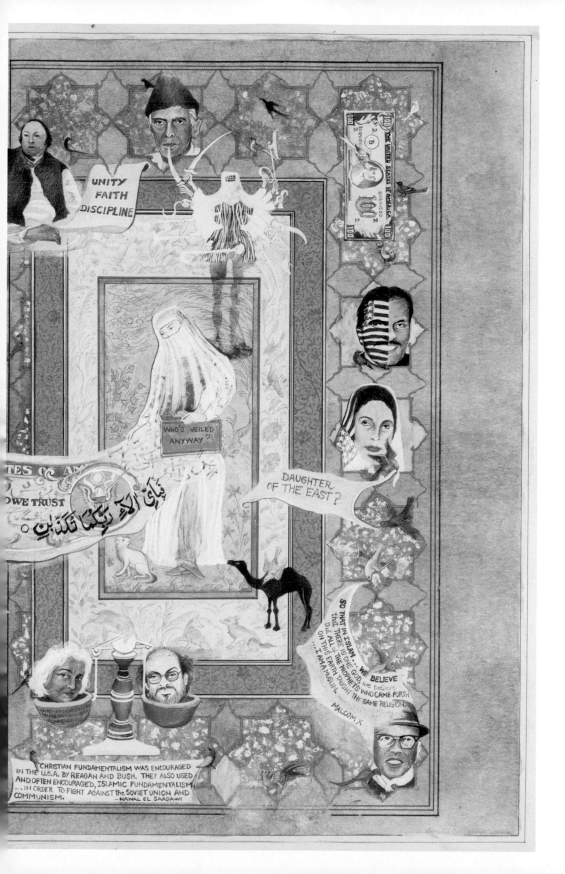

Born in Pakistan, **SHAHZIA SIKANDER** received her BFA in 1991 from the National College of Arts in Lahore. Sikander's breakthrough work received national critical acclaim, winning the prestigious Shakir Ali and Haji Sharif Awards for excellence in miniature painting, subsequently launching the medium into the forefront of NCA's program, and bringing international recognition to this medium within contemporary art practices. Sikander moved to the United States in 1993 to pursue her MFA at the Rhode Island School of Design. Informed by South Asian, American, feminist, and Muslim perspectives, Sikander has developed a unique, critically charged visual iconography to explore ideas of language, trade and empire, and migration. A recipient of a MacArthur Fellowship (2006) and the State Department Medal of Arts (2012), Sikander has been the subject of major international exhibitions around the world and has participated in more than four hundred group shows and international art forums.

The World Is Yours, the World Is Mine

Ink and gouache on prepared paper

The Many Faces of Islam

Dry pigment, gouache, gold leaf, tea wash on prepared paper

Fires

From the Journal of Ben Swift

Kranevo. The Black Sea. 1:15 a.m. May—what *is* today, anyway?—1999. Left L.A. 5/17 arr. Sofia 5/18, start road trip 5/19? So it's the 21st?

After a long lazy afternoon on the beach here, dinner tonight at an outdoor café. Kroum (pronounced "Kroom," name of some ancient Bulgarian khan) orders grape *rakia*, fills my shot glass. "Thanks, Kroum," I say, "but I don't drink."

"How is it possible? How can a man not drink?"

"Maybe I'm not a 'man.'"

"You must be kidding." (Picked up from American kids at that school in Switzerland where he and Eva met a thousand years ago?)

Reaction shot: Eva, wary, listens.

"I mean it. Bad stuff happens when I drink. And you don't want to see it."

"On the contrary, I do!"

"Look, I drank in order not to be there. I wasn't really present in the lives of my wife and kids." (American psychobabble, must sound like Martian to him.)

"Smart guy," he says. "Why would you want to give that up?!"

"Because my drinking became a sickness."

"We have a saying here: all diseases are the result of irregular drinking!"

"Until regular drinking turns into a disease."

He doesn't insist, but goes right ahead and gets absolutely wasted. We're eating spicy meat patties and fries and salads, and Kroum digs right in along with us, but having started with *rakia*, he moves on to the first of three enormous pitchers of beer. Mug follows mug follows mug until his speech slurs to gibberish. The guy is fucking hammered.

Later, Eva and I lock our arms under his and tow him back to the hotel through the Kranevo crowds while he belts out some hundred-year-old song about a hero named Popyordanov, who, Eva explains, was a guerrilla in VMRO, i.e., the Internal Macedonian Revolutionary Organization. Wounded he's lying, O woe he's dying, his old mother's grieving, etc. Eva says: when people get together in Bulgaria they sit around the table and eat and sing sad old songs about heroes who died fighting against the "Turkish Yoke." (Memo: Yesterday's visit to Shipka Pass. Site of huge battle 1877–1878, Russians and Bulgarians, who, when out of ammunition, heave gigantic boulders down the mountain onto stealthily climbing bayonet-and-scimitar-wielding Turks; would make a terrific scene in a movie.)

The Kranevo crowd here is mostly college-age—easily ten years younger than Harry would have been by now—and nobody pays the slightest attention to our sloshed Kroum, whose doleful ballad is in any case drowned out by relentless disco music throbbing from every café, restaurant and bar. This morning, over coffee, when I remark that this nonstop disco roar is almost all American, Kroum says, with a tight smile, "Of course. We are a shitty little unimportant outpost of your empire. And if we refuse to take orders you will bomb us the way you're bombing Serbia." Again, he's surprised when I don't disagree. Even though he knows I'm a communist he keeps expecting me to be a knee-jerk pro-American asshole.

Back in their room, we put him to bed. He's so sunburned from the day on the beach he looks boiled.

"What's with him?" I ask Eva at the door.

"Bitter disappointment."

"Didn't he vote for the 'Democratic Changes'?"

"He did. But democracy here has turned out to be a big fat lie."

"And that's a reason to get drunk?"

"One reason out of a thousand."

Now I'm in my room, next to theirs. Have walked and fed Kroum's sweet old German shepherd, Romy Schneider. I keep waiting for the jet lag to lift but it's too soon. I'm still goofy and loopy. The disco stuff could wake the dead.

If only.

4:20 a.m. Restless, wakeful (jet lag, of course) after sleeping a couple of hours. Wondering: what the hell am I doing here? My pixilated cousin Eva, after thirty years and more of absolutely no contact whatsoever with her ninth-grade Bulgarian beau at that fancy school they went to in Geneva (her father an infectious disease expert with the WHO, his father with the UN), gets back with him about three years ago after they reconnect through the school's alumni email list. Lo and behold they're both divorced and passion rekindles. So she starts coming here every summer, where they play house for three months and she paints and then in late August she goes home and starts teaching again. Eva and I have been pals forever and she knows me, and so we're on the phone five or six months ago and she says, knowing I'm stuck (that's putting it mildly), come stay with us for three months. You can visit all the old commie monuments and Kroum has a project you can help him with.

So why have I come? To get the hell out of an America I hate more and more every day, and to find out if, maybe, the "actually existing socialism" they supposedly had here between 1944 and 1989 in fact actually existed.

Still, now that I'm here, I don't know what I want. I don't even know what *wanting* is anymore. I want to want—but what? I don't know who the hell I am and by that I don't mean some cornball middle-aged identity crisis crap.

Harry's father? It feels like that's the only definite thing I am. Or *was.* That's not something I can run away from or even want to run away from, unbearable as it is. But what am I running away *to*?

The dog's ears twitch as I write and she opens her eyes and looks at me. I can almost hear her saying, *Go back to sleep, you dope. It isn't morning yet. If I can sleep through the disco cacophony, so can you.*

Dimitrovgrad, May 23?, 1999, 1:20 a.m.

From Kroum's car radio: yesterday NATO bombs accidentally killed dozens of Albanians in Kosare. Fucking idiots, even though I can't stand the KLA thugs. When I say this or "Humanitarian intervention my ass," Kroum looks at me in utter amazement. He just can't get it into his head that I'm a Yank and against this war.

Up at 6 a.m. yesterday. Over coffee I tease Kroum: He looks like the Platonic form of Hangover. Bloodshot lizard eyes, hair one big cowlick, face puffy. But he's an old hangover pro and orders *shkembe chorba*—a milky soup with chunks of chewy tripe, sprinkled with vinegar and paprika. Not bad at all and by God it seemed to revive him.

Driving south along the coast, the sea a deep blue (it's called the Black Sea because of fierce winter storms), we pass Golden Sands, where Kroum spent a priapic teenage summer working as a waiter and "chasing Swedish blondes," Eva remarks sotto voce. In one of our long phone conversations after she got back with him she told me he's always been successful with women but also that he really does "fall in love"—for me always a foreign language and complete disaster. (Thoughts of Jeanie. Boy, I really fucked that one up. So what if I already had two kids? Would it have been so hard to give her what she wanted and have a couple more? Selfish bastard.)

Then through Varna: faded pastel apartment buildings, wrought-iron balconies, the traces of tsarist-era refinement. During Communism Varna was called Stalin, not Stalingrad. Name changed back to Varna 1956, soon after the Khrushchev speech (boy, they didn't waste any time, did they). Funny thing here about changing names: when Bulgaria was an ally of the Nazis, one boulevard in Sofia was changed to Adolf Hitler, then during communism to Klement Gottwald, and now it's named for some Bulgarian philanthropist. "No one," Kroum says, "is fooled by these changes except the people who order them. They think they can just erase the history." (Memo: Bulgarian uses definite articles where we don't.)

• • •

Lunch about 2 in Nessebar, an ancient port town. Old churches, walls of brick and mortar mixed with shards of tile and colored glass. Too many tourists. Still, maybe Herodotus passed through? My aborted classics major keeps pointing an accusing finger at me (one of many).

After lunch we stop to refuel at a super-modern Shell (!) station. A brief explosive fight between Kroum and Eva about his having to explain for the umpteenth time how he fills the car with both "benzene," i.e., gasoline, and "gaz," that is, vapor, and has a mechanism for switching between the two he wants her to know how to use. He snarls, she scolds, I tune out, stroke Romy between the ears, hating couples' fights, wishing I'd just taken off for Cuba or Vietnam instead of coming here. When he returns from paying inside he's holding an ice cream cone and feeds it to Eva bite by bite, kisses her.

Sudden desolation. Scratch the dog between the ears. Tear up. No talent for love. No fun being a third wheel. Not sure how long I'll stay here except that I'm OUT of the lousy USA. They don't know and nobody else knows either but I'm gone. For good. *Never going back.*

On the road again Romy and I fall asleep. Her head in my lap. When I wake up it's almost five, inland, sea long gone. On both sides of the road acres and acres of sunflowers. They look at you as if they're psychiatrists. Or FBI agents.

A sudden catch in my throat, a dry tickle, and I'm just about to make a major public announcement that I've caught an airplane cold when Eva coughs and Kroum coughs and Romy coughs. Kroum pulls over. We get out of the car. Eva gives water to the dog. We had come to the Black Sea through the Balkans. Now we're in the Thracian Plain far to the south, and both to our left, in the distance, and now, to our right, up in the Sredna Gora, or "Middle Mountains," the sky overhead an evil gray-orange, the sun a sickly blur, and clusters of billowing flame.

"*Pozhari,*" Kroum says.

"Fires?" asks Eva.

He shakes his head: a Bulgarian *yes.* (For *no* you jerk your head upward. Go figure it.)

"And do you know what causes these fires?" Kroum shouts, startling both

Eva and me, his face contorted with fury. "These are forest fires that some-one deliberately makes to destroy the trees. This is how it works now in this 'democracy' that is so fuckin."

"So that's why there are no storks this year," Eva says. She coughs and turns to me. "Usually you see them all over Bulgaria this time of year. They build nests on village roofs. People say they bring good luck. But this spring I haven't seen even one."

Inside the car Kroum starts the engine. "You see how it is? They burn the branches and the leaves, and the skin"—"Bark," Eva interjects—"but not the trunks. These they cut down and sell."

"Wait," I say. "So what's the story?"

"When any *mutra*—that's a mafia guy, Ben, a criminal—who calls him-self a 'businessman' can hire some starving Gypsy to set a forest on fire, that is the story. Some gangster wants a burned forest because it will be cheaper. Or someone wants to destroy the forests to get the land to build new houses with, what do you call it—'washed' money."

"Laundered," Eva says.

"This is the deliberate, planned destruction of the Bulgarian economy, done on orders to prove to the Western masters we will be reliable slaves if they let us join the EU. And all we have to do is commit economic suicide, and let Western Europe fuck us in the ass."

"*Whose* orders?" I ask.

"You can very well guess yourself."

"The U.S., you mean?" His innuendos are exasperating.

"Of course the U.S. The IMF and the World Bank also follow the orders of the U.S. ruling elite."

"The 'ruling elite' again!" Eva says. "You and your tired old commie-speak. Anyway, why would people here agree to their own economic suicide?"

"Because, my naive American darling," he answers, as his Lada Samara grinds its way through the smoky haze, "the shits in control here think only of themselves and their personal profits. They sell off the government enterprises for ridiculous amounts and the IMF looks the other way and meanwhile these *mutri* guys give the enterprises to their twenty-two-year-old whores who are listed as the CEOs of fake companies while the criminal oligarchs put not millions but *billions* in their pockets and the U.S. ambassador congratulates them and says, 'Oh, very good, my dear neoliberal children, you are doing such a fine job privatizing everything!' and, 'Ooh, aah, how you are creating such a wonderful free-market economy! Now to prove yourself even more you must throw the people out of work and punish them for communism and teach them the magnificent ways of glorious capitalism!' which as you very well know is nothing but economic rape and thievery."

"And how," I say. Maybe this time he sees I mean it.

Our lovely apolitical Eva looks out at the fields on both sides of the road, dabbing her eyes and nose with Kleenex. "Um, guys," she says, "I read somewhere about a family that was incinerated in their car when they drove over a tiny cinder from a forest fire."

"That's not going to happen, darling." He reaches his hand over and squeezes the back of her neck.

I can still see flames. She's right to worry.

"Poor storks," she says. "Where do they go?"

"They die," Kroum says. "That's all. They die."

Finally, maybe fifteen, twenty miles later, the air begins to clear. The light is fading. This is such an old, old country. Who knows, maybe it was along this road that Thracian tribes or Roman legions built campfires and rested for the night. Somehow a comforting thought. A country that has outlasted everything perhaps?

I bought a tourist book on Bulgaria before I left L.A. and when I got to the part about Dimitrovgrad (named for my Reichstag-trial hero Georgi Dimitrov, yes!), it said that the city hasn't changed since the communist time and is so dreary and depressing you should just skip it.

Ah, my kind of town . . .

We get there around nine. Kroum disappears into a café and a few minutes later comes out with this tall guy, Niko, who speaks no English. He gets into the car with us and in seconds we're at one of these big concrete apartment "blocks" exactly like the ones Kroum showed me on the way from the Sofia airport to his house in the suburb of Boyana. Niko takes us up to a two-bedroom apartment he owns (?), and we dump our stuff. Then we all go back to the café where we'd picked him up and eat grilled sausages with *lyutenitsa*, a savory sauce made of red peppers and tomatoes.

Too tired for more, conking out.

Boyana. Tues., May 25, 1999—I think. Just past midnight.
The "Old Little House."

Yesterday NATO bombed Serb power grids. Blackouts in Belgrade, Novi Sad, Nis. Millions without water or electricity. Kroum says don't believe what they say about thousands of Albanians being expelled and disappearing. "It's all lies and propaganda to justify the bombing."

To pick up where I left off: In Dimitrovgrad we join Niko's entire clan (mother, sister, uncles, et al.) for breakfast at his apartment, in another high-rise block. Kroum takes me aside. "I am very sorry, Ben, but we are trapped. We will not be able to leave until very late today." He looks so grim I nearly burst out laughing.

"Rules of Bulgarian hospitality," Eva whispers to me.

But, for me, serendipity: Kroum wastes no time telling Niko (an old friend from university), who relays it to his uncles, that I'm "a real American communist." They have never met an American before, much less an American communist. They shake their heads like crazy, all the while smiling. Ben Swift the white Bengal tiger.

After breakfast, we drive with Niko to a hilly area within the city where the two uncles (on Niko's dead father's side) have gone ahead and are waiting for us. They are now in their late seventies or early eighties and "pensioneers," Kroum says, but years ago they built their side-by-side houses with their own hands. Traditional Bulgarian design: red tile roofs, white walls, brown wood trim, the second floor jutting out over the first.

Behind the houses, and parallel with them, twin gardens, where the uncles and their wives grow what must be every fruit and vegetable known to man. Beyond the gardens a sublime industrial vista like a Sheeler painting: cylinder after cylinder, miles of interconnected tubes and pipes. But only a few spout vapor and smoke.

The brothers' adult children and grandchildren live in cities (Sofia and one called Haskovo, I believe). As we talk the wives appear with orange juice, a bowl of sugar, and cookies. We all spoon the sugar into the OJ (my fillings ache!). Both women buxom, blocky, with muscular arms and strong wide backs like rafts you could float down the Mississippi on. The old guys are lean, tan, spry, wear immaculate jeans and running shoes. One is taller than the other; both still have a lot of hair, thick and white. The tall one chain-smokes.

With Kroum interpreting I ask questions. "Under democracy, how are you doing?"

"Not well. Bread keeps going up. Electricity too. We can't afford medicines. We never go to doctors now."

It's everything Kroum's been saying.

We sit on the back porch of the taller brother's house. Eva sketches the two gardens.

Under communism, they say in answer to more questions, they had good wages. Free education and medical care. The promise of a comfortable old age. No fear. Dignity and purpose: they were building socialism.

They both retired in the late eighties, just before the Changes. Until then the shorter one had worked in a cement factory. The tall one and both wives had worked at a chemical fertilizer plant (a Dimitrovgrad specialty). Today both factories are closed.

And what about now? The brothers both say the same thing: "We were lied to. Democracy has made our lives very uncertain. It is counterrevolution and a catastrophe."

As the two old guys take turns talking, unsmiling Niko says nothing, looks bored, glances at his watch.

The shorter one asks Kroum to ask me, "So, how does a communist live in the United States?"

My answer: "Now that the Cold War is over they think of you as a kind of harmless fossil. They used to think you were the devil out to destroy 'the great-est country on earth.' Now they say, like idiots, 'We won! We won!'"

With this the brothers burst out laughing and slap me on the back.

The taller brother asks me about my family. I keep it short: I'm divorced, have a daughter in her late twenties, a dancer. "I had a son, but he died." Sud-den silence, solemn faces. I tell them how beautiful their gardens are, sip my sugared OJ.

"Oh, Ben, you're such a red romantic," Eva says to me on the way back to the car. "These two guys walk right out of a Socialist Realism poster and you love them for it, don't you?"

"Why not? Communism worked for them."

"You really believe that?"

I have the weird feeling that it's someone else, a past me, who could get into a big argument with her, but all I do is nod: an American yes. I no longer have the energy for arguing. I'm still a communist (aren't I?) but no longer feel *mar-ried* to communism. Or anything else for that matter, though these old guys would be great subjects for a documentary film. Will I ever make another? It seems like somebody else made my own (including the one about Harry).

Huge lunch, back at Niko's. An incredible spread, all of it whipped up by his mother after this morning's huge breakfast. Of course when I refuse the *rakia* the old men look at me in disbelief. "Help me out here, Kroum," I beg him, and though I can see that in front of these old guys he's itching to tease me about not drinking, he tells them simply that we're going to share the driving back to Sofia and so we both have to abstain. DUI laws here are very strict, apparently.

Afterward, in the high dry heat, all I want to do is sleep, but Kroum, who seems, like Niko, anxious and impatient, says there's work to be done. So after parking Eva and Romy with Niko's sister, a woman in her early forties who can speak some English and whose very black hair is pulled back in a tight pony-tail, Kroum, Niko and I drive a couple of streets away to a little almost bare white office Niko rents while he tries to make a go of it in the life insurance biz. According to Kroum he isn't doing very well. Most people in this city are out of work. They can't afford to live, much less die.

A few minutes later the two nice old uncles show up and stand around kibitzing as we schlep three pairs of boxed PCs from the office to Kroum's old Lada Samara. While he fits two pairs of computers in the trunk and one in the back seat, Kroum explains that he'd originally brought the computers to D. because he and Niko were going to be partners in a computer club right where Niko now has his office. After months of silence from him, Kroum learned that Niko had never gotten around to setting up the club. So we've come to retrieve the computers because Kroum is going to open his own computer club, and very soon, in a couple of days. Hearing this jolts me out of the muzziness of jet lag. What had I been thinking? That he and Eva had nothing better to do than drive me around the country and take me to the beach? This has been a business trip.

Niko edgy, thin, round-shouldered, very short salt-and-pepper hair. Gives off a hyperactive desperation. Some kind of hustler? As we load the car he keeps going into his office to make phone calls to "*klienti.*" The big-shot "entrepreneur."

A little past five we're done and Kroum is eager to hit the road, but, eyes glazing over, he tells me we're expected to stay for an early supper—one last gargantuan feast. We go back to Niko's place, which is on the ground floor of the high-rise block and has a nice porch with a grape trellis, and Kroum and I take brief sitting-up naps on the sofa. I wake up to what I now can identify as the characteristic smell of this country: roasting peppers, and it's delicious.

Just when Niko's mother calls us to the table, who should appear from out of nowhere but Eva, all decked out in what she tells me is a traditional Bulgarian women's outfit: white linen shirt with long embroidered sleeves, under a heavy wool dress with embroidery and trim in a lot of bright colors. Also a red-checked linen apron and a wide sash.

Kroum stares at her with an expression I'd have to call astonished, admiring and amused; the outfit looks good on her but he so thoroughly sees her as American that he's obviously never imagined her in a peasant getup like this. Niko's sister stands beside Eva, with an odd fixed smile. "I give this

135

national dress to my new friend Eva," she says to me and Kroum, in English, "to remember us and our city Dimitrovgrad. This belong before to one good friend. She die few years ago—cancer from the fertilizers factory—and before she die she give me this dress, which belong to her mother in the near-to-here village of Rakovski."

"Thank you, Biliana, really, it's a wonderful gift," Eva says. It's very hot and in the heavy wool dress she's flushed and sweating.

"And I am so sorry, Eva, if I offend you by what I say about the Jewishes. I do not know you is a Jewish," she says, taking Eva's hand, smile gone, eyes brimming.

Whoa, what's this?

Eva looks at me as if to say, *Uh-huh, you heard that right*. Kroum, lighting one of his infernal cigarettes, looks up at the two women.

"It's okay, Biliana," Eva says. I sense she's being extremely careful. "A lot of people have this idea about us . . ." she begins. (Can't help it but here's a horrible pun: *Jewishes* my command. Ouch.)

"Yes!" says the sister, eyes now bright and eager. "That the Jewishes are behind the financial *manipulatsia* of the world."

"Well, as I said to you, Biliana"—Eva puts her arm around the sister—"don't believe everything you hear!" A forced smile and a kiss planted on Biliana's cheek. Kroum has turned to stone.

"Now, my brother Niko—" Biliana jerks her head toward her brother, who has just come in and has the pissed-off, running-on-empty look of someone who has failed to complete even one single economic transaction so far that day—"has many books against the Jewishes. He is—what you call it?—a real anti-Semite. Yes, Niko?" I can clearly hear the word *anti-seMEET*. She says something to him in Bulgarian.

"*Da*," he says, curtly, it seems to me, and, unsmiling, says something else to his sister in Bulgarian.

Niko's mother again calls everyone to the table, where the uncles and their wives are already sitting.

"You see," the sister says, her weird smile now reckless, "he say he cannot stand the Jewishes."

"It's *JEWS*," Eva says. "Not Jewishes."

"Because he say they are swindlers—*moshenitsi*. But I tell him you is a Jewish and your cousin here is a Jewish—"

"No," Eva says. "My cousin is not a Jew. I am, he's not."

The sister stares for a moment at me. She has no idea what to make of this.

"—and that you is very nice. You see"—her eyes fill again—"he is not tolerant but *I* am tolerant. My brother act like a cretin," which she pronounces in a sort of French way—*cre-tanh*. "When you say you is a Jewish and I say the Jewishes are the ones who do the financial *manipulatsia*, I see you face become sad, and I think you is going to make apology for the Jewishes, and so I see is not possible that you is one of the ones who do this *manipulatsia*."

"You think, Biliana, that I am going to *apologize* to you on behalf of the Jews?" Eva doesn't sound angry. Just flabbergasted.

My guess is that Kroum, seated beside me, is silently begging her not to lose her cool. She doesn't. On the contrary, she looks as if she's trying not to laugh.

At this point the mother comes in and speaks sharply to Biliana. Eva disappears and comes back in a minute in her jeans and T-shirt, the national outfit put away in a plastic shopping bag. Kroum and I and she and Biliana join everyone at the table. Niko seems to have disappeared.

No doubt he has important deals to make at his office.

What Eva tells me later is that Biliana reports on the democratically wrecked Dimitrovgrad economy for a newspaper in Sofia. From Niko she has "learned" that America, which is "owned by the Jewishes," is responsible for the destruction of Bulgaria and that "the Jewishes are trying to establish world domination." While Kroum and Niko and I were loading up the car, Biliana was asking Eva if she had ever read *The Protocols of the Elders of Zion*, showed her a copy of the book in Bulgarian, and recommended it highly. At that point, Eva told me, she lost it, and said "Surely you don't believe that absolute shit!" whereupon Biliana burst into tears and started apologizing and made her try on the peasant dress.

The really odd thing is that Eva had told me over the phone a year or so after she started coming here how Bulgaria saved its Jews—well, most of them—in World War II, and that Kroum had told her there's no anti-Semitism here. Now I thought of that old saying "An anti-Semite is someone who hates the Jews more than necessary." Niko, then, but maybe not hapless Biliana?

The hot, heavy meal, late in the hot afternoon, is like a drug. I'm almost stuporous and feel like passing out right at the table. Then comes baklava oozing with honey, and *lokum* (Turkish delight), very sweet, with powdered sugar, reminding me maybe even more than the visit to Shipka Pass that Bulgaria was under the Ottomans for five hundred years.

Though the drive back to Sofia is going to take at least four or five hours, we just can't up and leave. Finally, to appease the gods of hospitality, Kroum takes a shot of *rakia*, to the great joy of the uncles. As we're downing multiple tiny cups of sweet Turkish coffee—I swear to God I don't know what came over her—perhaps it's because she's by nature a peacemaker—Eva, who has been to these kinds of feasts here before, says to Kroum, "Why don't we have some singing!" Kroum relays her request in Bulgarian to everyone at the table, but Niko's old mother, who had been nearly invisible cooking all day, and had said nothing during the meal except to encourage everyone to eat more, throws Eva a stern look and says (I learned later), loud and clear, "We do not sing when they are bombing our Slavic brothers." ("Which," Kroum also tells me later, "made me want to laugh because between the Serbs and the Bulgarians there is a lot of bad blood.")

Eva's Bulgarian is good enough by now to understand immediately what the old lady has just said, and again she turns as red as one of those hot little Bulgarian chili peppers. She puts her hand to her heart and says, in English, as Kroum translates, "Forgive me. I meant no disrespect. You are of course right. There should be no singing. Both my cousin and I feel nothing but shame at what our country is doing to Serbia. We are completely against this criminal NATO war."

Everyone has gone silent. Biliana, who, having made an ass of herself, now understands that Eva has just done so too, shakes her head from side to side and smiles. Then the old mother shakes her head, Kroum shakes his head and I shake my head and the old uncles and their wives shake their heads in a general Bulgarian yes-fest and so Eva redeems herself as an American and even possibly as a "Jewish." As for me, I just help myself to another couple of pieces of *lokum*. Eva catches my eye and makes a gesture that, I realize, means that I should wipe the powdered sugar off my face.

It took us about four hours to reach Sofia.

In the late-spring twilight here you don't see how bad the roads are, how treacherous the potholes, how forlorn the villages with their left-behind old people, empty storks' nests and ravenous, diseased, homeless dogs.

"Look," says Eva, "how the shadows overtake the fields and mountains and turn everything into a deepening violet blue." I think of Harry and how much he liked to listen to her talk about color and light. Remember how, at Dad's place in Springs, when he was about fifteen, sixteen, before the sickness hit, he and Eva liked to do pastels together late afternoons at the beach? I think Nora still has those drawings. So I'll never see them again, I guess.

Just as we reach Sofia, huge clouds gather and by the time we get to Boyana a violent thunderstorm unleashes a savage downpour, with lightning and hail. This creates a serious dilemma for Kroum: with so much thievery here, to leave the computers in the car is a big risk, but taking them out and up to safety in the house, which involves climbing a steep incline and a flight of muddy and thus slippery concrete steps, in heavy rain, is perilous. He decides to leave the computers in the car, for now, but says he won't sleep well because he'll be worrying all night that they'll be stolen by Gypsies.

Christ, in one day, a full-blown shot of anti-Semitism, with an anti-Roma chaser.

Time to turn in. Tomorrow we will network the computers and open the club. This is what I need. Something to wake up for.

I can hear the rain clattering on the tin roof of the "Old Little House," the cottage they've given me for as long as I'm here. I asked Kroum if Romy could spend the night in my room and here she is, curled up on the end of my bed.

• • •

Later Tues., May 25, 1999. Postscript.

This morning (dry, sunny), after K. and I set up the computers in the space he's rented for his club, guess what we found: *porn* sites, dozens of them, on each desktop, not to mention missing and corrupted files galore on the operating systems. Niko hadn't said one word about any of this. The great "businessman" must have been inviting "*klienti*" to his office and charging them to look at the porn. Sure beats the life insurance game.

Kroum is beyond furious. "That fucking *moshenik*! He was my friend! Oh, this rotten democracy! It has brought us nothing but betrayal and degradation!"

So we have our work cut out for us. Some neighborhood boys—very polite—came around this afternoon on their bikes to ask when the club will open. Kroum gave them candy bars and Cokes and orange Fanta from the fridge he's installed near the front desk and promised them that the computers will be loaded with games and ready for play the day after tomorrow. He told them to bring their friends, their relatives, everyone they know.

Meanwhile, the three of us will be up all night working. I'm about to get Eva, who's making sandwiches, and drive the Lada over to the club. Kroum is already there.

He's tried capitalism before. After the Changes he had a shop in Sofia where he sold detergents and "household chemicals," but there was so much competition from other shops selling exactly the same thing that it failed. He then went into the export electronics business with a couple of friends but one turned out to be thoroughly corrupt and the partnership collapsed. Worst of all, what hard currency he had he lost when the bank he'd put it in supposedly went bust, though what really happened was a scam in which the owners put all the money in untouchable offshore accounts. Nobody was prosecuted, there was no deposit insurance, so Kroum and thousands like him couldn't get any of it back. When he and Eva reconnected on the alumni Listserv for the Swiss school where they'd met a thousand years ago, he and a pal had a business making car alarms. That too brought in hardly anything. Now he's about to open the first and, we all hope, the only computer club in Boyana. There's buzz in the neighborhood, and so he's almost hopeful.

As for me, well, it's good for me to have some kind of purpose. Something to wake up for. But the three months till my visa expires is a long time to hang out with a pair of lovey-doveys and their occasional fights. And if I do manage to see the past here, see how it worked? Then what? It's not coming back, for now—and now may last another couple hundred years. There's always Vietnam, I suppose, if I decide to just slip away in the night, pilgrim that I am, and poor wayfaring commie stranger.

ELIZABETH FRANK was born in Los Angeles. Her father, the producer-writer-director Melvin Frank, moved the family to London in 1960. Upon graduation from the International School of Geneva, she went to Bennington College, transferring two years later to the University of California at Berkeley, where she received her BA, MA, and PhD in English. Since 1982 she has been a member of the literature faculty at Bard College. In 1986 she won the Pulitzer Prize in biography for *Louise Bogan: A Portrait*. She writes frequently about art, and is the author of *Jackson Pollock, Esteban Vicente*, and *Karen Gunderson: The Dark World of Light* as well as the novel *Cheat and Charmer*, about Hollywood during the McCarthy period. The Joseph E. Harry Professor of Modern Languages and Literature at Bard College, she lives in New York, has an adult daughter, and in 1999 began spending every summer in Sofia, Bulgaria. She cotranslated two novels by Bulgarian screenwriter and novelist Angel Wagenstein, both published in the United States by Other Press, and is currently working on a novel about Bulgaria since the "Democratic Changes" of 1989.

Hate for Sale

Hate for sale. All the very best
Hate for sale. Vintage stuff.
Do my cries excite your interest?
Lovely hate. Your life is rough.

Buy my hate. You'll come right back for more.
Hate for sale. Enough to start a war.
Hate the rich, the brown, the black, the poor.
Hate is clean. And hate will make you sure.

Hate for sale. You'll feel superior.
Hate for sale. You'll make the news.
Hate the families who come here fleeing war.
Hate the gay, the trans, the new, the Jews.

Don't need to care who you detest,
hate makes you feel a whit less scared,
to know your people are the best
and burn to ashes all the rest
who will not face the real test
but showed up naked, unprepared
to be sent back, or drowned, or hurled

back into the abyss. Your world
will be so safe, so clean, so great.
And all you needed was some hate.

Hate for sale. All the very best
Hate for sale. Vintage stuff.
Do my cries excite your interest?
Hate for sale. Never enough.

NEIL GAIMAN is an award-winning author of books, graphic novels, short stories, and films for all ages. His titles include *Norse Mythology*, *The Graveyard Book*, *Coraline*, *The View from the Cheap Seats*, *The Ocean at the End of the Lane*, *Neverwhere*, and the *Sandman* series of graphic novels, among other works. His fiction has received Newbery, Carnegie, Hugo, Nebula, World Fantasy, and Eisner awards. The film adaptation of his short story "How to Talk to Girls at Parties" and the second season of the critically acclaimed, Emmy-nominated television adaptation of his novel *American Gods* will be released in 2018. Born in the UK, he now lives in the United States and is a United Nations Goodwill Ambassador for Refugees.

Unaccountable

This was on the outskirts of the capital, where Boulevard de la Révolution used to run through the shantytowns to the old aerodrome. In those days, three or four révolutions ago, we still had a base out by the north runway—we, the Americans: a half dozen hangars full of men and matériel, deployed to remind the Big Man, in his palace across the lagoon, that he was beholden to our interests. One of the Marine guards at the embassy had told me they had a pool table there, and a strategic supply of bourbon, and that if I wanted to partake, I could join him any Saturday. So that's where I was bound, behind the wheel of the absurd car I'd bought off my predecessor, a canary-yellow Buick Skylark that some long-ago diplomat had shipped in new in 1975, on the taxpayers' dime, and had been passed down through the years, through the embassy ranks, as it depreciated from showboat to relic to little more, by the time it became mine, than a gag. Saturday was market day, and the streams of pedestrians spilling along the road's shoulders in the shantytowns were particularly dense that afternoon. It was rainy season, the light mercurial and shuddering under greasy-gray clouds. And just as the skies opened, a black Mercedes appeared in my rearview mirror. A black Mercedes meant power; it was the car of rank among the Big Man's cronies, the car of those in a position to command the big bribes for the big favors—the car that signified that the person it carried was one of those whom everyone else in the country called "an unaccountable." This one, in my rearview, wasn't slowing down as it closed in on me. The headlights flashed. The horn sounded. It wanted me out of the way, and I wanted the same. The rain was crashing down too fast for my old

Buick's wipers. Everything was a blur. Then something hit my car with a juddering thump and crack, and a hideous grating sound came from below. I'd killed a man—I felt sure of it at once—a bicyclist who I swear wasn't there the split second before. His bike had flipped under my car, and he'd flipped over it, and as I stopped the car, right there in the road, a boy tapped my window and pressed his face as close to mine as the glass would allow, pointing to where the body lay, then running his finger over his throat, and popping his eyebrows in alarm as he mouthed the word: *"Vas-y! Vas-y . . ."* Go! Go . . .

That's what everyone always said there: if you hit someone, don't stop—the people will mob you, and hold court on the spot, rob you or stomp you or both, and you'll be lucky to live to tell of it. My predecessor, when he sold me the Skylark, when he handed me the keys, said, "Just hope you don't kill anyone." I told him I didn't plan on it. He said, "You should—it happens all the time here, and you'll have a lot better chance if you've got a plan." He told me that he'd heard that sometimes, when a poor child died, the family would wait by the roadside to throw the body in front of a foreigner's car and cry bloody murder until the whole neighborhood mobbed in for the shakedown. I thought that sounded far-fetched. "Very," he said. "I see no reason to believe it, except that one ignores such legends at one's peril."

None of this made any sense to me now. How could I go? Where could I go? You couldn't exactly disappear in that Buick. The rain was already spent, little more than a drizzle, and I could see that a great crowd had gathered around me, albeit at a wary distance, so that my car seemed to stand in a sort of clearing, and I had the sense that everyone was waiting to see what I would do to see what they would do. Probably I didn't think anything quite so clear as that, but that was the feeling, as I put the car in park and, leaving it idling, opened my door and stood in the road.

As soon as I appeared, a man peeled away from the crowd and strolled slowly toward me, holding his empty hands out in a consoling gesture, saying, "Don't worry about it, it's over, he's finished, be calm, it was an accident, an accident." He came at me, repeating himself, and sidled past, and was gone. Then there was another man, coming at the same angle. This man was brandishing a big stick, and muttering angrily, and as he came a woman's voice rose in fury behind me. I had forgotten about the black Mercedes, but of course it had to stop when I did, and out of it now erupted a magnificent woman in a flaming flower-print dress, with her head wrapped in a blazing orange turban. She flew at the man with the stick, this great grand fireball of a woman, crying out in a voice as loud as her outfit and even more adamant: "Stop! Don't you touch him. It was an accident! You animal. Look—this is a man. He didn't run. He got out. He has courage. He did right."

I didn't feel courageous or right, or like I had anything to do with this woman's spectacular passion, but the stick man shrank away, and she—suddenly calm, almost in a stage whisper, as if we knew each other well and were in this together—told me: "Go on, now, get out of here. I'll sort this out, like it never happened."

What did that mean? I started to protest: "It did happen. There's a body. That can't be denied." But she had turned away from me, and was moving into the crowd, dispersing it as she went.

Was that the moment I fell in love with her? I had no idea who she was. I didn't know her name. I wasn't even sure if she was real, or some apparition born of my state of shock. In my memory, she had no accent, which seemed as impossible as everything else about her. But when she spoke to me in that soothing conspiratorial voice, I had felt from her, all at once, a powerful warmth and a powerful corruption, and when she showed me her back and stepped away, I felt my heart lurch after her.

I must have done as she told me. I don't remember driving back to my house, but there I was—and I did not go out again for days. I didn't report the accident. I called the embassy without mentioning it, saying only that I had fever, and that was no lie. I slept an awful lot of the time, and spent my waking hours in a fugue state, with my collision replaying itself, as if on an unceasing loop tape in my mind. Or, I should really say my *collisions*—plural: the first with the bicyclist, and the second with that woman.

Both seemed to me at once unreal and inevitable. Perhaps a week passed in this limbo. My phone kept ringing—the same unknown number. When

I finally answered it, I knew her voice at once. She told me her name was Fatima. She said she'd been thinking of me, and I felt that lurch again in my chest. I didn't need to ask how she, a woman with such a black Mercedes and such an air of command, had found me, a guy with such a Buick. I said I'd been thinking of her, too. I said, "I mean, where did you come from?" "Right here," she said, but she'd gone to college in Wisconsin, which at least explained her accent.

I had been half expecting in the days since our encounter to be summoned by the police for an inquiry; and I asked Fatima now if it didn't seem wrong to her that a man had died, and that there were no consequences.

"I told you that I'd fix it," she said. "You know that's how it is here—you're an American, I'm not a nobody, either."

"Unaccountables," I said.

"Please," she said sharply. "Should I have left you to the mob there? Or had you arrested? Would that make anything better?" She waited for me to answer, and when I didn't, she said: "I want to see you. I don't want to talk about this. It's pointless. Okay? Can I come over?"

Fatima. She knew what she wanted, and when she got it, she had a great, full-throated, openmouthed laugh, made all the more joyous by a generous gap between her top front teeth. That's how I remember the first nonstop weeks of our affair, talking and touching, out on the town, or back at my place, in bed— as one long gust of unchecked, lusty laughter.

It was her town, so she led the way, and she was careful to keep a low profile, always driving a little Japanese car when she came to see me, never the black Mercedes. She wore jeans and T-shirts and baseball caps, making herself as nondescript-looking as she could, and took me to quiet little out-of-the-way places where nobody seemed to notice her, much less to know her. And we always returned to my place—she never once invited me to hers.

I didn't much mind. Of course she wanted privacy. Or that was how I figured it, anyway, until one night, as we lay naked beneath my ceiling fan, I told her, "You know what, Fati? I love you." And she said, "How much?"

That made me laugh. "You mean, like—would I die for you?"

"Don't be ridiculous," she said. "What good would you be to me dead? No. I mean, would you kill for me?"

What if I had said yes? Would I now be telling you a different story? I didn't say no. I told her: "I would prefer not to."

"That's not what I asked you," she said. She sounded irritated, and that irritated me. "Come on," I said, "has anybody ever loved you liked that, Fatima?"

"Without a doubt," she said. "The man I'm supposed to marry does."

That was the first I'd heard of such a man. She seemed surprised by my surprise. She thought it was obvious that we were only enjoying each other as a diversion until, inevitably, the rest of our lives reclaimed us. She said, "I've been pledged to marry him since we were six years old."

Their fathers had made the arrangement as part of a pact that ended nearly a century of bloody political and business feuds between two of the country's most powerful families. It was a gentleman's agreement, but to Fatima it had always seemed an inescapable destiny. Only in her Wisconsin years had she ever known what she called "the savage freedom of not belonging."

"I could have stayed there," she said. "I could have just become this Fatima-the-American you seem to fancy. Well, I didn't."

"So you're saying that you belong to him—this man who'd kill for you?"

"No more than he belongs to me."

I had pulled a sheet over my body, and Fatima got out of bed and got dressed.

"What about you?" I said. "Would you kill for him?"

"That's the deal," she said, "the pact our fathers made. Brutal—yeah, maybe. But breaking that pact would be way more brutal."

I found this note, slipped under my door, two mornings later—a single paragraph, without salutation or signature:

I can't blame you and I don't blame you. To blame you for wanting my wife would be to disparage her. That you want her means only that you are a man. So what? That she must have wanted you too—that is the problem.

That means you are a man whose existence is intolerable to me. You must understand my need for relief. There are many ways that I could dispose of you, just as there are many ways that I could end my own life. Those are the two solutions to our mutual predicament. A duel presents the most unprejudiced means of determining which of them will be our fate. I trust that a man worthy of my wife's interest will not hesitate to give me the satisfaction of accepting my challenge.

Was he joking—the fiancé? Apparently not, because as I sat rereading the note in bewilderment for the sixth or seventh time, he phoned and, after announcing himself, instructed me to meet him "for our contest" at dawn the next day at such and such a secluded pasture alongside the lagoon. Then, without waiting for a response, he hung up. Not fifteen minutes later, a messenger came to my door, handed me a large envelope, and hurried away. Inside was another note: "I will bring pistols. You will have the choice of weapons. In all other particulars we will proceed according to the rules detailed in the pamphlet here enclosed."

I never looked at that pamphlet. I didn't like being ordered around, and I couldn't have cared less about the rules of dueling. I knew nothing about pistols, had only fired one a few times in my life, and had never had even a fleeting wish to shoot another person. The absurdity of the situation maddened me—and, at the same time, the absurdity appealed to me, too. My thoughts spun and scrambled. It seemed obvious to me that I could not go through with this folly, and equally obvious that I must. No doubt it was a trap. Or perhaps the fiancé really did want to commit suicide by summoning me to shoot him. But then again he had made clear that he would do away with me if I didn't show up, so I might as well take my chances. And maybe I deserved it. Maybe all I had wanted since I struck that bicyclist was punishment, some commensurate measure of annihilating oblivion.

Time flew, and time stalled, and noon became dusk, and suddenly it was past midnight, and I did not know what I would do, and I knew I would do it. Was Fatima behind this? Was this the killing she wanted me to do for her to prove my love? I had no idea. I would never know. I had only one way to know.

"You must understand my need for relief." Yes, fiancé, yes, that was the only thing I understood absolutely, as I eased the Skylark through the fog-shrouded streets of the sleeping city in the first damp gray light of false dawn. When I pulled up to the field, a riot of crows tumbled from a stand of scraggly trees and filled the air overhead. The fiancé stood beside a black Mercedes. I had not seen him before and could not see him too clearly now. His second approached, carrying a box with a pair of pistols. The weapon I took felt good in my hand. The second spoke at length, with legalistic precision, explaining what was to happen, but I remember only the cawing of the crows and how that was drowned out, in turn, by songbirds going off everywhere at once in a manic collective euphoria as the night melted into day.

Then we were walking away from each other—the fiancé and I—wading, really, through the dew-heavy grass, holding our pistols, counting our paces. I lost count.

The second called: Halt.

I remember thinking I do not want to die like this. I remember thinking I do not want to live like this.

The second called: Turn and face.

We stood then at our little distance, two men, silhouetted in bright haze, pointing pistols at each other. Were we supposed to shoot now? Was he waiting for me? Was I waiting for him?

The second called: Gentlemen.

What was happening?

Gentlemen!

Why didn't that man shoot me?

The second called: Fire!

There was some commotion off to the side, a crow beating past, and my arm swung that way, and I shot it. I hit it. I could never do that again. Pure luck, an accident: the bird blew apart, feathers and blood. I was elated. The fiancé had to think that I could have killed him just as easily.

But why didn't he shoot?

The second called again: Fire!

And there was another commotion: a car swerved onto the field, and jerked to a stop, and out flew Fatima, wailing No! Then the fiancé fired, and Fatima fell.

He shot her in the thigh, and as she went down, he ran to her. It looked, from where I stood, like a tender reunion. He was binding her wounds. She was stroking his face.

I left them there then. I don't think anyone noticed. I dropped my pistol in the field, drove the Skylark to the aerodrome, and twenty-four hours later I was sitting in a rocking chair on my mother's porch in New Jersey.

I was sitting there still a couple months later when the mailman brought me a postcard: "It was only a flesh wound. He's a very good shot. I didn't even need a cane at our wedding. You see, as promised, everything's fixed like nothing ever happened. Love, Fatima."

PHILIP GOUREVITCH is a longtime staff writer for the *New Yorker*, the former editor of the *Paris Review*, and the author of three books: *The Ballad Of Abu Ghraib / Standard Operating Procedure*, *A Cold Case*, and *We Wish to Inform You That Tomorrow We Will Be Killed with Our Families: Stories from Rwanda*, which won the National Book Critics Circle Award, the Guardian First Book Award, and the Los Angeles Times Book Prize, among other honors. Gourevitch's books have been translated into twenty languages, and in 2010 he was named a Chevalier de l'Ordre des Arts et des Lettres in France. He is completing a new book, titled *You Hide That You Hate Me and I Hide That I Know*.

White Baby

A black American couple wanted a child. They wanted a child very badly but could not have one of their own. After many discussions, they went to an adoption agency. A heavyset black receptionist in a loose blouse greeted them in the reception area. She made them feel hopeful and welcome. The receptionist nodded sympathetically and gave them each a clipboard.

Soon, a woman with real authority came out. Her authority came partly from the fact that she had made them wait. Clearly, her time was more valuable than theirs. Also, she wore a stern expression and a dark purple tailored suit. From her dark, coarse hair, you might guess that she had black or Latin ancestors, but you couldn't tell for sure, even if you squinted, listened for an accent, or sought out certain inflections in her voice. She had an Anglo name, and she said nothing personal about herself. The woman took the couple's clipboards and looked them over. In the box where the adoption agency asked what race of baby they wanted, both the man and the woman had put an X in the box marked WHITE. The adoption agency woman pointed to the boxes to show them the X mark and asked if they had made a mistake.

"No," the wife said. "No mistake. We want a white baby."

"A white baby," said the possibly ethnic lady. "White babies are hard. Why a white baby?" It sounded to the couple as if she wanted to stop them from getting a white baby. It sounded as if she would not help them get a white baby.

The couple sighed. "We just want what anyone else would want," the husband said. His wife grabbed his forearm supportively and said, "This is

America!" which explained everything. But that did not satisfy the lady who might've been passing for white. The couple fidgeted and frowned.

Eventually the wife explained that they felt a white baby would have a better chance at success if black Americans raised him. "A white baby raised by black people could become the president of the United States," said the potential adoptive father. "Or he could become a rap star." The opportunities were boundless for a white baby raised by Negroes. "If not that, he could at least go top ten on the R & B chart."

"But plenty of white people are *already* raised by black people," the creamy-skinned woman said. The black couple got very offended. "We are doctors. We have medical degrees," the wife said scornfully. "We are not going to become domestics. We have the right to be parents, and we have the right to adopt whatever type of child we want." A white baby *needed* black parents, they agreed, in order to get the best of both worlds. The world of prosperity, abstract thinking, winter sports, technology, mayonnaise, and spiritual emptiness that white folks lived in, and the world of authenticity, ignorance, poverty, dancing, fattening food, and connection to God that black people lived in. The couple wanted a white baby, they said, because a white baby raised by black people could have extremely diverse friends and interests, and no one would question his ability to play basketball or his credibility as a financial advisor.

"If we can get a male, and he's good-looking, the sky's the limit," said the husband. "Everyone always wants to help a white boy."

Naturally, the maybe-not-white woman was taken aback by their candor, and at the same time seemed surprised by the couple's articulateness with regard to these issues. She also thought they might be insane. "Are you sure?" she asked.

"Oh, we definitely want a white baby," the black woman said.

"Yes, we do," the black man said, nodding gravely.

"And even if you can't find one for us," his wife said, blackening her attitude to emphasize her seriousness, "I'll be damned if I'm gonna sit here and let someone question our right to even *want* a white baby."

The black woman made her spine broom-straight and looked her in the eye. She stuck out her neck and shifted it a little, blackly. "Do you think we're not *good enough* to have a white child?"

The adoption agency woman looked perplexed, but she backed down. "It's just that white babies are so hard to get, even for white adoptive parents," the woman said. "There's so much demand and not enough supply." Her tone of voice had become high-pitched, soothing, afraid. "Plus, black children are so much more in need, and you could really help a black child more by raising it in its own culture. You could really make a huge difference in a black child's life."

"We know, we know. We've talked all that through," the black woman said, waving her hand in the air. "And we still want a white baby. Nothing you can say will change our minds. This is a free country, we want what we want, and why should we let anyone stop us from achieving our goals?"

"Please!" the lady suddenly snapped. "You know it isn't practical! Can I at least get you to consider the alternatives? I could place a Middle Eastern child with you."

"That's not white!" the black woman shouted.

The black man leaned forward in front of his wife and pointed to his mouth. "Read my lips," he said. "White! Baby!"

"Okay, okay, I understand your needs, and we really do want to place children with families who want them more than anything else. This won't be easy, but I'll see what can be done," the adoption agency woman said, blowing air through her cheeks. They knew she wouldn't do anything.

It took several years and a discrimination lawsuit, but eventually the stork delivered a white bundle of joy to the black couple. "Here he is," a new woman from the adoption agency announced. "Say hello to Jeremy!"

The black couple were overjoyed. They signed all the papers and brought Jeremy home. He had round blue eyes like fishbowls and skin as white as a bathtub. The new black mother rocked the baby in his blanket as her husband waved good-bye to the adoption agency woman through their picture window.

After the lady left, the black wife scooped the boy up and lifted him out of the crib. She undid the folds of his blanket and held the child up to her husband, who took a hearty bite out of Jeremy's face. The new mom chewed off Jeremy's tiny fingers. Blood went everywhere. The boy screamed and cried and kicked for as long as he remained alive. When the child finished struggling, the husband and wife picked his bones clean. Afterwards, the wife boiled them for soup stock.

"I can't believe how hungry I was," said the black man.

JAMES HANNAHAM's most recent novel, *Delicious Foods*, won the PEN/Faulkner Award, the Hurston/Wright Legacy Award, and the Morton Dauwen Zabel Award from the American Academy of Arts and Letters, was selected for the Barnes & Noble Discover Great New Writers program, was one of the *New York Times*' and *Washington Post*'s 100 Notable Books of 2015, and was a finalist for the Los Angeles Times Book Prize in Fiction. His debut, *God Says No*, was honored by the American Library Association's Stonewall Book Awards. He has published short stories in *One Story*, *Fence*, *StoryQuarterly*, and *BOMB*. He was a finalist for the Rome Prize. He teaches in the Writing Program at the Pratt Institute. He contributed to the *Village Voice* from 1992 to 2016, and his criticism, essays, and profiles have appeared in *Spin*, *Details*, *Us*, *Out*, BuzzFeed, the *New York Times Magazine*, *4Columns*, and elsewhere. He cofounded the performance group Elevator Repair Service and worked with them from 1992 to 2002. He has exhibited text-based visual art at the James Cohan Gallery, 490 Atlantic, Kimberly-Klark, and the Center for Emerging Visual Artists.

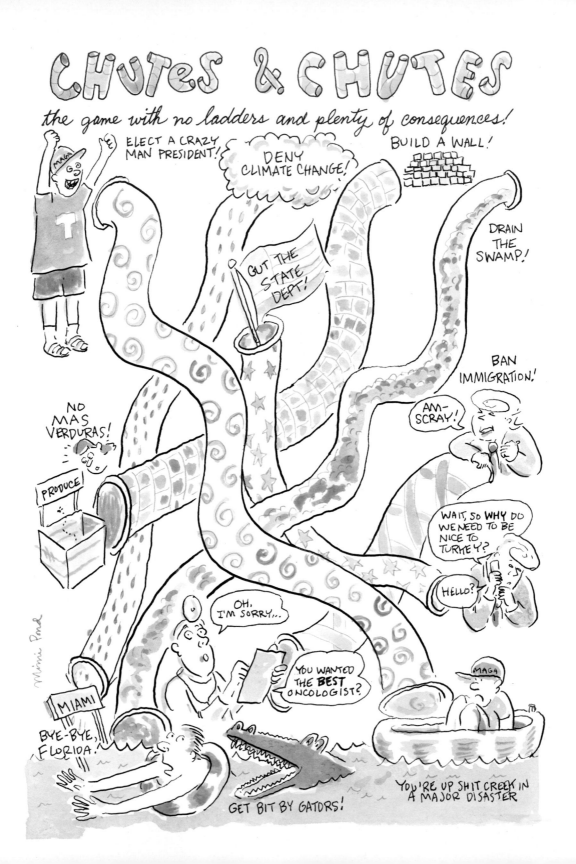

MIMI POND is a cartoonist, illustrator, and writer. Her most recent books are the semiautobiographical graphic novels *Over Easy* and *The Customer is Always Wrong*, about her late-1970s Oakland waitressing career. She has created comics for newyorker.com, the *Los Angeles Times*, *Seventeen* magazine, *National Lampoon*, and many other publications. She has also written for television: her credits include the first full-length episode of *The Simpsons*, "Simpsons Roasting on an Open Fire," and episodes for the television shows *Designing Women* and *Pee-wee's Playhouse*. She lives in Los Angeles with her husband, the painter Wayne White.

Your Sacred American Rights Bingo

Ink and watercolor

In the Trees

America the plum blossoms are falling.

When you have a secret in our town, you have to carry it close to your heart. You have to be careful even when you sleep to make sure you don't announce your crimes while you're dreaming. Everything is a crime here, even falling in love. That is what happened to me. My mother had warned me that being a woman could bring you sorrow, but I didn't listen. Not then. It was July, the time of year when the river is so blue it hurts to look at it. Fishermen come here from all across the country. My father owns a bait store, and everyone stops there, people from California and New York and Chicago. Men who are ruined, and those who are so rich they can't even count their money anymore. There's only one motel in town, but local folks open their houses, put their kids in tents in the yard, then rent out their bedrooms. You have to catch visitors from out of state while you can, my father says. We have a sort of trout that cannot be found anywhere else, called a blue rainbow. In school we've been told it was the original fish, the one that fed the multitudes, and that all other trout are descended from our rainbows. But we are taught many things I no longer believe. Less than a hundred years ago, there were countless wolves in our hills; now the last one to be caught is in the historical museum. I go there sometimes just to stare at him. You can see the stiches in his pelt, and his eyes are made of yellow glass. How can something so beautiful come to an end so quickly? Now we have hundreds of rabbits. It's the penance we pay. When I walk to school in the morning they're on everyone's lawn. There's not much grass left anymore, just patches of dirt. Sometimes the rabbits refuse to move out of the way; they block the sidewalk, and when I run, they chase me.

I fell in love with a boy who came from Chicago in July. His name was Will and his dream was to catch one of our rainbows, or so he said. Then after a while he said I was his dream. Maybe that was why I let him do things to me I'd never let anyone do before, but it was only part of the reason. I felt caught up in something when I looked in his eyes. I didn't understand that love is something that can ambush you, and there you are at the mercy of the forces of nature, like the wolves that had continued to come to the river to drink when they should have run as far as they could.

We met at night, in the parking lot of the motel, where he and his father and brothers were staying. I'd worked there one summer cleaning rooms, but I complained about some of the things I found, and they didn't hire me back. After that, I just worked in my father's shop. I'd wash my hands with lemon juice at the end of the day. I'd take off my clothes and change into clean jeans and a T-shirt that smelled of soap instead of fish. I'd let my hair out of the tight braids I usually wore and brush it till it shone. Then I'd walk to the motel. I'd try to walk slowly, so as not to give my heart away, but I'd always wind up running. I was fifteen, an age when a girl can be stupid and smart at the same time. We would go to his father's truck to be alone. The nights were starry in July and the trees whispered. There was a plum tree I knew about and sometimes, after we were done in his father's truck, we would walk to that tree and steal plums. Will believed things that I didn't. He was glad that the wolves had disappeared and he didn't care that polar bears were now found wandering down the streets in northern Scotland, and that the bees were all but gone. He didn't pay any attention to the lasts of things, but I did. I figured my little sister wouldn't even know honey had ever existed. Will had his eye on the future, he said. I, myself, didn't like to think about what would happen next. I was here now, with him, at the plum tree, listening to the cicadas and wondering why their song was so hard to hear. When I was a little girl they were so loud you could barely talk to each other outside at night. Now we could whisper and hear each other just fine.

I was in love with Will and with July and I never wanted the night to end. I dreaded the next day, which would force us further into the future. When I walked home alone on the dirt road that led to our house I was often dizzy. It was love that had done that to me, and the stars, and the way I knew that something would happen to ruin everything.

My mind is made up there's going to be trouble.

Will's father caught the biggest trout on record. I cried when I saw him on the dock, being photographed by the newspaper, with Will and his brothers flanking him. The fish was every color blue from sapphire to turquoise to cobalt. It shimmered in the sunlight, but its eyes were white. People said it was the granddaddy, the ancestor of all the other fish. Our mayor took Will's family to dinner. I was in the crowd but Will didn't wave. The truth is I don't think he even saw me. I was no one, after all. A girl he'd met by accident. I didn't go meet Will that night. Instead I went down to the river. My father always said it would take a day and a night to swim all the way across and that a person who tried to do so would likely drown. I took off all my clothes and I dove in. It was dark and the water looked black and I realized I was crying. I thought about a girl I knew who had once ruined her life with love. Ten years later, no one talked to her, although I always did.

Will came looking for me and told me I was wrong to think he'd forget me. He was still here, wasn't he? We held each other in the woods. I knew he would be leaving, but I did it anyway, as if this were the only day we would ever have. Still, I knew I'd have a price to pay.

My father found a letter I was writing to Will and he took me out and beat me with his belt. He told me I would thank him someday, but I doubted it. Someday didn't matter to me. I had welts on my skin and something had broken inside me. I packed a bag and ran down the dirt road, ready to leave town and everything I had ever known, but when I got to the motel, Will's father's truck was gone. I went into the office. Anna was there, the woman I worked with when I cleaned rooms. She was the one no one talked to, unless they were from out of town.

"Off to Chicago," she said. "You couldn't have thought he'd stay?"

I went to the river instead of going home. I knew what happened to girls like me. Everybody did. My secret hurt me, like a stone in my shoe. But worse. Much worse, because it was my heart.

I sit in my house for days on end and stare at the roses in the closet.

I did nothing for as long as I could, and then I went to the doctor. I'd known him all my life, so I kept my eyes lowered as I spoke to him. I told him I wanted to go to Chicago, where I'd heard they could free me of my misfortune. I knew someone who had been there, and she'd told me the address. I didn't tell him it was Anna, and that I had the address written down in my notebook. The doctor listened to my secret, then he told me to wait where I was. Instead of helping me, he called my father.

My father came in like a storm, cursing. He told me I had no right to do what I wanted to do. I was underage and my body belonged to him and he should have known I would turn out this way.

My father locked me in my room. I sat in the closet, thinking things over. When it was dark, I climbed out my window. I took the money my mother had buried in the yard in a coffee can. I felt bad, but not too bad, because she always said she was saving it for me and this was my time of need. I don't think about what happened after that. I don't think of the men in the cars, or the place I went to where they locked you in a room so you couldn't make a phone call, or the man they called Doc who wasn't a doctor. There were other girls there, but we didn't speak to each other. I heard them crying, but I swallowed my tears. I wished I weren't fifteen. I wished none of this had ever happened. I never think about the pain now, except when I still have it. They said that due to the circumstances, I would not be able to have children. I don't think about that either.

When I went home my father didn't speak to me, but my mother let me in. I didn't go back to school, I sat in my closet and thought about things that had passed. In time it was April and I could see the plum tree blossoms from my room. I thought of myself as the plum tree, standing alone in the woods.

I would be sixteen eventually, not that I cared. When it was July again people started coming to the river, but not Will, which was just as well. The trout were gone. People searched for them, they rented boats and came from all over the country, but there were no blue rainbows to be found. We didn't even have the last one in the historical museum. That one was on Will's father's wall in Chicago.

After that the future crept up on all of us, though I still try to keep it from my thoughts. Now when you go to the market, they sell trout that they paint with blue dye, but it doesn't fool anyone any more than the honey they make from sugar water and molasses. These things are lost. I know what it's like to disappear. I go to the river at night. It's mostly deserted now, but I swim out as far as I can. I swim until I'm hurting. I think about not going back, but I do. I can always find my way because the stars are still there.

ALICE HOFFMAN is the *New York Times* bestselling author of thirty novels, including *Faithful*, *The Marriage of Opposites*, and *The Dovekeepers*, which Toni Morrison called "a major contribution to twenty-first-century literature." Her newest novel, *The Rules of Magic*, is the prequel to her cult classic *Practical Magic*.

Getting Somewhere

"Sure," I told my husband, Jeffrey, "over my dead body." That was when he said he wanted to buy something spectacular in Boca. He'd always been Jeff, but he hit it big, owning forty shopping malls just before he turned fifty. The combo of true wealth as opposed to just lots of money plus his increasing girth (words like *girth* make everyone hearing me think *four-year college*) . . . Where was I? Oh, right. People just began calling him Jeffrey, like he was too important for a nickname. He didn't exactly object. He even thought about spelling it Geoffrey, but too much stuff was monogrammed. He took to playing golf, to say nothing of talking about it. He was getting that thick-waisted, bronzed, rich-guy look and once, as I caught a rear view of him going into the shower, I thought, *His ass looks like a schnecken.* Anyway, I said: "*Boca Raton?* So I can wear Missoni and join a book group?"

Palm Beach was out because Jeffrey knew the guys there were bankers and hedge-funders who thought a discussion of differential monetary policy was conversation. Also they made him feel insecure, because his malls weren't anchored by a store like Neiman Marcus. Not even Dunkin' Donuts. I told him: "Right. Me in pastel Chanel. Toots, you got me mixed up with your next wife."

So we picked Miami and when people asked us, basically, *Huh?*, we told them we loved that it was a real city. Culture and world-class restaurants. Also it was sooo international. That was true, and actually both of us had taken Spanish in high school, and when we spoke it, people were complimentary, but that's because Latinos have good manners, even the guys in the car washes, so I was glad I didn't take French.

Anyway, the first house the real estate agent wanted to show us was on Key Biscayne, over the Causeway from Miami, but Jeffrey said he didn't want to see it because the Key only had a public golf course, but then he said all right, he'd look at Paraíso—a house with a name! Was it gorgeous? At first glance his jaw dropped so low I had to give him the elbow before Marilyn, the agent who wore Armani, could see. Totally drop dead, so you could sit at the pool and, right ahead of you, there was the ocean. The house? I still can't believe it's ours.

But that's not the story.

This is what happened in 2002. Can you believe it was so long ago? I was driving my car, a BMW convertible since that was around the time it became chic to be unpretentious. So the last thing I wanted was a Bentley, which all but screamed faux modesty. Anyway, I was going over the Rickenbacker Causeway that's named for somebody and the news is on. It was about those snipers around Washington DC who got caught a few days before and I was thinking, *I am so sick of all this violence stuff*, because a little more than a month ago it had been the first anniversary of 9/11.

Whenever I drove, I made myself listen to NPR. It paid off. When I stopped at a traffic light, people in the other cars could think, *Intellectual*. Also, it was great for going to a cocktail party and having specific things to say about why Vice President Cheney was a putz and how much I adored *The Secret Life of Bees*.

The Causeway was five miles of total gorgeousness, a high bridge over Biscayne Bay that went from the Key to Miami. That day the air smelled like clams on the half shell. The early afternoon sun lit the tops of the waves in the bluish-green water and made them give off gold sparks. So I started feeling a little better. Top down, Anthelios sunscreen, Dolce & Gabbana sunglasses, wind in my hair, which didn't matter because I was on my way to get it done.

So I was over the Causeway and all of a sudden it's like everybody goes crazy. Cars are swerving, the giant Winn-Dixie truck in front of me slammed on its brakes so I slammed on mine. I couldn't see what was going on, just the back of the truck with a dumb slogan—"Beef, it's what's for dinner" and for a second thinking, *Feh, that picture looks like the cheap, mealy roast beef my mother used to put Adolph's Tenderizer on*—but then I realized something was wrong for this kind of sudden traffic chaos. Maybe a giant piece of concrete crashed down from the bridge into Biscayne Bay and there's a hole bigger than my car and theoretically I could survive crashing into the water as long as I remembered to take off my seat belt on the way down. Maybe it was something else. Could a car, God forbid, have hit a bike rider?

Very, very carefully, I inched the front wheels toward the left and moved up a teeny bit, so maybe I could see something beyond the truck. Nada. But all of a sudden there are people running across the road—black people, really black—coming up from the shore onto the Causeway. And I get from the way they're running and how many there are that it's not an accident or some kind of protest. They're wet. And so thin, not in a good way, like an African supermodel. Scrawny, and most of the men were shirtless. You could see their ribs, knots of bone on their shoulders. And the women—hardly any had shoes, or maybe they'd been wearing flip-flops and lost them. And there were some kids too, terrified looks on their faces, and a little girl with a white hair bow on one side. She kept patting the other side of her head, unable to believe the other bow was actually lost. More kept coming, like they were using the Causeway just to run away from wherever their boat left them.

I turned off NPR and that's when I heard some of the people shouting to each other, and police sirens in the distance. Miami stopped using regular sirens and now had those disgusting ones that make up and down sounds, like in World War II movies, *Yoo-hoo, Nazis coming.*

That's when I put it all together. The runners were Haitians trying to sneak into the States, except something had happened to their boat. You heard that a lot in South Florida. Maybe it fell apart or the currents took it to where they could be spotted. They were running as fast as they could because the sirens were so close. Across and down on the other side of the Causeway near the tollbooths, around where the road met the land. They needed to spread out and go . . . Who knew where they could get to that would be safe? They must've known America was no refuge for them, but in their hearts they believed it was.

What the hell could they do now, call a cab? And no matter how fast they were, some had kids—petrified little kids—and the grown-ups were screaming. To each other or just crying out, probably to God, to help them.

I opened my car door and got out, and stood on the metal thing beneath it that you kind of swing your legs over getting out. And then I saw, oh shit, a couple of cops had gotten on the bridge and were holding up traffic. I guessed they were doing it so that more cops could come and grab the Haitians. Refugees, that's what they were called. I'd been thinking immigrants, but that was like the island in New York that wasn't where the Statue of Liberty was. Ellis Island.

This was what got me. That when Cubans snuck into the U.S. on boats and made it, they were home free. But anybody else? Off to a detention center, then sent back to wherever they came from. Listen, I like Cubans and one of the women in my tennis group, Solana Diaz Ruiz, who for some reason didn't have a hyphen, was a total sweetheart and we had lunch once a week and knew all about each other's kids, and probably too much about each other's husbands. Also, Cubans really revived Miami, bringing so much talent and life to it. Plus Jeffrey's lawyer's last name was Mendoza, okay? Cubans = good. But is it fair that they got to stay just because there are tons of them who got citizenship and they vote?

So I'm standing on that metal thing on my car and the Haitians' screaming is cutting through me, though not my gut, but my throat. Like my air pipe is slit and I can't breathe. Those poor people, I thought, I bet they smell after being on a boat so long. And then I saw more cops, and they were running and grabbing people and making them sit over on the side of the Causeway. A cop watching over the ones they caught walked back and forth like he was just waiting for one to move so he could give him a klop. Meantime, other cops ran back and snatched up more refugees. Weren't their grandparents like mine, coming to America to escape something terrible? Listen, when things are okay, you stay put.

Bad to good. That's America. Okay, not the slaves who got brought here, who were forced from good to bad. But here on the Causeway there were blacks willing to die on a boat to get from horrible to good and I stared at an Irish-looking cop dragging one of them over to the side. Like his great-grandparents didn't cry out to come here when County Whatever ran out of potatoes and they were starving?

Oh God, the expression on one Haitian guy, he was no more than ten feet away from me when he sensed something and saw a big white hand circling the top of his arm. Sad, angry, defeated. But those are just three words. His long rectangle face showed thousands of emotions—every lousy feeling the human race has ever experienced. Otherwise, he would've been so handsome. Black satin skin, angled-up cheekbones and romantic Chinese-y eyes.

All of a sudden I was yelling out loud, "Fuck this!" Definitely not how I usually talk, though I thought it pretty often. Then I looked at that fat-ass Winn-Dixie truck and I blessed it—not because it's my favorite supermarket; truthfully when a major occasion is coming up I ask my housekeeper, Gloria, to go over the Causeway to shop at Publix. I blessed it because it blocked me off from view. I turned and saw a couple of Haitians behind me, about two cars back. I waved them over.

A man and—oh my God, I couldn't believe it—a pregnant woman who must've been at least in her sixth month. She wore cutoffs, khaki, and a T-shirt so faded I couldn't even make out what the design or writing was. They looked at me for like half a second, and then were about to turn away even though I was gesturing *Come here, come here*. Could my hair have been such a mess from blowing in the wind that I looked witchy and was scaring them? They just stood there, trans-something, whatever the word—who could think?— paralyzed-like, and then . . . they were running toward my car.

Then another two came, a man and a boy, maybe ten or eleven years old. So fast I couldn't believe it. I got the pregnant woman in the front passenger seat and the others in the back. Another guy came, close to old and so bony every rib showed. It was only then, *Duh*, I realized they weren't speaking English. Okay, except not Spanish either. Right, because Haitians speak some kind of French. But I got back into my seat and shook my head at the old guy and tried anyway. "*Sólo cuatro.*" Because it was a 328i and even if you didn't use seat belts there wasn't enough room, but he climbed over the door into the back. I motioned at them to get down, then kind of hunkered down myself for a second to show them. They got it.

Now what? At least ten people must've witnessed this happening. A jury would say *We have laws and who the hell is she to decide?* I'd go through menopause and beyond in some disgusting Florida prison with no air-conditioning and palmetto bugs crawling over my feet. All I could do was be grateful that I'd given a major hint to Jeffrey that if he got me a convertible without automatic top-up/top-down, I would definitely not jump for joy. Because a gift is a gift. Either you give with a full heart or you just say screw it and hand over a Saks gift certificate.

So I held the button to get the top up and yelled "*tête*" to them, which I was 100 percent sure was the French word for it, and patted the top of my head. Because this had to be a total trauma for them and it would be awful if they also got a concussion. I actually didn't have to give the demo because they all seemed to get it, and the pregnant woman in the front gave me a look that maybe said *Like we don't know?*, which I hoped wasn't the case because I didn't want her thinking I was condescending to blacks. I turned on the AC, closed the windows and said to her "*Je m'appelle Karen*" and she said something with an *M*, maybe Miriam.

But to tell you the truth by then I wasn't concentrating on her because Winn-Dixie started moving, crept up just enough to give me room to squeeze into the left lane, which was going a little faster now. Within a minute I was far enough ahead of the people who had seen me giving a ride to five illegal immigrants that my license plate would be unreadable.

Speaking of license plates, because Jeffrey gave me the total BMW luxury package, I personally drove to the DMV just west of Little Havana to get a Miami Heat plate. He was so touched by it because we had season tickets and sometimes I went with him. Anyway, my good deed paid off because as the left lane really started moving, I spotted two Miami cops waving *Move it* to get us all off the Causeway.

At first I thought, *What would happen if I fainted while I was driving?* That passed but I was worried that some corrupt cop who wasn't even being investigated would put handcuffs on me and pocket my Piaget watch as he shoved me into a police van. But then the two guys saw the Heat logo on the plate. One nodded and the other gave a big XL denture grin on seeing it, like he wanted to yell *Go Heat!* They were so thrilled by a stupid flaming basketball surrounded by a hoop that they missed five very black people in my car, though I admit the Haitians were thin and crouched down.

I got past the two cops, onto Twenty-Sixth. That was when I started to hyperventilate. I so much wanted to pull over and cup my hands over my mouth so I could get carbon dioxide. But I couldn't pull over because I had all these people whose lives were depending on me plus a baby who wasn't yet born. So I went right, left, right just to get rid of anyone who was tailing me, like in all those movies and TV shows where the guy keeps looking in his rearview mirror to see if someone's following him, and they usually are, so he keeps flooring it down weird streets. I prayed the boy in the back wasn't getting carsick. I swear I wasn't thinking about vomit on the floor mat, just that I remembered how my boys were at that age—such big shots, such babies.

As I turned onto Brickell, I said in a very loud voice, "To Petite Haiti." There's a Haitian neighborhood in Miami called Little Haiti, not that I knew where it was exactly or if *petite* was the right word for it in French or Haitian.

I wasn't sure whether they'd understood, but Miriam reached up from being practically down on the floor and patted the side of my leg. She said, "Okay," and then a bunch of other stuff that of course I didn't understand. Her voice was soft and deep, like you could record it and play it as spa music.

Once I announced where I was taking them, I realized I had to find it. I made another left and finally got to I-95 going north, because I knew that if you got to the Design District, you wouldn't be far from Little Haiti. Back then, the Design District wasn't as hot as it is now but it had lots of furniture stores and antique shops. I'd gone there with my designer, Susan, to pick out curtains and shades, and also had gone to a place that built gazebos, and someone there said that Little Haiti was up the road, but it was a bad neighborhood. Though Susan told me they had a great warehouse filled with incredible vintage deco furniture, I wasn't that into deco because a little goes a long way and I already had a fabulous vanity.

Going south on the other side of the interstate, it looked like every police car and National Guard van—or whoever the black uniformed guys were, maybe Immigration—was flooring it to get there and grab Haitians. I called out, "It's okay," so they wouldn't think we were in a car chase since now we were going sixty-five. Miriam tried to get up onto the seat, but I said, "No. Police. Cops," hoping they'd seen some American movie with subtitles and remembered the word. I wanted to raise my index finger and make a circle over my head like *They're all around and I think I heard a helicopter*, but no one would ever nominate me for the Miami-Dade Best Driver award and I was afraid we'd crash.

So we got to the Design District and I kept going, careful not to speed. If I knew it wasn't that far from Little Haiti, so did the cops, and I kept thinking, *We're getting closer and closer so maybe their hopes are getting up, but what if there's a roadblock?*

And dealing with cops? Because now I was a criminal, but except for this, with the Haitians, I'd always been very law-abiding. Maybe a little pot. Then I thought how these people had nothing, not even a change of underwear. Forget that, not even food. Except probably people in Little Haiti would help them. I had no idea how much cash I had in my handbag. Sometimes a few hundred, but it could be only twenty bucks because how often do I need cash, except when I'm on U.S. 1 and I see the guy under the overpass who sells the cheapest, best orchids?

I always forget the names of the roads that go through the Design District, even though now they've become like Rodeo Drive or Madison Avenue, with Prada and Tod's and Givenchy. But I kept driving on, through what looked like a wasteland of abandoned strip malls, so sun-bleached they'd turned near-death pale yellow. Hardly any people, but what there were didn't look Haitian.

Then I started to see more and more black people, not like American blacks who come in so many colors that it's stupid to call them black, so I probably should start saying African American. Except these people were Haitian. Or Haitian Americans. So finally I saw a man and a woman walking together. They had an air about them like they were going somewhere but weren't in a huge hurry, and they were talking to each other in the matter-of-fact, nice but not lovey-dovey way married people who really like each other talk. She was wearing navy cotton gauze pants and a lovely, crisp white shirt, cuffs turned up twice, which in my opinion is the only way to do it. So I pulled up the car right next to them and stopped. I rolled down my window. At the same time I was motioning *Up* to my passengers.

The couple turned and stared and either they'd heard about what was going on from the news or they just knew that these things happen. And I knew I picked the right people because the man had a cell phone, which wasn't a given in 2002, especially in poorer neighborhoods. I remember reading in the *Miami Herald* about how poor people need cell phones too, though I don't always finish every article I start. The woman was beaming at the refugees and motioning that they should get out of the car.

Anyway, in two seconds he was on the phone talking to someone and she had an arm around the boy, and amazingly the oldish man who'd been crouched down so long didn't even seem stiff. People were suddenly pouring onto the street, surrounding the Haitians who'd been with me. I hadn't even noticed them coming over. Just as I reached across the floor of the car to where Miriam had been sitting, to get my handbag, and I was opening it to get my wallet, I realized all five were already gone.

Gone. The woman turned to me and said, "They wanted me to thank you." I thought she'd have an accent, but she didn't.

"Oh, sure." I smiled at her, but honestly I felt like crying because I never got a chance to say goodbye. Of course, I didn't know them, and maybe the pregnant one's name wasn't even Miriam, but I felt like I knew them. Like I knew the father and the boy had a good relationship. I swear, I'm not making that up. "Can I give you some money for them?"

She shook her head. "No. I don't know where they went. People will take care of them. Don't worry."

"Is there a group that helps . . . immigrants?" She nodded. I took all the cash out of my wallet and gave it to her. "Can I—?"

She handed me back a ten, like a mother who wouldn't want a kid to go out without any money. She closed my fingers over it, then held my hand between both of hers. "Thank you," she said. "I'll never forget you."

Usually, that kind of stuff embarrasses me. If I have to say something back, it's like the worst, because I hate mush. But the words rushed out. "I'll never forget you either. You're a good person, and so is the man—"

"My husband."

"Yes. You both were so kind to stop and help like that," I said back, sincerely, wanting to stay with her, even though I knew I'd completely missed my hairdresser appointment and Marco wasn't great about clients being late, but that's why God made me a generous tipper.

"You were more than kind," she said back, and she did sound a little bit French or Haitian when she said that. Anyway, we wound up kissing each other, the two-cheek Euro kiss.

As I got back into my car, she vanished. Then I did too.

I think of them, the Causeway people and the good couple, a lot. More than you'd believe. Sometimes I smile. Sometimes my eyes fill up. Can you believe it's been fifteen years?

Maybe we're all Americans now. I hope so.

SUSAN ISAACS was dubbed "Jane Austen with a schmear" by NPR's book critic. Among her thirteen bestselling novels are *Lily White*, *Shining Through*, and *After All These Years*. She has written screenplays for two films, *Compromising Positions*, an adaptation of her novel, and *Hello Again*. She also has one nonfiction work to her credit, *Brave Dames and Wimpettes: What Women Are Really Doing on Page and Screen*. Before she took to books, she was an editor at *Seventeen* magazine and a freelance political speechwriter. An alum of Queens College, Susan currently chairs the board of the literary organization Poets & Writers. She is a past president of Mystery Writers of America and belongs to the National Book Critics Circle, Creative Coalition, PEN, and the International Association of Crime Writers. Among her honors are the John Steinbeck Award, the Writers for Writers Award, and the Marymount Manhattan Writing Center prize. Her most recent work is the novella *A Hint of Strangeness*. She is finishing her fourteenth novel (and first of a series), *Takes One to Know One*. She lives with her husband, a criminal defense lawyer, on Long Island.

Guantánamo, ERF Team: Macing Prisoner in Eye (detail)

Charcoal on paper

SUSAN CRILE's paintings and works on paper have been addressing war and its outcomes since 1991: the burning oil fields of Kuwait, 9/11, Abu Ghraib, and Guantánamo Bay. Her work is in the collections of the Metropolitan Museum of Art, the Hirshhorn Museum and Sculpture Garden, the Solomon R. Guggenheim Museum, and the Cleveland Museum of Art, among others, and has been exhibited in many museums in the United States and Europe, including the Museo di Roma in Trastevere, the Museo di Palazzo Mocenigo in Venice, the Phillips Collection, and the Saint Louis Art Museum. She has had over fifty one-person shows. She has received two National Endowment for the Arts awards, and two Residency grants, to the Bellagio Study and Conference Center, at the Rockefeller Foundation in Bellagio, Italy, and to the American Academy in Rome. She is a professor at Hunter College, CUNY, where she has been on the faculty since 1982. Currently, Crile is working on a series of works on paper using the Statue of Liberty as a metaphor for our times, continuing work on the BP oil spill, and starting investigation into the US prison system. Visit her website at www.susancrile.com.

Guantánamo, ERF Team: Waterboarding Prisoner

Charcoal on paper

Mr. Crime and Punishment and War and Peace

Roger Rabid, we called him. Jabbertalky. Evermore. But mostly we called him Gunner—Gunner Summers. And it wasn't just the Asian Americans. It was pretty much all his fellow 1Ls—the immigrants from Azerbaijan and Poland and Brazil. The students who were born here, but who had been brought up to be respectful of others—kids of cops, of farmers, of teachers. We analyzed Gunner en masse: It was his upbringing. His genes. His ego. It was his insecurity— related, perhaps, to the fact that this was not exactly Harvard Law School we were attending. I was not of the persuasion that it was Gunner's looks, too, that gave him the idea that he was entitled to more airtime than other human beings, but others maintained there was a chart somewhere showing correlation if not causation: rugby build plus blond locks put you at risk, especially if you played tennis, sailed, and had really wanted to take Swahili but in the end had been forced to admit it wasn't as useful as French. In truth, there weren't a lot of people like Gunner in our ranks—people born with silver spoons in their mouths and their hands in the air. This was a fourth-tier school. But he inspired an expansion of our vocabularies, anyway. By the end of the first month, everyone in our section could not only define but spell *logorrheic*. *Pleonastic*. *Periphrastic*. Indeed, you might have been forgiven for thinking we were strangely supersized contestants, preparing for the Scripps Spelling Bee.

As for the sesquipedalian adjectives, those were courtesy of Arabella Lee, of course—Arabella who was born in China but who had grown up here and

GISH JEN

who everyone knew was smarter than Gunner, and more prepared, too. For example, in Property Law, when Professor Meister asked for examples of disabilities protected by the Americans with Disabilities Act, Gunner immediately supplied that significant myopia constituted "a physical or mental impairment that substantially limits one or more major life activities." And such was the spell of his utter self-confidence that even normally perspicacious Professor Meister agreed until Arabella lifted her elegant hand.

"What about *Sutton v. United Airlines*, 1999?" she asked.

"Yes?" said Meister.

"This was an employment discrimination case involving two myopic individuals who had applied to be airplane pilots, were rejected for failing the eyesight requirement, and then sued United Airlines, alleging discrimination on the basis of disability."

"And?" said Meister.

"And they were found by the Supreme Court not to be disabled for purposes of the law," said Arabella.

"Ah. Well. That is indeed relevant." Meister flushed with embarrassment even as he grinned with delight. "What a great example of how critical it can be to look up the leading interpretations of the statute," he went on. "Especially those by the Supreme Court. Thank you."

Gunner scowled.

But would Arabella ever wield the oomph she really should in society? Or, out in the real world, would the Gunners always somehow triumph? She was, to begin with, most impressively unimposing. When the Red Cross came through asking for blood donations, she couldn't give; she didn't weigh enough. Rumor had it she was a size 0. Worse, she not only thought before she talked, she never seemed to forget that there were forty of us in the section, so that if everyone talked for five minutes straight, as Gunner was wont to do, classes would be two hundred minutes. Did this not spell defeat?

Of course, it bugged a lot of us, not just that Gunner was the ideal and knew it, but that he was the ideal to begin with. It bugged a lot of us that the professors wanted us to talk like him even if we were bound to get off topic and end up having to finish covering what we were supposed to cover on our own. And it bugged a lot of us that Arabella's being judged "too quiet" was potentially disastrous.

But this last injustice bugged me especially. Not that I was her boyfriend—she was practically engaged, of course. I was just your garden-variety five-foot-nine friend who was also born on the Mainland and also named Lee, and who was also raised in the States by brave, illegal parents, as a result of which I could appreciate as others perhaps could not just how special she was. A lot of us immigrants had the test scores and the work ethic, after all. She had something else. This clarity. This poise. This touch. Things I no doubt noticed because I was what my parents called "the good-for-nothing-artist type." She knew how to argue without hammering—something our Constitutional Law professor was always trying to teach us. Professor Radin would never have singled out anyone in public, but when she talked about how it really was possible, even at our level, to be deft, we knew she was inspired by the example of Arabella—that Arabella had sparked a flicker of hope in her for us all. Arabella was, what's more, the only member of our class who could ever admit she didn't know something. And she was kind. When people were at one another's throats, she sang funny songs like "So sue him, sue him, what can you do him?" Once she drove three hours to get a depressed classmate's cat from her house and smuggled the animal into her friend's apartment; the friend found her cat under her covers, purring.

I don't mean that Arabella was an angel. For one thing, she disliked Gunner as much as anyone; whenever his name came up she would move her mouth fast and wink. For another, she sometimes signed up for two slots on the treadmill at the gym when you were only allowed to sign up for one. Like she'd use her initials in the right order for one slot and reverse them for the other. AL then LA. It was such a pathetic ruse you had to think she was going to get caught, especially as she did it all the time. But this was Arabella: though everyone at the gym knew, no one wanted to bust her.

One more imperfection. She was, it must be said, a little unliterary. I once told her that *Crime and Punishment* was my favorite book, to which she answered that today someone would no doubt help poor Dostoyevsky, and that if talking weren't enough he would probably be put on something nice. Also, she said she didn't like the word *punishment*, as she strongly believed rehabilitation to be the appropriate point of all sentences, especially incarceration. It's true that, when I pointed out that *Crime and Rehabilitation* lacked a certain je ne sais quoi, she conceded that I was probably right. But she maintained that she didn't like the title anyway and thought Dostoyevsky should have gone back to the drawing board and come up with something completely different.

"Like *War and Peace*?" I said.

To which she replied that I could make fun of her but honestly? That was a great title and while the historical record could not, of course, prove this conclusively, it did lend support to her contention.

If you were looking for help for a title for something, in short, she might not be your go-to.

To return to her cardinal flaw, though—her failure, according to the professors, to be more Gunner-like—she said it was a species of Western hegemony that people like her and me were always being pushed to do something fundamentally at odds with our culture. It stressed her out, she said. It stressed us all out. She said that as a rule she just listened to her body and talked as much as felt comfortable, and that if her breath shortened up, suggesting a certain pulmonary preset, then she stopped. And if that kept her from getting a good grade, while people like Gunner were physiologically equipped with some manner of embarrassment override, well, so be it. She didn't need to finish first in our class. She was only in law school, she said, to learn to help ordinary people with their ordinary problems anyway.

And that was the truth. She really did just want to help people with their immigration problems. She did not want one of those fancy paneled offices with the in-house cappuccino and the million-dollar view. She wanted the kind of office you saw in forties movies, with worn wood floors and frosted glass doors. She wanted to tilt her head and give a kindly look to clueless people sitting on the edge of their chairs and ask, "What brings you here?" People like her parents and mine. She wanted to teach immigrants how to become citizens. She wanted to teach them how to stick up for themselves.

Other people, though, wanted her to be a judge. In fact, in my heart of hearts, I wanted to see her on the Supreme Court. The first Asian American on the Supreme Court! Or didn't she want to work for the ACLU? I asked her once. Talk about making a difference! Not just for one family at a time, but for lots of families, for all time. Of course, to even begin to think about it, you had to have a minimum of six years of litigation experience—that's what it said on their website. And to get litigation experience you had to get a public defender or prosecutor job. Or, if you had loans and needed to make more money—as she did, perhaps?—she nodded—you needed to do the litigation track at a top-notch firm, from which spot you could then go to a U.S. Attorney's Office or DOJ, the whole sleep-no-more slog.

"Sell my soul, you mean," she said, but I could tell she was thinking about it. The ACLU.

"No, no," I said. "You wouldn't have to sell your soul." Never mind that all I knew about a life in law came from Scott Turow novels; still, I sagaciously went on. "You'd just have to talk enough in class for Professor Radin to stop describing you as quiet. You'd have to channel your inner Gunner and, you know. Gun a little."

She looked at me and crossed her eyes.

"Have you always fastened on the utterly quixotic?" she asked. Then she uncrossed her eyes and smiled and said, "Actually, Eric says the same thing. About talking more, I mean."

As Eric was her boyfriend, this was and wasn't what I wanted to hear.

But the next day, she began to try, and that was what I wanted to see.

Not being a big-name law school, we were not exactly overrun with visits by Am Law 100 firms. It was mostly regional firms that came to recruit. A smattering of powerhouses did come through, though—typically because someone had some connection to the university—and every once in a while, a student subsequently landed a big-deal summer associate job. Once in the known history of the school, too, it had happened that, after the big-deal summer associate job, a person from our school had gone on to land a permanent position at the firm—to become an honest-to-God big-deal associate. That was a decade ago, but still. Why shouldn't the second person be Arabella?

She scoffed. But when the class rankings came out, and there she and

Gunner were—number 1 and number 2—she did wonder if maybe, when the time came, she should interview?

"Yes!" I all but yelled at her. "Yes! You have to do it! You do! You have to do it for all of us!"

"Whoever 'us' is, I think you should do it for yourselves," she said. "Starting with you."

In the end, though, she agreed that I was no lawyer. As for why, then, I was in law school? I didn't really have to tell her. For while she herself wasn't in law school because of her parents, she *was* here at Podunk Law because they wanted her nearby; she knew how Chinese parents could be. But never mind. When an on-campus interview sign-up sheet was posted, she held her nose and did it. She signed up.

It started out that three Biglaw firms were coming. But first there was a hurricane and Westfall & Howe canceled. Then Berger, Berkman and Leebron canceled, too, also because of the storm. That left Goodman, Thompson and Pierce, who were scheduled to come a week later than the other firms. I helped Arabella prepare, combing the internet for advice, and found that most of it fell into three categories. The first was existential—Be positive! Be assertive! Be confident! The second was gnomic: Show that you are agreeable but show that you are no pushover. Show that you are unique but show that you fit in. Show that you are well informed but show that you would like to be informed. And so on.

The third, toughest category was spatial. Take up room with your arms, went this advice, especially if you are a woman. Take up room with your voice. Take up room with your manner. Take up room in your chair.

Take up room in your chair? Arabella tried mansplaying her legs; it hurt her hips, she said. As for thrusting her chin out and squaring her chest, she simply could not do these things with a straight face. But she could, she figured, wear her roommate's size 4 jacket and, under it, a vest for bulk. And after a few tries, she found that pretending she was Gunner helped with her manner. Suddenly she could respond at length to what we agreed were lamer-than-lame prompts like Tell us about yourself, and Do you have any weaknesses?

She answered, answered, answered, answered. I nodded.

"Anything else we should know about you?" I asked finally.

"I broke up with Eric," she said.

"Ah." I jotted that down on my clipboard.

"Also," she said, "since I know we don't have a lot of time, I'd just like to make sure you realize I'm available for dinner after the interview."

"Six o'clock?" I said.

"If that's how business is done in your firm."

"It is," I said. "I mean, I hope it isn't. But it is. It is."

"Good," she said.

As for what she was supposed to do if the interviewer threw his clipboard up into the air for joy, I decided not to test her.

Instead I just said, "You're going to be great, Arabella."

"Thank you for your time," she said. And, "You are most generous person I have ever known."

The day of the interview, I did one more thing. I greased the seat of Gunner's bicycle with Vaseline, and for good measure greased his handlebar grips, too. Not so much that he would be in an accident, but enough that he'd have to spend twenty minutes in the men's room trying to get the grease off before he could shake anyone's hand. And then, of course, there would still be the issue of his crotch. Were anyone's interview chances ever dashed because he had grease in his crotch? Of course not. Still, I hoped that it would disconcert and distract him. As for whether this was my finest moment as a human being? Well, no. Still I did it. Then I waited.

Arabella's interview, she reported, went well enough. No surprises—for which she had to thank me, she said. I really had prepared her beautifully. But she did think the interviewer a bit inscrutable.

"Or maybe I should say guarded," she said. "He looked like he had the nuclear codes and thought I might ask for them."

"Hmm."

"He did smile at the end, at least."

"That's good."

"Then he asked me how tall I was."

"Oh no. Did you tell him?"

"Yes. And then I said that if he was wondering, I weigh ninety-one pounds."

"You didn't."

"You're right, I didn't. But I almost did."

We laughed. I had picked a hippie restaurant nearby with every variation of tofu and brown rice possible, and with four kinds of kale smoothies. We tried all four, and then three of the Buddha bowls, and then an udon-miso thing, and all the world glowed with warmth and happiness and antioxidants until I told her about the grease.

Gunner did not get a summer associate position even though his great-uncle, it turned out, was the "Goodman" in Goodman, Thompson. Gunner was so crushed he missed a week of classes; people said he was thinking about transferring to business school. Was that true? Who knew. What was clearer was that classes were not the same without him. We missed having someone to irritate us, and the professors—the poor professors—were suffering. Indeed, they were getting so discouraged, having to cold-call people for every single question, that after a day or two we started to put our hands up more, just to help out. They were nice people who already wished they had better jobs, after all. We felt sorry for them. And so a bunch of us tried gunning—even me— until we were all gunning and gunning and gunning. It wasted a lot of time, to be honest. But it was fun, and did make the professors perk up.

As for Arabella, she, too, got a thumbs-down from Goodman, Thompson. Still, she was glad she had interviewed, she said, because it helped her figure a few things out. For example, it helped her figure out that she should try and transfer to a higher-ranked school. She was going to apply and see what happened, she said, and if she got in, bring it up with her parents.

"I am also going to start lifting weights," she said. "I am too small."

"Isn't that selling your soul?" I said.

"No," she said. "It's strength training."

Meanwhile, I got thrown out of school altogether. Arabella had called me a reprobate and a miscreant for the Vaseline business but she hadn't reported me. It was Gunner who eventually figured out who'd smeared him, so to speak, and, though I apologized and had his suit cleaned twice, he nonetheless filed an official complaint.

Of course, my parents were apoplectic.

"I don't think you're even sorry," observed Arabella, however.

"About Gunner?" I said. "Because I am sorry about Gunner."

"About school," she said.

"Well, about school let's just say I'd rather be punished than rehabilitated," I said. "I'm not about law."

"No, you are about crime and punishment and war and peace," she agreed.

"And justice for the people I love," I added—which was kind of an overly venturesome thing to say, really. I didn't think before I said it; in fact, you could say I was just gunning. But she turned and gave me a kiss, and when I plunged on and said I was going to try to find a job near whatever school she ended up at, she looked serious.

"Rich Lee," she said thoughtfully. "Mr. Crime and Punishment and War and Peace." And then, deft as ever, she didn't tell me not to.

GISH JEN's stories have appeared in *The Best American Short Stories* four times, including *The Best American Short Stories of the Century*, edited by John Updike. Featured in a PBS TV *American Masters* series, Jen is the author of four novels and a collection of stories. She has received support from the Guggenheim Foundation, the Radcliffe Institute, and the Lannan Foundation, as well as a Mildred and Harold Strauss Living Award from the American Academy of Arts and Letters. She delivered the Massey Lectures in American Studies at Harvard University in 2012.

Her most recent book, a work of nonfiction, is titled *The Girl at the Baggage Claim: Explaining the East-West Culture Gap.*

Finally I Am American at Heart

I have often been asked two questions. One is: What was the most surprising incident when you served in the Chinese People's Army? The other: What surprised you most in America?

To both questions my answers are rather personal and internal. I served in the Chinese army for five years and saw terrible accidents. Soldiers got killed in military exercises and in collapsed constructions, but what surprised me most is something that none of my comrades might remember. A fellow soldier in our company was a wonderful basketball player, handsome and agile and six feet two inches tall. His parents were both senior officials in Beijing, in the Ministry of Railways. By contrast, most of us were from remote provinces, and many were sons of peasants. Toward the end of my third year in the army, word came that the basketball player's mother was dying in Beijing and left him her final words. We all knew she was a revolutionary, and thought her last words must be wise and edifying, so we were eager to learn about them too. Then her final words for her son came: "Don't ever give up your Beijing residence certificate."

Without a residence certificate, one couldn't live in Beijing permanently. But if you were not born in the capital, the only chance for you to get such a certificate was to find a permanent job in an official department or company that could help you get it. I was shocked by the mother's last words, because they suddenly revealed to me that people in China were not born equal. Her words stayed with me and went deeper and deeper in my consciousness. For decades afterward I carried the bitterness, not just for myself but also for tens of millions of people who could never have such a privilege of living in the capital and who, by birth, were citizens of lower class, although China's constitution guarantees equality to all its citizens. This inequality in residential status among the citizens actually contravenes China's constitution, which has become meaningless in the eyes of the public.

As for what surprised me most in America, it was also a personal moment that turned out to be charged with meaning, but mainly for myself. When I came to the States to do graduate work in 1985, my family couldn't come with me, both my wife and son having to remain in China, because at the time the Chinese government didn't allow families to go abroad together. Like my compatriots, I accepted this rule without questioning it because it was made by the country. Among my fellow graduate students at Brandeis, some were from other countries. They knew I was married but was here without my family. Sangeeta and her boyfriend, Chuck, were from India, living one floor below me. At a party one evening, she asked me why I'd left my wife and child behind. I told her because the Chinese government did not allow them to come with me. I couldn't explain further, since nobody could see the logic of such a rule. Out of the blue Sangeeta asked me, "Why don't you sue your country?"

Her question stunned me, and I turned tongue-tied, unable to get my head around it. Could she sue India? I wondered. She must be able to if she had a legitimate case and also the means. But never had I heard of any Chinese citizen suing the country. Sangeeta's question remained on my mind for many years and affected my view of the world. Gradually I came to realize that her question pointed to the core of democracy, namely that in the eyes of the law, the individual and the country are equal. If a country is wrong, a citizen is entitled to confront it.

It took one and a half years for my wife to join me here, but she couldn't bring our son with her. So he couldn't come to live with us until another two and a half years. By then, having stayed in American already for four years, I realized that all the forced separations among my compatriots and their families had been gratuitous, serving no purpose, as if the role of the powers that be was to make people suffer. Of course I couldn't sue China. For citizens to be able to sue their country, there has to be a legal system that can guarantee their civil rights, both on paper and in practice. Because there has been no such practice in China, people tend to just cower to the state. Many even worship the country like a deity, willing to serve it unconditionally. Owing to China's long ban on religions, people's religious feelings have been diverted to the deification of the country. God is amoral, and so is your country, and all you can do is obey.

When the Tiananmen massacre broke out in June 1989, I was traumatized and remained in shock for weeks. I was so outraged that I became very outspoken, publicly condemning the killing of the unarmed civilians. As a result, the next spring when I sent in my passport for renewal, the Chinese consulate in New York confiscated it. Afterward, for seven years I had no passport. I couldn't travel outside the States and became a man without a country. I had always planned on returning to China to teach, but that was out of the question now.

Finally in the fall of 1997 I was naturalized. At the ceremony, the new citizens were formally asked to renounce our loyalty to our former countries. Like the other new citizens, I swore my oath of allegiance to the US Constitution. A new citizen must be willing to perform noncombatant service in the armed forces to defend the Constitution. I assumed that this was equal to pledging loyalty to America, the country. I didn't feel completely comfortable about the oath, but this was a necessary step for me and my family if we wanted to become US citizens. In essence, it was a move for survival. Prior to the naturalization ceremony, I had read the Constitution, which struck me as something like a contract between the country and the people. It specifies repeatedly what rights the people keep or give to the government.

Nevertheless, unfamiliar with how this was enforced in practice, I didn't think much of the Constitution, which seemed to be just words few people could abide by. That was my misconception, partly due to the despondency that sank deep in my heart. What disappointed me most were American double standards. To put this simply, the US government's words and deeds didn't match. During the Tiananmen massacre, President George H. W. Bush spoke a great deal about supporting the democratic movement in China and condemned the Communist regime roundly, but in no time he dispatched his secret emissary to Beijing to pacify the Chinese government. The White House's double-dealing reflected crude American pragmatism. Americans tend to calculate everything in dollars. For the sake of business opportunities, the United States grew reluctant to defend human rights and even willing to relinquish our principles. On President Obama's first visit to China in 2009, Hillary Clinton, secretary of state then, said on NPR that human rights were no longer an issue on the negotiation table because we owed China a huge debt and our economy was struggling to recover from the previous year's recession. She said, "How can you talk about human rights to your creditor?" Hearing those words, I felt betrayed, my belief in American idealism shattered. Later I learned that Bill Clinton, after leaving the White House, had collected hefty fees when he gave speeches in China.

Besides pragmatism as a distinct trait of the American character, there is another aspect of the American character that I have always admired and cherished. That is American idealism. One can argue that because of having a black-and-white mind-set, Americans can become destructive, shaping the world according to our ideas or ideals. Such a tendency is dramatized vividly in Graham Greene's novel *The Quiet American*, specifically in the main character Alden Pyle, who turns blind to the human cost and suffering in carrying out the American plan for combating Communism and establishing a democratic force in Vietnam. Greene's novel is a condemnation of US imperialism and might have its legitimacy, considering the violence the United States has unleashed in the world. However, he addresses only one aspect of the American character, which to me also embodies strength and integrity and even nobility, inseparable from idealism. In fact, we often talked about honesty, justice, equality, all of which show the other aspect of the American character, rooted in the belief in universal values.

I believe in noble ideas, which differentiate humans from animals. Some governments of non-Western countries oppose universal values, and instead emphasize their countries' peculiarities and differences. In essence, such an emphasis is their way of defending the power of the state and justifying their ideologies or dictatorships, which can never be measured against the standards of democracy and social justice. To me, it's fundamental to hold on to some ideals so as to show the distance between sordid realities and the dream we might strive to realize. Without such a distance or room in our vision for improvement, we would be stranded in the quagmire of particulars and differences. In this sense, I admire American idealism and cherish the image of America as a shining city upon the hill.

Because of my despondency about American pragmatism, I tended to stand aloof, observing life flowing by. Rarely would I get involved in politics. I even grew a little cynical about social activities, believing that everyone acted out of personal interests. During the last election when the final two candidates, Hillary Clinton and Donald Trump, emerged to compete for the presidency, I would vote for neither. Clinton was an insider, a practical politician, whom I couldn't trust, whereas Trump was too outrageous and bigoted in his views on many issues. I also knew that Trump's family had business connections with China, so the Chinese government could find ways to influence him. I simply couldn't vote for Trump. There was no viable third-party candidate for me to root for. I again stood aside and just observed, my despondency deepened by the political rhetoric and controversies I often encountered. I didn't expect that Trump would win the election, and his success cast gloomy shadows on my mind about America and made me wonder if my adopted country had failed as a democracy.

However, my attitude was utterly changed early this year when Judge James Robart blocked President Trump's travel ban on citizens of seven Muslim-majority countries from being implemented. Robart was only a district judge but could overturn the president's order on the grounds that it did "not comport with our Constitution."

This public incident was very personal to me. It meant several things. Despite my despondency and cynicism, American society's general acceptance of Robart's ruling against Trump's order showed that our democratic system was still sound and intact, and it was also a blow to those who were gloating over the US retreat from democracy. It demonstrated that this land was still ruled by law—no one, even the most powerful man on earth, is above law. No matter how great a political issue is, it must find a solution in the law, which everyone must serve and obey. Robart's ruling struck a sharp contrast with the incident on July 9, 2015, when more than three hundred lawyers and legal workers in Chinese cities were detained and interrogated and imprisoned, and some simply disappeared, because they had been helping petitioners and common citizens defend their civil rights. Now I finally understand why at the naturalization ceremony we were asked to swear an oath of allegiance to the Constitution, not to a government or a country. The Constitution embodies the true America, a land based on ideas and principles. I was touched by Judge Robart's ruling, which signifies to me that it's still possible to live by ideas and ideals. If I have the law on my side, I can sue my country when it violates my rights guaranteed by the Constitution. As I recall the oath of allegiance that specifies "noncombatant service" in armed forces as a new citizen's duty to defend the Constitution, I am more than ever willing to perform such a duty. If need be, I will be willing to do even "combatant service" for such a defense, because unlike China's constitution that promises citizens so many rights without ever ensuring the implementation of them, the US Constitution has the supreme legal force and we can rely on it to exercise our civil rights.

Finally, after living in America for thirty-two years, I feel at peace with my role as a US citizen and can accept myself as an American at heart. This conviction was possible only after I had witnessed the public acceptance of Judge James Robart's ruling.

HA JIN grew up in mainland China and came to the United States in 1985 to do graduate work at Brandeis University, from which he earned his PhD in 1993. In 1990 he began to write in English. To date, he has published three volumes of poetry—*Between Silences*, *Facing Shadows*, and *Wreckage*—and four books of short fiction: *Ocean of Words*, which received the PEN/Hemingway Award; *Under the Red Flag*, which received the Flannery O'Connor Award for Short Fiction, *The Bridegroom*;

which received the Asian American Literary Award and the Townsend Prize for Fiction; and *A Good Fall*. He has also published eight novels: *In the Pond*; *Waiting*, which received the National Book Award and the PEN/Faulkner Award; *The Crazed*; *War Trash*, which received the PEN/Faulkner Award; *A Free Life*; *Nanjing Requiem*; *A Map of Betrayal*; and *The Boat Rocker*. His work has been translated into more than thirty languages. He has been elected a fellow of the American Academy of Arts and Sciences and a fellow of the American Academy of Arts and Letters. He taught poetry writing at Emory University for eight years. Since 2002 he has been a professor of English and creative writing at Boston University and lives in the Boston area.

Arlington Street

It's a long time ago now that Cilla Hall walked into the high school gym, heels ringing on the worn maple boards of the basketball court. I'm not sure we would have been more surprised if Joe McCarthy had come through the door. Only four of us had shown up to the meeting. It was an old Republican town. Just me, Ponti the hairdresser, Kosmos the dressmaker, and now Cilla Hall in her black capris and cashmere turtleneck. Kosmos made a fuss of getting her a chair from the stack against the wall. Imagine the fuss she must always have to put up with, I thought.

I'd seen her around. She'd come to town earlier in the year with her bony husband and fierce-eyed toddler and a newborn that got wheeled around by the nanny. She came in a wave of young brides brought here by their Harvard grads who'd seemed to collectively decide that our harbor town was the next step after the Fly Club.

I had that feeling of becoming less female because a beautiful woman has entered the room. People liked to say she looked like Grace Kelly but she was more willowy, with a Nefertiti neck, sharp cheekbones, and wide, wary eyes. She hooked her heels on the rung beneath her seat and pulled out a Flair pen and a notebook stained with coffee rings. Ponti and Kosmos were hopeless, and stumbled through their reports on the selectman meeting and the housing commission. Cilla took quick notes that filled up several pages while we griped about our town administrator and our state rep. When we had run out of complaints, Cilla took out a few newspaper clippings from the back of her notebook. The first was about something called the Boston Action Group that was organizing a boycott against Wonder Bread, she said, for its discriminatory hiring practices. She wanted to put up signs at the grocery store, reminding people. The second was about the Birmingham Sympathy Rally the next weekend in the Common that she thought we should go to. And the third was a short article about a congressional candidate we'd never heard of, who represented black families in housing cases, wanted to abolish capital punishment, and believed we should get out of Vietnam before we got into a proxy war with the Soviets and China.

I want to host a fundraiser for him, she said.

We tried to tell her that none of our candidates would ever win, that our district had voted Republican since 1875. But she just smiled, and wrote it down—1875—in her notebook, and underlined it twice.

As we suspected, the grocer wouldn't let us put posters about the boycott anywhere near his store, so we lingered in the bread aisle, urging people away from the white bread made by white workers. The grocer called the cop, who was his brother, and he kept us at the station for the whole day, until our husbands got out of work and could sign for our release. You have to remember how it was then. We weren't allowed to have a credit card or get our tubes tied without our husbands' consent. The cop kept us in a hallway with a narrow little bench. He needed to go down the hallway to get anywhere and we got into the habit of asking for something each time he came through. A deck of cards, a sheet of paper, a pencil. He refused us everything. But he came through so often and we got so hungry and punchy that soon we were asking him for a shoehorn or a bobby pin or—and this made us slide down from the bench onto the floor in senseless hysterics—a small piece of cheese.

At the end of the day my husband came first and was mostly amused so I missed the arrival of hers, who was not.

Undaunted, Cilla invited a cross section of ladies to her house for tea. The only thing we had in common was that we bought bread at the grocery store. I thought the plan was for Cilla and me to casually mention the boycott here and there to the other women, but once everyone was served their tea and sugar cookies Cilla tapped a spoon against her cup, silenced the room, and told them I would be saying a few words about Wonder Bread and the Continental Baking Company. I could not have been less prepared. But the words came. I said Jim Crow was right here, in our white town and in our white bread. Wonder Bread has been exposed this month, but these policies are in every part of our society, I said, from housing to schooling to the workplace, every aspect of black life was debilitated by our racism, our denial, our ignorance, and our silence. The ladies had not expected this. But Cilla had. She bent over her teacup with a satisfied little smile.

On the way to the Birmingham Sympathy Rally she told me about meeting her husband in the summer of '59. She had her bare feet up on the dash, her hands laced around a thermos of coffee she'd brought from home. They were packed with rings, those hands, two or three on every finger, old-money rings.

You know how when you try to break a branch you have to find the weak part? she said. That summer was her weak part. Her mother's third marriage was falling apart and Cilla was losing her favorite stepfather and the house in Georgetown she loved. The three of them were in Northeast Harbor with friends for a week, putting on a good face, which seemed to be easier for her mother and stepfather than for her. Before a boat picnic she cried in an empty maid's room on the third floor. Drew stepped out of a rowboat onto the dock, she said. He was the sailing instructor, all bones and knobs and a smile he couldn't keep in when he saw Cilla coming down the ramp, steep at low tide. He asked her to come for a sail when she returned from her picnic. He asked her to a dance at the community hall that weekend. He asked her to marry him six months later, on Christmas Eve.

When I said yes, she told me, I felt a sharp, unpleasant vibration, like the zap you get on your palm when you fail to put the car into the right gear, except it was all over my body, inside and out. It was the whole universe ruddering. I remember Cilla said that, *ruddering*, as if she needed to make up a word to explain the feeling.

And then it stopped, she said, and Drew was grinning a wicked grin, and we both knew we could finally have sex.

They planned the wedding for June, after she graduated from junior college, but in April she started getting headaches so bad her vision dimmed and her teeth felt like they were falling out. Her mother was in Palm Springs trying to attract a fourth husband before the money ran out, so Cilla went back to Northeast Harbor to stay with Drew's mother, a widow with no daughters who put her in a suite of rooms that looked out at three small islands, one with a lighthouse at its tip. She told herself she would get better there, then break off the engagement. It wasn't logical, she said, considering that the engagement was causing the headaches, but she didn't figure that out until it was too late, until the flowers had arrived and Drew's mother was doing up the front of her dress because she couldn't see the buttonholes. Her own mother didn't come. She couldn't support the idea that her daughter would now have a husband and she would not.

She spoke about that time just before she married Drew often while we canvassed or drove to protests and rallies, while we set up and broke down events and benefits, but never about the years that had followed. If it was summer she'd invite me up to the house for a swim and I'd bring Markie, my littlest, and she'd pry her girl from the nanny and they'd float around the shallow end in orange life preservers. Drew's station wagon might pull up or leave the driveway, but he never came over to our chairs by the pool and she never waved hello or goodbye. She hosted fundraisers, fancy affairs on the side patio out the French doors that overlooked the English garden. I got used to her asking me without warning to introduce the candidate, expound on the issues, shrink the problems of the day into a few digestible sentences for a cocktail crowd. Drew was never among them. When people asked, she said he was upstairs watching the Red Sox with their son, even if it was the dead of winter.

We worked tirelessly for many candidates who never won and a few who did, including her obscure congressional candidate who ended the eighty-year

Republican lock on the seat. We marched with Reverend King from Roxbury to the Common. And three years later she came over to my house when we heard King was shot in Memphis. She drove over in her nightgown and we watched on the old black-and-white set in my bedroom—my husband had left by then, no longer amused by me and my politics—as Bobby Kennedy gave his speech in Indianapolis to a black audience, many of whom hadn't heard the news. I can only say that I feel in my heart the same kind of feeling, Bobby said. I had a member of my family killed, he said. Cilla and I burst out crying. We wailed together like twin babies delivered into an unholy world.

Outside of politics we traveled in different circles that rarely overlapped. I had a cocktail party once, when my nephew Brad was in town, and Cilla and Drew came. Brad worked at the Service Board for Conscientious Objectors in Washington. Cilla had grown up in DC, or at least spent a few years there—the geography of her childhood was complex and involved at least six states in the US, Egypt, Mexico, and a West Indian island I'd never heard of—and they spent a while in the kitchen talking about Georgetown during the war. Drew glowered near the bar, and after less than ten minutes he got her coat and purse and went into the kitchen. He held the coat open for her and she slid her arms in.

Don't worry, little Commie, Drew said to Brad. You can't afford her.

When my divorce was final I could no longer receive the host at mass. Cilla came with me every Sunday for six months and sat beside me so I wouldn't be alone in the pew as all the other adults and children over seven rose and stood in line and let the priest drop the sacrament onto their tongues.

The day before Nixon's second inauguration we decided to drive down and join the protest of the Christmas bombing of North Vietnam. We gathered at the Lincoln Memorial and the FBI took pictures of us all the way to the Washington Monument. The day after we got back she called me and told me to meet her outside on Walker Street across from the dry cleaner's. She brought me up to a two-bedroom apartment.

I'm leaving him, she told me in the galley kitchen. And I need a job.

Ponti had heard that the lieutenant governor's cousin, who was in charge of fundraising, was looking for a new assistant. I drove her to the State House for her interview.

I've never had an interview, she said. Never had a job. Her voice caught. She held a finger to each lower eyelid. I can't cry, she said, laughing. I can't afford to reapply my makeup. Drew's lawyer was outgunning hers. He wrote her child support checks for half the amount they'd agreed on. You're a Democrat, Drew had said to her. You love the poor.

We went up the front steps of the State House. I pointed up to the corner office. We'd worked hard to help elect the governor. I took her up to the third floor, where the cousin was holding the interviews. I felt like I was leading in a skittish racehorse. We sat in the old leather seats of an outer waiting room. I don't think she took a breath from the time we sat down to when he called her in.

When it was over it was lunchtime and people were streaming out of the building and down the capitol steps. The governor was ahead of us, on the other side of the stairs, ringed by a small cluster of men in suits and overcoats. Otherwise, all around us, were women, receptionists and secretaries and assistants and fundraisers—all the anonymous women it takes to prop up one male politician.

We went to the deli a half block away on Park Street. We stood in line with the other women. The men were at nicer places, the Parker House or Locke-Ober. But Cilla was gleaming. She was gleeful. We ordered Reubens and extra pickles and she told me she had handed him her list of donors, a typed stack of pages of all the guests from her parties, names, addresses, and donation amounts. Big amounts. She must have had five thousand names, names you would have said were Republican names. He pored over it slowly.

So—he looked up—do you want to get paid like this? He held his hand out flat above his desk. Or like this? He put his hand beneath the desk. She said she pretended not to understand the question. We shrieked with laughter in the corner of that deli.

We crumpled up our napkins and tossed our plates. She said that we should now go pay a visit to Mr. Firestone.

I thought she was joking but she wasn't. I followed her across the Common to the awning of the Ritz on Arlington and into Firestone and Parson. Mr. Firestone was reaching into the last of the curved jewelry cases. He straightened up quickly. He was pleased, you might even say moved, to see her. They shook hands and then he took both of hers. They were bare of her rings. Drew's mother had demanded all of her jewelry back. She told Mr. Firestone they were at home soaking and he scolded her for not letting him clean them properly.

Mr. Firestone went into a back office and came out with a manila envelope from which he slid another smaller manila envelope from which he shook out two rings. Each had a diamond the size of big lima bean in the center. This is a cushion cut, he explained, slipping it onto Cilla's finger. And this is a cabochon, he said, putting it on mine. Her diamond had a halo of bright sapphires. Mine was all diamonds, all around, even on what Mr. Firestone called the shoulders of the ring. He urged us take them outside.

Diamonds need to be seen in the sun, he said.

We went out to the sidewalk on Arlington Street with the rings on our fingers. Cilla laid her right hand over her left as if asking herself for her hand. Her diamond exploded with color.

I think you should run against Kenny Lorde in the primary, she said to me.

What? Kenny Lorde was running for state senator in our district.

He's weak. You'd thrash him.

You're crazy.

Let's see the ring, she said.

I hadn't dared hold up my hand yet. I was sure someone would come around the corner and pluck it off my finger as soon as I did.

C'mon, she said. Let's see it.

I brought the ring up into the sun. It flashed at everything all around it. Magnificent, Cilla said.

Run against Kenny Lorde, I thought, a thick rope of energy forming fast inside me.

I had been the racehorse all along.

LILY KING is the author of four novels: *The Pleasing Hour*, *The English Teacher*, *Father of the Rain*, and, most recently, *Euphoria*, winner of the Kirkus Prize for Fiction, finalist for the National Book Critics Circle Award, and named one of the 10 Best Books of 2014 by the *New York Times Book Review*. King lives in Maine and is committed to the increasingly threatened ideals of American democracy, including freedom of speech, freedom of the press, and equal rights for all.

The Harlot and the Murderer: Sonia's Story

The hero of my story—whom I love with all the power of my soul . . .
who was, is, and ever will be beautiful—is the truth.
—TOLSTOY

She still comes to me here, stepping out of the shadows, in this savage place. None of my memories of men, even of R., are lit up quite like my memory of her. Lizaveta. So tall, dark-skinned, with her wide-spaced eyes, her big smile, her bright and hopeful gaze, she walks toward me in the muddy street, coming into the uncertain sunlight. Broad-shouldered like a man, dressed like a soldier, with her crooked legs and big goatskin shoes, I see her approaching, clothes in her arms like an offering. Brutally killed so young, she lingers on in my mind like a sacred object, a bronze icon, a glow around her braided head. It was she who found the clothes I wore for my work. She dressed me up, disguised me, changed me as much as she could. Did I become the part I played?

One afternoon, soon after I arrived here, on a high bank by this desolate river, in the great quiet of the wide spaces of the Siberian steppe, an unfortunate shuffled up to me in his heavy shackles. He took off his pancake-shaped hat and bowed his half-shaved head: *"Matushka! Matushka!"* "Little Mother! Little Mother!" he called out to me. "Pray for me. Please pray for me."

What did he see in my thin face, in the dark circles beneath my eyes, in my drab attire? Is the life I have lived branded in my skin? Is it there in my gaze, my gait, my gestures? Something in my mien, my stance, as faltering and timid as they may seem, led him to single me out, to watch me walk, to approach me freely, without fear and even with affection, as though he knew me, had always known me intimately, like an ever-flowing river, or even as one of his own family. Did he understand I am in a sense one with him, an equal who would not condemn him whatever he might have done, that I am as great a sinner as he might be? Yet he asked me to pray for him, which I have gladly done.

God bless them all, the ones in chains, in dank cells, the prisoners in this place where I have accompanied them.

It all began with a moment of which I have never spoken. It lingers on in my mind static and silent, like a photograph. Some of my story has already been told and told so well by a genius, but by a man. There were secrets that he could not know, things left out, not said, not seen, not felt, and not heard. He was wrong about me at times—how could he not be?

I know that his word will almost certainly be considered more reliable than mine: a man's word against a woman's. How easily women are accused of lying, of not knowing how to distinguish good from bad. Who will believe the words of a young woman, a woman of ill repute, a prostitute, branded with the yellow ticket, when her story has been told by a famous writer, a celebrated man? Yet what he ignored was that R. was how I escaped my shame, how I reached God or anyway ecstasy—if ecstasy is that moment of exit when the soul takes wing, like a flying fish, and seems to swim from the body.

Now I see myself as the lodgers in that crowded room must have seen me, as my father recognized me, as R. must have noticed me for the first time, hesitating in the doorway: a puny girl with a narrow face, dressed incongruously.

She is young but not innocent. Though she has never experienced desire, pleasure, the possibility is within her. It is visible in the avid eyes, the open mouth, the trembling hands. It is the strength of that desire that drives me, despite the difficulties I know I will encounter, to speak up, to speak out, to dare to tell my own version of the story, the real story of a woman of ill repute, now.

I see my own image from without, from a distance, as though seeing someone else, someone cut off and separate, standing in the entrance to that crowded room, a breathless girl, surrounded by opprobrium, unmistakable in her gutter finery.

I am eighteen years old. It is Saint Petersburg where the pale light lingers late in the sultry July night. I have been, as I do most evenings, wandering the streets, watching my step, keeping my wits about me, glancing around hopefully in the summer stench of stagnant water, lime, and dust. It was well after eight when I heard a clatter on the cobblestones. In the clear light I saw the girl's thin, pretty face. It was little Polenka, the eldest child of my stepmother, K.I., running toward me out of the shadows at the end of the street, in her thin dress, a kerchief around her head, her cheeks pink, her fair hair streaming out wildly behind her.

"Come quickly, Sonechka!" she shouted even before she had reached me. I hurried toward her, and she grasped my hand, pulling me along the street in my garish attire, the train of my yellow dress dragging in the dirt behind me, my hand hanging on to my feathered hat, my parasol. Together we ran through the streets, my light-colored shoes spattered with mud and mire. There was no time to ask what was wrong, and I knew it must be death or extreme illness. I thought something had happened to K.I., my stepmother, as of course it eventually did.

Once we reached our building, I told Polenka to go ahead, taking a moment to get my breath and smooth out the flounces of the worn silk with trembling fingers. She ran up the stairs before me, disappearing into the crowd already congregated in the doorway and down the stairs, the curious, the idle, and the gossipers. All of the landlady's lodgers seemed to have streamed from their innumerable closets and were squeezing through the doorway into our corridor to see what was going on. I made my way as best I could through the crowd and stood in the doorway.

There is a lot about doors in the book that was written about R. and me and my family. There are many sudden exits and mysterious entrances. Strangers lurk and listen behind doors. There are struggles at doors, pulling and pushing, bells ringing repeatedly. Like a series of scenes on a stage, there are the necessary furniture, the props, the reader, the audience. The characters squeeze into crowded spaces: apartments, taverns, hotel rooms with mice. They meet by chance in streets and stairways, police stations. They talk to one another at length. Words pour from them for pages. They tell the whole stories of their lives. They overhear conversations as they move along the boulevards, across the bridges and the crowded squares of Saint Petersburg, going from one building to another, down steps into dark, dank taverns and sordid eating places, watched over by landladies, concierges, good-tempered maids.

But it was not like that, not at all, not for me. So little was said in my life, or if it was, it was said to conceal and not reveal. Words did not reflect reality, or not the one I perceived. There were long silences, many sighs, groans, sobs. More was conveyed with a glance or a gesture—a flash of hate, a sudden slap on the side of the head, the pulling of hair, the thrust of the cane, a hand slipping down a bodice like a snake, an unexpected gift.

Mostly I remember hunger, the lack of means to buy something to satisfy the crying children, to protect them from K.I.'s blows.

Money changed hands repeatedly in shadowy rooms in silence or with just the glad chink of it on a dresser. Things happened in doorways, it is true, but there are places in the book where the writer felt obliged to close the doors firmly, to draw the shutters down like eyelids on eyes that prefer not to see.

In Saint Petersburg, as it says in the book, we were housed in a building owned by a German cabinetmaker. The street was near the Haymarket, that huge square where vendors set up stalls to sell whatever they can, a place peopled by pickpockets, hucksters, and peasants in greasy sheepskin coats and knee-high boots as well as the occasional merchant or even an aristocrat looking for a bargain. The air was filled with the clatter and rumble of carts and carriages, the cries of vendors, with soot from the new factories that had sprung up in the city and the stench of garbage and sewage that rose suffocatingly in the air.

It was there that I met Lizaveta by chance one summer evening. She lived with her much older stepsister, the pawnbroker. I came across her standing in the flickering sunlight, talking by a stall, a bundle of old clothes she was hoping to sell in her arms. Somehow she knew my name. "Sonia!" she called out with a glad glance of recognition, and, despite the clothes, reached out her large hand to clasp mine, holding on to me.

I felt we had always known each other. We became instant friends, sisters in misfortune. When we managed to meet we discovered our similar lives, our similar hearts. We seemed to come from the same family, though we looked so different: Lizaveta, so tall, strong, and bronze-cheeked, and myself so small, light-boned, and pale-skinned.

Sometimes we met at the pawnbroker's small apartment if Alyona was out, but she rarely left her premises. Alyona never approved of me. At rare moments when we met, passing in the corridor or in the entrance to the apartment, she would smile thinly and call me "dearie" in her reedy voice, but she glanced at me with a flicker of suspicion in her small, bright eyes. Besides, she was often busy with her constant customers, students coming and going, the doorbell ringing, and she was wary of strangers on her premises, rightly, as it turned out. She probably felt my presence an intrusion, an unwelcome distraction, even a danger in their hardworking lives.

More often Lizaveta came to my room, and we had a moment alone. Or we met somewhere on the banks of the Neva or in the shadows of a church.

Like me, she had lost her mother soon after birth. Her father, though he loved Lizaveta, indeed favored her, was so much older than she and not often home. Her care fell to her stepsister, who treated her like her slave, beating her. Her father made things worse, slipping her surreptitious presents from his pockets: an apple, a good-luck charm, a copper cross, when he came home late and found her dutifully carrying out her stepsister's wishes.

After his death she was entirely at the mercy of her stepsister, and like me, she was often glad to escape, coming to me with some object, an offering. She would braid my fine hair, threading a bright ribbon through my pale tresses or dangling a glittering glass earring from an ear; she showed me how to saunter with a slow sway, hands on my hips, how to sigh suggestively, rouged lips parted and damp eyelids lowered, long lashes lingering on the cheeks. Once she brought me a short-tailed goldfinch in a little cage, which I hung on a long cord from the ceiling of my room. I could hear it perpetually hopping about and chirping, dropping birdseed, rocking back and forth cheerfully above my head. We exchanged crosses once, and Lizaveta gave me her copper one, and I gave her one of mine, as I was later to do with R.

I see myself from afar in that first moment I saw R. and everything began: a girl in a photograph in someone else's album, the kind tinted with color, she already has that same face, the clear blue eyes without innocence, eyes that have seen and accept all. She wears the wide crinoline that fills the doorway, the hat with its flaming fuchsia feather, and mechanically twirls the parasol with the ruffle around the rim.

A tall, slender man in gray hovers in the flickering shadows of that crowded, candlelit, and smoke-filled room. He leans close over her stricken father, spattered with her father's blood, and looks up at her. He stares at her, studying her face, her form, her clothes. He watches her leaning against the jamb, lowering her gaze with shame, her head to her chest, as if trying to hide her face, so that she has difficulty breathing and the beat of her heart thunders in her head.

Murderer! This man has murdered my father! she thinks when she sees his pale face, the dark tormented gaze, blood all over his clothes.

It was Lizaveta who had acquired my secondhand clothes. She had done her best. The train of the dress was thin and worn in places, but it was silk; the hat was dented at the brim, but stylish with its bright-colored feather, the parasol still a faded pink. In the daylight it cast a pink shadow on my face. "Look how pretty, Sonechka," Lizaveta had said, twirling the parasol behind her head, looking down at me from her great height—she must have been six feet.

Occasionally we would escape to the islands and wander in the greenness and freshness, watching with wonder the elegant carriages or a smart woman on a horse tapping its dappled flank with an English riding crop. Or we looked into windows of fine houses at a luxurious life we could only imagine. Sometimes we went to Vasilievsky Island in the summer and sat beneath the trees and talked.

Or we came to my own place, where I would read to her from the New Testament she had found for me with its worn leather cover, the yellowed pages.

I am not sure she knew how to read, though she could juggle figures in her head quickly and without error. No one had taught her the alphabet. They called her a half-caste with her swarthy skin, her crinkly hair. Yet her eyes were a pale, innocent blue.

She was good-natured, openhearted, and merry. How we would laugh together! Tucked away in the room with the icons at the pawnbroker's, where she was so brutally murdered. We would giggle like adolescents, which I was. I am not sure of her age when she died. Perhaps she was thirty-five or -six, but her café au lait skin was bright like a girl's, and burnished as though polished on her high cheekbones. She never told me her age. Perhaps she did not know it. I hear us speaking, sometimes both at once, in our eagerness to share the secrets of our hearts.

The girl is aware that her face, her figure are incongruous, shocking in these clothes. As in a dream, I see her as she stands there, Sonia, my double, my reflection, my other, as though looking into a mirror. She is me and yet not me in the flickering candlelight, the smoky air, the grotesque faces grimacing disapprovingly all around her in the shadows of the narrow room. She pauses painfully, staring at the priest, who is at her father's side, too.

"What is it?" she asks, and someone answers in a loud voice that the drunkard has finally been brought home half-dead.

She pushes her way forward and faces the sight of her father lying on the sofa, a pillow beneath his head, blood oozing from the corner of his mouth, perspiration on his forehead, the gashed, crushed chest.

At the same time, she notices a badly dressed stranger in gray trousers holding a cap by his side. The man is so thin he looks as if he might be ill or has been ill. Even in the dimly lit room, she notices his close-set, intense dark eyes, pale skin, aquiline nose, his gray waistcoat spattered with her father's blood. It is then that she thinks, irrationally, *This man has murdered my father!* and at the same time, *This murderer has pierced my heart.*

"What has happened to him?" she asks, and someone murmurs that Semyon Zakharovich Marmeladov has been run down by a carriage in his drunken state while she wandered the streets in her streetwalker clothes.

On the last day I saw Lizaveta, she came to my room before I went into the streets. We sat at my table and drank a cup of tea and ate some honey cakes she had brought for me, as she often did, saying I needed to eat more than I did.

Then she said someone was waiting for her between six and seven in the Haymarket. It might be a profitable sale, with something I could wear among the clothes. She would bring me something soon. If only she had stayed instead of hurrying off to fulfill a promise so punctually!

It was a hot day in late July. I still see her standing at my door in her strange worn-out shoes, lifting her big hand in a sort of soldier's salute, her dark hair so neatly braided flat against her head, her slanting eyes smiling at me, promising to be back soon.

But she never came back. When I had not seen her around in the Haymarket where I could usually find her and feared she might be ill, I went to the pawnbroker's.

Somehow it was the smell of fresh paint that alerted me to danger, and I felt uneasy as I climbed the stairs. To my surprise I found the door ajar and two painters busy repapering and painting. The paper was no longer yellow but white with little purple flowers. I looked around, disoriented.

The sofa with its curved back, the geraniums, the prints of German damsels, even the icon stand with its oil lamp had disappeared, though it had left a visible mark on the wallpaper in that corner of the room.

I asked the painters what had happened, but they just shook their heads in a strange, almost guilty way, maintaining they knew nothing. It was the concierge whom I found in the courtyard who told me. "Both murdered, blood all over the place," he said.

"Not Lizaveta! Why Lizaveta?" I asked, unable to believe such a monstrous thing.

"The money, I suppose—the old lady must have had quite a lot of money and many pledges, probably hidden in some trunk under the bed. I always said something like this might happen with all those people tramping up and down the stairs day and night to pawn things."

"What people?" I asked.

"Mostly students who needed money."

"How were they killed?" I couldn't help asking.

"Some blunt instrument. Probably an ax," he said.

"Did you see anyone?" I asked, imagining a dark shadow with an ax lifted high. He shook his head.

K.I. asks the priest angrily, waving her hands, her cheeks crimson, what she is to do now, gesturing toward the three small children kneeling beside her: Polya, Kolya, and the youngest girl, little Lidochka, her hair rising up like a baby hedgehog's spines on her head. At the same time, K.I. is giving her husband water to drink, wiping the blood and sweat from his face, his chest. She almost flies at the priest when he accuses her of sinful words. She coughs all the time, while her husband stares up at her, asking for her forgiveness with his eyes.

Then he looks up and sees the girl standing in the doorway and sits up, grimaces, and says, "Who's that?" his voice filled with disapproval. K.I. tells him to lie down. Her heart dipping low with shame and sadness, the girl realizes that her father does not recognize his own daughter in this shameful attire. She considers turning back and slipping away down the stairs in ignominy and tears.

Suddenly her father calls out in a voice filled with sorrow. *"Sonia! Daughter! Forgive me!"* he cries. He reaches out his arms to her with such violence that he falls from the sofa, a fall into nothingness like her own.

How she has stumbled and tumbled, going precipitously down a cliff, falling ever faster, clutching on to whatever she could to stop her descent, breathless, carried down into the dark and terrifying abyss of the labyrinthine streets at night.

Of course I was wrong about R. He had not murdered my father. It was alcohol that had done that. On the contrary, R., a stranger, had tried to save him. This young man had found him, rescued him, carried him through the streets and all the way up the stairs into our corridor, brought him home once again.

The girl stands there, leaning against the jamb of the door as if it were the mast of a rocking ship on a rough sea, aware for the first time in her life of desire. She wants this man. She wants a savior.

And yes, you are right, reader. This is R., or if you like, the one with all the *R*'s. R. R. R. The Russians carry their father's name with them for life, and the writer, apparently, liked alliteration. As R. he has already made his famous entrance onto the literary scene. You will recognize him perhaps, you may even remember what he has actually done, that I was wrong about him but not entirely. I met him in the midst of that crowd, the night Father died.

I wept bitterly when I heard of Lizaveta's brutal end. I could not imagine how anyone could have wished the innocent creature ill. How could anyone bring an ax down on her defenseless head? Despite her great height, her sturdy build, her large feet, and her strange dress, she was vulnerable in so many ways. She was unable to refuse anything to anyone, particularly the men who asked for her favors, which she gave away so easily and almost without noticing, or so it seemed. Her body was a gift, given to any taker. She was constantly pregnant and often had recourse to the "angel maker."

Lizaveta was not as simple as she might have seemed. She did a good business in the sale of old clothing and even furniture, though whatever she earned she would give to her wealthy stepsister, who beat her and had promised her fortune to a monastery to say prayers in perpetuity for her soul. Somehow Lizaveta felt she owed Alyona her life.

"You put it on, show me," I would say when Lizaveta brought forth some garment she had found for me.

She would take off her clothes without shame. She did not bother much with undergarments or stays or corsets of any kind. I would catch a glimpse of her heavy, innocent body, her big, shiny, bronzed breasts. "You put it on," she would say.

"You do not look quite right, Sonechka," she might murmur when I obeyed, turning shyly before her. Then she would show me how to lift my petticoats and give a glimpse of my ankles—one of my better attributes.

But really, hard as I might try and though it is true, she gave away for free what I was obliged to sell, Lizaveta was much more successful than I was, and despite her awkwardness, her crooked legs, the men flocked around her.

Even at that moment, with the crowd of lodgers still pressing around curiously, breathing down on my father, with the candlelight flickering on R.'s face, and spattered as he is with my father's blood, I am aware of something strange in his thin, sensitive face, his tragic eyes, and his dark-blond hair, which falls untidily from his cap onto his glistening forehead. But it is his choice of words, his tact at that moment that moves me most. He tells K.I. that her husband has told him how much he loved and respected her and how devoted he was to all the children, his own child and hers, words that ring true.

I remember then that Father has mentioned this young man. Father has met him in a tavern—a former law student who made an impression on him. He had spoken of R. with admiration, someone who had the kindness to bring him home when he could hardly stagger from the tavern and did not dare return to K.I. with no money left in his pocket, and straw from the barge where he had spent several nights in his hair; a stranger who left a few kopeks, all he had in his pocket, Father imagined, for the family on a windowsill.

Indeed, it is true, Father loved K.I. and all of the children, his own and hers, despite his inability to care for us.

R.'s words are the words of someone who has thought about others and understood them, something I have not often come upon in my short, sad life.

R. begs K.I. to allow him to assist her at this moment of need as though she were doing him a favor, and he thrusts twenty rubles into her hand so quickly and firmly that she has no opportunity to decline. I realize later, when I see his coffin-like room, it must have been all he had.

I will learn that R. is capable of these great gestures of generosity, that he has noble impulses and is able to offer money, the right words, or just his hand to end a misunderstanding.

R. was the one to rescue Father as far as he could be rescued, the one who had brought him home to us, wounded and near death. It was he who had insisted on calling the doctor, though it was obvious his services were useless; it was R. who had offered to pay, with such solicitude, as though his own life depended on it. I can never reconcile such loving acts, such generosity and tender tactfulness, with what I will discover R. has done before.

Then, before any of us can gather our wits to thank him, he leaves. It is then that I tell Polenka to run after him, to find out his name and where he lives. Suddenly I do not want to lose this man who has already entered my heart, become part of my dreams and fears.

"Yes, yes," K.I. says. "Hurry, Polya, and find our benefactor."

When Polenka comes back she tells me R. has asked who sent her. "He asked me if I loved you," Polenka tells me, staring at me with her large gray eyes as though seeing me anew.

"And what did you say?" I ask her. She says she gave him a kiss. "The kiss was for you," Polenka says, weeping in my arms and kissing me. It is the first kiss R. and I exchange, through Polya, K.I.'s ten-year-old child.

•   •   •

Much later, R. does come to me. He comes in as I sit at my table, my head in my hands, worn out with worry, thinking of him.

He walks restlessly around my barnlike room, talking about the right to kill. Are there circumstances when we have the right? If a life is useless or even harmful to society, and a death could bring help to many, should the life be preserved?

He speaks of his great poverty, his poor mother, his beloved sister, her betrothal to a despicable man, even his dreadful coffin-shaped room.

He talks about his idea of a superior being, someone who is above the law, like Napoleon. All I know about Napoleon is that he had risen through the ranks and seized the crown, which had fallen into the gutter after the French Revolution. R. seems to believe he was someone of genius, a man above the law, to whom all was permitted because of the great deeds he accomplished.

He speaks of chance, fate, even the devil and the role he plays.

He looks at me with hate now, and I drift out of myself, doubling, as I think of Lizaveta and see her standing there with the ax raised over her head.

In the moment when the words are spoken, when she cannot deny what he is saying, when she realizes she has known all this from the start, she sees him looking at her with fear in his eyes. He is terrified she will turn from him, abandon him, leave him in the terrible isolation his crime has created. She can only hold him fiercely in her arms.

How strange and contradictory is desire, she thinks. How can she reach out to this man who has murdered twice? Yet at the same time all her own guilt is wiped away by his acts. Before the murderer she, Sonia, the whore, is innocent, pure. They are already one. She is free to feel all her body, all her need for him.

What happens between them happens in the pale Petersburg light. As she plunges into the depths of her desire, Lizaveta comes to greet her through the opaque light; the murdered girl swims to her, reaches out her long arms, her big, giving hands through the silt and the seaweed of the deep. She grasps her hands, her breasts, her body. Then the swimming begins. They are swimming together with large strokes, the three of them, the light shimmering down through the surface of the water. On they swim, passionately plunging through the water, coming up to the surface from time to time to gasp for great breaths of air.

Now I sit alone on the bank of this desolate river where I have accompanied R. and stare out across the endless open countryside in these long spring days. I am surrounded by a cloud of gnats as the dark Irtysh flows swiftly by me. I gaze at that distant point where sky and earth meet in a pure line with the impression that something is out there waiting for me.

Simultaneously, in my heart, a knot tightened by the years, habit, and suffering is slowly loosening. I stare at the nomads' encampment with longing. Nothing stirs among the black yurts, and yet I think of these men and women whose existence is barely known to me. There, homeless, cut off, they wander, a few souls ceaselessly voyaging, possessing nothing but serving no one, poverty-stricken but free lords of a strange kingdom. It is as if this kingdom has been promised to me and a sense of freedom, of inner strength has come to me in this savage place—a place of extremes: wild wind, flying insects, and sand, great heat and intense cold, endless fields of snow—the right to speak up, speak out, to tell what only I, Sonia, a girl branded with the yellow ticket, know, to confide the true secrets of my suffering heart, those thoughts that have never been heard.

SHEILA KOHLER is the author of ten novels, three volumes of short fiction, a memoir, and many essays. Her most recent novel is *Dreaming for Freud*, based on the Dora case. Her memoir *Once We Were Sisters* came out with Penguin in 2017. She has won numerous prizes, including the O. Henry twice, and been included in *Best American Short Stories* twice. Her work has been published in eighteen countries. She has taught at Columbia, Sarah Lawrence, and Bennington, and now teaches at Princeton.

Her novel *Cracks* was made into a film directed by Jordan Scott, with Eva Green playing Miss G. You can find her blog at Psychology Today under "Dreaming for Freud."

ELINOR LIPMAN

"People Are People"

I am the namesake of a great-aunt murdered by the Nazis, as were her husband and two of her adult children. Most sacred to me is her surviving daughter's story, in part because I loved and admired her, in part because I grew up believing that my mother had a role in her rescue.

Born in 1912 in Riga, Latvia, Adele Rewitsch survived two ghettos (the so-named Large Riga and Small Riga ones), three labor camps, and finally, Bergen-Belsen concentration camp. She'd been there just three weeks when British troops arrived on the afternoon of April 15, 1945. Said the eighty-four-year-old Adele in her Shoah testimony, smiling at the memory, "It was the most beautiful joy a person could feel."

She was thirty-three years old and weighed sixty-five pounds. She was tiny, five feet one inch, yet as a prisoner she'd worked in munitions factories making barbed wire, had chopped wood, dug peat; at Kaiserwald had moved stones from one side of the road and back—cruel and pointless invented work overseen by German women I fervently hope were eventually sentenced to worse fates. Then Bergen-Belsen, where, for an extra so-called meal, and hardly able to lift the shovel, she volunteered to dig graves for the "mountain of corpses—the most horrible sight of all the time of the war." That first measly ration of bread she allowed herself to eat. The second she sneaked back to her barracks for "her group."

Adele's surviving brother, Eugene, a doctor, had immigrated to the United States in 1937. Anti-Semitism, ironically, had served a purpose: his homeland, Latvia, claiming not to recognize his French medical degree, wouldn't grant him an internship. After serving in the Latvian army (mistakenly in the ski patrol; couldn't ski), after coming to America and marrying, his wife wrote to dozens of American hospitals, in search of internships. Finally, one said yes, come. Or more likely, *"Oui, venez,"* because it was a hospital run by an order of French nuns, Saint Peter's Hospital in New Brunswick, New Jersey.

Remembering that city as his last known home before communication ceased, a very ill Adele sent a letter from Bergen-Belsen to her brother at Saint Peter's in "New Brunswick, New Brunswick." At the bottom of the envelope, in German, she noted that he'd been working there as an intern in 1941. It reached him, forwarded to the U.S. Army, finally arriving in Missoula, Montana, where he was stationed.

But a long six months had passed, and the war was over. Not knowing if she'd survived, and because "it was a letter that could not be understood" according to Adele, he, a psychiatrist, was inconsolable. "Help me," she'd written. "I'm so sick. I dreamed about strawberries. Maybe you can get me some strawberries." Eugene's daughter, Judy, born in 1940, told me that her mother, fearing her husband would spend the rest of his life reading it, eventually destroyed the letter, so late to reach him, his only sister's fate unknown.

From Adele's Shoah testimony: After "two or three" months in the makeshift Belsen infirmary, unmoored and refusing "like a crazy woman" to be repatriated to Russia (Latvia was under Russian rule, but the transport would have taken her to Russia proper), she was "like a little cadaver," brought by the Red Cross to Sweden to recuperate. There she was quarantined, housed, fed, clothed. ("The Jewish people of Sweden! There are no words for them!") Among the amenities—paper napkins! Toilet paper! Shoes! Coats! Kronor!—survivors received paper, pencils, and stamps, encouraging them to get in touch with whomever they remembered in a safe place.

Somewhere in America was the older brother she'd already tried to reach, but where now? She wrote to her uncle—my grandfather—and though addressed only "Louis Masur, Tailor, Lowell, Boston," the letter reached him. Written in German, it described her plight and her location. Could someone help? Did they know the whereabouts of her brother?

Only my mother was home when the blue airmail letter arrived. She didn't know German but she knew who it was from and what it must mean: Adele was alive! She ran—a mission she never described in any other way except "I ran"—to the synagogue to ask the German-speaking custodian to translate. Her cousin had survived! She was in Sweden, alive and safe. My mother called Eugene and another cousin, now safe in New York, and from there no doubt ran straight to Western Union. Everyone contacted sent telegrams. *Your letter received! We will get you out!*

And they did.

Adele obtained a visa in December 1945, which had to be used within three months. Just short of that expiration date, she found passage: from Göteborg to Liverpool (where three hundred war brides and their children boarded—quite the circus!) to Halifax, then America.

On April 8, 1946, after rough seas the whole way, the SS *Drottningholm* arrived in New York Harbor. It would be most narratively fulfilling to report that the Statue of Liberty loomed large in Adele's memory, that Lady Liberty had a role in the family story. It did not. But the sight that did make it into the narrative, which she reported to me herself, fifty years later, over lunch, was that her beloved brother had been granted a twenty-four-hour furlough by the U.S. Army, and was there to meet her.

Her brother-doctor Eugene worried that New York, where she'd been living with her cousin, would be too hot in the summer; she should come live with him and his wife and daughter in Missoula, "high in the mountains and very beautiful."

Fluent in three languages, Adele once told me, looking stumped, "It's funny, but the language I've forgotten is Latvian." (To which I, the excellent grudge-holder, think: Murderers! Ninety-eight percent of Latvian Jews were murdered by Nazis and all-too-cooperative Latvian citizens—the largest percentage loss of any Jewish community in the world during the Shoah.) Yiddish, too? "Well, yes, but that I learned later in the camps."

Adele moved back to New York in the fall of 1946, and worked for the next thirty-five years for the International Ladies' Garment Workers' Union as a bookkeeper. Her first day on the job was also the first day for handsome Ludwig Honigwill, a lawyer, a displaced Jew from Poland, who'd made it to the U.S. in 1941. "We went for our Social Security cards together," she told me with a smile. "We were two numbers apart—we would have been just *one* number apart but because he was such a gentleman he let the woman behind him go first." They married five years later, and were together until his death in 1977.

When the first cousins eventually met, Adele told my mother that the day the American relatives' telegrams arrived was the day she'd set as a deadline for herself: if she'd heard back from no one, she'd have to start over, alone.

Adele died in 2004, strong to the end. If only someone could have told her in 1945, newly liberated but deathly ill with typhus, emaciated, grieving, lost: "You will live! You will make it to America, to safety and to family. You will find work there, and love. And not only will you regain your health, but you will live to the age of ninety-two in the borough of Queens in the great city of New York. You will look back at the pathetically small acts of kindness performed only rarely by monsters, and say with a shrug and a sweet smile, 'People are people.' And, most amazingly, sixty years from that hell on earth, you will sum up your life, on the record, as good and long and lucky. Imagine such a beautiful thing, newly liberated survivor Adele Rewitsch, because all of that came true."

ELINOR LIPMAN is the author of thirteen books of fiction and nonfiction, including *Then She Found Me*, *The Inn at Lake Devine*, *Isabel's Bed*, *I Can't Complain: (All Too) Personal Essays*, *The View from Penthouse B*, and *On Turpentine Lane*. Her rhyming tweets were published in 2012 as *Tweet Land of Liberty: Irreverent Rhymes from the Political Circus*. She was the 2011–12 Elizabeth Drew Professor of Creative Writing at Smith College, and lives in New York City.

The Trout Fisherman

I wake up—dog on feet, dog on head, dog on face—around five thirty. There's a house here, but Jolene and I choose to sleep in the little boathouse on the water, where I can hear the frogs and loons all night long and see the moon on the lake.

Hop out of bed, into my bathing suit, down the ladder, dive into the water. (Sometimes there's mist rising, and it looks a little chilly. If so I recite my mantra: *I never regret a swim.* Because as difficult as it may be on occasion to make that first plunge, it's always true. I never regret that I did.)

I'm not completely by myself here. Every morning I see the same lone fisherman, rod in the water, in search of his trout. I call out my hello. He answers with his.

Now here is a surprising fact about my fisherman friend. (His name is John, as I learned, early on in my summer of swimming.) He's black.

This might not surprise you if you don't know that much about very small towns in New Hampshire. But when I grew up here, in the fifties and sixties, months might go by in which you did not encounter a person of color. Later on in my growing-up years, a single African American family attended my school of probably four hundred kids. One Asian girl. One from India. That was the extent of our diversity, and though this has changed considerably now in my home state—in the larger cities or even medium-sized towns—it is still a surprising thing, when swimming in a small lake in a town whose population is under a thousand, to run into a fisherman who's also a person of color.

Over the summer, we've gotten to talking a little during these early-morning encounters. In this lonely summer after my husband's death, his presence, even on mornings when we said nothing, offered a form of quiet comfort. Though I knew only his first name, and little else besides the fact he liked to fish, as the weeks passed, on those rare mornings when he failed to show up in that little boat of his, I missed him.

The trout are excellent in this lake. So is the swimming. And gradually, as June moved into July, and then August, I learned more about my fisherman friend.

It turns out John and his wife retired here from Missouri. No particular ties to the state of New Hampshire except that they both attended the university here many years ago. As it happens, my father taught English there during those years, but John was more the engineering type and never took a class with him.

This morning John mentioned a surprising fact. Despite a lifetime of fishing, he cannot swim.

"I guess you didn't grow up around water," I said—thinking of my own hometown, which didn't have a lake like this, but did offer a wonderful pool where I took swimming lessons every summer. All year long I looked forward to times at that pool, and on the last day before they closed, I could hardly bring myself to get out of the water.

"There was a pool in our town," John told me, quietly. (He in his little metal boat. I in the lake. Not far off, a loon.) "Blacks weren't allowed to go in. They thought we might contaminate the water."

I should have known, I guess. I am old enough to remember images from television, of black churches burned, white policemen standing at the door of a school, barring entrance to a child just my age, but a different color. Governor George Wallace, manning the barricades.

But John's words caught me up short. I felt something like guilt, to be there in that lake at that moment. While he sat in his boat, a man a few years older than I, wearing his life jacket. I was familiar with the not entirely accurate stereotype that African Americans were unlikely to swim. But I had never considered this part of the story. *Why?*

All could say was "I'm so sorry."

A few minutes after, I swam back to my house. Had my shower, made my coffee. Turned on my laptop to find out what new abomination our current administration had cooked up overnight. If pancreatic cancer hadn't killed my husband, I have been saying for a while now, what's going on now might have.

Today, I learned, the Civil Rights Division of our Justice Department—an office whose creation came out of the intent to rectify decades of injustice in our country toward persons of color and preserve educational opportunities of the sort that allowed my friend John to come to my hometown from Missouri to study engineering—has been directed to focus its energies on a new goal: the mission of this division will now be "investigations and possible litigation related to intentional race-based discrimination in college and university admissions."

In plain language, they have been directed to seek out evidence of discrimination against that put-upon and downtrodden group of which I am a member: white people.

I didn't grow up rich. But when I entered the water of my town swimming pool every summer morning I never gave a thought to the idea that some children might not be allowed to do this. For a few years there, I watched so many of the smartest boys in my school head off to an elite Ivy League prep school one town over that did not allow girls. But in my senior year, I got to attend that school. Same as, a year later, I got to attend another fine university that had once admitted only men.

When I did, my classmates included many persons of color like John, who came from places where the schools were probably not the best. The schools they were allowed to attend, anyway. It was affirmative action that made it possible for those students to gain access to that level of education. They were not the only ones whose lives were enriched by this. So was mine. So were we all.

When I read the small-minded, entitled, hate-filled invective of those who would deny affirmative action, my mind returned to the trout fisherman in his boat this morning, who does not swim. Until his retirement, by the way, John worked as an engineer. He is a man of no small accomplishment. He just didn't get to go in the pool.

. . .

I asked him, before swimming back to shore, about his children.

He has four. All grown now. Grandchildren too. They're all swimmers. That's what happens when you let a person get in the water. He brings the next generation along.

JOYCE MAYNARD is the author of sixteen books, including the novels *To Die For* and *Labor Day* and the memoir *At Home in the World*. Her most recent memoir, about finding and losing her husband, is titled *The Best of Us*.

Listen

—We were all so surprised.

—You were surprised? I wasn't surprised.

—Shocked.

—It was surprising how unhappy.

—No one saw.

—No one could see.

—No one wanted to see.

—They saw.

—Didn't really think about it.

—So they were right.

—Of course they were right.

—They were wrong.

—Who's they?

—They were.

—They are.

—Seeing what they weren't.

—Feeling left.

—Who're they?

—Wanted what everybody else.

—Left out.

—Who's everybody?

—Reasons for it.

—Can't ignore the numbers.

—People want.
—The numbers say it all.
—People hoping.
—What the numbers mean.
—People always want.
—What the rich.
—People always want something.
—What the poor.
—People always something new.
—Want something more.
—People always.
—Who're people?
—The uncounted.
—They can't.
—The ignored.
—They won't.
—They try.
—Just ignore.
—They're forgotten.
—They know who they are.
—They're to blame.
—Who's the problem?
—They're corrupt.
—They're the future.
—Liars.
—They're what's happening.
—They're the heart.
—They won't.
—Who're they?
—Never on our side.
—They were never.
—They don't care.

—They're insane.
—They used to be great.
—Why can't they get along?
—They're clueless.
—Trying our best.
—Symbols of hate.
—Doesn't work anymore.
—Symbol of hope.
—Used to be great.
—Not trying.
—Have to fix.
—Have no choice.
—Making it worse.
—Did our best.
—Human behavior.
—Must do better.
—Having no choices.
—The rich.
—Wrong of them.
—The poor.
—Can't handle.
—Leaving.
—Never leaving.
—Must do something.
—Time for a change.
—Out of complacency.
—Not mine.
—Doesn't work anymore.
—Time to act.
—Not theirs.
—Who're they?
—We'll show them.

—What they're saying.
—They are.
—What they want to say.
—What they couldn't say.
—What they're thinking.
—What are they thinking?
—They couldn't say.
—No one was listening.
—The rich always.
—Can't be helped.
—Human nature.
—Can't be changed.
—Must be saved.
—Weirder every day.
—Nature unbridled.
—What I heard.
—Did something else happen?
—Can't watch.
—Can't listen.
—How can they?
—Can't dismiss.
—Can't blame.
—So surprising.
—More each day.
—Less each day.
—Have to leave.
—Never leaving.
—What can we do?
—I thought we were.
—What will they do?
—Isn't fair.
—We didn't know.
—Seen it all.

—What the kids?
—It's never been.
—Truly insane.
—Lost his mind.
—Never had it.
—He was great.
—Never in my lifetime.
—Only the rich.
—Like it was before.
—99%.
—Keep fighting.
—Really worried.
—How do you like your meat done?
—Can't listen anymore.
—What're they saying?
—Can't watch.
—Can't stop watching.
—How can people?
—Can't sleep.
—What do they want?
—Please hold.
—How can people not?
—More.
—Stop complaining.
—Feeling threatened.
—Upon themselves.
—Did something else happen?
—You mean Charlottesville?
—No, since then.
—Anyone better?
—Sorry I'm late.
—Somebody must.
—Who?

—She couldn't.
—She could have.
—She didn't.
—He did.
—He heard them.
—He was great.
—They hated him.
—We loved him.
—They loved him.
—He heard them.
—Can't believe this.
—Nothing like this yet.
—Can't be happening.
—Had to happen.
—They've finally gotten.
—Can't go on.
—Can't stand to listen.
—Can't bear to watch.
—Has to change.
—Message is clear.
—What's the message?
—Can't bear.
—They're insane.
—Must condemn.
—Has to stop.
—Blame the rise.
—Feeling threatened.
—No one listening.
—Accept the differences.
—Deliberate strategy.
—No strategy.
—No one listening.

—He heard them.

—No one heard.

—They heard him.

—Which them? Which him?

—Across the aisle.

—This is how I like to cook my meat.

—Great again.

—Really worried now.

—Like the world has never seen.

—Not the way I like it.

—Lies.

—Getting what they want.

—No, thank you.

—Hell, yeah.

—Must ignore it.

—All lies.

—Has to change.

—Nothing new.

—Never before.

—Once again.

—Feeling threatened.

—Haven't a clue.

—Never will.

—This is where I work.

—Not anymore.

—Threatened.

—I never did before.

—Can't stand it.

—Not anymore.

—Have to for my family.

—Still can't believe it.

—Can't imagine.

—Can't bear.
—Can't look.
—Not another word.

SUSAN MINOT is the author of the novels *Monkeys*, which was published in a dozen countries and won the 1987 Prix Femina Étranger in France; *Folly*; *Evening*; *Rapture*; and *Thirty Girls*. She has written a collection of short stories, *Lust & Other Stories*, and of poems, *Poems 4 A.M.* She wrote the screenplay for Bernardo Bertolucci's *Stealing Beauty* and coauthored the screenplay of *Evening*, based on her novel. Most recently she wrote a one-act play, *Summer*, which was performed at Waterman's Community Center in North Haven, Maine, in 2017. She also likes to paint.

Between Storms

After the storm Michael Trey just didn't want to leave his apartment anymore. There was something about the booming thunder and the dire news reports, the red line across the bottom of every TV show warning residents to stay inside and away from windows even if they were closed and shaded. Subway tunnels were flooded, as were the streets. The airports would be closed for the next four days and the Hudson had risen up over the West Side Highway to cause millions of dollars in damage in Lower Manhattan.

The mayor interrupted TV Land's repeat of an old *Married with Children* episode to report that the National Guard had been called out.

The president had taken a train (a train!) to Manhattan to address New Yorkers everywhere, telling one and all that he had declared them a disaster. He wore a white dress shirt with thin green and blue lines across it. He didn't wear a tie because he was getting down to business—that's what Michael thought. Even the president was afraid of the havoc that nature had wrought.

It didn't matter that the sun was shining the next day or that the skies were blue and cloudless. The storm was only hiding behind the horizon. And there with it was a hothouse sun; crazed terrorist bombers; women with HIV, hepatitis C, and thoughts of a brief marriage followed by a lifetime of support. In North Korea they were planning a nuclear attack and there was probably some immigrant on the first plane in after the storm carrying a strain of the Ebola virus that would show signs only after he had moved past the customs area.

Michael didn't go to work the next morning. The radio and TV said that most public transportation was moving normally. Traffic was congested, however. Three sidewalks in Manhattan had collapsed from water damage. Just walking down the street someone might get killed or paralyzed.

Europe's economy had almost failed again except that the Germans bailed out the Greeks with money that neither of them had. China was going to take over the American economy and make Michael and everyone he knew into communist slaves living in dormitories and eating rice.

But if no one could buy the goods, then China's economy might fail and it would engage its two-hundred-million-man army to reclaim all the money we borrowed to pay for the health insurance of undocumented, Spanish-speaking, job-stealing illegal immigrants.

There were microbes in the water after the storm. Militant Muslims had used the cover of the downpour to move explosives under churches and big businesses. They weren't afraid of the rain like Michael and other poor Americans who just wanted to work until retirement . . . never came.

The phone rang on the morning of the third day that Michael had not gone in to work at Prospect, Farr, Grant, and Heldhammer.

Michael picked up the receiver but did not speak.

"Mike?" someone said. "Mike, is that you?"

"Michael is not here," Michael heard himself say. He felt safe behind the subterfuge of those words. He wasn't at home and therefore couldn't be reached; couldn't be touched, burned, infected, blown up, or experimented on by sales scientists working in subterranean desert laboratories for the superstores.

"Mike, it's Finnmore, Ron Finnmore. Mr. Russell is wondering where you are."

"I'll leave him the message," Mike said, and then he put the phone back in its cradle.

After hanging up Michael had the urge to giggle but suppressed it. He knew that if he showed any emotion so soon they'd say he'd gone crazy and take him away.

• • •

It rained the next day and so Michael felt justified in calling PFGH and telling them that he wasn't coming in due to the inclement weather.

"It's just a few showers," Faye Lesser, Thomas Grant's assistant's secretary, said.

"That's how the last storm started. What if I got there and it came down like that again? Who would feed my cat?"

Michael didn't have a cat. He didn't have a fish or even a plant. If he had had a plant it would have died because he hadn't pulled up the shades since the storm.

The television took on a new role in the young man's life. It spoke of conspiracies and disasters both domestic and foreign that were increasing in severity like the storm that had raged over New York. There were mad cows and rampant use of hormones and antibiotics. The Y chromosome in men had shrunk to the point where men might cease to be men and would soon have to learn how to be women without wombs.

There were prisons across the country that together released at least a hundred convicted killers every week and banks that created bad debt (Michael was never sure how they did this) and then sold the nonexistent interest to pension plans that subsequently failed.

Michael started taking notes. He had five folders that he'd bought for his financial records but never used. He labeled these folders: DISEASES, NATURAL DISASTERS, MANMADE DISASTERS, FINANCIAL DISASTERS, and HUMAN THREATS. Five folders was just right for the notes he needed to compile. He saw this as a sign that he was meant to stay in his fourteenth-floor apartment and study the truth that so many people missed because they went to work and therefore somehow, inexplicably, betrayed themselves.

He spent whole days looking up fires, floods, serial killers, and food additives on his cell phone. He ordered hundreds of cans of beans and tuna, concentrated orange juice and powdered milk from delivery services. He made them leave the foods at the apartment door and collected them only when he was sure that no one was in the hall.

He used his phone to pay his bills until his accounts went low.

The super brought up his mail and left it at the threshold for him.

He had been fired, of course. His girlfriend, Melanie, told him that either he would meet her at the Starbucks on Forty-Second Street or she was breaking up with him. His mother called but Michael fooled her by saying that Michael wasn't home.

And he was getting somewhere with his research.

At first he thought that the problem was that there were too many people but he gave up that theory when he realized that people working together would be benefited by great numbers. Finally he understood that it wasn't the number of souls but the plethora of ideas that bogged down the world. It was like the old-time Polish parliament in which nothing could be decided as long as anyone held a contrary point of view.

The problem with the world was a trick of consciousness: people believed in free will and independent thinking and were, therefore, dooming the world to the impossibility of choice. Yes. That was the problem. Together all the peoples of the world—Muslims, Hindus, and Jews; Christians, atheists, and Buddhists—would have to give up disagreements if they wanted the human race to survive the storm of incongruent consciousness, which was even worse than the weather that had brought New York to its knees.

Michael felt that he was making great progress. He was beginning, he was sure, to articulate the prime issue at the base of all the bad news the *New York Times* had to print. He was trying to imagine what kind of blog or article he could author when the eviction notice was shoved under his door. It had only been six weeks . . . no, no, no, nine. Just eleven weeks but he was rent stabilized and the collusion of city government and greedy landlords made prompt evictions possible when there was potential for rent that could soar.

After midnight, working for two weeks, Michael drilled forty-eight holes along the sides, top, and bottom of his door and similarly placed holes in the doorjamb and along the floor. He used a handheld wireless drill to do this work. Through these connective cavities he looped twined wire hangers, two strands for each hole. This reinforcement, he figured, stood a chance of resisting a battering ram if it came to that.

He also used melted candle wax to seal the cracks at the sides of the door so that the police couldn't force him out with tear gas.

His beard had begun to sprout and his hair had grown shaggy. He looked to himself like another man in the mirror: the man who answered the phone for the absent Michael.

He filled the bathtub to the drain in case the super turned off the water.

On his iPhone he read the newspapers, studied the Middle East, Central America, and the Chinese, who, he believed, had gained control of capitalism without understanding its deteriorative quality.

Finally all those boring political science courses—the ones he'd taken when he thought he might want to be a lawyer—had some use.

He was well on his way to a breakthrough when the landline rang.

He always answered the phone because, in a discussion with the man in the mirror, he deduced that if no one answered they might use the excuse that there was some kind of emergency behind his coat-hanger-reinforced door.

"Hello?"

"May I speak to Michael Trey, please?" a pleasant man's voice asked.

"He's not here."

"Then to whom am I speaking?"

This was a new question and it was very smart—very. This was not just some befuddled contrarian thinker but one of those unofficial agents who pretended to protect freedom while in reality achieving the opposite end.

"My name is X," he replied, and suddenly, magically, Michael ceased to exist.

"X?"

"What do you want?"

"My name is Balkan, Bob Balkan. I'm an independent contractor working for the city to settle disputes."

"I don't have any disputes, Mr. Balkan Bob. As a matter of fact, I might be one of the few people in the world who does not disagree."

"I don't understand," the independent contractor admitted.

"I have to go, Bob."

"Can you tell me something first, Mr. X?"

"What's that, Bob?"

"What do you want?"

The question threw X out of Michael's mind. The man who was left felt confused, overwhelmed. The question was like a blank check; a hint to the solution of a primary conundrum from a superior alien life-form. It had ecclesiastical echoes running down a corridor heretofore unknown in Michael's mind.

"What do I want?" Michael repeated the words but changed the intonation.

"Yes," Balkan Bob said.

"I want . . . I want people everywhere to stop for a minute and think about only the essential necessities of their lives. You know, air and water, food and friendship, shelter and laughing, disposal of waste and the continual need for all those things through all the days of their lives."

Balkan Bob was quiet for half a minute and so Michael, not X, continued, "If everybody everywhere had that thought in their mind, then they would realize that it's not individuality or identity but being human, being the same, that makes us strong. That's what I've been thinking in here while the rain's been falling and the landlord was trying to evict me."

"But Michael hasn't paid the rent, Mr. X."

"I have to go, Bob," X said, and then Michael hung up.

Eight days later the electricity was turned off. The grocery delivery service had brought him twelve fat nine-inch wax candles, so he had light. It was all right to be in semidarkness, to be without TV, radio, or internet. Michael had his five folders and the knowledge of a lifetime plus four years of college to filter through.

Two days after the electricity went off it came back on. Michael wondered what bureaucratic and legal contortion had the man with his hand on the lever going back and forth with the power.

The phone rang again.

When it sounded Michael realized that there had been no calls for the past forty-eight hours, not his mother or Melanie, who worried that her demands had brought him to this place.

Our Cuntry Needs You

Photograph

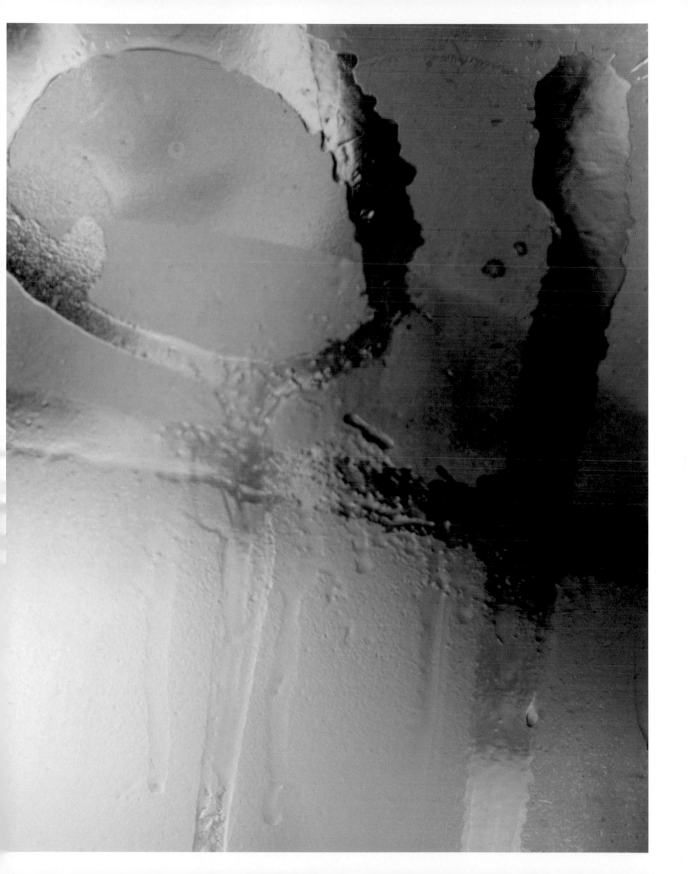

Tic-Tac-Toe

Photograph

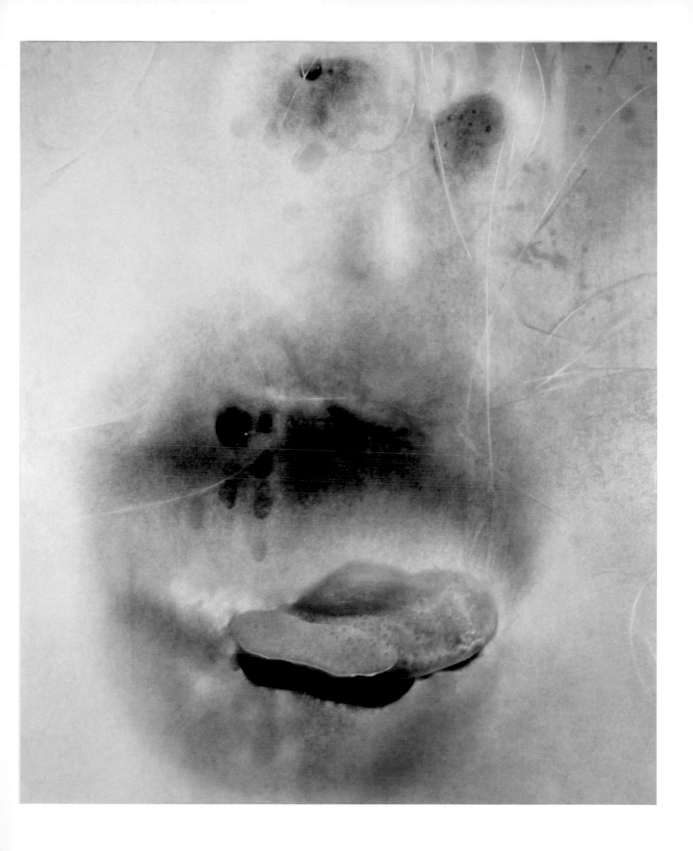

MARILYN MINTER lives and works in New York. She has been the subject of numerous solo exhibitions, including the San Francisco Museum of Modern Art in 2005; the Contemporary Arts Center, Cincinnati, Ohio, in 2009; La Conservera, Centro de Arte Contemporáneo, Ceutí, Murcia, Spain, in 2009; the Museum of Contemporary Art Cleveland, Ohio, in 2010; and the Deichtorhallen in Hamburg, Germany, in 2011. Her video "Green Pink Caviar" was exhibited in the lobby of the Museum of Modern Art in 2010 for over a year, and was also shown on digital billboards on Sunset Boulevard in L.A. and the Creative Time MTV billboard in Times Square, New York. In 2006, Minter was included in the Whitney Biennial, and, in collaboration with Creative Time, she installed billboards all over Chelsea in NYC. In 2013, she was featured in *Riotous Baroque*, an exhibition that originated at the Kunsthaus Zürich and traveled to the Guggenheim Bilbao. In 2015, her retrospective *Pretty/Dirty* opened at the Contemporary Arts Museum, Houston, Texas, then traveled to the Museum of Contemporary Art, Denver, and on to the Orange County Museum of Art. *Pretty/ Dirty* opened at the Brooklyn Museum in November 2016.

Deep Frost

Photograph

He always answered the phone but never stayed on for more than a minute.

The phone didn't depend on the power system. Maybe the phone company had cut him off for not paying his bill and then, at the behest of the city, had turned the service back on.

"Hello," X said.

"Mr. X?"

"Bob?"

"How are you?"

"Things are becoming clearer all the time, Bob," X said. "I just don't understand why you cut off my power and then turned it back on again."

"I didn't do it," he said.

"But you're working for the people who did, or at least their friends and allies."

"Do you feel that you are at war, Mr. X?"

"I'm just an innocent bystander who has made the mistake of witnessing the crime." X was much more certain about things than Michael was.

"I recorded your statement about what you wanted. Someone in my office released the recording to the media. You have lots of friends out here, Mr. X. If you look out your window you'll see them in the street."

"I'd like to but there might be something there I don't want to see. And I don't want anyone seeing me."

"No one wants to hurt you," Bob said in a very reassuring voice.

"No one wants to kill children in Afghanistan but no one cries over it either."

"You haven't come out of your apartment since we got hit by the hurricane."

"And here I don't know anything about you." Somewhere Michael was aware of the difference in the way he and X talked.

"What do you want to know?" Bob Balkan offered.

"You ask good questions, Bob."

"And?"

"Do you think that we're equal to our technology?"

"Maybe not."

"So why are you on my ass? That's all I'm saying."

"Let me ask you a question, Mr. X."

"What's that?"

"Do you think that we're equal to our biology?"

Neither Michael nor X was ready for that question. It got down to the crux of what they had been trying to figure out. If the human mind, Michael thought, was the subject of biological instinct, then there was no answer, no agreement, nor any exit from madness.

Stroking his beard, Michael forgot about the phone call and wondered if his own body was an unconscious plot against the idea of humanity, human-ness. Machines and techniques could be torn down and abandoned but what about blood and bone, nerves and hormones? Was he himself an aberrant machine set upon an impossible mission amid the insouciant materials of exis-tence? Was his resistance futile?

While he was considering these questions the phone went dead and the lights cut off. There came sounds of heavy footfalls in the hallway. Suddenly there was a great thumping wallop against his steel-reinforced, hanger-looped fire door. The police battering ram hit the door nineteen times, by Michael's count. The locks and hangers, doorjamb and metal infrastructure held. The pounding ceased and voices sounded up and down the outside hall.

There were shouts and curses. One man suggested that they break through the wall.

Michael armed himself with a butcher knife but then put the cooking weapon down.

"I can't hurt anybody," he said to no one.

That night Michael slept on the living room floor in front of the door. His iPhone was dead and the lights were cut off but under candlelight he read *Man's Fate* by André Malraux. He felt for the characters in the novel although, for the most part, he did not identify with them. Revolution, Michael thought, was both personal and shared, and everyone, and everything, had a part in it. His only affinity was with the feeling of doom and dread threaded throughout the book. He believed that soon he would be killed because he had decided to stop moving forward with the herd toward slow but certain slaughter.

"Mike. Hey, Mike," a voice hissed.

Michael had fallen asleep. He believed that his name was part of a dream but he didn't know why someone calling out to him would be important.

He tried to lift his right hand but it wouldn't move.

"Mike!" The whisper became more plaintive.

Suddenly afraid that people had secretly come in and bound him, Michael lurched up, jerking his right hand from whatever held it.

His fingers were encased in wax. The candle had burned unevenly and warm wax had pooled and dried around his hand. Michael laughed to himself, relieved that he was safe. He blew out the burning wick.

"Mike!"

The ventilation plate in the living room had a faint light glowing between its slats.

Michael's first impulse was to cover that opening with plastic and masking tape, but he hesitated.

He pulled a chair to the wall and got up on it so that he could stand face-to-face with the brass plate.

"Who is that?" he asked.

"Mike?"

"Yeah."

"It's Tommy Rimes from the apartment next door."

"The tall guy with the mustache?"

"No," the voice said. "I'm the guy who goes bowling all the time."

Michael remembered the squat middle-aged man with the potbelly and the red bowling-ball bag.

You wanna go run down some pins? he once asked Michael.

"What do you want, Mr. Rimes?"

"They got you all over the news, Mike. From Occupy Wall Street to the *Wall Street Journal* they all been talkin' about you. You went viral on the internet now that the cops couldn't beat down your door. Fisk, the guy with the mustache on the other side'a you, videoed it and put it up on YouTube. You're a celebrity."

Michael was peeling the wax from his fingers, wondering what notoriety would get him. Would it hold the hurricanes back or keep the communists from conquering capitalism? Would it get Melanie to take him back?

"Mike?" Michael had all but forgotten that Tommy Rimes was there.

"What?" the newly minted celebrity asked.

"Can you take off the ventilation plate?"

"Why?"

"I'm gonna push through a power strip and this aquarium hose I got. That way you can have power again and if they cut off your water you can have that."

"Why?"

"This rich guy from uptown put what you said to the city psychologist up on a billboard down the street. I like it. I mean, I think you might have somethin' there. And even if you're wrong, I like it that you're stickin' it to the landlord."

By morning Michael had light, and once he powered up his phone he found that it was still working. There was an email from Melanie telling him that she had paid his phone bill. On his tiny phone screen he could see newscasts covering a thousand people in the streets outside his apartment building protesting the police, the mayor, the landlord, and everyone who uses the law to keep people apart.

"I believe that Mr. Trey is trying to speak for all of us," a young black woman with braids that stood out from her head like spikes said to an interviewer. "I mean, here we are working hard and barely able to live. We eat junk food and watch junk TV and our schools are being closed down because they're so bad. The police will frisk anybody except if they're rich or something and we're fighting a war. Mr. Trey has just stopped. He's saying that he doesn't want to be a part of all this [*bleep*] and that we should all do the same."

"I'm a conservative," a white man in a dark-blue suit told a camera. "I believe that we have to fight the war and bail out the banks but I still wonder about what this guy says. I think he's crazy but you can't deny that there's something wrong with the world we're living in."

Both the liberal and conservative press praised Michael. They called him a people's hero who was refusing to take one more step before the other side made changes. They bent his words, however—that's what Michael thought. They didn't understand that the whole idea was *not* to have a hero but to discover a natural credo to unite people and keep them from destroying themselves.

"We love Michael Trey!" two beautiful young women shouted at one camera.

The city or the landlord cut his water off; Tommy Rimes turned it back on through the aquarium hose.

The iPhone sounded.

"Melanie?" Michael said after seeing the screen and answering.

"They've closed down the street in front of your building," she said.

"The police?"

"No, the protesters. They want the city to leave you alone. One group is raising money for your rent and four lawyers are working for injunctions against the landlord. Other tenants are making complaints about health and safety infractions. A journalist asked the president about you but he refused to comment and it's been all over the news."

"What has?" Michael asked his ex.

"The president not saying anything."

Michael tried to remember why he had decided to stay in his apartment. It was the storm. He was just too afraid because of the threat the news media made out of the storm. He was afraid, not heroic.

"Michael?" Melanie said.

"Uh-huh?"

"Max Strummer, who owns Opal Internet Services, wants you to do a daily podcast from your phone. He wants me to be the producer. Isn't that great? You could make enough money to pay your rent and lawyers. He said that if you couldn't think of anything to say we could send you text files that you could just read."

"I have to go, Mel," Michael said.

"What about Mr. Strummer?"

"I'll call you later," Michael uttered and then he touched the disconnect icon.

After turning off the sound on his phone, Michael went to sit in his favorite chair. It was extra wide with foam-rubber cushions under white cotton bro-cade. There was a lamp that he'd plugged into the power strip hanging halfway down his wall from the ventilation grate hole. The light wasn't strong enough to illuminate the whole room, just the area around his chair.

Reclining in the oasis of light, Michael tried to make sense of the storm and his street being closed down; of the young women who loved a man they'd never met; and Melanie, who had changed from an ex-girlfriend to a maybe-producer.

When no ideas came he turned off the lamp, hoping that darkness would provide an answer. It didn't. He was trying to recapture the moment when everything had made sense and he'd taken action without second-guessing his motives.

Feeling lost, he looked across the room and saw a blue luminescence. It was the phone trying to reach out to him.

Half an hour later he went to see who was calling. There had been a dozen calls. Most of the entries were unfamiliar, but one, instead of a number, was a name that he knew.

"Hello?"

"Mr. Balkan?"

"Mr. X?"

"No, no, this is Michael."

"Oh."

"Did you call me on city business?" Michael asked.

"They wanted me to call but this is your nickel."

"I've been looking at the internet," Michael said. "People all over the place want to protect me. They're offering money and legal support. One guy named Strummer wants to hire me and my ex to do a podcast for him."

"That's what you wanted, isn't it?"

"No."

"I thought you said that you wanted people to realize what they had in common."

"But between them," Michael said, "not outside."

"I don't get you."

"Not like a natural disaster or some enemy," the young bearded man replied. "I don't want to be the discounted meal at the fast food chain that you can buy in Anchorage or the Bronx. I don't want to be anything except an idea."

"But you're a man."

"Thanks for that, Bob."

"For what?"

"I needed to talk to somebody about these thoughts in my head. I couldn't get them out if I didn't have anybody to talk to. I know that you're working for them but right now they don't know what to do. In that little window you helped me. You really did."

"Helped you what?"

"I got to go, Bob."

"Where can you go, Michael?"

"You always ask the best questions."

The next morning Michael was standing in his kitchen eating from a can of pork and beans with a teaspoon when he noticed that the spigot had a slow drip. Michael wasn't sure if it was the dripping or his talk with the city psychologist that made up his mind.

He tested the hot water and then called Melanie. She was surprised to hear from him and happy that he had decided to do his first podcast. He was careful, and she was too, not to talk about love.

At four in the afternoon Michael was ready. He had refused to allow Strummer to dictate what he said. He ignored the checklist of subjects his internet listeners might want to hear about.

Michael had the bathtub draining when he started recording and had to close the bathroom door to keep out the noise.

"My name is Michael Trey," he said into the receiver with no notes or even a notion of what exactly he'd say. "I have lived in Manhattan for seven years and I was scared about Hurricane Laura, so scared that I haven't left my house since it broke. Because I wouldn't go out I lost my job and my girlfriend, and the landlord has been trying to evict me. I'm broke and they keep turning my utilities on and off. I have hot water right now and so I'm going to take my first real bath in weeks.

"My neighbor, Tommy Rimes, pushed a power strip and a little hose through the ventilation duct and so I've been able to get by. I've seen videos of people down in the street supporting me. I like that but it's misguided. What they should do, I believe, is lock themselves into their own houses and turn off the world outside. I don't know if this would be possible or if it would make any difference at all but that's all I've got.

"What I'm saying is that the president didn't talk about me because there's nothing to say. It is us who should be talking to him. It's us who need to get the red lines out of the bottoms of our screens because we're in it together as far as we go. But maybe, maybe that's impossible because we do things primarily as mammals, not men and women.

"That's really all I have to say. I know there are people out there who want a daily report from my musty apartment but really all they have to do is listen to this, what I'm saying right now.

"Goodbye."

Michael turned off his phone before running the hot bath in the deep, cast-iron tub. It was this tub that had made him take the apartment in the first place. The hot water felt so good that he groaned when he first sat back. The stinging in his wrists subsided and he wasn't frightened except if he concentrated on the hue of the water.

He was exhilarated at first and then tired the way he used to be as a little boy getting into his bed. He wondered if anyone would ever make sense out of the fear-herding that all the people, and maybe all other creatures, of the world lived under.

He would have liked Melanie to say that she loved him but only if he didn't have to ask.

WALTER MOSLEY is one of the most versatile and admired writers in America today. He is the author of more than fifty critically acclaimed books, including the major bestselling Easy Rawlins mystery series. His work has been translated into twenty-five languages and includes literary fiction, science fiction, political monographs, and a young adult novel. His short fiction has been widely published, and his nonfiction has appeared in the *New York Times Magazine* and the *Nation*, among other publications. In 2013, he was inducted into the New York State Writers Hall of Fame, and he is the winner of numerous awards, including an O. Henry Award, the Mystery Writers of America's Grand Master Award, a Grammy, and PEN America's Lifetime Achievement Award. He lives in New York City.

"Good News!"

1.

Or so at first it seemed.

I'd been named valedictorian of my class at Pennsboro High School. And I'd been the only one at our school, of five students nominated, to be awarded a federally funded Patriot Democracy Scholarship.

My mother came running to hug me and congratulate me. And my father, though more warily.

"That's our girl! We are so proud of you."

The principal of our high school had telephoned my parents with the good news. It was rare for a phone to ring in our house, for most messages came electronically and there was no choice about receiving them.

And my brother, Roderick, came to greet me with a strange expression on his face. He'd heard of Patriot Democracy Scholarships, Roddy said, but had never known anyone who'd gotten one. He was sure that no one had ever been named a Patriot Scholar while he'd been at Pennsboro High.

"Well. Congratulations, Addie."

"Thanks! I guess."

Roddy, who'd graduated from Pennsboro High three years before and was now working as a barely paid intern in the Pennsboro branch of the NAS Media Dissemination Bureau (MDB), was grudgingly admiring. Smiling at me strangely—just his mouth, not his eyes. I thought, *He's jealous. He can't go to a real university.*

I never knew if I felt sorry for my hulking-tall brother, who'd cultivated a wispy little sand-colored beard and mustache and always wore the same dull-brown clothes, which were a sort of uniform for lower-division workers at MDB, or if—actually—I was afraid of him. Inside Roddy's smile there was a secret little smirk just for *me*.

When we were younger Roddy had often tormented me—"teasing," it was called (by Roddy). Both our parents worked ten-hour shifts and Roddy and I were home alone together much of the time. As Roddy was the older sibling, it had been his task to *take care of your little sister*. What a joke! But a cruel joke that doesn't make me smile.

Now that we were older, and I was tall myself (for a girl of my age: five feet eight), Roddy didn't torment me quite as much. Mostly it was his expression—a sort of shifting, frowning, smirk-smiling, meant to convey that Roddy was thinking certain thoughts best kept secret.

That smirking little smile just for me—like an ice sliver in the heart.

My parents had explained: It was difficult for Roddy, who hadn't done well enough in high school to merit a scholarship even to the local NAS state college, to see that I was doing much better in the same school. Embarrassing to him to know that his younger sister earned higher grades than he had, from the very teachers he'd had at Pennsboro High. And Roddy had little chance of ever being admitted to a federally mandated four-year university, even if he took community college courses and our parents could afford to send him.

Something had gone wrong during Roddy's last two years of high school. He'd become scared about things—maybe with reason. He'd never confided in me.

At Pennsboro High—as everywhere in our nation, I suppose—there was a fear of seeming "smart," which might be interpreted as "too smart," which would result in calling unwanted attention to you. In a True Democracy all individuals are *equal*—no one is *better than anyone else*. It was okay to get Bs, and an occasional A–, but As were risky, and A+ was very risky. In his effort not to get As on exams, though he was intelligent enough, and had done well in middle school, Roddy seriously missed, and wound up with Ds.

Dad had explained: It's like you're a champion archer. And you have to shoot to miss the bull's-eye. And something willful in you ensures that you don't just miss the bull's-eye but the entire damned target.

Dad had laughed, shaking his head. Something like this had happened to him.

Poor Roddy. And poor Adriane, since Roddy took out his disappointment on me.

It wasn't talked about openly at school. But we all knew. Many of the smartest kids "held back" in order not to call attention to themselves. HSPSO (Homeland Security Public Safety Oversight) was reputed to keep lists of potential dissenters/MIs/SIs, and these were said to contain the names of students with high grades and high IQ scores.

Of course, it was just as much of a mistake to wind up with Cs and Ds— that meant that you were *dull-normal*, or it might mean that you'd deliberately sabotaged your high school career. Too obviously "holding back" was sometimes dangerous. After graduation you might wind up at a community college hoping to better yourself by taking courses and trying to transfer to a state school, but the fact was, once you entered the workforce in a low-level category, like Roddy at MDB, you were there forever.

Nothing is ever forgotten; no one is going anywhere they aren't already at. This was a saying no one was supposed to say aloud.

So Dad was stuck forever as an MT2—medical technician, second rank— at the district medical clinic, where staff physicians routinely consulted him on medical matters, especially pediatric oncology—physicians whose salaries were five times Dad's.

Dad's health benefits, like Mom's, were so poor, he couldn't even get treatment at the clinic he worked in. We didn't want to think what it would mean if and when they needed serious medical treatment.

I hadn't been nearly as cautious in school as Roddy. I enjoyed school, where I had (girl) friends as close as sisters. I liked quizzes and tests—they were like games at which, if you studied hard and memorized what your teachers told you, you could do well.

But then, sometimes I tried harder than I needed to try.

Maybe it was risky. Some little spark of defiance provoked me.

But maybe also (some of us thought) school wasn't so risky for girls. There had been only a few DASTADs—Disciplinary Actions Securing Threats Against Democracy—taken against Pennsboro students in recent years, and these students had all been boys in category ST3 or below.

(The highest ST—SkinTone—category was 1: "Caucasian." Most residents of Pennsboro were ST1 or ST2, then there was a scattering of ST3s. There were ST4s in a neighboring district and of course dark-complected ST workers in all the districts. We knew they existed but most of us had never seen an actual ST10.)

It seems like the most pathetic vanity now, and foolishly naive, but at our school I was one of those students who'd displayed some talent for writing, and for art; I was a "fast study" (my teachers said, not entirely approvingly), and could memorize passages of prose easily. I did not believe that I was the "outstanding" student in my class. That could not be possible! I had to work hard to understand math and science, I had to read and reread my homework assignments, and to rehearse quizzes and tests, while to certain of my classmates these subjects came naturally. (ST2s and ST3s were likely to be Asians, a minority in our district, and these girls and boys were very smart, yet not aggressive in putting themselves forward—that's to say *at risk*.) Yet somehow it happened that Adriane Strohl wound up with the highest grade-point average in the class of twenty-three—4.3 out of 5.0.

My close friend Paige Connor had been warned by her parents to hold back—so Paige's average was only 4.1. And one of the obviously smartest boys, whose father was MI, like my dad, a former math professor, had definitely held back—or maybe exams so traumatized him, Jonny had done poorly without trying, and his average was a modest/safe 3.9.

Better to be safe than sorry. Why had I ignored such warnings?

Fact is, I had just not been thinking. Later in my life, or rather in my next life, as a university student, when I studied cognitive psychology, I would become aware of the phenomenon of "attention"—"attentiveness"—that is within consciousness but is the pointed, purposeful, focused aspect of consciousness. Just to have your eyes open is to be conscious, minimally; to *pay attention* is something further. In my schoolgirl life I was conscious, but I was not *paying attention.* Focused on tasks like homework, exams, friends to sit with in cafeteria and hang out with in gym class, I did not pick up more than a fraction of what hovered in the air about me, the warnings of teachers that were nonverbal, glances that should have alerted me to—something . . .

So it happened: Adriane Strohl was named valedictorian of her class. Now I can see that no one else who might've been qualified wanted this "honor"— just as no one else wanted a Patriot Democracy Scholarship. Though there'd been some controversy, our principal was said to favor another student for the honor, a boy with a 4.2 average but also a varsity letter in football and a Good Democratic Citizenship Award, whose parents were of a higher caste than mine, and whose father was not MI but rather EI1, a special designation granted to Exiled persons who had served their terms of Exile and had been what was called 101 percent rehabilitated.

Maybe the school administrators were worried that Adriane Strohl would say "unacceptable" things in her valedictorian's speech?

Evidently I had acquired a reputation at school for saying things that other students wouldn't have said. Impulsively I'd raise my hand and ask questions. And my teachers were surprised, or annoyed—or, maybe, scared. My voice was quiet and courteous but I guess I came across as *willful.*

Sometimes the quizzical look on my face disconcerted my teachers, who took care always to compose their expressions when they stood in front of a classroom. There were approved ways of showing interest, surprise, (mild) disapproval, severity.

Of course, all our classrooms, like all public spaces and many private spaces, were monitored. Each class had its spies. We didn't know who they were, of course—it was said that if you thought you knew, you were surely mistaken, since the DCVSB (Democratic Citizens Volunteer Surveillance Bureau) chose spies so carefully, it was analogous to the camouflaged wings of a certain species of moth that blends in *seamlessly* with the bark of a certain tree. As Dad said, *Your teachers can't help it. They can't deviate from the curriculum. The ideal is lockstep—each teacher in each classroom performing like a robot and never deviating from the script under penalty of—you know what.*

(Was this true? For years in our class—the class of NAS 23—there'd been vague talk of a teacher—how long ago, we didn't know—maybe when we were in middle school?—who'd deviated from the script one day, began talking wildly and laughing and shaking his/her fist at the "eye" [in fact, there were probably numerous "eyes" in any classroom, and all invisible], and was arrested, and overnight Deleted—so a new teacher was hired to take his/her place; and soon no one remembered the teacher who'd been Deleted. And after a while we couldn't even remember clearly that one of our teachers *had been* Deleted. [Or had there been more than one? Were certain classrooms in our school *haunted*?] In our brains, where the memory of _____ should have been, there was just a blank.)

Definitely, I was not aggressive in class. I don't think so. But compared to my mostly meek classmates, some of whom sat small in their desks like partially folded-up papier-mâché dolls, it is possible that Adriane Strohl stood out—in a bad way.

In Patriot Democracy History, for instance, I'd questioned "facts" of history, sometimes. I'd asked questions about the subject no one ever questioned—the Great Terrorist Attacks of 9/11/01. But not in an arrogant way, really—just out of curiosity! I certainly didn't want to get any of my teachers in trouble with the EOB (Education Oversight Bureau), which could result in them being demoted or fired or—vaporized.

I'd thought that, well—people liked me, mostly. I was the spiky-haired girl with the big, glistening dark-brown eyes and a voice with a little catch in it and a habit of asking questions. Like a really young child with too much energy in kindergarten, whom you hope will run in circles and tire himself out. With a kind of naive obliviousness I earned good grades, so it was assumed that, despite my father being of MI caste, I would qualify for a federally mandated State Democracy University.

(That is, I was eligible for admission to one of the massive state universities. At these, a thousand students might attend a lecture, and many courses were online. Restricted universities were far smaller, prestigious and inaccessible to all but a fraction of the population; though not listed online or in any public directory, these universities were housed on "traditional" campuses in Cambridge, New Haven, Princeton, and so on, in restricted districts. Not only did

Island of Tears . . .

Oil pastel on "JR" photos

Inset panels of *Island of Tears*: India ink with Photoshop digital color

ISLAND OF *HOPE!*

POSED AS MAN FOR FIFTEEN YEARS

SECRET AT LAST DISCLOSED

Tells Ellis Island Board That She Adopted Men's Attire to Get On In the World—She Also Had a Mustache

"Frank Woodhull, 50 years old, a Canadian; thirty years in the United States; bound for New Orleans," is the record of Mary Johnson on the manifest of the SS New York. There was no question as to the sex of the passenger during the voyage. Her voice is soft and rather low. In addition her long life in male attire has trained her to take a man's part with unconscious ease. When being interrogated by Deputy Commissioner Joseph Murray she dug both hands into her trousers pockets just as a man might have done in perplexity. The discovery of her sex was made by chance. One of the Marine Hospital surgeons "on the line" was rapidly passing the New York's passengers when he came to Mary Johnson. He looked over, and deciding that she was rather slight of build for a man, asked her to step to one side, intending to put her through a tuberculosis test. It was then that the woman, knowing that discovery was imminent, confessed her sex.

"My life," she said, "has always been a struggle. I come of an English-Canadian family, and I have had most of my fight to make all alone. Thirty years ago, when I was 20, my father died and I was thrown entirely on my own resources. I came to this country a young girl and went West to make my way. For fifteen years I struggled on. The hair on my face was a misfortune. It was often the subject of rude jest and caused me endless embarrassment. The struggle was awful, but I had to live somehow, and so I went on. God knows that life has been hard, but of the hardness of those years I cannot speak.

"Then came a time fifteen years ago when I got desperate. I had been told that I looked like a man, and I knew that in Canada some women have put on men's clothes to do men's work. So the thought took shape in my mind. If these women had done it why could not I, who looked like a man? I was in California at the time. I bought men's clothes and began to wear them. Then things changed. I had prospects. My occupation I have given here as a canvasser, but I have done many things. I have sold books, lightning rods, and worked in stores. Never once was it suspected that I was other than Frank Woodhull. I have lived my life and tried to live it well. Most of the time I have been in California, but now I am going to New Orleans, where there are chances of employment.

"I have never attempted to take out citizenship papers. I knew that to do so would be either to reveal my sex or else become a lawbreaker. I have never been the latter. I did not know that there was a law against women wearing male attire in this State or I would have sailed to another port.... My folks came originally from England and it had long been my wish to go there and take a look about. So with a measure of success the longing grew and I began to save up for my holiday. I went over in the steerage two months ago and returned the same way."

The woman was assigned to a private room in the Ellis Island Hospital, and there she awaits the word of the Board of Special Inquiry that may allow her to go out and as Frank Woodhull again face the world. If discharged she must go from Ellis Island as a woman to meet the requirements of the law, but thereafter she will be free to choose her own manner of life.

—NEW YORK TIMES, Oct. 4, 1908

(Note: Frank Woodhull was welcomed into the US on Oct. 9, 1908, and proceeded by train to New Orleans, a free man.)

Island of Hope!

Oil pastel on "JR" photos

ART SPIEGELMAN has almost single-handedly brought comic books out of the toy closet and onto the literature shelves. In 1992 he won the Pulitzer Prize for his masterful Holocaust narrative *Maus*. He continued the remarkable story of his parents' survival of the Nazi regime and their lives after in *Maus II*. His comics are best known for their shifting graphic styles, their formal complexity, and controversial content. Spiegelman studied cartooning in high school and went on to study art and philosophy before becoming part of the underground comix subculture of the 1960s and '70s. He founded *Raw*, the acclaimed avant-garde comics magazine, with his wife, Françoise Mouly, in 1980. In 2005 Spiegelman was named one of *Time Magazine*'s 100 Most Influential People; in 2006 he was named to the Art Directors Club Hall of Fame; in 2007 he was made an Officier de l'Ordre des Arts et des Lettres in France; in 2011 he won the Grand Prix at the Angoulême International Comics Festival; in 2015 he was elected a member of the American Academy of Arts and Letters. His project *WORDLESS!*, a multimedia look at the history of the graphic novel, had its world premiere at the Sydney Opera House in October 2013 and its US premiere at the Brooklyn Academy of Music in January 2014. His work has been published in many periodicals, including *The New Yorker*, where he was a staff artist and writer from 1993 to 2003.

Ghost of Ellis Island

Oil pastel on "JR" photos

we not know precisely where these centers of learning were, we had not ever met anyone with degrees from them.)

In class, when I raised my hand to answer a teacher's question I often did notice classmates glancing at me—my friends, even—sort of uneasy, apprehensive: *What will Adriane say now? What is wrong with Adriane?*

There was nothing wrong with *me*! I was sure.

In fact, I was secretly proud of myself. Maybe just a little vain. Wanting to think *I am Eric Strohl's daughter.*

2.

The words were brisk, impersonal: "Strohl, Adriane. Hands behind your back."

It happened so fast. At graduation rehearsal.

So fast! I was too surprised—too scared—to think of resisting.

Except I guess that I did—try to "resist"—in childish desperation tried to duck and cringe away from the officers' rough hands on me, wrenching my arms behind my back with such force I had to bite my lips to keep from screaming.

What was happening? I could not believe it—I was being *arrested.*

Yet even in my shock, thinking, *I will not scream. I will not beg for mercy.*

My wrists were handcuffed behind my back. Within seconds I was a captive of Homeland Security.

I'd only just given my valedictorian's speech and had stepped away from the podium to come down from the auditorium stage when there came our principal, Mr. Mackay, with a peculiar expression on his face—muted anger, righteousness, but fear also—to point at me, as if the arresting officers needed him to point me out at close range.

"That is she—Adriane Strohl. That is the treasonous girl you seek."

Mr. Mackay's words were strangely stilted. He seemed very angry with me—but why? Because of my valedictory speech? But the speech had consisted entirely of questions—not answers, or accusations.

I'd known that Mr. Mackay didn't like me. He didn't know me very well but knew of me from my teachers. But it was shocking to see in an adult's face a look of genuine *hatred*.

"She was warned. They are all warned. We did our best to educate her as a patriot, but—the girl is a born *provocateur*."

Provocateur! I knew what the term meant, but I'd never heard such a charge before, applied to me.

Later I would realize that the arrest warrant must have been drawn up for me before the rehearsal—of course. Mr. Mackay and his faculty advisors must have reported me to Youth Disciplinary before they'd even heard my speech— they'd *guessed* that it would be "treasonous" and that I couldn't be allowed to give it at the graduation ceremony. And the Patriot Democracy Scholarship— that must have been a cruel trick as well.

As others stood staring at the front of the brightly lit auditorium, the arrest warrant was read to me by the female arresting officer. I was too stunned to hear most of it—only the accusing words *arrest, detention, reassignment, sentencing*—*treason-speech* and *questioning of authority*.

Quickly then, Mr. Mackay called for an "emergency assembly" of the senior class.

Murmuring and excited, my classmates settled into the auditorium. There were 322 students in the class, and like wildfire news of my arrest had spread among them within seconds.

Gravely Mr. Mackay announced from the podium that Adriane Strohl, "formerly" valedictorian of the class, had been arrested by the State on charges of treason and questioning of authority; and what was required now was a "vote of confidence" from her peers regarding this action.

That is, all members of the senior class (excepting Adriane Strohl) were to vote on whether to confirm the arrest or to challenge it. "We will ask for a show of hands," Mr. Mackay said, voice quavering with the solemnity of the occasion, "in a full, fair, and unbiased demonstration of democracy."

At this time I was positioned, handcuffed, with a wet, streaked, guilty face, at the very edge of the stage, a few yards away from the flush-faced, indignant principal. As he spoke, from time to time he glared at me, even pointing at me once with an accusing forefinger. As if my classmates needed to be reminded who the arrestee was.

Gripping my upper arms were two husky officers from the Youth Disciplinary Division of Homeland Security. They were one man and one woman, each with razor-cut hair, and they wore dark-blue uniforms and were equipped with billy clubs, Tasers, Mace, and revolvers in heavy holsters around their waists. My classmates stared wide-eyed, both intimidated and thrilled. An arrest! At school! And a show-of-hands vote, which was not a novelty in itself except on this exciting occasion.

"Boys and girls! Attention! All those in favor of Adriane Strohl being stripped of the honor of class valedictorian as a consequence of having committed treason and questioned authority, raise your hands—yes?" There was a brief stunned pause. Brief.

Hesitantly, a few hands were lifted. Then a few more.

No doubt the presence of the uniformed Youth Disciplinary officers glaring at them roused my classmates to action. Entire rows lifted their hands—*Yes!*

Here and there were individuals who shifted uneasily in their seats. They were not voting, yet. I caught the eye of my friend Carla, whose face too appeared to be wet with tears. And there was Paige all but signaling to me—*I'm sorry, Adriane. I have no choice.*

As in a nightmare, at last a sea of hands was raised against me. If there were some not voting, clasping their hands in their laps, I could not see them.

"And all opposed—no?" Mr. Mackay's voice hovered dramatically as if he were counting raised hands; in fact, there was not a single hand, of all the rows of seniors, to be seen.

"I think, then, we have a stunning example of democracy in action, boys and girls. 'Majority rule—the truth is in the numbers.'"

The second vote was hardly more than a repeat of the first: "We, the senior class of Pennsboro High School, confirm and support the arrest of the former valedictorian, Adriane Strohl, on charges of treason and questioning of authority. All those in favor . . ."

By this time the arrestee had shut her teary eyes in shame, revulsion, dread. No need to see the show of hands another time.

The officers hauled me out of the school by a rear exit, paying absolutely no heed to my protests of being in pain from the tight handcuffs and their grip on my upper arms. Immediately I was forced into an unmarked police vehicle resembling a small tank with plow-like gratings that might be used to ram against and flatten protesters.

Roughly I was thrown into the rear of the tank. The door was shut and locked. Though I pleaded with the officers, who were seated in the front of the vehicle, on the other side of a barred Plexiglas barrier, no one paid the slightest attention to me, as if I did not exist.

The officers appeared to be ST4 and ST5. It was possible that they were foreign-born indoctrinated NAS citizens who had not been allowed to learn English.

I thought, *Will anyone tell my parents where I am? Will they let me go home?*

Panicked, I thought, *Will they vaporize me?*

Heralded by a blaring siren, I was taken to a fortresslike building in the city center of Pennsboro, the local headquarters of Homeland Security Interrogation. This was a building with blank, bricked-up windows that was said to have once been a post office, before the Reconstitution of the United States into the North American States and the privatization and gradual extinction of the Postal Service.

(Many buildings from the old States remained, now utilized for very different purposes. The building to which my mother had gone for grade school had been converted to a Children's Diagnostic and Surgical Repair Facility, for instance; the residence hall in which my father had lived as a young medical student, in the years before he'd been reclassified as MI, was now a Youth Detention and Reeducation Facility. The Media Dissemination Bureau, where my brother worked, was in an old brownstone building, formerly the Pennsboro Public Library in the days when books existed to be held in the hand—and read!)

In this drafty place I was brought to an interrogation room in the Youth Disciplinary Division, forcibly seated in an uncomfortable chair with a blinding light shining in my face and a camera aimed at me, and interrogated by strangers whom I could barely see.

Repeatedly I was asked—"Who wrote that speech for you?"

No one, I said. No one wrote my speech, or helped me write it—I'd written it myself.

"Did your father, Eric Strohl, write that speech for you?"

No! My father did not.

"Did your father tell you what to write? Influence you? Are these questions your father's questions?"

No! My own questions.

"Did either of your parents help you write your speech? Influence you? Are these questions their questions?"

No, no, *no*.

"Are these treasonous thoughts their thoughts?"

I was terrified that my father, or both my parents, had been arrested, and were being interrogated too, somewhere else in this awful place. I was terrified that my father would be reclassified no longer MI but SI (Subversive Individual) or AT (Active Traitor)—crimes punishable by Deletion.

My valedictory speech was examined line by line, word by word, by the interrogators—though it was just two printed double-spaced sheets of paper with a few scrawled annotations. My computer had been seized from my locker and was being examined as well.

And all my belongings from my locker—laptop, sketchbook, backpack, cell phone, granola bars, a soiled school sweatshirt, wadded tissues—were confiscated.

The interrogators were brisk and impersonal as machines. Almost, you'd have thought they might be robot interrogators—until you saw one of them blink, or swallow, or glare at me in pity or disgust, or scratch at his nose.

(Even then, as Dad might have said, these figures could have been robots, for the most recent AI devices were being programmed to emulate idiosyncratic, "spontaneous" human mannerisms.)

Sometimes an interrogator would shift in his seat, away from the blinding light, and I would have a fleeting but clear view of a face—and what was shocking was that the face appeared to be so *ordinary*, the face of someone you'd see on a bus, or a neighbor of ours.

My valedictory address had been timed to be no more than eight minutes long. That was the tradition at our school—a short valedictorian address, and an even shorter salutatorian address. My English teacher, Mrs. Dewson, had been assigned to "advise" me—but I hadn't shown her what I'd been writing. (I hadn't shown Dad, or Mom, or any of my friends—I'd wanted to surprise them at graduation.) After a half dozen failed starts I'd gotten desperate and had the bright idea of asking numbered questions—twelve in all—of the kind my classmates might have asked if they'd had the nerve (some of these the very questions I'd asked my teachers, who had never given satisfactory answers)—like *What came before the beginning of time?*

And *What came before the Great Terrorist Attacks of 9/11?*

Our NAS calendar dates from the time of that attack, which was before my birth, but not my parents' births, and so my parents could remember a pre-NAS time when the calendar was different—time wasn't measured as just a two-digit figure but a *four-digit figure!* (Under the old, now-outlawed calendar, my mother and father had been born in what had been called the twentieth century. It was against the law to compute birthdates under the old calendar, but Daddy had told me—I'd been born in what would have been called the twenty-first century if the calendar had not been reformed.)

NAS means North American States—more formally known as RNAS, Reconstituted North American States—which came into being some years after the Great Terrorist Attacks, as a direct consequence of the Attacks, as we were taught.

Following the Attacks there was an Interlude of Indecisiveness, during which time issues of "rights" (the Constitution, the Bill of Rights, civil rights law, etc.) versus the need for Patriot Vigilance in the War Against Terror were contested, with a victory, after the suspension of the Constitution and the Bill of Rights by executive order, for PVIWAT, or Patriot Vigilance. (Yes, it is hard to comprehend. As soon as you come to the end of such a sentence, you have forgotten the beginning!)

How strange it was to think there'd been a time when the regions known as

(Reconstituted) Mexico and (Reconstituted) Canada had been separate political entities—separate from the States! On a map it seems clear, for instance, that the large state of Alaska should be connected with mainland United States, and not separated by what was formerly "Canada." This too was hard to grasp and had never been clearly explained in any of our Patriot Democracy History classes, perhaps because our teachers were not certain of the facts.

The old, "outdated" (that is, "unpatriotic") history books had all been destroyed, my father said. Hunted down in the most remote outposts—obscure rural libraries in the Dakotas, belowground stacks in great university libraries, microfilm in what had been the Library of Congress. "Outdated"/"unpatriotic" information was deleted from all computers and from all accessible memory—only reconstituted history and information were allowed, just as only the reconstituted calendar was allowed.

This was only logical, we were taught. There was no purpose to learning useless things, which would only clutter our brains like debris stuffed to overflowing in a trash bin.

But there must have been a time *before that time*—before the Reconstitution, and before the Attacks. That was what I was asking. Patriot Democracy History—which we'd had every year since fifth grade, an unchanging core of First Principles with ever-more-detailed information—was concerned only with post-Terrorist events, mostly the relations of the NAS with its numerous Terrorist Enemies in other parts of the world, and an account of the "triumphs" of the NAS in numerous wars. So many wars! They were fought now at long distance, and did not involve living soldiers, for the most part; robot-missiles were employed, and powerful bombs said to be nuclear, chemical, and biological. In our senior year of high school we were required to take a course titled Wars of Freedom—these included long-ago wars like the Revolutionary War, the Spanish-American War, World War I, World War II, the Korean War, the Vietnam War, and the more recent Afghanistan and Iraqi wars—all of which our country had won—"decisively." We were not required to learn the causes of these wars, if there were actual causes, but dates of battles and names of high-ranking generals and political leaders and presidents; these were provided in columns to be memorized for exams. The question of *Why?* was never asked—and so I'd asked it in class, and in my valedictory address. It had not occurred to me that this was *treason-speech*, or that I was *questioning authority*.

The harsh voices were taking a new approach: Was it one of my teachers who'd written the speech for me? One of my teachers who'd "influenced" me?

The thought came to me—*Mr. Mackay! I could blame him, he would be arrested...*

But I would never do such a thing, I thought. Even if the man hated me and had had me arrested for treason, I could not lie about him.

After two hours of interrogation it was decided that I was an "uncooperative subject." In handcuffs I was taken by YD officers to another floor of Homeland Security, which exuded the distressing air of a medical unit; there I was strapped down onto a movable platform and slid inside a cylindrical machine that made clanging and whirring noises close against my head; the cylinder was so small, the surface only an inch or so from my face, I had to shut my eyes tight to keep from panicking. The interrogators' voices were channeled into the machine, sounding distorted and inhuman. This was a BIM (Brain-Image Maker)—I'd only heard of these—that would determine if I was telling the truth or lying.

Did your father—or any adult—write your speech for you?
Did your father—or any adult—influence your speech?
Did your father—or any adult—infiltrate your mind with treasonous thoughts?

Barely I could answer, through parched lips—*No. No, no!*

Again and again these questions were repeated. No matter what answers I gave, the questions were repeated.

Yet more insidious were variants of these questions.

Your father, Eric Strohl, has just confessed to us, to influencing you—so you may as well confess too. In what ways did he influence you?

This had to be a trick, I thought. I stammered—*In no ways. Not ever. Daddy did not.*

More harshly the voice continued.

Your mother, Madeleine Strohl, has confessed to us, both she and your father influenced you. In what ways did they influence you?

I was sobbing, protesting—*They didn't! They did not influence me . . .*

(Of course, this wasn't true. How could any parents fail to "influence" their children? My parents had influenced me through my entire life—not so much in their speech as in their personalities. They were good, loving parents. They had taught Roddy and me: *There is a soul within. There is "free will" within. If—without—the State is lacking a soul, and there is no free will that you can see, trust the inner, not the outer. Trust the soul, not the State.* But I would not betray my parents by repeating these defiant words.)

At some point in the interrogation I must have passed out—for I was awakened by deafening noises, in a state of panic. Was this a form of torture? Noise torture? Powerful enough to burst eardrums? To drive the subject insane? We'd all heard rumors of such torture interrogations—though no one would speak openly about them. Shaken and excited, Roddy would come home from his work at MDB to tell us about certain "experimental techniques" Homeland Security was developing, using laboratory primates—until Mom clamped her hands over her ears and asked him to *please stop.*

The deafening noises stopped abruptly. The interrogation resumed.

But it was soon decided that I was too upset—my brain waves were too "agitated"—to accurately register truth or falsity, so I was removed from the cylindrical imaging machine, and an IV needle was jabbed into a vein in my arm, to inject me with a powerful "truth-serum" drug. And again the same several questions were asked, and I gave the same answers. Even in my exhausted and demoralized state I would not tell the interrogators what they wanted to hear: that my father, or maybe both my parents, had influenced me in my treasonous ways.

Or any of my teachers. Or even Mr. Mackay, my enemy.

I was strapped to a chair. It was a thick, squat "wired" chair—a kind of electric chair—that sent currents of shock through my body, painful as knife stabs. Now I was crying, and lost control of my bladder.

The interrogation continued. Essentially it was the same question, always the same question, with a variant now and then to throw me off stride.

Who wrote your speech for you? Who influenced you? Who is your collaborator in treason?

It was your brother Roderick who reported you. As a treasonmonger and a questioner of authority, you have been denounced by your brother.

I began to cry harder. I had lost all hope. Of all the things the interrogators had told me, or wanted me to believe, it was only this—that Roddy had reported me—that seemed to me possible, and not so very surprising.

I could remember how, squeezing my hand when he'd congratulated me about my good news, Roddy had smiled—his special smirk-smile just for me.

Congratulations, Addie!

JOYCE CAROL OATES is the author most recently of the novel *A Book of American Martyrs* and the story collection *DIS MEM BER*. She is a recipient of the National Book Award, the National Humanities Medal, the PEN/Malamud Award in Short Fiction, and a Lifetime Achievement Award from PEN America, among other honors. She has been a professor at Princeton University for many years and is currently Visiting Distinguished Writer in Residence in the Graduate Writing Program at New York University; in the spring term she is Visiting Professor of English at the University of California, Berkeley. Her forthcoming novel is *Hazards of Time Travel*.

Safety First

She guessed cameras, or at least microphones, were hidden in the cell. Possibly in the showers, the cafeteria, even the attorneys' meeting rooms. From the moment of her arrest until the day of the trial, she said nothing inside the prison, except immediately after her arrest, and that was only to repeat a demand for a phone call. Finally on the fifth day, when she'd been kept sleepless and could no longer be sure of time, a guard handed her a cell phone and told her she had thirty seconds, and if she didn't know the number, they weren't a phone directory, so tough luck.

Once she'd made the call, she became mute. She didn't speak to the assistant attorneys for the Northern District of Illinois sent to interrogate her, nor to the guards who summoned her for roll call four times a day, or tried to chat with her during the exercise period. Because she was a high-risk prisoner, she was kept segregated from the general population. A guard was always with her, and always tried to get her to speak.

The other women yelled at her across the wire fence that separated her from them during recreation, not rude, just curious: "Why are you here, Grandma? You kill your old man? You hold up a bank?"

One day the guards brought a woman into her cell, a prisoner with an advanced pregnancy. "You're a baby doctor, right? This woman is bleeding, she says she's in pain, says she needs to go to the hospital. You can examine her, see if she's telling the truth or casting shade."

A pregnant woman, bleeding, that wasn't so rare, could mean anything, but brought to her cell, not to the infirmary? That could mean an invitation to a charge of abuse, malpractice. She stared at the pregnant woman, saw fear in her face and something less appetizing, something like greed, or maybe unwholesome anticipation. She sat cross-legged on her bunk, closed her eyes, hands clasped in her lap.

The guard smacked her face, hard enough to knock her backward. "You think you're better than her, you're too good to touch her? Didn't you swear an oath to take care of sick people when they gave you your telescope?"

In the beginning, she had corrected such ludicrous mistakes in her head. Now, she carefully withdrew herself from even a mental engagement: arguing a point in your head meant you were tempted to argue it out loud.

She sat back up, eyes still shut, took a deep breath in, a slow breath out. Chose a poem from her interior library. German rhymes from her early childhood. English poems from her years in London schools. *Über allen Gipfeln ist Ruh* and *Does the road wind up-hill all the way?*

When her lawyer finally arrived, three weeks after her arrest, she still didn't speak inside the small room set aside for attorney-client meetings. The lawyer explained that it had taken them that long to discover where the doctor was being held. "They're fighting very dirty," the lawyer said.

The doctor nodded. *Come back with an erasable board*, she wrote on an edge of the lawyer's legal pad. When the lawyer had read the message, the doctor tore off the handwritten scrap and swallowed it.

She was being held without bond because she was considered a flight risk, the lawyer explained. "We tried to fight for bail, but these new Homeland Security courts have more power than ordinary federal courts. We are challenging the constitutionality of both your arrest and your post-arrest treatment. We have our own investigators tracking down information and witnesses in your support. Keep heart: there are hundreds of thousands of people in America and across the world who are aware of your arrest and are protesting it."

After the lawyer left, the guards took the doctor to a new cell, one with three other inmates. Those women were noisy. One had a small radio she played at top volume at all hours. Another heard voices telling her to pray or scream or, on their third day together, to attack the doctor. The radio player was shocked into calling for a guard. When no one came, the radio player grabbed the woman hearing voices; the fourth cellmate joined her. Together they subdued the voice hearer.

"You gotta file a complaint," the radio player said. "You can't let people be trying to kill you. That's what they want, you know, they told us they hoping you'll die, or that we'd annoy you so much, you'd attack one of us. They didn't say you was an old lady who wouldn't hurt a flea. So you gotta file a complaint."

The doctor almost touched the radio player's shoulder, remembered in time that a touch could be turned into a sexual caress by clever camera editing, and clasped her hands in front of her. The following day, she was back in her old cell, one bed, just her, alone.

After that, she was sent to exercise with the general population. The woman who'd attacked her tried to do so again, joined by several others who liked to prey on the old or friendless—including the woman who'd been brought to her with a problem pregnancy. "She's a doctor but she only treat people with money!"

The radio player intervened. She had plenty of friends or at least followers within the prison, and she summoned enough help that the attackers withdrew.

"You a doctor?" the radio player demanded. "Why you in here?"

The doctor shook her head. Because they were outside, presumably far from microphones—although these days you probably were never far from a camera or a mike—she risked a few words.

"I don't know." Her voice was hoarse from disuse.

"How come you don't know? You know if you killed a patient, right? You know if you stole money from Medicare. So what you do?"

The doctor couldn't help laughing. "True, I'd know if I did either of those things. I didn't do them. I don't know why the United States government arrested me."

"You got some big fish pissed off," the radio player nodded sagely.

After that, people approached the doctor during exercise in the yard. The radio player served as an informal triage nurse. Swollen nodes in necks or armpits, varicose veins, heavy periods, no periods, bruises, knife wounds.

The doctor had limited ability to treat, no way to conduct a proper exam, but she would recommend the infirmary or a demand for hospital care or, in most cases, wait it out—which is what the inmates would have to do in any event, even the women whose swollen abdomens didn't indicate pregnancy but ovarian tumors.

Finally, seven months and twenty-three days after her arrest and arraignment, the trial began.

The clerk of the court: "Docket number 137035, *People v. Charlotte R. Herschel, MD*, Homeland Security Court, Justice Montgomery Sessions presiding.

"Dr. Charlotte Herschel is accused of violating United States Act 312698, An Act to Guarantee the Security of the Borders of the United States, known as the 'Keep America Free Act,' paragraphs 7.97 through 7.183 inclusive, relating to the medical treatment of undocumented aliens and to the willful concealment of undocumented aliens from the federal government. She is charged further with violating paragraphs 16.313 through 16.654, relating to the sanctity of the life of all United States–born citizens, from the moment of conception."

Justice Sessions: "Today's hearing is held in camera. Because the Security of Borders Act addresses Homeland Security, neither journalists nor civilian observers can be present. I must ask the bailiff to clear the courtroom of everyone but the lawyers and their assistants."

Some forty people from the Ex-Left were in the courtroom. Predictably, they raised outraged howls at being ordered to leave. In fact, many of them lay limp on the floor. The bailiff and federal marshals didn't suppress grins as they banged the protestors into the benches or against the doorjamb on their way out of court.

About the only legislation the 115th Congress had passed was the Keep America Free Act, and its follow-on, the law funding the Homeland Security courts. Dr. Herschel's case was one of the first to be heard in a Homeland court.

The law was sketchy on what defendants could do to support themselves.

They could not have a trial by jury—a tribunal of five federal judges was empaneled for each trial. Defendants could call witnesses, but it wasn't clear on the presence of citizens in the courtroom. Justice Sessions had decided that matter, at least for Dr. Herschel's trial.

From the moment of her arrest, Dr. Herschel's case had been drawing attention from the Extreme Left and their fake news machines. The *New York Times* huffed and puffed so furiously that a Real News cartoon, showing the paper as the Big Bad Wolf unable to blow over the government's case, went viral. Of course, in response, the Ex-Left tried to paint the government as a trough full of pigs, but everyone agreed that the *Times* response was a lame knockoff of the Real News original.

However, the *Times* coverage meant that the Ex-Left fat cats put up so much money for the doctor's defense that Ruth Lebeau had agreed to take the case. Lebeau was a formidable constitutional lawyer with a team of experienced research lawyers at her side. Except for the court reporter and Dr. Herschel, she was the only woman in today's courtroom, and the sole African American, but she seemed to pay no attention to that distinction, nor to the insults lobbed by Real News, comparing her to a talking chimpanzee.

Opening statement of Melvin Coulter, federal attorney for the Northern District of Illinois:

"Dr. Herschel is well known to federal agents throughout the Northern District. She runs what she calls a medical clinic, but is in reality a squalid den where the most vile crimes are committed. She not only harbors known enemies of the United States, but is a self-proclaimed murderer of the most innocent lives in our midst. So heinous are the crimes, and so intent is this *doctor* on keeping them from public view, that she spent a small fortune in turning her abattoir into an armed fortress."

Coulter droned on for over an hour. Ruth Lebeau, dressed in navy suiting with an Elizabethan collar framing her face, made a few notes, but spent most of Coulter's speech either smiling reassuringly at her client, or mouthing comments to her second, who seemed to find Lebeau very witty.

Dr. Herschel was a small woman, with graying hair cut close to her head. She wore no makeup and no jewelry. The court reporter thought she looked like the kind of doctor you could trust, not the formidable monster described in the government's brief. It troubled the reporter that the doctor didn't look at Coulter or Sessions during the opening statement. The reporter believed innocent people could stare down their accusers. She didn't know that sociopaths could also stare down their accusers and that innocent people might be looking at their clasped hands so that judge and prosecutor couldn't see the furious contempt in their eyes.

When the prosecutor sat down, Ruth Lebeau made her own opening statement. She sketched Dr. Herschel's history: an orphan, a refugee, who had dedicated her life to the health and welfare of women in the United States. The many awards she had received for her humanitarian work, for her innovations in perinatal medicine and in surgery. Lebeau spoke about the Constitution as well, and how the law under which Dr. Herschel was charged set up two classes of people.

"We're skating perilously close to Nuremberg laws here. Americans reject the idea that one class of person has higher value than other classes, whether the division is between black and white, Christian and Jew, foreign-born or native born. We will show that Dr. Herschel's whole life and career have been devoted to caring for women and children who most need help, and that she has used her own resources to bring free medical care to Americans who can least afford it, but need it most."

The court adjourned for lunch. Melvin Coulter was seen eating with Justice Sessions and the other judges on the tribunal. A photograph of them together in the Potawatomi Club circulated on Fake News websites, but Real News assured Americans that there was nothing wrong with two old friends meeting for lunch. The Ex-Left also put up videos of the federal marshals dragging protestors from the courtroom; Real News showed patriots cheering the marshals.

In the afternoon, the evidence part of the trial began. The government had been surveilling Dr. Herschel and her clinic for many months. Even before

Look Away

Oil on canvas

BEVERLY McIVER is widely acknowledged as a significant presence in contemporary American art and has charted a new direction as an African American female artist. She is committed to producing art that examines racial, gender, social, and occupational identity. McIver was named one of the "Top Ten in Painting" in *Art in America* in 2011. *Raising Renee*, a feature-length documentary produced in association with HBO that tells the story of the impact of McIver's promise to care for her sister when their mother dies, was nominated for an Emmy Award and is now streaming on Amazon Prime. McIver's work is in such collections as the North Carolina Museum of Art, the Weatherspoon Art Museum, the Baltimore Museum of Art, the NCCU Museum of Art, the Asheville Art Museum, the Nasher Museum of Art at Duke University, and the Mint Museum, among others. McIver has received grants and awards including the 2017 Rome Prize Fellowship, a 2017 award from the American Academy of Arts and Letters, an Anonymous Was A Woman Award, a John Simon Guggenheim Fellowship, a Radcliffe Institute Fellowship from Harvard University, a Marie Walsh Sharpe Foundation Award, a Distinguished Alumni Award from Pennsylvania State University, a Louis Comfort Tiffany Foundation Award, and a Creative Capital grant.

Loving in Black & White

Oil on canvas

the Keep America Free Act, ICE agents had paid particular attention to her Damen Avenue clinic because she treated so many low-income women, not just immigrants from Muslim countries and Mexico, but poor Americans as well.

Coulter began with photographs of the Radbuka-Herschel Family Clinic projected onto the three screens in the courtroom. These days the clinic was padlocked, the windows covered with obscene graffiti, including swastikas and "death camp" in jagged capital letters, but the pictures had been taken during the surveillance and data-gathering phase of the case.

The clinic stood near the corner of Damen and Irving Park Road in Chicago. The sidewalks were dirty, the nearby storefronts run-down or boarded over. The court watched two women in head scarves approach the building, one with toddlers in a double stroller, the other carrying an infant while an older child held her skirt. The women glanced around furtively, then rang the clinic bell.

"You can see the armor-plated glass"—Coulter tapped the windows in the photograph—"and the video cameras. Once the women gained entrance through the first door, they were sealed in the equivalent of an airlock while clerks videoed them. Only then did they gain admittance to the death chambers inside."

The testimony of all the Immigration and Customs Enforcement agents, along with the FBI, took close to two weeks to hear. The most dramatic testimony actually came from one of Dr. Herschel's own nurses: Leah Shazar had worn a tiny body camera to record many of Dr. Herschel's patients and procedures, even patients she herself was examining.

When Ruth Lebeau rose to cross-examine her, Shazar broke down into sobs. "They threatened to deport my own mother, my sisters, back to the men who raped them. What else could I do?"

"Find someone to help you fight them," Lebeau said. "What did you think you were doing to the patients entrusted to your care?"

After Shazar's weeping went into its second inarticulate minute, Justice Sessions ruled that Lebeau was badgering the witness and to stop such an emotional line of questioning. When Shazar stepped out of the witness box, she tried to approach the doctor, but Dr. Herschel turned her head away and refused to look at her.

The court reporter didn't know how to react. If she'd been a patient in the clinic, she sure wouldn't have wanted her private business shown in a courtroom. And had it really been fair for the FBI to coerce her into recording people? But the nurse was truly sorry—shouldn't Dr. Herschel at least accept Shazar's apology?

During Shazar's testimony, Coulter showed videos that she had taken. "Yes, Dr. Herschel routinely performed abortions in her abattoir. And she helped illegal immigrants avoid federal agents."

The five male judges, the bailiff, the clerk, and the two armed marshals gasped in delighted indignation as a camera focused on a woman's vulva, where the doctor was inserting a speculum. A nurse, back to the camera, was bathing the woman's forehead with a towel. After a moment, blood flowed. The camera zoomed in on a blood clot, which Coulter identified as a dead baby.

After letting Justice Sessions and the rest of the all-male court lick their lips for a long moment, Coulter showed a video of the alley behind the clinic. A dark van was backed up to the clinic's rear door.

"We can't see who is coming out at this particular moment, but we do know that Dr. Herschel used this and other vehicles to whisk away illegals before ICE agents could demand their papers. Of course, once we spotted the ruse, we stopped the vans and arrested the occupants."

Here, the video showed stalwart Immigration and Customs Enforcement agents stopping several different vehicles. They pulled out women and children, cuffed them, and thrust them into government cars. Dr. Herschel's lawyer directed a contemptuous smile at the prosecution table and made a point of writing an exceptionally long note. She whispered something to her own assistant, a young man whose impeccable tailoring matched her own. The young man bit back a guffaw, earning a frown from Justice Sessions.

The final charge against the doctor claimed she'd helped spirit away the notorious immigration activist Sofia Pacheco. Since going onto the FBI's Ten Most Wanted list, Pacheco had been hidden in churches and attics by sympathizers across the nation. Every time the government seemed poised to make an arrest, it turned out they had the wrong information, or, worse, someone at the FBI or ICE had leaked the raid and given Pacheco time to make her getaway.

Finally, thirteen months ago, they were sure they had cornered Pacheco in a Chicago garden shop. The shop made a delivery of gladioli and daylilies to Dr. Herschel inside a long carton; Pacheco, apparently, lay underneath the flowers.

At the clinic, someone, perhaps the doctor, perhaps one of her staff, styled Pacheco's hair to resemble the doctor's own, streaked it with white dye, put her in a lab coat, and brazenly sent her outside.

"The agent detailed to follow the doctor had stepped away from his post for three minutes—even our ICE agents sometimes have a call from nature" (laughter from Sessions and the other four judges).

"The clinic staff seemed to be watching our agent, because they used that window of time to send Pacheco out; she drove off in Dr. Herschel's own Audi."

The Audi had been found in the meatpacking district; the doctor was in surgery all day and claimed to know nothing about Pacheco. "Of course she knew about Pacheco: why else did she leave her Audi at the clinic instead of driving herself to the hospital?"

Ruth Lebeau cross-examined the agent to no avail: Wasn't it true that Dr. Herschel often used a car service between the clinic and the hospital? Wasn't it true that she was often in the operating room for ten or even fifteen hours, so that she was too fatigued to drive herself at the end of surgery?

"You're arguing generalities," Justice Sessions rebuked Lebeau. "We're looking at a specific day and a particular crime."

At the end of the eighth day, the prosecution rested. "The government has irrefutable evidence that warrants that Dr. Herschel be stripped of her U.S. citizenship. However, we believe her crimes rise to the level of deliberate treason against the United States by refusing to acknowledge the power of the government to pass the Keep America Free Act, and to enforce its provisions."

Coulter wiped his mouth with the red handkerchief he kept in his breast pocket for such moments and resumed his seat. Justice Sessions adjourned the court and said they would hear the defense in the morning. He and Melvin

Coulter rode down the elevator together and were later seen yet again at the Potawatomi Club, laughing over their drinks—martini for the prosecutor, iced tea for the abstemious justice.

All during the final day of the prosecution's case, Coulter had been smirking with his juniors at the prosecution table, watching as Ruth Lebeau sent her own juniors out in flocks.

In the morning, it became clear that the defense was in trouble, and why: their key witnesses had disappeared. The detective V. I. Warshawski, who had gathered much of the defense's evidence, was in prison herself: she'd been arrested two days earlier, charged under the same sections of the Keep America Free Act as Dr. Herschel.

The court reporter thought Dr. Herschel was going to faint. Her dark, vivid face turned pale and waxy and she swayed in her seat. Ruth Lebeau, her attorney, asked if she needed a break.

"I require water," the doctor said.

Ruth Lebeau's chief assistant produced a large thermos of hot water from his case and poured a cup for the doctor. Since the rest of her witnesses had been disappeared, Lebeau called the doctor to the stand.

As the doctor spoke, her vocal cords gradually regained their flexibility. The court reporter had strained to understand her at first, but after half an hour, the grating harshness left the doctor's voice. She spoke clearly, almost musically: the reporter realized it was a pleasure to listen to her after all the men she'd been recording during the prosecution phase. Too much bullying and swagger, none of this evenness, this effort to be clear that the doctor exhibited.

"I treat everyone who comes to my clinic," Dr. Herschel said. "I don't need to see a driver's license or a passport to diagnose measles or an ectopic pregnancy."

On cross-examination, Coulter demanded to know why she'd refused to treat the pregnant woman who'd been brought to her jail cell.

"I am curious about your knowledge of this woman," the doctor said. "Did you direct the guards to bring her to my cell?"

The members of the tribunal seemed to gasp, but Justice Sessions said, "You are on the stand, doctor. You don't get to ask questions."

The doctor bowed her head.

"You must answer the attorney," Sessions said.

"The woman was not pregnant," Dr. Herschel said.

"You refused to examine her, so how can you possibly know this?" Coulter asked.

"How many pregnant women have you examined in your legal career, Mr. Coulter?" the doctor said. "Oh, yes, I must not ask you questions. But we will assume it is one woman, your wife, who produced two children with you. I have seen thousands. I know the difference between an abdomen with a fetus inside it, and a body with a pillow buckled to it. Perhaps you would have been fooled, but I was not."

"You can't know that!" Coulter snapped.

The doctor shrugged but remained silent.

"Have you nothing to say?" Sessions demanded.

Before Lebeau could jump to her feet to remind the court that Coulter had made a statement, not asked a question, the doctor said, "I have lived a long life. I have seen governments taken over by ravening weasels, I have watched them incite a bored or ignorant or fearful mob to violence. That you would bribe or coerce a woman to pretend a pregnancy does not surprise me, but it does sicken me."

Coulter sat down again. There was a moment of silence and then Ruth Lebeau asked the prosecution to put up one of their videos of a couple of women being pulled from an SUV in handcuffs. She zoomed in on their faces and asked the doctor if she recognized them.

"Yes, they were patients, first in my clinic, and then, because the daughter had complications, I saw her in surgery at Beth Israel."

"And can you identify them, by name, I mean?" Lebeau asked.

"I can, but I will not. It is enough that these strange men can look at them and know they sought medical help, but I will not violate their privacy further by naming them."

"Did you know that the older woman was Justice Sessions's housekeeper?" Lebeau asked.

The doctor's eyes widened: the court reporter, barely keeping back a gasp herself, thought the doctor hadn't known. "I did not know that, but I do not discriminate among those I treat."

"And did you know the daughter, whose abortion you performed, had been raped by the justice?"

At that, Sessions slammed his gavel and demanded an end to the proceedings. "The defense will rest. They cannot call independent witnesses to this calumny—"

"Yes, we cannot call your housekeeper, who looked after you for twenty-three years, because she was deported last week, was she not?" Lebeau said.

"That was a decision by Immigration and Customs, not by me. The court is adjourned for today. The tribunal will meet tomorrow to discuss a verdict."

The court reporter couldn't sleep that night. She was shocked by today's testimony. Abortion was evil, and the doctor was wicked to perform them. But Justice Sessions—when the black lady lawyer said he'd raped his housekeeper's daughter, he'd ended the trial. If he'd been innocent, surely he would have denied the accusation.

The court reporter had a high security clearance, which required her to sign papers promising never to speak to anyone of the proceedings she attended. She thought of her oath, she thought of the doctor, the presiding justice, the men licking their lips at the video of the naked woman's vagina.

At five in the morning, she got up and went down the street to her local drugstore. The clerk was yawning, barely awake, counting the seconds until her overnight shift would end. The reporter, her hands shaking, paid cash for a cheap phone. She made a call to the cousin who had helped get her the job with the federal courts.

In the morning, the tribunal met for less than an hour before summoning the prisoner. The court reporter could see that the doctor had probably not slept any more than she had herself. The doctor's walnut-colored skin was pale, her eyes a pair of black holes sunk deep in her face.

Justice Sessions said, "The court has voted four to one to find you guilty on all counts under the Keep America Free Act. We debated stripping you of your citizenship and deporting you, but we are well aware that your native country, Austria, is prepared to make you an international heroine and martyr, and so we are sentencing you to natural life in a federal prison in the United States. The Federal Bureau of Prisons will inform your attorney when they have decided where to house you. For now, you will remain in Chicago in the care of the Metropolitan Correctional Center. Court is adjourned."

A marshal seized Dr. Herschel and marched her through the side door that led to the fenced-in yard at the back of the building where prisoners were transferred into the buses that returned them to the various jails around town.

Her lawyer and the lawyer's chief assistant walked with the doctor as far as the exit: they weren't permitted beyond the doorway. As she tried to thank the lawyer, the doctor seemed to stumble. The assistant attorney caught her as she fainted.

He pulled his thermos from his briefcase and unscrewed the top. No one could agree what happened next, but one of the marshals thought the young lawyer poured a glass bottle labeled "sugar" into the thermos. Smoke billowed out. It covered the doctor, the lawyer, and the marshal, and spread through the fenced-in courtyard. The marshals pulled their weapons and began firing into the thick fog, but someone screamed: they'd hit the driver of the prison van, who'd been standing behind it waiting to lock the doctor inside. By the time the fog cleared, the prison van was gone.

The van was discovered at Belmont Harbor on the Chicago shore of Lake Michigan. The Coast Guard began a search of all boats on the lake, but they didn't find the doctor, the lawyer's chief assistant, or the federal marshal who'd handcuffed the doctor as she was taken from the courtroom. No one noticed that the court reporter had also disappeared.

Months went by; the Department of Justice kept close surveillance on anyone who might be in touch with the doctor, even the imprisoned V. I. Warshawski, who'd been the doctor's close friend for decades. They monitored the doctor's family members in Canada, her medical colleagues, even some of her high-profile patients. No one spoke of her. No one heard from her.

Time passed. Crops were rotting in the fields because the immigrants who used to harvest them were denied entry or had been deported from a safe America. Construction sites languished. The 117th Congress overturned the most stringent sections of the Keep America Free Act, although the criminal penalties for performing abortions on U.S.-born women remained in place.

Somewhere along the way, V. I. Warshawski was released from prison. She, too, disappeared without a trace, despite the FBI's continued monitoring of her actions.

Every now and then, the FBI or ICE would follow up on a report of a small, black-eyed doctor performing miracle cures among indigenous Americans, or in Congo or Central America. She had a few assistants, who helped trace rapists or murderers or thieves in whatever village or jungle they found themselves, but by the time U.S. agents were dispatched across the deserts and mountains, these legendary figures had moved on.

SARA PARETSKY's husband describes her as a pit dog, willing to go against anyone as long as they are at least four times her size. This means she's often exhausted, as is her iconic fictional detective, V. I. Warshawski, star of eighteen of Paretsky's twenty novels. The granddaughter of undocumented immigrants who escaped certain death by seeking refuge in America, Paretsky believes our country thrives on immigrants and diversity. She has worked for women's reproductive rights since 1970, and clings to a romantic notion that the Framers were serious when they said the Constitution exists to "establish justice and promote the general welfare." The recipient of many awards, she is one of four living writers to hold both the Cartier Diamond Dagger and the Edgar Grand Master.

Bystanders (April 2003)

A Wednesday evening, the air cool and diaphanous. Everyone in Greenwich Village seemed to have taken to the sidewalks. Dave Soloff and Rachel Tobias made their way down West Fourth Street toward their gallery rendezvous with Rachel's parents, who were grudgingly making the trip from the Upper West Side at Rachel's insistence.

She had seen the listing in the *New Yorker* and had read the notice aloud to Dave four nights earlier in his Hudson Street sublet as they ate Chinese take-out from the restaurant they had nicknamed Hunan Resources.

"'*These starkly juxtaposed photographic images of human rights violations, assembled and mounted by Jacobi in a muted, claustral, winding passage, cut across all ideological and geographical borders, from WTC to Palestine, and together make up a kind of* Family of Man *of suffering. Warning: the images are extremely disturbing, and not for the delicate.*' It's all photographs by different photographers, amateur and professional. It was put together by somebody named Lilith Jacobi. Have you heard of her?"

"Nope," Dave said. "Great name, though. Is it going to tell us anything we don't already know?"

"We should bring Abe," she said.

Rachel and her father, Abe Tobias—legendary book publisher, World War II veteran, and staunch Israel supporter—had been conducting an escalating, monthlong guerrilla war of words over the Iraq invasion. In the two years since Dave and Rachel had graduated from Hollister College, Dave had sat through enough dinner-table battles in the labyrinthine apartment where Rachel lived with her parents to recognize a disaster in the making. Rachel called the building the *Angstschloss*—the Castle of Anxiety. It certainly was that for Dave, whose part-time job at a down-market travel magazine was a ready target for Abe between skirmishes with his headstrong daughter.

"Come on," Dave said. "You'd kill each other."

"Abe is exactly who needs to see this," she said.

Dave dropped it in hopes that she might forget the idea. But she didn't, and that next Wednesday found them walking through the Village streets on their way to the gallery.

Since the 9/11 attacks nineteen months earlier, the lift of possibility that New York offered on a spring evening, the intimation that any turn of a corner could open a new chapter, was not quite enough to drown out the lingering sense that something loud was about to happen overhead. When Rachel was very young, the city was still dangerous in an old-fashioned way; there were pockets of unreconstructed poverty and crime, homeless people sleeping on sidewalk grates, and lunatics roving the streets and the subways. Still, in those young days one could prepare oneself with knowledge and lore to minimize the possibility of trouble. That was now officially a thing of the past. An airplane could plow into a building right above your head. But on an evening like this, despite the ambient anxiety, the reflexive hunch of the psychic shoulders against the coming blow, the Village exhaled poetry along its tree-lined streets and behind its charming brick façades, and you could almost forget about a lot of things.

"Jesus," Rachel said as they walked down West Fourth Street. "I want to live down here. The Upper West Side is so . . . literal."

"Literal?" Dave said.

"It's like . . . 'You want living space? Here's a big cube divided into little cubes, on rectangular blocks . . .' There are no twists and turns. Like, you'd never have Chumley's on the Upper West Side."

"Well . . . ," Dave said, "you've got Zabar's."

"You've got the White Horse," Rachel said.

"You've got the Museum of Natural History."

"No fair."

"What do you mean, 'no fair'?"

"Look," Rachel said, "you've got Music Inn."

Across West Fourth, the gated storefront, its windows crowded with strange instruments and African masks and junk, a throwback to an earlier era. "Great place. Hey," he said, pointing up at a yellow sign hanging overhead, "we've got Tio Pepe's. This place has been here since the Huguenots. I came here on a field trip for eighth-grade Spanish class."

"Little Jersey boy. Little bridge-and-tunnel rat."

They arrived at Sixth Avenue, with its traffic streaming uptown, and the same sudden vacuum hit them both in the stomach, the absence of the towers in the distance against the dimming sky.

"Let's cut across West Third," Dave said. "We can see what used to be world-famous Folk City, where Bob Dylan had his first New York appearance, except Folk City was in a totally different place when that happened."

"Still cool, though," Rachel said.

From West Third they turned south on MacDougal, where the tenements along the narrow street disguised the hole in the sky. They strolled along as the warmth of the day faded from the sidewalks. Across Houston, they entered the rust belt of SoHo, clanking over the metal doors in the cement and walking around the loading platforms with their looming lofts overhead, cutting left on Prince Street. On Mercer they found the address, a loft building with galleries on every floor. They stood outside for a moment, looking around.

"It's so fucking beautiful out," Dave said.

"I know," Rachel said. "I don't want to go inside."

Abe and Ruth were waiting for them upstairs. "Good, you're here," Abe said. "I'm going to find the men's before we descend into the abyss."

"I think it's over there, Abe," Ruth said.

"Hold my jacket," Abe said, handing his sports coat to Ruth, who shook her head and gave Rachel a look as he walked off.

"He's in a state," Ruth said. "You know how he can be."

"Oy," Rachel said. "This will be fun."

"Why don't you two get started going through the exhibit and we'll catch up with you. Abe will be a few minutes."

An artist's statement stenciled on a wall began by asking viewers to take a moment to prepare themselves for the images they were about to see. *"As a Jew, and as a human being,"* the statement read, *"I have a right and a responsibility to ask when enough will be enough—not just for the people of Israel under siege, but for the people of Palestine. Not just for those who lost their future at the World Trade Center on September 11, but for those who lose their future every day in Lebanon and Afghanistan, in Iraq and Jerusalem. When will we stop using righteous victimhood as an excuse for barbarism?"*

They entered the exhibition through a narrow opening into a darkened, curving, carpeted passageway; along the walls hung spotlit images, color photographs blown up so large that they backed the viewers up, crowded them.

The first image showed a body on a sidewalk littered with ash and shards of glass, blood spattered out onto the cement as if from a broken bottle. The body had twisted at an impossible angle but the head had landed face-up on the ground, still recognizable as a head, although the back of it had been smashed and sat in a puddle of raspberry-colored blood, with the face peering up at the sky as if out of a shallow bowl of soup. The tag read: *"WTC; 9/11."*

"Oh no," Rachel said under her breath. She gagged and Dave put his hand on her arm; she waved him off.

Next to it on the same wall loomed a five-foot-square image of a small boy, plainly dead but with his eyes open and a smile on his face, all the flesh on the front of his chest gone, ribs and intestines visible. The legend on the wall, neatly printed on a small card, read: *"Baghdad, March 27, 2003."*

The viewers were led onward to a mountain road, where a group of soldiers had gathered, laughing, in a semicircle around a man contorted in agony on the ground. The rags around his midsection were drenched deep maroon with blood; the legend on the wall said the American-backed Northern Alliance soldiers had castrated and eviscerated him but he was still alive and was begging the soldiers to shoot him. Next to this, a closeup of a man's black boot on the ground next to a confused mess of crimson meat and hair, and the legend reading *"Woman executed by Taliban for adultery, Kandahar, October 1999."*

Sounds of weeping, involuntary expressions of shock and anger could be heard throughout the winding passageway. Around the next bend, another pair of huge photos, at first impossible to believe, a man whose head was already violated, partly off skew from his spine, his eyes open and a huge blade making its way into his neck, gouts of blood up the arm of the figure who was cutting the head off, head held by the hair, still plainly conscious as he was butchered alive.

Dave and Rachel were waiting as Abe and Ruth emerged from the exhibit.

"Let's get out of here," Abe said. His face was red and he dabbed at his nose with a rumpled handkerchief.

"The elevators have been slow," Dave said.

"Then let's take the stairs," Abe said. "Do they have stairs in this place? Excuse me," he said to a woman with a laminated ID tag around her neck, "did anyone think to put stairs in this building? How do we get out of here?"

The woman smiled faintly and pointed to red EXIT letters plainly visible over a fire door, and Abe began walking toward it, leaving the others to follow.

They walked two blocks to a restaurant where Rachel had made dinner reservations. Inside, an efficient young woman showed them to their table and handed out menus. As they were sitting down Abe said to her, "Bring me some club soda, please."

"Your server will be with you in a moment," she said, and walked away.

"You have to see a specialist to get a glass of seltzer in this place," Abe said.

Little by little, the familiarity of being in a restaurant, handling menus, sitting at a table, hearing other people talking, began to relax them. Dave asked if they'd had trouble finding the gallery. Ruth said no, they had just been a little late getting out of the apartment. Abe hadn't been feeling particularly well.

"What's wrong?" Rachel said.

Ruth said, "Nothing, for God's sake, Rachel. It was nothing. He was just feeling a little slow on his feet."

"Don't get old," Abe said. "Even if you have the opportunity."

Rachel frowned and studied the menu. Complaining about being old had never been in Abe's repertoire, and it had come up several times recently.

Their waiter was thin and pale, with three small earrings going up the edge of his right ear. Dave ordered crab cakes, Rachel ordered a salade niçoise, Ruth a bowl of gazpacho anglaise, a name that made Rachel laugh.

When the waiter's attention turned to Abe, Abe said, "Club soda, that's all." The others looked at him with mild surprise and puzzlement.

"Abe, eat something," Ruth said.

"Ruth," he said, raising his fingertips an inch off the table where his hand rested. He turned to regard the waiter and repeated, "Club soda," managed a slight smile and a nod, the server said, "Very good," and walked off.

After a few moments in which nobody seemed to know where to start, Dave jumped in and said, "I've never seen anything like that."

"Really?" Abe said, wiping his nose again with the handkerchief. "Where have you been?"

Undaunted, Dave said, "I mean with everything arranged together like that. The impact of it together . . ."

"I know what you mean," Abe said, suddenly angry. "It's the same story, over and over: everything is the Jews' fault, and the Americans' fault. Everything bad comes from America and the Jews."

Dave was taken aback at the intensity. Ruth sat there, nodding, which surprised him, and Rachel was getting ready to say something.

"I don't think she was saying that," Dave said. "I think she's saying that after a certain point it doesn't matter whose fault it is."

Abe gave Ruth a significant look across the table.

"But it *is* our fault . . . ," Rachel began.

"Rachel . . . ," Abe said, sharply, "please . . ."

"*What*," Ruth said to her daughter, "is our fault?"

"Operating as if the whole world is our plantation."

"Please . . . ," Abe repeated, more urgently.

"Wait . . . ," Dave said.

"We fund Israel while the Palestinians live in tents and hovels," she began.

"They always lived in tents and hovels," Abe said.

"No they *didn't*, Dad."

"Look," Dave said, "before we get into World War Three, I think what the artist is saying is that there has to be a recognition of our common situation, instead of finger-pointing all the time."

"David," Ruth said, "are you saying that it *doesn't* matter who committed an atrocity? Nobody is responsible for their actions?"

"I think she's putting it in a broader context, like with the Gandhi quote she put in about how if everything is an eye for an eye and a tooth for a tooth we'd all end up blind and toothless."

"So what's the alternative?" Abe said. "You sit there and let people round you up and put you in boxcars because you want the moral high ground, and then there's one blind, toothless person—he's called a scapegoat—and everybody else is walking around singing *'Deutschland über alles'*? People have to take responsibility to figure out who is right and who is wrong. People don't have automatically equal claims just because somebody got hurt. That's what the Holocaust denier Nazi bastards like this guy in England always bring up the bombing of Dresden, like it gives them some kind of parity, and that's just what this woman is saying, and it's a lot of shit. Who started it? *Who started it?*"

Abe's face was red, and his hands were shaking, and people from other tables were looking.

"Drink some water, Abe," Ruth was saying.

"Where's water? Do you see water? You have to die in this place before somebody brings you something to drink."

At that moment the waiter was approaching their table with their drinks. The four of them sat silently as he distributed the glasses and asked, "Everything okay? Do you need anything?" Abe waved him off, reached for his glass, and drank.

"But," Dave began again, "someone has to let go of the rope sometime, right? Someone has to say it doesn't matter—we don't want to live this way. Can we all agree we don't want to live this way?"

"Try doing that when someone is walking toward you with a suicide bomb," Abe said. "What are you going to do? Are you going to shoot him or are you going to let him blow you up?"

"But what led up to that point?" Rachel said. "This is what nobody asks.

People don't just go around blowing each other up for no reason. There's a context . . ."

"I don't know if I agree with that," Dave said.

"What are you talking about?" Rachel said.

"I think Jacobi's saying that the broader context is our common humanity, and we can choose to either have the killing define our common humanity, or the refusal to kill can define our humanity."

"That's not badly put, David," Ruth said.

"That is such a privileged position to take," Rachel said. "You're out of the context and you don't have to deal with the reality, so you say everybody should just stop all that silly fighting . . ."

"People have a right to defend themselves," Abe said. "When someone is walking up to you with a bomb it doesn't matter that his kids don't have new shoes or his brother has a hangnail."

"Oh," Rachel said, "then context *doesn't* matter? First you say, 'Who started it?' and now it doesn't matter?"

"Don't twist what I'm saying, young lady."

Rachel looked at him, mouth open, half smiling. "Twist it?" she said. "It's all twisted up on its own. I don't have to twist anything."

"Rachel . . . ," Ruth said.

"When we bomb people and destroy their houses that's okay, but when the powerless fight back that's terrorism."

"Stop it this minute, Rachel," Abe said, his voice quaking with rage and his face deep red. "Ruth, let's go." His hands were shaking as he reached around for his wallet.

"Abe," Ruth said, looking from Dave to Rachel and back again, as if for help. "Let's all just take a few deep breaths . . ."

Abe had pulled out his wallet and was counting out three twenty-dollar bills. "This will be enough," he said, putting them on the table. "Come on." He pushed his chair out from the table.

"Abe," Ruth began, "can we just take a minute here . . ."

"Come on, Ruth," he said, standing up. Rachel, as stubborn as her father, sat there without a word. "Let the dust settle."

"Abe," Dave said, "can we just maybe shelve this and finish out the evening?"

Abe was helping Ruth up from her chair. "Do you have your bag?"

"Yes," she said, with muted annoyance, tired, shaking her head a little.

Abe started for the door, and Ruth said, "I don't know what else to do. You spoke very harshly to him, Rachel."

"*I* spoke harshly to *him*?" Rachel said.

Ruth held up her hand. "I'll call tomorrow," she said. "Goodnight, David," and headed off after Abe.

Dave and Rachel sat there as if underneath a giant bell, its sound fading slowly away. Their server approached after a moment, saying, "Is everything all right?"

Rachel looked up at him and said, "What's *that* supposed to mean?"

"Stop twitching."

"I can't help it," Rachel said. "My legs are restless."

Dave stared at the dim lights from the courtyard crisscrossing the ceiling. Out in the city the tumblers clicked and the ducts spewed. Somewhere across the world, God only knew what was happening. He felt for the clock on the nightstand, picked it up, and peered closely. 3:24.

"Jesus," he said.

"*What*," Rachel said, shifting onto her left side and adjusting the sheet around her shoulder.

"Now I'm awake."

No response. Then: "What time is it?"

"Three thirty."

Rachel rolled onto her back.

"I feel like the world is falling apart," she said. "How can somebody as smart as Abe watch five pushcart drivers and a tank pull that statue down and think it's anything but some fake photo op? They probably got a bag of chickpeas from the CIA and that was it. How can he defend this insanity . . ."

"I don't know. I thought he made some good points."

"Good points? Like what?"

"He's from a different generation," Dave said. "He was in World War Two . . ."

"That isn't it. Noam fucking Chomsky was probably in World War Two. . . . Seriously, how can the same person be so smart and so . . . oblivious? Or something."

"Yeah," Dave said, staring at the ceiling. Somewhere in the distance a car alarm blared. "It's a good question."

TOM PIAZZA is celebrated both as a novelist and as a writer on American music. His twelve books include the novels *A Free State* and *City Of Refuge*, the post-Katrina manifesto *Why New Orleans Matters*, and the essay collection *Devil Sent the Rain: Music and Writing in Desperate America*. He was a principal writer for the innovative HBO drama series *Treme*, and the winner of a Grammy Award for his album notes to *Martin Scorsese Presents the Blues: A Musical Journey*. His writing has appeared in the *New York Times*, the *Atlantic*, *Bookforum*, the *Oxford American*, the *Columbia Journalism Review*, and many other periodicals. He lives in New Orleans.

Lucky Girl

On the Saturday before the presidential election, a new volunteer showed up at the dog shelter. Joelle's step-aunt Candace owned the place, and Joelle spent most Saturdays here. When the front door opened, she had been staring at her iPhone and the polls that favored the not-enraging candidate. A black man, and one in his thirties like her, was entirely without context in this dank, overcrowded bunker in Dutchess County. His head was shaved and he had knowing, almost sly eyes, the shadow of a goatee, and a cleft chin. He wore tiny silver hoop earrings and a faded brown leather jacket, and stood about six inches taller than Joelle. He introduced himself as Anthony and said, "Candace told me to come by and look around."

"Great!" Joelle said. "The dogs are back there." She motioned behind her to the kennel room. She cleared her red-gold hair from her face and adjusted her shoulders outward, as if opening a window. "Come on, I'll introduce you." She wanted to sound welcoming.

A chorus of barks exploded as she pushed through the swinging door. The humid air in the kennel room reeked of kibble and dog shit. Almost all fifteen animals reared up behind their metal cage doors.

Anthony stopped next to Wanda, a fluffy tan spaniel mix whose hair was kept back from her face with a pink plastic barrette. He scratched the top of her snout and said, "Hello, cutie."

Joelle headed past Wanda and Waffle, a terrier mutt, and stopped in front of the blind Maltese. "They found this guy, Mo, in a Dumpster outside a Walmart. People can be real beasts, you know?"

"Amen to that." Anthony knelt down and got a closer look at Mo. "Hey, little man. The worst is over now. You're in good hands here."

A hollow, moony howl rang out above all the other barks and yips.

"That one sounds like a person," Anthony said. He stood and turned his eyes to Joelle.

"She's the new bloodhound. She lost one of her rear legs," Joelle said. She led him toward the russet-colored dog in the last pen. Congealed drool lined the bloodhound's jowls and a mitten-shaped piece was missing from one droopy ear. She had one green eye and one brown. When she saw the two of them, she rose and hobbled closer on her three legs.

"Damn, she's not easy to look at," Anthony said.

"She was found chained up outside a flag factory near Chattanooga," Joelle said. She felt compelled to explain the sad history behind every dog here. "She doesn't have a name yet. You want to give her one?"

"How about America? For that flag factory."

"All right." She did not love his choice. In the lead-up to the election, the American flag had become a sort of threat. Someone down the road had mounted a swimming-pool-sized flag across the front of their garage and a red sign on their lawn that read TRUMP THAT BITCH.

"*America*," Joelle said. The bloodhound grunted and licked the nub where her fourth leg would be. "Let's hope that next week, the country is better off than this dog. The polls have been making me nervous since that Comey thing about her emails. I mean, let it go already."

"Right," Anthony said.

Given the tenor of the election and all that was at stake, Joelle spoke more freely about politics than she ever had in years past.

Anthony glanced at his watch, then over at Joelle. He ran his eyes across her shoulders and toward her stomach. He thanked her for showing him around and said, "I should head out. I won't be able to come back here and start until February." He explained that he had a studio apartment down in the city, that he had to go to London and Madrid for work, and he had promised to take his niece on vacation to Mexico after Christmas. "She lives five minutes from this place."

"Mexico? Lucky girl," Joelle said. She led him toward the front of the shelter again.

"I work for Hyatt, so I get to stay in their hotels at a discount," he said. "And my niece is going through a rough time."

"You're a generous uncle."

He looked down and shrugged. When his eyes returned to her, his face changed. "So, will we get to be here together, you and me?"

"Maybe. Probably."

"Good," he said, and pointed a finger at her. "Lucky you." He smirked.

"Oh yeah?"

"We'll see." He rolled his eyes in a way that was hard to read.

She flushed and laughed, and they said goodbye. She watched him cross the dirt parking lot in an appealing half saunter.

Seven months ago, Joelle had moved up from Flatbush. She had left her job in Brooklyn Heights. She had left her boss, Sean O'Donnell, who had liked to hide brown and black dildos in her desk drawers and watch her unexpectedly find them. She had left her married boyfriend of ten months, a third-grade teacher, although technically Evan was the one to initiate the breakup a polite two weeks after her abortion.

She got a job in Peekskill at a new venture capital firm that specialized in women-run tech companies. She Ventures, located in a renovated mill, consisted of five people: Joelle; three local women in their forties; and their assistant, Beryl, a recent Vassar graduate. For lunch, the five women often walked together to the salad bar at a nearby health-food store. Joelle rented a tiny but charming low-ceilinged farmhouse just a few doors down from the dog shelter. Her new life in the small, quiet town was good and virtuous, but also chaste, as if she had moved out of a Jackson Pollock painting and into a landscape, maybe a Monet.

The country elected the enraging candidate, the months passed, and everything was going to hell. Before heading to She Ventures each morning, Joelle called the offices of her congressional representatives with concerns about threatened immigration and health-care laws. With her colleagues, she attended the Women's March in New York. She set up monthly donations to the ACLU and gave a hundred dollars to a Kickstarter fund for a Jewish cemetery, where dozens of grave markers had been tipped over and spray-painted with swastikas. At a gas station in her town a man ripped off a Muslim woman's hijab and yelled at her and her infant son: "Go back home." What was previously a quaint and pretty town had come to feel menacing, the possibility of hatred lurking in every trip to the grocery store or CVS. In general, Joelle had been hovering just above despair with the occasional dip into hopelessness. Her mood was not buoyed by the news updates that she ingested regularly on her iPhone, despite her best efforts to limit her intake.

Her own life became as uncertain as American democracy. Two of She Ventures' biggest investors backed out and reinvested elsewhere. Beryl found a job working for the Planned Parenthood headquarters in New York City and for more than two months now, She Ventures had been without administrative support. Joelle's inbox ballooned, a paralyzing sight that too often drove her to procrastinate by checking various news websites. *Was he still president? Had anything changed?* Despair, despair, and yet another vow to stop reading so much news.

On the last day of January, Joelle's father was diagnosed with breast cancer.

"Jesus, Mom," she responded to her mother when she first called.

"His doctor caught it early and thinks he'll be fine. There's no reason to share this with anyone, Jo. To be honest, Dad's a little embarrassed."

"Oh, come on, Mom." Such gender-based humiliation irritated Joelle perhaps more than it would have if the country did not seem like a sexist swamp now that a woman had been robbed of the presidency.

"Jo, the man has cancer," her mother said. "Give him a break."

That day, Joelle saw Anthony's name on the volunteer schedule alongside her own for the following week. Was it possible that this was in fact a setup? When she moved up here, Joelle had poured out her sorrows about Evan to her step-aunt, a longtime widow whose one adult child had moved away. Candace, who was short and wore her gray hair in a bun like a baker woman in a nursery rhyme, was heavy with unused love. Lately she had been suggesting that Joelle try dating again, but Joelle had balked. The only men she had met up here were either married to her colleagues or living with their parents and clearly depressed. The sight of Anthony's name on the schedule was a small but real beam of light in an otherwise dim time.

When the morning arrived, she washed and blow-dried her hair and put on a pair of skinny jeans that Evan once said made her ass look amazing. She applied some mascara and her favorite shade of lip gloss and headed to the dog shelter.

"Long time, no see," Anthony said. He sat on the front stoop.

"How was Mexico?" She went for her keys.

"Other than a bad case of food poisoning, one lost suitcase, and a totally insane cabdriver, pretty good." He explained that his niece, not he, had gotten sick, but that she was all right now. In fact, he had just come from her house.

"Things have been so quiet here since the election," she said once inside the shelter. "I swear, it feels like everyone is bracing for something catastrophic. Who wants to commit to owning a new dog right now, let alone some shelter mutt that might turn out to be sick or bad with kids? Waffle did get a nice home last week, this really sweet family who drove up from Tarrytown. But America's still here." Most days, the dog just rested her head on the torso of a purple teddy bear and slept. To prospective owners, Joelle had talked up the dog's soulful howl and kind, unique eyes—two different colors! People inevitably smiled, nodded sympathetically, and moved on to the dog in the next cage. "Poor, hobbled America. She's down one leg and the respect of the rest of the world."

"What?"

"Remember, the bloodhound? You named her."

Anthony nodded in a way indicating that he did not remember.

In Joelle's estimation, to name one of them was to establish a link. She herself had named dozens of dogs here. Last month, when Seymour's new owner came to take him home, she had cradled the old dachshund mutt, reluctant to walk him out front. Seymour had been the name of Joelle's guinea pig when she was a child.

"Hold on—I'll be right back," she said, and strode toward the kennel room. Over the months, she had gotten to know and like America, the way the dog nuzzled her snout against Joelle's arm or dropped it like a heavy sponge onto her leg when she was sitting. Candace had tied a red bandanna around her neck that worked as a bib and mostly took care of the drool problem. Joelle opened the latch on America's pen and hooked a leash to her collar.

"Oh man! That ugly three-legger," Anthony said when he saw Joelle and the dog.

"She's a sweetheart. Give her a chance."

"Those dogs don't get killed if they don't find a home, do they?"

Joelle vigorously shook her head. Most likely, though, America would live here for a year or two, no one would take her, and she would get sick and die. Joelle had seen it happen before. This was a no-kill shelter but not, of course, a no-die one, and plenty of dogs spent their final days here.

Now seated behind the front desk, Anthony pulled his sweatshirt over his head, revealing a green T-shirt that said *What part of "meow" don't you understand?* A pro-woman message, Joelle thought—or was it simply pro-cat?

"Joelle, right?" he asked.

She nodded and unclipped the leash from America. The dog hobbled around the desk and sat next to him. He reached over and stiffly patted her big head.

"There you go," she said. America began to lick the knee of his pants. "She likes you. Look at her!"

He half smiled. "I'd rather look at you," he said.

Her face burned. She understood that she might sleep with him, if only once or twice. She had slept with a Pakistani guy two years ago and her college boyfriend was half-Hispanic, but she had never hooked up with a black man. She liked the thought of it.

"Any chance you want to grab something to eat after we're done here?" he said. "It's a long drive back to the city."

"Yeah. I know a great pizza place two minutes from here."

Fourteen months earlier, Joelle and Evan had sat at a bar in Flatbush drinking dirty martinis. His wife was visiting her parents in Ohio. Heart's "Barracuda" played overhead as they ordered their third set of drinks. Joelle told him what her boss had been hiding in her desk, and Evan burst out laughing.

"How is that funny?"

"Were they huge? I mean, you know."

Joelle rolled her eyes. For a third-grade teacher, Evan could be awfully raunchy, and lately he had been pushing into thornier, uglier territory. She thought of the first time that she had slept with this married person, when she had been a raw nerve as they ripped off each other's clothes on her roommate's sofa and he covered her collarbone with hickeys. Honestly, had she ever been more alive? He and his wife rented an apartment in the same building. Joelle had met him folding his boxer shorts in the laundry room.

"Sorry," he said at last. "Your boss sounds like an asshole."

"He is. Yesterday, he asked me for a paper clip, and then he just stood there staring at me, obviously waiting for me to see what he'd put in my top drawer. I literally screamed."

"Must have been a shock," Evan said, trying not to smile.

"You want me to hide a plastic vagina in your desk at school?"

"Actually—" His eyes shimmered.

"Fuck off."

"Come on, Jo. You know I'm kidding." She was supposed to be the fun one, the guy's girl who was game for anything.

She watched Evan move his swizzle stick around his glass, his slow blinks revealing that he was more than a little tipsy. He had a pale baby face with crystalline blue eyes that had once made her smolder, but lately he called to mind an acclaimed movie actor who had just been outed for sexually harassing his costars.

"Hey," he said, "men are terrible, horrible, no-good creatures. Is it okay if we go back to your place now? Because those jeans make your ass look fucking amazing." His breath warm in her ear, he sang, "You'd have me down, down, down on my knees. Now wouldn't you, barracuda?"

Later, she berated herself for stepping in line, for ending up in bed with him that night, for allowing him to forgo a condom a few weeks later, for ceding herself to sex again and again, for returning repeatedly to a married man.

She knew better than to commit such an act against another woman. She had been a women's studies major at Smith, for God's sake.

"What made you want to volunteer so far from the city?" she asked Anthony after explaining her own move north. They sat across from each other in a wooden booth, a small pizza on the table between them.

"My niece lives up near here with her mom. I guess it's a chance to see her. We both like dogs, and I figure I can bring her with me when I volunteer. It'd be something for us to do together. She couldn't come today because she had a basketball game."

Joelle wondered if he had told Candace of his plans to bring his niece every week. "You two are close."

"Yeah, we are," he said, and reached for a second slice. "My brother, her dad, used to say that he liked dogs more than people, that dogs were easier for him to be around."

"He 'used to'? What changed? The dogs or the people?" She smiled.

"He got killed. A cop shot him."

"Oh my God." Joelle could guess the rest—white cop, car on the side of the road. The girl left with no father. His niece, of course, his niece. It was a story that never got easier to hear—and had to be infinitely harder to tell. "I'm so sorry."

"Thanks," he said, his eyes on the pizza.

She grew embarrassed for what she had just said, which had been nowhere near enough or the right thing, whatever that was.

A Taylor Swift song played. Two lanky teenage girls skulked past in North Face jackets. Some guys behind the counter bantered about Tom Brady. Everything was Caucasian and vapid. "Can I ask what happened? You probably don't want to talk about it," she said.

"It's okay. It was on the news a lot—it was in the Bronx last year? Couple of white cops. Marcus was standing outside a Duane Reade."

She vaguely remembered reading about a man selling packs of cigarettes near some drugstore, or was she thinking of another shooting? There had been so many.

One of the teenage girls began to cackle. She made a scene of laughing and choking on her drink.

"I wish she would shut up," Joelle said. She shot a disapproving look at the girls.

He turned to see them. "Kids being kids."

The girl's friend held her phone sideways in front of them. *Care what other people think of you*, Joelle could have said. *Be better people as young white females.* "Her friend is taking a selfie of them licking each other's faces."

"Nice," he said, laughing.

Maybe he was right. Maybe in some way, there was something obliquely funny about it.

Afterward, he offered to walk Joelle home and touched her lower back as he moved behind her. "You cold?" he asked, and she shook her head. The air was bearable outside the restaurant, and she lived only a few minutes from here. "Come on, take my hat. You're so small. You have to be cold." He pulled a red-and-blue-striped ski hat from his pocket. Worried about seeming like a germaphobe or worse, she took it.

Inside her house, he wandered around her antique kitchen, stopping to look at the bumper stickers she had affixed to her fridge: RESIST; WELL-BEHAVED WOMEN RARELY MAKE HISTORY; BLACK LIVES MATTER, one that right now made her both proud and self-conscious. "Drink?" she asked him.

She poured him a glass of pinot, and he set it on the counter, reached down and tucked her hair behind her ear. She stood on her tiptoes and kissed him, and he lifted her and she wrapped her legs around his waist. His body was dense and strong and irresistible, and their mouths sealed together, his breath strong with pepperoni pizza. She guided him toward the bedroom. They fell backward on her mattress, she on top, but then he lifted her and turned her so that she was beneath him as they continued to kiss.

Anthony pulled off her shirt and easily unclasped her bra. He traced his finger around the words tattooed across her left breast, just atop where her heart was located: *I Am Enough*.

"Hey now," he said.

"It's a feminist thing. I got it with some friends when we worked for a rape crisis center."

"That and the dog shelter? Are you trying to be everybody's hero?"

She smiled in a twitchy way.

He pulled off his shirt and engulfed her right nipple with his warm mouth. She arched her back as the sensation of his soft tongue registered inside her spine. "That's why I'm here?" he whispered. Leaning on one arm, he went to unbutton her jeans. "You going to try to save me or something?"

"What do you mean?"

"A black man whose brother got shot by a white cop?"

"No." Her skin tightened everywhere. She shrank away.

He said, "I don't have a problem with it. I'm good with this." He began to tug her pants down.

"You shouldn't say things like that. You should think better of yourself."

"Oh yeah?" His hand on his own zipper, he froze. "What else do you want to tell me to do?"

"It's not, I don't—I mean—I like you and you're really hot. This has nothing to do with—" She could not manage to say the word *pity*. They had lurched so quickly onto this horribly thin ice.

"Can we get back to business?" he said. He slid off his pants and they began to kiss again.

But her mind was stuck in the previous moment. She had to make things right before they went any further. "We're not so different, you know, women and black men, people of color, I mean in terms of the harassment and the persecution, all the violence. The micro- and macroaggressions—like every day. Believe me, I have stories. Yes, I don't have to worry about white cops and being shot, but it's not so easy for us women, even white women. We get lumped in with white men—and blamed because so many white women voted for him, but it's not so simple." She had meant to sound woke—she thought she *was* woke—but her words moved in the air like desperate little flies buzzing around for some kind of food that did not exist.

He looked at her. "Do you still want to fuck?"

She blinked and nodded.

He slid on a condom, and they moved efficiently and quietly and quickly. She told herself to enjoy his toned arms and muscular ass and his flawless dark skin, but she could not manage to shake a binding self-consciousness.

Afterward, he caught his breath, gave her a peck on the forehead, and went for his clothes. She could have guessed that he would not want to stay. Still, she felt a choking grief, as if she had finally inhaled a toxic smog that had been closing in on her for some time. "Don't feel like you have to leave," she managed.

"I've got a long drive—and I have plans tomorrow." He appeared to take note of her blue button that read STRONGER TOGETHER. She had gotten it at the Women's March and had clipped it to her curtain.

"This country sucks," she said. "Even more since November eighth." She might never have the heart to take down that button.

"Well, people picked who they wanted."

"No, the Electoral College did. I didn't. The popular vote didn't."

"I guess that's part of the deal," he said, reaching for his shirt.

"Well, the deal sucks too." How was she more upset about this than he was? "Wait, you didn't vote for—"

"If I'd voted, I guess I would have gone for Hillary, but honestly, she reminded me of this stuck-up teacher I had at Horace Mann. I did kind of like Bernie. But in this blue state? My vote wasn't going to change any damn thing."

"God. What if everyone said that?"

"You're funny. You're cute." Now dressed, he moved toward her and set a few fingers on her tattoo again. "*I am enough.*" He chuckled. "I should go. I'll see you at the shelter sometime?"

"Yeah," she said, tugging the sheet over her chest. "You want me to walk back to your car with you?" She had no image of where he might be headed, no clue even where in the city or in which borough he lived.

"That's all right. I'm good."

Joelle's father had a lumpectomy. America suffered through a long bout of kennel cough, after which Joelle began to toy with the idea of adopting the dog herself. She Ventures found a new investor, a motorboat heiress from Albany, as well as Aruna, an administrative assistant who had recently moved up here from Brooklyn with her husband and young son. Joelle continued in vain to try to limit her consumption of news. There were so many articles online, more and more details revealed about the president's entanglements with Russia, the rapid-fire executive orders that punished everyone from women to immigrants to disabled children to wolf pups.

Several weeks after their evening together, she and Anthony were scheduled to cover the same shift again at the dog shelter. She had often replayed the evening, and each time cringed at the words she had used, although if she had to say or do things differently, she was unsure just how she would.

That Saturday morning, he showed up at the shelter, his goatee now grown in, a girl of about twelve or thirteen beside him. She looked a little like him. He introduced her as Eve, his niece.

"Hey," the girl said.

"Nice to meet you," Joelle said. Maybe it was good that Eve was here. Her presence could mitigate the inevitable awkwardness.

Eve wore red cat-eye glasses and a purple-and-white-striped scarf. She was adorable. Although Candace had a strict age threshold for volunteers—no one under sixteen—Joelle offered to take Eve's mint-green jacket.

"No thanks," the girl said. "It's freezing in here. And it smells like toilets."

Anthony chuckled and said, "She's not wrong."

Joelle held forth the dog food bowl of butterscotches that Candace kept on the front counter, but Eve said, "I don't eat sugar. No one should. Do you know what sugar does to a body?"

"I do," Joelle said, returning the bowl to its place. She reminded herself that this girl had lost her father.

Eve went off to look at the pamphlets about dog adoption and health.

"You've been okay?" Anthony asked Joelle.

"Pretty okay. My father had his surgery and it looks like they got all the cancer."

"Cancer?"

Hadn't she told him that night? She swore that she had at the pizza restaurant, when they talked about their families. "In his, well, his chest."

"Oh man. My uncle had lymphoma. It was rough for a while, but he's fine now."

A few dogs barked and a sad howl rose up and wound through the place like a silk ribbon. "That's America," she said. "You know what? I've been thinking of taking her home myself."

"Really?"

"Yeah," she said. The other day, she had mentioned it to Candace, who reacted with relief. "In fact, I will. I just decided. I'll bring her home later. Why not?"

"Lucky girl," he said with a surprised look.

Eve returned to them and complained again about the smell.

Anthony said, "How about we go back and see the dogs?"

Joelle grabbed a few Milk-Bones, and the three headed toward the swinging door.

"These are some really sorry-looking animals," Eve said, standing at the center of the loud room. "Who's going to want them?"

"It's a shelter, Evie," Anthony said.

"It's a dump."

"Maybe you could make them some clothes? Some cute dog shirts and stuff? Evie sews," Anthony told Joelle. "She made me a bag for my laptop, and she sewed a shirt for her mom."

"Wow, nice," Joelle said. She imagined America and the others ambling around in dog-sized coats, dog-sized shirts, carrying dog-sized bags.

"Um, no thanks," Eve said. "Anthony, how long do we have to be here?"

He did not answer.

Joelle wandered to the last pen, where America stood, staring out at them, her teddy bear torso and a fleece Yankees blanket wadded up behind her. Anthony and Eve followed.

"Would you hate it if I changed America's name?" Joelle asked Anthony. The president was about to sign an executive order repealing all legal protections for wolves and bears. In a tweet that morning, he had accused the previous president of tapping his phones before the election. The country might never be the same again. "America is a really big name for a dog. And that flag factory where she was found? For all we know, it made POW or rainbow flags and not American flags."

"Go for it," he said.

"I've been thinking I might call her Iris. She has two different-colored irises, but I also just like the name. And the flower too. You sure you don't mind?"

"Of course not. Why would I?" He had only volunteered a few times, hardly enough to grow attached to any of the dogs.

America, or Iris, watched them standing there outside her pen now. She rose up awkwardly on her three legs and went to lick Joelle's hand through the bars.

Eve said, "Oh my God. You let that disgusting thing lick you?"

"*Evie*," Anthony said.

The girl spun around and marched off, and Anthony followed her.

Joelle watched them disappear through the swinging door. Was it possible for a person to age twenty years in just six months? She went to unlatch the dog's cage and held out a bone for America, who snapped it up and cracked it between her teeth, gazing up kindly. *Iris*. Maybe it was too late, even cruel to change the dog's name now, after all she had been through. There was no way to know how long she had been chained up outside Chattanooga, how she had lost her leg or what brand of hell she had endured before that.

When Joelle knelt down and looked directly into the dog's green and brown eyes, one and then the other, the only thing she saw was the reflection of herself.

"What a good girl," Joelle told the dog. When she crunched the rest of the bone between her rear teeth, America almost looked as if she was grinning.

HEIDI PITLOR has been the series editor of *The Best American Short Stories* since 2007. With Lorrie Moore, she coedited *100 Years of the Best American Short Stories*. She is the author of the novels *The Birthdays* and *The Daylight Marriage*, and is currently working on her third novel. Her writing has appeared in *Plough-shares*, the *New York Times*, the *Boston Globe*, the *Huffington Post*, and elsewhere. She teaches at the low-residency MFA program at Regis University in Denver and lives outside Boston with her husband and twin daughter and son.

S. J. ROZAN

If They Come
in the Morning

Finally, they came again.

I knew always that they would.

The first time when they came I was fourteen years old. This was 1944. For me they came, and for my little brother, Ludvik. Ludvik: Chaim his name was, in Hebrew. It means life.

They put us in a truck, the children only.

Our Mami had died before the War. So endlessly sorrowful it seemed to us then, but no. She never knew what happened, so for her it was a blessing. Tati by the time the truck came was also gone. I knew: the SS troops shot him, they took the men away and shot them all. Grandmother didn't tell me and I didn't tell Ludvik, but I knew.

Ludvik was mine to raise after Mami died, mine and Grandmother's. She said I must be Ludvik's Little Mami. Tati was sweet, and funny, but so sad about Mami, and children? You might have thought we were from the moon. Sometimes his face became so puzzled, he tilted his head so far trying to understand us—Ludvik and I had to laugh.

Ludvik laughed a lot. He was a happy boy, full of jokes and pranks. Grandmother and I tried to shield him from what was happening around us. This was not really possible, especially after the men were taken away, but I think he understood we were trying and so he pretended. And he had such a happy nature.

Early one morning, a neighbor ran to Grandmother to say a truck was coming to take away the children. Grandmother's face went white and she tried to hide us. She told us to lie flat on the bed slats and she put the mattress over us and made up the bed. The mattress was heavy, the slats were hard and I held Ludvik's hand, though he was eight years old and not a baby. We lay facing the floor, trying to breathe between the slats. We heard pounding on the door, then men's voices yelling. Pots crashed in the kitchen and dishes broke. Boots stomped closer; the men came into the bedroom. They threw the closet open, pulled the wardrobe down. It crashed to the floor. Great-grandmother's bowl fell from the top of it and shattered.

Then the coverlet flew off the bed. The mattress, that heavy weight, was lifted off and Ludvik was pulled from my hand. Then I, too, was pulled up. I staggered. Grandmother was crying, she was on her knees. She begged them not to take us. A soldier hit her with the back of his hand, sent her sprawling across the floor. He grabbed up Ludvik under his arm like a sack and carried him out of the room, out of the house. Ludvik kicked. The soldier punched him. Grandmother wailed. Hands pushed me forward and I went, stumbling out the door. The soldier threw Ludvik onto the back of a truck already filled with children, some crying, some frozen in silence. The soldier grinned at me, a horrible face, and he pointed. I climbed onto the truck, skinning my knee.

The journey was very long. More children were picked up, loaded together with us. Many of them we knew. We were friends, we had played together, had gone to school together when that was still allowed to Jews. The older children stood so the babies had room to sit. Ludvik insisted on standing, too, with me. So many were crying. As it got dark, and cold, the crying slowly stopped. Everyone huddled together, trying to keep warm.

Late at night the truck drove through the gate of a place we'd never seen. It stopped and loud-voiced men told us to get out, to line up. The lights shone very bright. The soldiers went down the line and I could see: they were pulling out the older girls, taking them away. When a soldier came to me he ordered me to step forward. I heard my voice shaking as I said to him I would do anything they wanted—I knew full well what they wanted, it terrified me—anything they wanted, but please let my little brother come with me.

Skinny, he was, this soldier, with glittering, small eyes. He said, *You will do whatever we want, in any case. Which is your brother?* I showed him.

Step forward, he said to Ludvik. Ludvik took a step and reached out his hand to me.

The soldier raised his pistol and fired.

The noise was very loud. Another child screamed. Ludvik made no sound. Eyes still open, his hand still held out, he fell forward in the dirt. I tried to run to him but another soldier lifted me and dragged me away. I kicked and shrieked. He hit me hard.

For nearly a year I was there. I sat in a room, on a bed, waiting for the men. The things they did to me, I won't describe to you. Some of the other girls I could hear screaming or sobbing in their rooms. Some of them died.

When no man was there I watched out the window in case Ludvik was not dead, in case he had only been hurt and would soon march past carrying a shovel or pushing a wheelbarrow. As other little boys did. The boys whose sisters had not tried to save them.

When the Americans came, I hardly knew. They gave us clothes and blankets and they gave us food, and I ate and wrapped myself but I thought they were just more men and would do more things to me. They moved us, the older girls, to a different building. Then, a few days later, again in trucks, they took us to another place. A different kind of camp, they said, but it was the same to me. Doctors examined us. They asked my name but I didn't speak. Since Ludvik died, I hadn't spoken. *Do you not know your name?* one man asked gently. I knew what my name had been before I came here, but now, I was someone else. Her name, I didn't know.

So I said nothing, and went wherever in the new camp they told me, and sat in my blanket, and ate the food they brought, and waited for the men.

But no men came.

What happened was, they brought the children.

From where, I don't know. Young children, skinny and crying and scared. Some they carried in, some walked. They had beds for them in another big room past the room for us. One little boy tried to walk with the others but he was unsteady and he fell down, right in front of my bed. He looked so sad but he didn't cry. He just sat where he'd fallen, watching as the Americans led the other children away. After a time I got out of my blanket, picked him up, and carried him back with me. I wrapped us up together and rocked him, and he fell asleep. When he stirred and started to cry, *Hush*, I said.

I stayed in that camp, a relocation camp it was, for two years. I ate and grew strong. I helped with the children. From the soldiers I learned English. The people in charge, many different agencies, they tried to find families, if anyone was left. Many children had no families anymore, or didn't know who their families had been, knew only *Momma* and *Pappa*, *Mami* and *Tati*.

In the end the camp was closed. The children who no longer had families were taken in by families who no longer had children, or by agencies in Israel, in Canada, in America.

I had no family; I was sent to America, here to this quiet, pretty town. A kind couple whose son died in the War took me into their home, sent me to school. I will not say their names because both are gone now and I do not want their memory dishonored by what has come after.

All my life since I came here I have lived in this town. I did not marry. After the camp, never again would I let a man touch me. I went to college and became a teacher. In the public school I taught and also in the Hebrew school in the town's single synagogue, Temple Sinai. Why did I do this? After all that had happened, all I had seen, did I still believe in a benevolent God? Or at least, a righteous one, a God who would avenge the wrongs done to His people?

I did not.

I taught in the Hebrew school because these children, these beautiful children, they had to know who they were. If knowledge is in any way truly power, then knowing the past would help them be prepared, more prepared than we had been, when the Nazis came.

But knowledge is not the only power. Very early, I bought a gun. I would not be helpless again.

306

• • •

And to our quiet town, our pretty town in the middle of America, more than seventy years later, the Nazis came.

Neo-Nazis, they call them; alt-right, and skinheads, and nativists. We have now a president who allows it, who says some of them are fine people. I know who they are. The swastikas on their armbands and the eagles on their flags, I know. Their loud voices and mean faces, their fists, I know.

The Nazis decided they would march here, down our Main Street, from the playing fields—the children's playing fields!—to City Hall. In our town we have many churches. To one of them most of the black people go, Mount Horeb Baptist Church. It sits down the street from Temple Sinai. Sinai and Horeb: different names for the same mountain. The route these Nazis chose went in front of both.

We knew the route in advance because the mayor announced it. *We cannot stop them from coming but we will fight them with knowledge*, he said. *And with peace. Everyone along the route, close your doors, stay inside, turn your backs. Deny them what they want: attention.*

We were not sure. At Mount Horeb Church, they also were not sure. The minister came to meet with our rabbi. His Elders came, and our Board of Assembly, and we met together. We discussed and debated and together we prayed. In the end there was no vote: consensus was unanimous. Peace, yes, we agreed; but we would be seen. We did not think the Nazis wanted only attention. We thought—I knew—they wanted to frighten us. To scare us into hiding ourselves. Once they saw we were scared, they would grow stronger. So we refused.

They came at night. Lifting high their torches, they stomped and chanted, they shouted and saluted. We saw them coming up the street. Our congregations had chosen to mix ourselves together. In front of Temple Sinai and also in front of Mount Horeb Church Jews stood silently. Black people stood at Mount Horeb and at Temple Sinai. Men and women together, in lines. Also with us, many people from the town, neither Jew nor black but people who wanted also to be seen.

307

The children had been told to stay at home, but at Temple Sinai the recent bar and bat mitzvahs, the thirteen- and fourteen-year-olds, had a meeting the adults did not know about. They took a vote and came out as one to stand in the lines. *We are adults now*, said their spokesman, a boy whose voice had not yet broken. *We share the responsibility for our community.*

I was so proud of the children.

I was there, in the line. I am on the Board of Assembly and I had been part of the debate. My duty was to be there, but people said, *You are eighty-six years old.* They said this gently, but I answered, *Yes, and my greatest regret is that I was so frightened when the Nazis came the first time that I obeyed.*

We stood. They came. At first, they just raised their fists, they shouted louder. Black people and Jews standing together, unafraid, it incensed them. Then they broke ranks, charged right up to us. They cursed, screamed *Heil Hitler* and *Niggers burn in hell.* The police came, pushed them back. That the police were there, fighting against them, it made them furious. *This is our country.* Someone threw a bottle. *Die, nigger.* Someone threw a punch. *Fuck the Jews.* So many people shouting. Scuffles and fights. One of the bat mitzvahs, a freckled girl named Leah, yelled to a Nazi. A troublemaker, Leah, a girl I always liked. To the Nazi, a boy who looked no older than she was, she screamed, *Your mother is ashamed.*

The Nazi pulled Leah from the line, threw her down, and started punching her.

I pulled out my gun, fired into the street beside him. I would have shot him without hesitation but I was afraid for Leah.

Concrete sprayed. The Nazi boy leapt fast and fell over. He looked frantically for the person with the gun. I had it fixed on him, not four feet from his face. Lying on the ground, eyes wide, he begged. *No, no, please.* He raised his hands. *Please don't shoot me.* I was holding the gun so hard my arms shook.

So badly, with my whole body, I wanted to shoot him. More, I thought, than I had ever wanted anything. But as soon as that thought came I knew this: even more, I had wanted to see Ludvik from the window of my room. And then I thought, this Nazi boy, he is someone's grandson. He is someone's little brother. I let the gun lower slowly. My whole body slumped.

The Nazi boy jumped to his feet and pulled away my gun. I staggered.

Jew bitch! Jew bitch! He pointed it at me. Leah lunged up from the ground to knock his arm away. The gun fired. Two policemen also then shot their guns.

Leah's funeral was this morning. Within twenty-four hours, we bury our dead. The entire synagogue was there, and the Mount Horeb congregation came, too. The Nazi boy, I don't know when his funeral will be, or who will come. His name was in the newspapers but I don't remember it.

At the funeral, everyone came and said, *Are you all right? I hope you know this isn't your fault.* I know. Directly from the funeral I came home. I sat on my bed and wrapped myself in my blanket and I took these pills, all these pills. But not because I think it was my fault.

It's only, nothing has changed.

If we're silent, if we speak up; if we're cowardly, if we're brave; if we're unwary, if we're prepared; if we're harsh, if we're merciful: the ending is the same.

I wanted to save Ludvik.

I wanted the children to know who they were, to be ready.

I wanted to show the Nazi boy pity, to let him live.

I wanted to save Leah.

Finally, now, there is nothing I want.

S. J. ROZAN has won multiple awards, including the Edgar, Shamus, Anthony, Nero, Macavity, the Japanese Maltese Falcon Society Falcon, and the Private Eye Writers of America Life Achievement. She's written fifteen novels, thirteen under her own name and two with Carlos Dews as "Sam Cabot." She's edited/coedited two short story anthologies, and many of her own seventy-five-plus short stories have appeared in various "Best of the Year" collections. S. J. was born in the Bronx and lives in Lower Manhattan. She is a card-carrying member of the ACLU. www.sjrozan.net.

Top Step

My maternal grandfather served in both world wars, too young for the first, too old for the second. In the Pacific he contracted malaria, from which he never fully recovered. What killed him, though, was emphysema, the result of breathing leather dust (he was a glove cutter) and smoking cigarettes. In other words he was poisoned on the job and also poisoned himself. The last years of his life he spent hooked up to an oxygen tank, gasping, his chest convulsing violently, as if it contained a trip-hammer. When my mother and I moved to Arizona from upstate New York to begin what we imagined would be new lives, I think we both understood that we were absolving ourselves of the duty of being present when his abused heart finally gave out.

He'd bought the house we shared—my mother and I on the top floor, he and my grandmother on the bottom—so we'd have a place to live after my parents split up. Having himself grown up in a disorderly home, he prized order. Our lawn was mowed and edged in summer, our leaves raked and disposed of in autumn, our sidewalks shoveled in winter, our house repainted at the first sign of flaking. The clothes he wore were never expensive or showy, but they were always clean and, thanks to my grandmother, crisply ironed. He always hiked his trouser legs an inch or two at the knee before sitting down, the first human gesture I can recall imitating. Other gestures of his I've imitated my whole life and been the better man for it. I loved him with my whole heart and love him still.

That said, I don't imitate everything about him. During the Civil Rights Movement, I remember him making fun of a young black mother on the news when she complained about "not even having enough money to feed my little babies!" A natural mimic, his impersonation was spot-on and devastating. Had he been asked to explain his lack of sympathy for the woman's plight, her hungry kids, I doubt he would've mentioned her race, and in his defense he was equally merciless in his imitations of white southern lawmen and politicians. But there can be no question he was stereotyping her. There would've been no doubt in his mind that the kids in question all had different fathers and that producing more hungry kids was her only life skill. On the basis of this one anecdote, it would be hard to argue that the man I loved and love still was not racist. But I also remember the afternoon he ordered off his front porch a neighbor who was circulating a petition to keep a black family from buying a house on our street, explaining that this was America and we didn't do things that way here. He must've seen how many names were already on the petition and known how many of his neighbors had accepted the man's specious argument—that it wasn't about these particular people and whether or not they were decent and hardworking, but rather a question of property values. If you let this family in, where do you draw the line?

Where my grandfather drew it was right there, on our front porch, just one short step from the top.

My father drew lines, too.

"Well," he said, finally waking up and rubbing his eyes with his fists. "No need to tell me where we are."

Out late the night before, he'd slept most of the way to Albany. I'd just returned home from the university and next week would start working road construction with him. Before that could happen, I had to check in at the union hall where he and I were members. At the moment we were stopped at a traffic light in a predominantly black section of the city.

"Please," I begged him, because of course I knew where this was headed.

"You're telling me you can't smell that?"

On more than one previous occasion my father had claimed he could smell black people. Their blackness. Whether they were clean or dirty made no difference. Race itself, he claimed, had an odor.

"You're sure it isn't poverty you're smelling?" I ventured.

"Yep," he said. "And so are you. You just won't admit it."

Mulignans, he called them, the Italian word for eggplant ("Ever see a white one?"). The irony was that by the end of August, after a summer of working in the hot sun, his own complexion would be darker than most light-skinned blacks. Certainly as dark as Calvin's. When my father was spouting racist nonsense, I'd often remind him that one of his best friends was black, an incongruity that was not lost on Calvin either. Indeed, in a playful mood he would sometimes put his forearm up next to my father's for comparison's sake. "Except for the smell," he'd say, grinning at me, if I happened to be around, "you can't tell us apart." One drunken night my father had apparently shared with Calvin his theory of smell.

Another story. It's a few years later and my father and I are driving a U-Haul across the country from Tucson, Arizona, to Altoona, Pennsylvania, to my first academic job at a branch campus of Penn State. I'm pushing thirty, married, a father myself now, and broke. The plan is for my wife, who is pregnant with our second daughter, to join me later in the summer. My father is now in his fifties, but lean and strong from a lifetime of hard labor, his black Brillo Pad hair only just beginning to be flecked with gray. He's a D-day guy. Bronze star. A genuine war hero. That he's not prospered in the peace, as so many returning vets have, doesn't seem to trouble him. That he's alive and kicking seems enough. I myself am soft by comparison, soft in so many ways. Thanks to a series of deferments and then a high draft number, I've managed to stay out of Vietnam. My father's opinion of that clusterfuck war was pretty much the same as mine, but I know it troubles him that I stayed home when others of my generation served and came back, like him, profoundly changed. But the "conflict" is finally over and I'm alive and I know he's glad about that.

His war we've never talked about, not due to any lack of interest on my part, but because men like my father and grandfather simply didn't. Is it the realization that, with Vietnam over, I will probably never experience war first-hand that starts him talking today? Or just the fact that we've been cooped up in the cab of that U-Haul truck for so long? The worst was the Hedgerows, he begins, surprising me. (Not Normandy? Not the Hürtgen Forest?) Every time you turned around, there were more Germans stepping out from behind the hedges, hands in the air, wanting to surrender. (He slips unconsciously into present tense now, suddenly more in France than here in the cab of the truck.) We're driving, going flat-out, miles and hours ahead of our supply train. Maybe days, for all we know. Here come another seven Germans, hands in the air. Then nine more. Another mile up the road, more hedgerows, more surrendering Germans. A dozen this time, maybe two. Hands in the air and guns on the ground at their feet. What do you do with them? You can't take them with you. You can't leave them behind because who knows? Maybe they take up their weapons again, and now they're behind you, these same guys who have been shooting at you since Utah Beach.

Did I ask the begged question? I don't remember, but anyway, no need. He's going to tell me. It's the point of the story. And maybe the point of my *not* serving in Vietnam. In any company, he tells me, his voice thick, there's always one who doesn't mind taking these guys down the road.

Down the road?

Right, he says. Around the bend. Out of sight. If you don't see it, it didn't happen. None of your business. *Your* business is up ahead.

And that was pretty much all my father had to say about the Second World War. And the one I managed to avoid.

"It occurs to me that I am America," Allen Ginsberg wrote.

The same thing occurs to me. I'm proud, like my grandfather and father, but also ashamed. I write this the week after young white men waving Nazi flags and members of the KKK and conspiracy-theory-stoked militiamen converged on Charlottesville and were not unambiguously denounced by the president of the United States. Is this the country my father and grandfather fought for? I ask because the shame I felt seeing those swastikas on display in Charlottesville was deeply personal, a betrayal of two men I loved, who at their best were brave men and good Americans and at their worst were far, far better than these despicable, pathetic, deluded fuckwads. My father and grandfather both believed, and not without justification, that America was the light and hope of the world. They also believed, with perhaps less justification, in *me*. Okay, not me, exactly, but the possibility inherent in my existence, in this time and this place, which, not coincidentally, is how I feel about my own children and grandchildren. Like my grandfather and father, I don't demand or expect perfection in those I love. But I do hope that when their neighbor climbs the porch steps, petition in hand, my children and grandchildren will say, as my grandfather did, "That's not the way we do things here. Not in America." And I want them to know about the day when my father, in an uncharacteristically serious mood, took me aside and said, "Listen up, Dummy." (Yeah, Dad?) "You're ever in a tough spot? You need somebody you can trust? Go to Calvin." I want them to understand that in the final analysis, as far as my father was concerned, Calvin wasn't black. He was Calvin. I want them to understand that even though you couldn't talk him out of the idea that black people had an odor and he held the entire race in low esteem, he made exceptions, as many as were necessary, in fact, and there *were* many. He preferred black men who worked hard to white men who didn't. Like Whitman, he didn't trouble himself about contradictions.

What I most want my daughters and grandchildren to understand is that it's okay to love flawed people with your whole heart and soul because if you don't, you'll end up with a low opinion of yourself. I want them to understand that the world poisons you, but that most of us are to one degree or another complicit in that poisoning. Inherent in being an American is cherishing ideals that are impossible to live up to, that invite failure and self-loathing when we don't. Why commit to the impossible? Because it's the only way forward. Because the many paradoxes of democracy demand nothing less. Because timid people don't find the courage to face their neighbors on that top step. Cowed, they sign the petition. And not knowing what else to do with their enemies when at last they surrender, they take them down the road.

• • •

RICHARD RUSSO is the author of nine novels, two collections of short stories, a memoir, and several produced screenplays. *Empire Falls* won the 2002 Pulitzer Prize for Fiction, and his adaptation of the book for HBO was nominated for an Emmy. His collection of essays, *The Destiny Thief,* will be published this spring. He and his wife, Barbara, live in Portland, Maine.

Hope

The car creeps across the Pulaski Skyway. Hope stares out the window at brackish water, the Hackensack River, and thinks of her father, a lawyer and intermittent tyrant, and how her mother waits on him like a slave and what he would say if he could see her right now.

Off the bridge the car skids, the road slick in late February—not quite two weeks after Hope's nineteenth birthday—a sheer icy drizzle varnishing the windshield.

"Nothing to worry about," says Barry, gripping the steering wheel, her boy-friend's brother-in-law who has been enlisted for this job.

The New Jersey Turnpike is better, wider, the ice not sticking as they cruise past elevated power lines and towers belching black smoke into a slate-gray sky.

"God, it stinks here," says Barry.

It is very early on a Sunday morning, not many cars on the road and what sun there is, a hazy globule lolling just above the horizon, adds a sour lemony hue to the atmosphere.

Her boyfriend, Artie, beside Hope in the back seat, turns to look behind them, the blue rental sedan still there.

"What's the exit again?" Barry asks.

Artie, directions rumpled and clenched in his palm, says, "Thirteen."

Unlucky thirteen, Hope thinks, shutting her eyes.

"You okay?" Artie asks.

Hope looks at him then away, thinks of a conversation she had about art school, her mother saying Hope could go if she studied Art Ed, how she could teach and support a husband through medical school or law school, how she would have "something to fall back on," and how, when she told that to Artie, they both laughed.

The large green sign looms into view.

Down the exit ramp to a stop sign, one turn then another, Artie supplying directions, Hope twisting in her seat, trying not to watch.

"They're still there," says Barry, eying the sedan in his rearview mirror.

The service road runs parallel to the turnpike, close-set one-family homes lined up along its perimeter absorbing carbon monoxide like dermal patches. The road ends in a T.

"Take a left over the highway," Artie says, reading from the paper in his hand.

On the overpass Hope looks down at cars whizzing beneath them, for a moment thinks she will shout: *Stop! Let me out! I'm going to jump!*

"Take a right," says Artie, his tone flat. "Then two blocks to a mall."

Through her window Hope surveys small signs of life: attached houses, a few leafless trees, boarded-up shops. No, she thinks, no signs of life at all.

They pull into the strip mall—drugstore, supermarket, coffee shop, discount shoes—everything closed, New Jersey blue laws in effect.

"Drive around back," Artie says, "to the parking lot."

Hope holds her breath as they make the turn.

"I guess dis is da place," Barry singsongs, trying for cheerful. He parks at the edge of the lot.

The blue rental follows and parks beside them.

Artie's college roommate, scrawny with glasses, an anti-Vietnam radical of some notoriety, gets out of the car, his girlfriend, Rochelle, dark-haired and petite, just behind him.

Artie opens his door and gets out too. Hope doesn't move. He leans back in, extends his hand, but she just sits there. "It's going to be okay," he says. Hope sucks in a breath then struggles out of the car, nods at the roommate's girlfriend, whom she hardly knows though they are in this together, a freakish coincidence.

The four of them stand together but apart, as if glued to their individual squares of asphalt.

Hope asks, "What time is it?"

"Ten to eight," Artie says.

His roommate says, "It stopped raining or snowing or whatever it was doing," tugs a pack of Marlboros from his pocket and offers it around. Both girls shake their heads no but Artie takes one, lights up and inhales, looks back at the car, Barry sitting rigid behind the wheel. Hope is surprised but thankful Artie's brother-in-law has not joined the group, telling jokes in his frat-boy way.

Hope can't focus on anything, not Artie, his roommate or his roommate's girlfriend, her brain like a loaded shotgun ready to go off. Artie pulls her close.

They hear the car before they see it round the corner, their heads cocked at the sound; Hope stiffens against Artie's side.

"It will be okay," he says again.

A black car, in need of a wash, angles alongside theirs and stops. A woman gets out, scarf over her hair, cat's-eye sunglasses, a bulky blue parka.

Hope watches as Artie hands the woman the envelope, red fingernail slashing it open, fingering the bills, lips moving as she counts before she stuffs it into her pocket.

His roommate hands over a second envelope. The woman counts again.

Hope studies the woman's face, the lines around her mouth, guesses she is somewhere in her late thirties, possibly forty. The woman looks up, arcs her chin toward the car idling behind her, a man at the wheel, fedora low on his forehead, cigarette dangling from the corner of his mouth like a gangster.

Hope thinks, *No way*, but then the roommate's girlfriend nods at her and they head toward the car holding hands like little girls.

The woman in scarf and sunglasses flicks a smile at them, then says to Artie, "Be back here at eleven," opens the car's back door for the young women, who climb in.

Artie wants to say something, to call out, but can't think of what before the door slams shut and the car takes off. He watches it disappear from the lot.

"Well," his roommate says, a cloud of smoke surrounding the word.

Barry calls from the car. "You guys want to get something to eat? There's a diner across from the mall."

The roommate shakes his head, "I'm going to stay here," tugs a copy of their college newspaper, of which he is editor, from his back pocket. The headline reads: IMPEACH JOHNSON.

"I'll stay with you," Artie says.

"No, go with your brother."

"In-law," Artie says. "You sure?"

His roommate nods, adjusting his wire-framed glasses.

Barry says, "C'mon, Artie, I'm starving."

The diner is all hard surfaces, tiled floor, tin ceiling, metal cases filled with cakes and pies that look as if they are made of Styrofoam, cold fluorescent lighting, disinfectant thickening the air.

Artie slides into a booth, drums his nails on the scratched Formica tabletop.

"Coffee?" the waitress asks, thirtyish, eyes smudged as if she is exhausted or wearing last night's mascara.

Barry nods and she fills his cup. Artie says, "Tea," the idea of coffee nauseating. Barry orders two eggs over easy with bacon and hash browns, rye toast.

"How about you, Artie?" he asks.

"Can't eat."

"C'mon. Eat something."

Artie sighs, says, "One egg, scrambled. Toast, whole wheat."

When the waitress leaves, Barry says, "Don't worry, it'll be fine, it's not a big deal."

Artie is about to say *Are you kidding?* but the waitress is already back with his hot water and tea bag. A few minutes later she delivers their food. He eyes the eggs, clots of yellow and white, pushes the plate aside, pries a small butter container open and scrapes it onto a piece of toast while Barry shakes ketchup onto his eggs and potatoes, tears open three packets of saccharine for his coffee.

Artie watches Barry eat, ketchup on the edges of his brother-in-law's mouth while he talks, thinking how his businessman father had given him the $500 needed for today without hesitation, without the usual criticism or the ongoing question: "What are you going to do with a degree in *art?*"

"Be an artist," Artie always says, though he has no idea what *being an artist* means or requires.

He wonders if his father has told his mother about the money. He figures he has; his parents are close.

"Does my sister know?" Artie asks.

"I had to tell her something," Barry says, staring into his coffee.

Artie finishes his tea. "We should get going."

"It's only ten."

Artie sags back against the booth's plastic, stares at the large wall clock above the chrome counter, ticking off seconds. He tries not to think about what's going on, what she is going through, if she will be okay; he's heard many bad stories.

Barry starts to say something but Artie cuts him off. "Let's go," he says.

"We're only five minutes away," says Barry, but Artie is already edging out of the booth.

The windows of the roommate's rental car are fogged.

Artie raps on the glass, simultaneously wiping away the icy mist, the frost starting up again. His roommate flinches, cracks the door, says, "Guess I dozed off," the newspaper with IMPEACH JOHNSON crumpled in his lap. "What time is it?" He takes off his glasses, rubs at his eyes.

Artie can't believe the guy fell asleep. He feels as if his nerve endings are electrified, his mind sparking. He walks to one end of the parking lot and back, replaying everything—Hope crying as she told him she was two months late—"and I'm never late"—asking around until he got a name—everyone seemed to have one—making the call and the way he felt in the phone booth on Commonwealth Avenue, small and scared as the unidentified man on the other end of the line told him the cost, where and when to meet.

He is sweating inside his coat though it's frigid, his face pricked by icy needles. He thinks: *What if something goes wrong?*

Barry ambles over, tells him to relax, pats his shoulder.

The three of them huddle together, a helpless trio of boys with no idea of what to do, what to think, how to imagine what is going on. Artie grubs another cigarette from his roommate, blows smoke rings into the bitter winter air.

Barry says, "It's freezing," heads back to his car, but Artie and his roommate do not, pacing and smoking until the black car rounds the corner and comes to a stop. The back doors open and the girls get out.

Artie thinks, *She's alive!*

He runs toward her, notes how pale she looks, gets an arm around her and asks, "Are you okay?"

"I feel—empty," she says, and sags against his chest.

His roommate's girlfriend, Rochelle, is crying as they get into their rental.

No one says goodbye.

In the back seat of the car Artie and Hope hold hands but look in opposite directions as Barry drives them to Newark Airport for a flight back to Boston where they are both in school.

Hope thinks about the appointment she has tomorrow with a gynecologist, who will check her out, someone she's never met, a recommendation from a girlfriend who has assured her that the doctor will be "cool." How many stories has she heard about botched abortions, about women who could never bear children again though she is not sure she wants to have children, not after this.

"Everyone okay back there?" Barry calls over his shoulder.

Hope doesn't answer. She curls up, arms across her belly, crying softly now, like a mewing kitten, Artie's hand resting lightly on her back.

On the flight Hope falls into a deep sleep and Artie watches her, still the observer, looking for signs of what she has gone through.

Back in Boston things are strained and he just wants everything to be the way it was, carefree, easy, two young people in love, but it isn't; Hope is moody, wounded, seemingly mad at him and she doesn't want to do anything, no movies, no parties and he is beginning to resent it. He keeps asking her if she is okay; she is always crying.

It is several weeks before she tells him the details.

It was a house, a small private home with a room decked out like a doctor's office but there was no sheet on the metal table which was stained and rusty and the doctor—if that's what he was—was smoking!—his cigarette ash falling onto the table, onto the floor, and the place looked so dirty—and the woman, the one who took the money, was his assistant, maybe his wife or girlfriend—I can't remember if either of them wore gloves but I don't think so. The woman kept telling me it would be okay and held my hand—Oh, I remember now, I can feel her hand in mine—she wasn't wearing gloves, both of them smoking as they attached my legs to stirrups, and all I kept thinking was . . . I am going to die.

Artie listens, afraid to say anything wrong because once when he said, "But you *wanted* to do this," she snapped: "No one *wants* to have an abortion!"

The roommate and his girlfriend break up soon after. "She was always mad at me," he says to Artie, "and what did I do?"

"Well," Artie says, his tone slightly mocking: "You *did* get her pregnant," and they almost smile the way young men do because there is something powerful in the idea that a man can get a woman pregnant—a way to prove you are a man.

Five years later Artie and Hope marry and she supports him through graduate school by teaching and they have one child and lose another to a miscarriage, but they never talk about the abortion.

Artie loses touch with his roommate, but one day, thirty years later, he is reading his monthly college newspaper, an article titled "Where Are They

Now: The Student Radicals," an interview with his roommate who refers to "my husband" and how he has always been gay but how "back in the day, you could call for the impeachment of the president of the United States—and I did—but admit I was *gay?* Not a chance."

Artie lays the paper aside, processes this new information—that his roommate, who got a girl pregnant, a girl who had an abortion along with Hope—was gay. He feels sad that his roommate could not tell him and sad that he didn't understand what Hope was going through and sadder still that everything his generation fought for feels as if it could be lost.

JONATHAN SANTLOFER is a writer and artist. He has published five novels, including the *The Death Artist*, the Nero Award–winning *Anatomy of Fear*, and many short stories. He has been editor/contributor of several anthologies as well as the *New York Times* bestselling serial novel *Inherit the Dead*. His artwork has been exhibited widely in the US, Europe, and Asia, and is in such public and private collections as the Art Institute of Chicago, Tokyo's Museum of Contemporary Art, and the Newark Museum, among many others. Santlofer is the recipient of two National Endowment for the Arts grants and serves on the board of Yaddo. His memoir, *The Widower's Notebook*, will be published by Penguin Books in July 2018. Visit Jonathan at www.jonathansantlofer.com.

The Walk

About his children, something was wrong.

This came to Denny Pelletier as he walked alone on the road one night in late December. It was a chilly night, and he was not dressed for it, having only a coat over his T-shirt, with his pair of old jeans. He had not intended to walk, but after dinner he felt the need in him arise, and then later, as his wife readied herself for bed, he said to her, "I have to walk." He was sixty-nine years old and in good shape, though there were mornings when he felt very stiff.

As he walked, he thought again: something was wrong. And he meant about his children. He had three children; they were all married. They had all married young, by the age of twenty, just as he and his wife had married young; his wife had been eighteen. At the time of his children's weddings—the last, his daughter's seventeen years ago—Denny did not think about how young they were, even though now, walking, he realized that it had been unusual during that time for kids to marry so young. Now his mind went over the classmates of his children, and he realized many had waited until they were twenty-five, or twenty-eight, or even—like the really handsome Woodcock boy—thirty-two years old when he married his pretty yellow-haired bride.

The cold was distracting and Denny walked faster in order to warm up. Christmas was two weeks away, and yet no snow had fallen. This struck Denny as strange—as it did many people—because he could remember his childhood in this very town in Maine, and by Christmastime there would be snow so high he and his friends would build forts inside the snowbanks. But tonight as he walked, the only sound was the quiet crunching of leaves beneath his sneakers.

The moon was full. It shone down on the river as he walked past the mills, their windows lined up and dark. One of the mills, the Washburn mill, Denny had worked in starting when he was eighteen; it closed thirty years ago, and then he had worked in a clothing store that sold among other things rain slickers and rubber boots to the fishermen and to the tourists as well. The mill seemed more vivid to him than the store, the memories of it, though he had worked there not nearly as long as he had at the store. But he could remember with surprising clarity the machines that went on all night, the loom room he worked in; his father had worked as a loom mender there at the time, and when Denny began he had been lucky enough to go from sweeping the floors for three months to becoming a weaver and then, not long after, a loom mender as his father had been. The earsplitting noise of the place, the frightening scoot a shuttle could take if it got out of place, whipping across the cloth and chipping pieces of metal—what a thing it had been! And yet it was no more. He thought of Snuffy, who had never learned to read or write, and who had taken his teeth out and washed them in the water trough, and then a sign had been put up: NO WASHING TEETH HERE! And the jokes about Snuffy not being able to read the sign. Snuffy had died a few years ago. Many—most—of the men he had worked with at the mill were now dead. Somehow, tonight, Denny felt a quiet astonishment at that fact.

And then his mind returned to his children. They were quiet, he thought. Too quiet. Were they angry with him? All three had gone to college, and his sons had moved to Massachusetts, his daughter to New Hampshire; there seemed to be no jobs for them here. His grandchildren were okay; they all did well in school. It was his children he wondered about as he walked.

Last year at Denny's fiftieth high school reunion, he had shown his eldest boy his yearbook, and his son had said, "Dad! They called you *Frenchie*?" Oh sure, Denny said, with a chuckle. "It's not funny," his son had said, and he had gotten up and walked away, leaving Denny with his yearbook open on the kitchen table.

Times changed.

But Denny, who had turned to walk along the river, now saw his son's point: to be called "Frenchie" was no longer acceptable. What Denny's son had not understood was that Denny had never had his feelings hurt by being called Frenchie. As Denny kept walking, digging his hands deeper into his pockets, he began to wonder if this was true. He realized: what was true was that he, Denny, had *accepted* it.

To accept it meant to accept much: that Denny would go to work in the mills as soon as he could, it meant that he did not expect himself to go on to school, to pay attention to his studies. Did it mean these things? As Denny approached the river, and could see in the moonlight how the river was moving quickly, he felt as though his life had been a piece of bark on that river, just going along, not thinking at all. Headed toward the waterfall.

The moon was slightly to the right of him, and it seemed to become brighter as he stopped to look at it. Is this why he suddenly thought of Dorothy Prescott?

Dorie Prescott had been a beautiful girl—oh, she was a beauty! She had walked the halls of the high school with her long blond hair over her shoulders; she was tall and wore her height well. Her eyes were large, and she had a tentative smile always on her face. She had shown up at the end of their sophomore year, and she was the reason Denny had stayed in school. He just wanted to see her, just wanted to look at her. Otherwise he had been planning on quitting school and going to work in the mill. His locker was not far from Dorie's, but they shared no classes, because Dorie, along with her astonishing looks, had brains as well. She was, according to teachers and even students said this, the smartest student to have come through in a long time. Her father was a doctor. One day she said, "Hi," as they were at their lockers, and Denny felt dizzy. "Hi there," he said. And after that, they were sort of friends. Dorie hung around with a few other kids who were smart, and those were her real friends, but she and Denny had become friends too. "Tell me about yourself," she said one day, after school. They were alone in the hallway. "Tell me everything." And she laughed.

"Nothing to tell," Denny said, and he meant it.

"That's not true, it can't be true. Do you have brothers and sisters?" She was almost as tall as he was, and she waited there for him while he fumbled with his books.

"Yeah. I'm the oldest. I have three sisters and two brothers." Denny finally had his books and he stood and looked at her. It was like looking at the sun.

"Oh wow," Dorie said, "is that wonderful? It sounds wonderful. I only have one brother and so the house is quiet. I bet your house isn't quiet."

"No," said Denny. "It's not too quiet." He was already going out with Marie Levesque, and he worried that she would show up. He walked down the hall away from the gym where Marie was practicing—she was a cheerleader—and Dorie followed him. So at the other end of the school, near the band room, they talked. He could not now remember all they said that day, or the other days, when she would suddenly appear and they headed toward the band room and stood outside it and talked. He did remember she never said he should go to college, she must have known—of course, "Frenchie"—he did not have the grades, or the money, to go; she would have known because of the classes they were not in together, just as he knew she would go to college.

For two and a half years they did this, talked maybe once a week. Mostly they talked during the basketball season when Marie was practicing in the gym. Dorie never asked him about Marie, though she'd have seen him in the halls with her. He saw Dorie with different guys, always a different fellow seemed to be following Dorie, and she'd laugh with whoever it was, and call out, "Hi, Denny!" He had really loved her. The girl was so beautiful. She was just a thing of beauty.

"I'm going to Vassar," she said to him the spring of their senior year, and he didn't know what she meant. After a moment she added, "It's a college in upstate New York."

"That's great," he said. "I hope it's a really good college, you're awfully smart, Dorie."

"It's okay," she said. "Yeah, it's a good college."

He could never remember the last time they spoke. He did remember that during the graduation ceremony, when her name was called, there had been some catcalls, whistles, things of that sort. He was married within a year, and he never saw Dorie again. But he remembered where he was—right outside the main grocery store here in town—when he found out that she had finished Vassar and then killed herself. It was Trish Tucker who told him, a girl they had been in school with, and when Denny said, *"Why?"* Trish had looked at the ground and then she said, "Denny, you guys were friendly, so I don't know if you knew. But there was sexual abuse in her house."

"What do you mean?" Denny asked, and he asked because his mind was having trouble understanding this.

"Her father," said Trish. And she stood with him for a few moments while he took this in. She looked at him kindly, and said, "I'm sorry, Denny." He always remembered that too, Trish's look of kindness as she told him this.

So that was the story of Dorie Prescott.

Denny headed back to his house; he went up Main Street. Over him came a sudden sense of uneasiness, as though he was not safe; and in fact the town had changed so much over these last years that people no longer strolled around at night as he was doing. But he had not thought of Dorie for quite a while; he used to think of her a great deal. Above him the moon shone down; its brightness continued, as though the memory of Dorie—or Dorie herself—had made it so. "I bet your house isn't quiet," she had said.

And suddenly it came to Denny: his house was quiet now. It had been getting quieter for years. After the kids got married, moved away, then gradually his house became quiet. Marie, who had worked as an Ed Tech at the local school, had retired a few years ago, and she no longer had as much to say about her days. And then he had retired from the store, and he didn't have that much to say either.

Denny walked along, passing the benches that were near the bandstand. A few leaves scuttled in front of him in the harsh breeze. Where his mind went he could not have said, nor how long he had walked. But he suddenly saw ahead of him a heavy man bent over the back of a bench. Almost, Denny turned around. But the large body was just draped over the back of the bench—such an unusual thing—and appeared not to be moving. Slowly Denny approached. He cleared his throat loudly. The fellow did not move. "Hello?" Denny said. The man's jeans were slightly tugged down by the way he was hanging over the bench, and in the moonlight Denny could see just the beginning of the crack of his ass. The fellow's hands were in front, as though pressed down on the seat of the bench. "Hello?" Denny said this much more loudly, and still there was no response. He could see the fellow's hair, longish, pale brown, draped across his cheek. Denny reached and touched the man's arm, and the man moaned.

Stepping back, Denny brought out his phone and called 911. He told the woman who answered where he was and what he was looking at, and the dispatcher said, "We'll have someone right there, sir. Stay on the line with me." He could hear her speaking—into another phone?—and he could hear static and clicks and he waited. "Okay, sir. Do you know if the man is alive?"

"He moaned," Denny said.

"Okay, sir."

And then very shortly—it seemed to Denny—a police car with its blue lights flashing drove right up, and two cops got out of the car. They were calm, Denny noticed, and they spoke to him briefly, and then went to the man who was draped across the back of the bench. "Drugs," said one of the policemen, and the other said, "Oh yeah."

One of the policemen reached into his pocket and brought out a syringe, and in a flash—it seemed to Denny—the policeman injected the man, in his arm, in the crook of his elbow, and very soon the man stood up. He looked around. It was the Woodcock boy.

Denny would not have recognized him, except that his eyes, deep-set on a handsome face, looked at Denny and said, "Hey, hi." Then his eyes rolled up for a moment, and the policemen had the fellow sit down on the bench. He was not a boy any longer—he was a middle-aged man, and yet Denny could think of him only as a kid in his daughter's class years ago. How had he turned into this person? Large—fat—with his longish hair and all doped up? Denny stayed where he was, looking at the back of the fellow's head, and then an ambulance drove up, siren screaming and lights flashing, and within moments, two EMT men jumped out, and spoke to the policemen, one of the policemen saying, Yes, he had injected him with naloxone right away. The two EMT men took the Woodcock boy's arms and walked him into the ambulance; the door shut.

As the ambulance drove away, one of the policemen said to Denny, "Well, you saved a life tonight," and the other policeman said, getting into the car, "For now."

Denny walked home quickly, and he thought: it was not his children at all. This seemed to come to him clearly. His children had been safe in their childhood home, not like poor Dorie. His children were not on drugs. It was himself about which something was wrong. He had been saddened by the waning of his life, and yet it was not over.

Hurriedly he went up the steps to his house, tossing his coat off, and in the bedroom Marie was awake, reading. Her face brightened when she saw him. She put her book down on the bed, and waved her hand at him. "Hi there," she said.

ELIZABETH STROUT is the author of six books of fiction, most recently *Anything Is Possible* and *My Name Is Lucy Barton*, a #1 *New York Times* bestseller. Her other books include *The Burgess Boys*, *Abide With Me*, and *Amy and Isabelle*, which was nominated for the PEN/Faulkner Award and also won the Art Seidenbaum Award for First Fiction. In 2009 her book *Olive Kitteridge* won the Pulitzer Prize. She divides her time between New York City and Maine.

DEBORAH KASS is an artist whose paintings examine the intersection of art history, popular culture, and the self. Her work is in the collections of the Metropolitan Museum of Art, the Museum of Modern Art, the Whitney Museum of American Art, the Solomon R. Guggenheim Museum, the Jewish Museum, the Museum of Fine Arts, Boston, the Cincinnati Art Museum, the New Orleans Museum of Art, the Smithsonian National Portrait Gallery, and the Fogg Museum at Harvard, as well as other museums and private collections. Kass's work has been shown nationally and internationally, including at the Venice Biennale, the Istanbul Biennial, the Museum Ludwig, Cologne, and the Andy Warhol Museum. Her monumental sculpture *OY/YO* in Brooklyn Bridge Park became an instant icon, appearing on the front page of the *New York Times*, currently installed at the North 5th Street Pier in Williamsburg. Kass was inducted into the New York Foundation for the Arts Hall of Fame in 2014. Her print *Vote Hillary* was an official commemorative print for Hillary Rodham Clinton's presidential campaign.

Vote Hillary

Silkscreen on Stonehenge 320-gram paper

Stop & Shop

"Follow me, kid," Ray Mammola said, pushing through the basement door, untying his long white apron with one hand and using the broken nail of his dirty thumb to slide an inch of blade out of his box cutter. "You tell anyone where I am and I'll use this on you." His low, snarly voice was worse than a shout. "Think I don't know how? Ask anyone. I was in Korea. I seen action."

He slipped his apron over his head and heaved a wide carton labeled BATH-ROOM TISSUE from a stack, placing it end to end with another carton the same size, all the while swinging the box cutter and talking, his voice seeming to come out of his big broken nose.

"Them crates behind me—it's all jerkins in jars, so heads up when you stack them on the deck."

His back was turned to me, and now with wicked swipes of his knife he began slicing off the top of one of the wide cartons, in a sequence of thrusts, each like a beheading, zipping off, first the long side, then the ends, leaning and slashing the cardboard until he'd freed it, lifting it open like a lid. His recklessness excited me, but I was thinking, *Jerkins?*

"You were supposed to do this yesterday."

"I had soccer practice."

For the first time he turned around to face me, still holding his box cutter.

"You any good?"

"No."

He laughed, not in a mocking way, but a surprised appreciative laugh. My answer surprised me, too.

"All this stuff needs to be priced. You got your stamp?"

"Right here." I tugged open the roomy front pocket of my apron and showed him the upright chrome contraption, with numbers on adjustable wheels that printed the price on the jar cap or box top in purple ink.

"Twenty-nine cents each," he said, turning away and starting on the second carton, knifing the top open with what seemed savagery calculated to intimidate me. But his efficiency with the box cutter thrilled me. "After that, there's more cases for the pickle aisle, them quart jars of kosher dills and the sweet ones, them bread and butters. Start loading the dolly." Still running the blade through the top edge of the cardboard carton he said, "By the way, what's your name?"

"Andy Parent."

"You a Canuck?"

"I'm an American."

"Okay." He leaned over the open carton and began to claw out rolls of toilet paper, creating a long trough through the middle in each carton and then cutting a section of cardboard where the boxes met. Concentrating on this he didn't say anything more, and now he was digging out loose toilet rolls, putting some on the basement floor and rearranging others in the end-to-end cartons.

"And the jars of mustard," he said. "Same aisle. Price them, stack them on the dolly. Stock all them shelves, and look alive."

I tried not to look shocked as he climbed into the bed-like trough he'd made in the two cartons of toilet paper. He knelt and then lay down and sank into the softness, yawning, extending his legs, folding his arms across his chest like a corpse in a coffin, still holding his box cutter in his fist.

"Remember what I said, Andy." He wagged the box cutter at me, then closed his eyes and seemed to gargle luxuriously and go to sleep.

Upstairs, I was stocking the shelves in the pickle aisle, when Mr. Crotty the store manager approached me, looking fussed, pinch-faced, his thin cheeks glowing with exertion. His blue smock was a sign of his seniority, his name KEVIN CROTTY embroidered on the pocket.

"There's a black kid up front by the registers looking for you, Andrew. Keep it short." Saying *shawt* in the blunt Boston way was his being fierce. "This is a supermarket, not a social club."

I slipped the crate of gherkins that I'd held jammed between my chest and the shelf, and eased it to the floor.

"And where's Ray Mammola?"

"I haven't seen him."

"You sure?" He peered at me, the eyes and teeth of a small nibbling animal. His confident authority made me evasive and I found it easy to lie.

"Yes, sir."

He glared at me and in my lie I felt older, like a conspirator, an outlaw, doing whatever I wanted.

Roy Junkins was waiting behind one of the registers. He looked uncomfortable among the shoppers, dancing from one foot to the other as though controlling a soccer ball. He widened his eyes and said, "Coach Umlah sent me. I'm supposed to tell you we got an extra practice tomorrow for the Governor Dummer game."

"That's not for two weeks. Anyway, I'll be on the bench."

"Everyone plays. He'll put you in."

"For five seconds. Third string. First string wins the game. Roy, come on."

"We're unbeaten!"

"No thanks to me. Anyway I might have to work. I got promoted."

With a note of sorrow in his pleading voice, he said, "It's a team, Andre."

A blue figure twitched at the far end of the aisle, Mr. Crotty glaring at me. "Cheezit, Roy, I can't talk. Okay, I'll see you at practice on Monday."

That I got promoted was not an exaggeration. I had started in the summer rounding up shopping carts in the parking lot and hating it, especially on rainy days. I still attended soccer practice regularly and was on the verge of quitting the Stop & Shop when a new boy, Felix Perez, was hired and I was moved inside, bagging groceries, while Felix did the shopping carts. A month of that—and soccer games at Newton High and Phillips Academy—and the grouchiness of customers saying "Careful with my eggs" and "Don't put the Ajax in with my chicken." I was a servant, at a buck an hour, and ready to quit when I was moved again to help Ray Mammola, stocking shelves, and Felix was promoted to bagging.

Lying about Ray should have made me feel bad—Umlah the soccer coach had an honesty policy ("Hands up if you fouled someone"); but lying to Crotty had the opposite effect. It made me smile inside; it suggested that Ray trusted me. Roy Junkins was my friend, and he believed in the team, but he was a starter, and starters were gung ho. I was not gung ho about anything, not even the Stop & Shop.

I had just raised the crate of gherkins to my chest again—the technique was to use both hands—when Mr. Crotty approached me again.

"I don't want your friends coming around. Understood?"

I wondered if he was saying that because Roy was black, but I said, "Yes, sir."

"And what about Ray?"

"I still haven't seen him." It now gave me pleasure to defy him.

"He was supposed to tell you to take a break. You can go at four." It was another fierce Boston pronunciation, *foh-wah.* "I want you back here in twenty minutes." He hesitated, then said, "Another thing, Andrew. Mr. Hackler the area supervisor is making a surprise inspection."

"When would that be, sir?"

"Did you hear me? A surprise inspection. We don't know. That's why it's called a surprise."

"Right. I see what you mean."

"Everyone on their toes, like a fire drill." And he walked away, narrow shoulders, narrow head, blue floppy smock. *Fy-ah drill.*

The United Food and Commercial Workers Union, of which I was a fifteen-year-old card-carrying member, specified that we workers were to be given a twenty-minute break for every three hours on the job. The break room was in the back, next to the employee toilets. On my way through the stockroom I stole a jelly donut out of a box, and a carton of chocolate milk out of the dairy case. The break room was clouded with cigarette smoke and chatter, three men at the card table, Omar from produce, Vinny the head of the deli section, and Sal the butcher talking together. Sal's bloodstained apron over his knees gave him a kind of brutal majesty. Felix sat eating something from a paper plate he held close to his face.

"What's that supposed to be?" Sal asked Felix.

Still eating, Felix said, "My mother tamale."

"I want a taste of your mother's tamale," Sal said, and the others laughed, though Felix went on eating.

"Where's Ray?" Vinny said. When I stammered he said, "You can tell us! Never mind—we know he's sleeping."

"Right," I said, and saying that made me feel conspiratorial again.

"We need a fourth here—you'll do," Vinny said to me, and began to deal cards for whist, the usual break-time game. As he snapped the cards down he pointed to my jelly donut and said, "If you'd eat that you'd eat anything."

We played whist quickly, gathering and piling tricks. We were in the middle of one hand, when Ray flung the door open, yawning. He took the cards from me, tapped my shoulder. I got up and gave him my chair.

"Did he ask?"

"Two times."

"What did you tell him?"

"What you told me," I said. "And there's going to be a surprise inspection from Mr. Hackler."

"Hitler," Ray said. "The mystery man."

"I'll give him a hit on the head," Vinny said.

Sal said, "Ray was in the service. He never leaves his buddies behind." He nudged Felix, "Get it?" Then he said to Ray, "That's his mother's tamale he's eating."

Staring at his cards, Ray said, "Who dealt this mess?"

Soccer practice the following Monday started with a prayer, and then Mr. Umlah, the coach, read from his clipboard the order we'd be playing. I was third string, so I sat on the bench, between Fesjian and Brodie, waiting for my turn. Coach Umlah came over and sat heavily next to me, bumping my shoulder as a rough companionable greeting.

"Missed you on Saturday, Andrew."

"I had to work."

"Work is a good character builder, but so is teamwork. The Governor Dummer game is coming up. We have a good chance to stay unbeaten."

Roy Junkins had drifted over and heard what the coach had said. "We'll win, no sweat."

"We'll win if we work together as a team," the coach said in a reprimanding voice.

"Bunch of percies," Roy said.

"I don't want to hear that word," Coach Umlah said.

The belief at our public high school was that only wealthy, overdressed, fairly stupid boys went to private school, their parents buying them an education; and poorer, tougher, more athletic, highly motivated boys attended public schools. I was a junior, a wing on the soccer team, skinny and not particularly strong, but fast enough and accurate when I had an opening in the box, which was seldom. Because so few high schools had soccer teams, we played the Tufts freshmen and the Harvard freshmen and the prep schools, and we had not lost a game.

"This is a team," the coach said at the end of the Monday practice. "Everyone plays. No heroes, no glory boys."

But I knew that when the game was on the line only the first string mattered, and the scorer would be a hero, and it wouldn't be me. Still, I ran, I kicked, I headed the ball, Coach Umlah praised me, and afterward we went to Brigham's for ice cream.

We crowded into a booth and talked, the usual hot whispers about the names for different parts of girls' bodies. I glanced at the soda jerk, Joe Slubsky, digging his scoop into the tubs of ice cream; his apron, his high-crowned paper hat, saying nothing. His English was poor, his face was averted, but he was listening and I knew what he was thinking. We were sweaty, and dirty from practice, and monkey-like, talking about what girls looked like naked, and he half envied us and half hated us.

School, and more soccer practice the rest of the week, Friday evening at the Stop & Shop; Friday night at my grandmother's house because her home was walking distance from the store—I got out of work too late to take the bus home. Sunday church, Monday school and more soccer, then the weekend, Stop & Shop.

Work, school, and soccer seemed like a whole life but it was a life I barely inhabited. I was somewhere else, helplessly yearning, yet constantly reminded—by Crotty, my teachers, the coach—of their importance. Your future, they said. But my future was a blank. How do you get from here to there?

My dilemma was easy to explain, if anyone cared to hear it, though no one did. I was not adrift, I was stuck. Being fifteen years old was like being on the lower floor of my grandmother's three-decker house where, on the floor above, a man was speaking to a woman out of earshot in a different room, who couldn't hear him, but was talking back to him, though he couldn't hear her. To a shout, which might be tedious or revealing, or shocking, or life-altering, or wise, each yelled, "What?" Other people, too, calling to each other on the floor above them, each deaf to the other.

Though I could hear every word, they didn't know I was listening, or even that I existed. But that was not my dilemma. My dilemma was: what do I do with all the things I am hearing?

It was an intimation, not that I would be a writer in any important way, but that writing this down might help ease my mind.

My secret dreams were of success, of good fortune, of heroism, and I could not understand how work or school or soccer mattered. No heroes, no glory boys, the coach had said. Yet I longed to be a hero—not a scorer on the field, or a brain at school, but big and dangerous. Heroism was like a blessing. It came unbidden: you were chosen, you were someone reckless, like Ray Mammola saying, "Who dealt this mess?" and some of the other men at the Stop & Shop, Vinny saying, "I'll give him a hit on the head," and Sal with his bloody apron, and Omar in produce who could juggle oranges, and Felix who brought me a tamale to try. The Stop & Shop was a team, too, but a more complex one, old guys and young guys.

I loved the heartlessness of their talk. I remembered Ray's gusto with the box cutter, swiping open the cartons of toilet paper and making himself a nest for a nap. He was a full-time employee, in charge of inventory, but he also broke the rules and got away with it. Mr. Crotty needed him, which was why he was always looking for him.

"Kevin Crotty," Ray said. "He doesn't know whether to scratch his watch or wind his ass." He was the talker, the smoker, the winner at whist. Seeing Felix and me coming out of the toilet he said, "You guys comparing tools?"

"Stop and Shop's merging with the A and P," he said one day. "They're going to call it the Stop and Pee."

Sal said, "What's with this surprise visit of the supervisor?"

"Hackler," Vinny said.

"Hitler," Ray said. "No one knows what he looks like. He sneaks in and rats on us. If I ever find out who he is I'll pinch his head off."

Except for Felix and me, they were all older men. They smoked, they swore, they teased each other, Ray talked about Korea.

"Best feeling in the world?" Ray said. "It's not sex. It's after a long march, all day. You sit down and take your combat boots and socks off. And you feel the breeze on your toes and you wiggle them a little."

They jokingly complained about their wives. "My wife says to me—"

"My day off tomorrow," Vinny said.

"Doing anything special?"

"Stay home. Make babies."

I tried not to smile, but it excited me to hear it.

Sal said, "It's not how long you make it, it's how you make it long."

"I live in a duplex," Ray said, studying his cards. "You know, those places attract some strange people. Last year I was sleeping in my room and three naked women were pounding on my door. They just would not stop."

"So what did you do?" Omar asked.

"I got up and let them out." Then Ray pitched a card. "Trumps!"

"Union meeting on Sunday," Sal said.

This was news. The men conferred about going there, who would ride with whom. Ray nudged me. "You can go with us, kid. You, too, Felix the Cat."

• • •

On that Sunday I went to church with my grandmother. I sat, I stood, I knelt. Even the flowers and the candles on the altar seemed meaningless, but I went through the motions; I prayed, feeling that no one was listening. My old unanswered question: How do you get from here to there? "Have faith," the priest said in his sermon. Back at her house, my grandmother said, *"Andre, qui sont ces hommes?"*

They were in the car, beeping the horn.

"Les gars—mes amis. Gram, I got a union meeting."

Ray and Vinny in the front, me and Felix in the backseat. Ray was ending a story he was telling Vinny about a Korean. "I'm drunk, I'm bollocky, I tip her over and she screams, 'Me no dog!'" Then to me and Felix, "Hey, the union men!"

I had no idea where we were going and was surprised when, after half an hour, we were in open country—narrow roads, a pond, woods in leafless November.

"They hold these things in the sticks," Ray said. "They can get a bigger function room that way, more parking, cheaper rental."

The hall was a high school gym, filled with Stop & Shop workers, all older men, sitting on folding chairs, talking among themselves, until a man on a platform called them to order. A banner over his head was lettered UNITED FOOD AND COMMERCIAL WORKERS 595.

"We want more money," someone called out.

"Keep your shirt on," the man said.

It was not a team, it was more like an army—I thought of them as soldiers, and many of them like Ray had probably been soldiers, either in World War II or Korea. They had the heavy faces and the look of exhaustion and the tattoos and the toughness. One man near me was saying to another, "I've gotta put food on the table." This wasn't soccer or school; it was serious, their livelihood. They were all sorts, mainly white guys, and some women—I saw Veronica and Lucy from the cash registers talking with other workers—but also some black men conferring in a group, and Omar who had found some Arabs to joke with, and Felix relieved to be in a secure corner of Puerto Ricans.

"Maybe they'll vote you a buck ten," Ray said.

Men called out from the floor, some stood and made short speeches, which provoked arguing and interruption, and all of it happened in the air above my head, the talk, like the smoke, until a vote was taken and hands were raised and the men roared.

"Know what I like about this?" Ray said, leaning back, relaxed, his hands behind his head. "Guys like Hitler aren't allowed in. He's management. We're the workers."

"And like I say, if he tried to get in I'd give him a hit on the head," Vinny said.

"If we knew what he looked like," Ray said.

Darkness had fallen by the time the union meeting ended. In the car, driving away, Ray murmured to Vinny, "Why not?" and farther down the road suddenly slowed the car and drove into a field at the far end of which was a tent decorated in Christmas lights.

"Where are we?" I asked.

"Little surprise," Ray said. "It's a carnival."

He parked and we walked across the shadowy field of wet grass to the tent, where we slipped through a thick canvas flap. A man just inside asked us for fifty cents and gave us a ticket. Inside, men in heavy coats pressed against a bare, brightly lit stage. Some of them I recognized from the union meeting, all of us standing on grass. Behind me, Felix muttered, "*¿Qué pasa?*" After a while, a few of the men began calling out in impatience.

Then an old man in a derby hat and bow tie and a striped vest walked onstage and said, "Welcome, gentlemen. Welcome! Let me present Miss Lana Lane!"

A woman wearing a red two-piece bathing suit and a beret appeared from the curtains, did a few dance steps, and then paced back and forth, wiggling a little and laughing and waving. The men hooted at her. One called out, "Take it off!" She teased with her fingers and then reached behind her, unhooked her top, and held it carelessly against her breasts, teasing some more, while the men shouted. I was shoved on both sides by the much bigger men, and then pushed nearer the stage, separated from Felix. The woman quickly revealed her bare dog-nosed white breasts, then laughed and skipped offstage.

"Gentlemen!" It was the man in the bow tie, returning. He fanned his face with his derby. He was white-haired, with yellow teeth in a wicked grin. He said, "If you want to see more, it'll cost you more."

He shook his derby hat and handed it into the crowd of men. They passed it around, putting money into it, mostly coins, and some dollar bills, like a collection in a church.

And that was when it struck me that this tent and this gathering was like a church—the attentive men, the flickering lights, the stage like an altar, the old man like an evil priest, taking the money, the painted pictures on the tent walls adding to the effect of a ritual or a mass.

"Once again, Miss Lana Lane!"

The woman walked onstage from the side curtains. She was entirely naked, except for her black beret, the first live naked woman I had seen in my life. Without her high heels she was flat-footed, and walked like a soldier, her yellow feet slapping the stage. Her breasts were small, her legs heavy. She lifted her arms and laughed, then walked in a circle, smiling, not looking vulnerable in her nakedness, but defiant in the glare of lights and the raw upturned faces of the men.

The tent became more church-like, the men very quiet, concentrating, leaning and looking closely. When the woman walked near the edge of the stage I could see her flesh move, her arms, the nod of her breasts, the shake of her fattish thighs.

The silence of the men seemed to embolden her. She laughed out loud and snatched off her beret and rubbed it against her belly and the hair between her legs, seeming to exult. She held the beret on her secret spot, clutching herself, then flung it.

The beret sailed like a Frisbee towards me. I reached to smack it away and when it snagged on my fingers, a shout went up from the men.

"The kid caught it!"

By then the naked woman had walked offstage. Ray said, "Show's over," then "Put it on, kid."

I tugged the beret on my head.

"On you it looks good." Ray led the way back to the car and slammed the door and sighed. "Work tomorrow."

"I got school."

"Good. Get an education, kid," he said. He squirmed in the front seat and faced Felix and me. "Or you'll end up like us."

Monday: soccer practice. I wore the beret ("What's that supposed to be?" Coach Umlah said) but did not tell anyone where I'd gotten it or what I'd seen, even afterwards, at Brigham's, when they were talking about girls' bodies and sex and how to buy Trojans at a drugstore.

"Big game Saturday," Roy said.

We practiced twice that week, doing sprints, exercises, headers, Umlah saying, "This is a team. Never mind that it's Governor Dummer. We can win if we all work together."

That Friday afternoon, Roy said, "See you tomorrow on the bus"—he meant the game, the trip to Governor Dummer.

And I thought, maybe—my last game. I'll ask Crotty for Saturday off. Going with the team, I knew I wouldn't play any serious time, I wouldn't score, I'd be on the bench; but it also meant that I would not make myself conspicuous by staying away.

"We're collecting for the March of Dimes," Mr. Crotty said, before I could ask for Saturday off. He handed me a large can with a slot cut in the top. "I want you at the front door."

A cold dark early evening in raw mid-November, I wore my winter coat over my apron, and my beret pulled over my ears; and I shook my collecting can, "March of Dimes!" ambushing the shoppers leaving the store pushing their carts, wagging the can at them, making it jingle. I wanted it heavy with coins to present it to Mr. Crotty: "Look—it's full," as a way of getting the day off on Saturday to go with the team to Governor Dummer.

By seven thirty, the can was weightier, the coins slewing and clanking. I obstructed the departing shoppers and surprised them with the can. The store closed at nine, then empty shelves to be restocked; and the walk to my grandmother's, and the game tomorrow. I did as I was told, I obeyed and behaved; yet I did not see where, in any of this, I belonged.

As I shook the can I imagined the soccer game, and saw myself on the bench. Shake, shake. Shelves to stock. Shake, shake. School, work, shake, shake. The can like the derby hat at the carnival show, filling with money. I didn't know what to do. Shaking the can was like shaking dice, trying to discern my fate, yet my belief that I was no one, I was nowhere.

Absorbed in this I did not see the man approach me. I looked up and there he was, standing before me, too near, as though he knew me. He wore an overcoat and a wool scarf, and a green Tyrolean hat, a feather in the band. Carrying a briefcase, he peered at me through his gold-rimmed glasses, closing in, taking charge, as though he had chosen me and had an answer for me.

I held him at bay with my collecting can, tipping it towards him.

"March of Dimes, sir."

He leaned over the can and put his face against me, but he was not looking me in the eye.

"I don't think I like your hat."

He had a well-fed face, smooth cheeks reddened in the cold, his green velour hat tipped to the side, with the jaunty feather. He was too close to me— ridiculously so for a customer; nor did he have a coin for the can.

I said in his voice, "I don't think I like *your* hat."

Instead of laughing, as I'd expected, he panted and became fierce. "You don't get it." He panted some more. "I don't like your hat."

"Right." It seemed a game, a contest in which it was a mistake to back down. "And I don't like yours." It seemed when I said it that his hat did seem much sillier than mine.

"Don't talk to me that way," he said, one of his front teeth snagging on his lower lip.

"You just said that to me!"

It seemed unfair—perverse. He could criticize my hat, but I couldn't say the same to him? And all this time I was darting at the customers, calling out, "March of Dimes," so they could put a coin in my can.

"I like my hat," I said, though until he had spoken to me I had barely been aware that I had it on. His mention of it provoked the memory of the carnival tent, and the naked woman, her flinging the beret at me, and Ray saying, "Put it on, kid."

"Just who do you think you are?" the man said, his cheeks tightening with anger. He began to shout at me, then gagging on his words and seeing that he was attracting attention he seemed to think better of it. He rushed back into the store. I sneaked a look inside and saw that he was talking to Mr. Crotty, chopping the air with his hand. When he was done, he rushed towards me, red-faced, his arms working, swinging his briefcase, and for a moment I thought he was going to hit me. But he hurried past, into the parking lot, and the darkness.

Mr. Crotty was beckoning. I went inside.

"What happened out there?" *Out thay-ah.*

"The man said, 'I don't like your hat.'"

"And?"

"I said, 'I don't like *your* hat.'"

Mr. Crotty winced, then said, "What else?"

"He kept saying it. So did I. I thought he was joking."

Mr. Crotty did not look angry. He wanted detail, and the detail did not distress him—it seemed to fascinate him, as though he was hearing something reckless and bold, a kind of daring, and that he had found out something new and interesting about me. He did not want to betray his fascination yet I could see it a little like mirth, in his eyes, and in his nibbling lips.

"Do you know who that man is?"

"No, sir."

"He's Mr. Merrick Hackler, the area supervisor. He's very important. He doesn't joke. It was his surprise inspection." Mr. Crotty did not seem angry, and yet I fully believed I was going to be fired. But that did not dismay me. Being fired was something final—it was a direction, like knowing I was no good at soccer. "You upset him."

I said, "What should I do?"

"Don't do it again, ever." *Evah.* Was he smiling?

Now and then I'd had a glimpse of what it meant to be an adult, like seeing Ray at the carnival, or hearing "Making babies" or "I've gotta put food on the table." Now I saw for the first time that Mr. Crotty had suffered, and hated Hackler, and that I had been an instrument of his revenge. But he could not reveal it to me. He looked sad and beaten, like a servant in his blue smock-like coat with his odd name stitched on the pocket. I had thought of him as powerful, yet he was like the rest of us, Ray and Omar and Sal and Vinny and Felix—perhaps more punished.

By the next coffee break everyone knew—more proof that Mr. Crotty had approved, probably told the assistant manager, who spread the word. The others were laughing when I entered the room.

Ray put his arm around me. "Tell us exactly what you said to Hitler."

I told it haltingly. In this telling I was older and stronger, and the story more orderly; I was defiant and satirical, a wise guy.

"Know where the kid got that hat?" Ray said, and described the carnival, the naked woman, using the dirty words that came naturally to him.

As though coaching me, he said, "Sit down, kid. I want to hear it again. This is beautiful." He quieted the room with a shout. "Listen!"

I told the story again, more slowly, and in this version I was a hero, standing my ground, and Hitler was red as a beet and had spittle on his lips.

"I don't like your hat!" Vinny shouted.

"I thought Crotty was going to fire me."

"They can't fire you. You're union! We're all union. We'd go on strike!"

Early the next day, Saturday, Roy Junkins appeared in the aisle I was stocking with jars of grape jelly, standing on a stepladder. He was carrying his gym bag. "The bus is leaving at noon." And in his sorrowing voice, "Andy."

I kept putting the jars on the shelf, sliding them back, lining them up.

"The team needs you."

I kept the crate against my chest. I didn't think of how I'd mastered this, pricing them and then using both hands. I thought of the break in about an hour, and a donut, and two or three hurried games of whist, and Vinny and

Ray and Sal and Omar and Felix, and "Who dealt this mess?" I'd listen to their talk, and maybe they'd ask me to tell the story again.

"I'm working," I said.

Roy shrugged, and scuffed the floor with his foot to show me he was disappointed. He looked small from where I stood on my ladder, as I watched him walk away, burdened by his gym bag bumping his leg, down the aisle, past Ray, past Mr. Crotty, out the door to the game. Then I resumed stocking the shelf, and whistling.

PAUL THEROUX, former grocery store employee in Medford, Massachusetts, of Native American, French, and Italian ancestry, is the author of more than fifty books—novels, short stories, travel books, and essays. His most recent books are *Deep South: Four Seasons on Back Roads* and the novel *Mother Land*. His *Figures in a Landscape: People and Places* will be published in 2018.

LITTLE HOUSE ON THE PRAIRIE HOLDING COMPANY LLC

DAVID STOREY is an artist who lives and works in New York. He makes paintings, drawings, and prints that compound and condense the interaction of image and abstraction. His work is in such collections as the Museum of Modern Art and the Boston Museum of Fine Arts. He has been awarded fellowships from the Guggenheim Foundation and the National Endowment for the Arts, in addition to residencies at Yaddo and the MacDowell Colony. He currently teaches at Fordham University in New York.

Little House on the Prairie Holding Company LLC

Acrylic on paper

The Way We Read Now

On the feed it's the hurricane, great big snaking lines of folks in need—and they want you to write a story? On the feed it's words in a grown man's mouth—someone's president—about let me tell you how much your suffering is affecting my budget. On the feed it's the familiar and unsurprising but no less dispiriting spectacle of the morally bankrupt lording over the willfully, colonially bankrupted and tossing out paper towels to the masses. Five frowny faces and seventeen angry, but mostly it's thumbs-up.

On the feed it's a clip called *RuPaul Explains the Difficulties of Being a Go-Go Dancer in 1988*. Vintage VHS footage of Ru tipsy backstage after a gig, wearing a cream bodice and a platinum wig, both candid and performing, pleading and defiant, aware the camera is rolling but looking elsewhere, around the room, for her shoes, her lipstick, before finally giving up the search. *Oh well, I don't have any lips, I kissed them away.* She's looking at herself in the makeup mirror, talking to herself, talking to her reflection, about these men she allows to touch her all over, for the money, but then she finds the camera to land the line, to ask the question *Isn't that terrible?* And it's the tone here that kills, at once searching and mocking and vulnerable, amused and amusing. Is it terrible? *What else is there? What am I going to do? I'm in show business. I've got to live, right?* Ru asks, and a disembodied voice from behind the camera jokes, consoles, maybe commands, *You've got to live, Ru. You've got to let men touch you.*

On the feed a message: *Are you okay? Do you know folks there?*

And then you're looking for that older message, from months ago, to which you've yet to respond—but no, it was a post to your wall—a second cousin, a decade younger than you, saying she's not sure the two of you have ever met, but hey, you're family, right? And isn't the world just so small and strange—she saw something you posted and she wanted to find you, and she did, could. But you have met—she was too young to remember, but you remember well, the apartment in Brooklyn, this sweet little toddler, bumping cars around the kitchen floor, her mother's people from China, her father's from Puerto Rico, and it's a fucking stunning combination in this kid, she looks beautiful and like she will look more beautiful still, but already drugs and old wounds and bullshit and sexuality are pulling you away from the family and you don't suspect you'll see her again, and maybe for her too there will be drugs and bullshit and beatings and sexuality—or perhaps not—but it's the unknowing that causes you to ache for her, what the world can and might do, and what's going to become of all that potential? And then there she is, or this profile pic of her, next to her post on your wall, and all the years apart flatten into the present and you're looking for the seed of the girl in the woman, and nothing to say, searching and finding ain't nothing to say, thumbs-up—no, heart. No heart.

Return to Ru, who is herself returning to her reflection, conversing with herself about a prior conversation she had earlier in the night, again with herself: *I said to myself, I said, you know, what do you want? These guys, they look at you, they want to touch you, charge them for it, dammit.* And then back out, back to the camera, and again that tone—searching, defensive, defiant—*What's the damn wrong with that, huh?* Then Ru's back whispering to herself, turning away from the camera, about some protective mats they've placed on the bar, protective mats that the dancers must use because of recent renovations made by the owners to the surface of the bar itself. *They've touched it up*, Ru says, *Made it new.*

On the feed, superimposed, a notification that someone unmet yet friended has donated their birthday to the Red Cross, which reminds you of posts you've half read about how the Red Cross is everything from a bureaucratic money-suck to actually doing evil in the world, a think piece referring to another think piece about the Red Cross, and there's one about the Jones Act, which you've always understood to be another colonial tool in the subjugation of the island—but hold on, there's a think piece about the merits of protectionism—

and everyone has a point. The lawyers have a point, the doctors have a point, the marchers have a point, the mamas, the daughters, the nobody's mamas, the nobody's daughters, the politicians, the peaceniks, but you can't help laughing at one comment by a dyke friend that says, simply, *My pussy ain't pink, though.* And here's a piece about colorism in Latinx communities, and here's one on whether Afro-Latinx folks have a right to the n-word, which is really just someone mad at Cardi B. And J. Lo's throwing some money to the First Lady of Puerto Rico, many thumbs-up and a prayer-hands emoji, and Beyoncé's doing . . . something . . . you're scrolling too quickly past the celebrity efforts to investigate, but you do notice that someone has posted a reminder in the comments of the J. Lo post that, yo, the Red Cross is straight-up evil.

Read about the Puerto Rican diaspora, read again about the Spanish American War, and now the algorithm has you figured, on the feed it's Rough Riders, Buffalo Soldiers, articles about statehood, independence, somehow there is Lolita Lebrón, elegant, restrained by three cops after shooting up Congress, but mostly it's images of folks wading through water, a clip of San Juan's mayor all at once overwhelmed with grief and insisting on resilience. Try to make it real, research where best to send money—send money—fearing any aid, any resources accumulated, will be repaid, with terrible interest, terrible appreciation, over the months and years ahead. Vulture capitalists have vowed to pick the island dry, this is a promise, una PROMESA, but try instead to believe in the potential of a reconstruction.

You're supposed to write a story, but on the feed somebody's president is popping off about nuking millions. On the feed somebody has sold a book, somebody has failed to sell a story, to place a poem, somebody you love has been held by TSA because trans and arrested and released, and this is the first you're hearing about it. You try to picture them in a faraway city.

Are you okay? Do you know folks there?

Trump Furious Tillerson Refused to Deny Calling Him a Moron Trump Rolls Back Obama's Birth Control Trump Talks of Calm Before the Storm Donald Trump Is a Textbook Racist Trump: Puerto Rico "Quite a sight. We are doing a great job there."

Try to make it real. Try to resist making it all into a lyric, into blurred lyri-

JUSTIN TORRES

cism, look at all the photos, watch all the clips, all the cell phone footage somehow uploaded despite a total blackout on the island, all the articles, the op-eds, try to make it real, real, real, real, real—but on the stream Roberta Flack asks, *Compared to what?*

Thirty years ago RuPaul is tipsy backstage, and it is a semiprivate moment, a moment of transition, coming from being a persona, from being a public figure fully available, in all senses of the word, for public consumption, and now retreating to a private space, backstage. 1988, the end of Reagan, the thick of the AIDS crisis, ACT UP, the thick of the response. This is all well before RuPaul became a household name—and while it's impossible not to see the seed of the future media empress Ru in this twenty-something queen, it must have been equally impossible for this young Ru to know with any certainty what the future held. *Isn't that terrible?* she asks, and the way she's asking, it's as if she's keeping herself from knowing the answer.

On the feed someone leaves a sincere comment in reply to a cynical post: It's easy to live like we know what the future is going to be like; we don't.

They've touched it up, Ru is saying, *Made it new.* You're watching the first half of the clip on a loop, like a broken record, until you realize what's grabbed you—in less than a minute, the very meaning of "touching up" has been transposed from an act of violation to one of improvement. Ru has performed a kind of linguistic alchemy. Maybe that's the extent of what's possible; maybe that's the goal.

Cousin, I've been watching news of Maria's aftermath come in for a week now. I've been drinking a lot and feeling immobilized, and also thinking of you.

Cousin, I thought I might tell you about the time we met, when you were very young and you were bumping toy cars around the kitchen floor. No, that's imprecise; there was only one car, which you ran very deliberately along the linoleum, tracing the pattern.

Cousin, we did meet once, I was a teenager, and was terrified I'd die from exposure.

Cousin, you've got to live. You've got to let men touch you.

Cousin, I've been trying to parse out what the difference is between believing in progress and believing in potential.

352

Cousin, you've got to make it new.

A million false starts, but at least you've begun; something semiprivate about the desire to be pierced and not numbed by the news of the world, about keeping a cynical kind of knowingness at bay, about finding new ways to use the old words.

Cousin, I wondered what life was like for you at home, your parents were very handsome and only kids themselves, and I wondered what would become of you.

Still the wrong tack, but closer. Anyway, you can act, write, start, now, now the response begins.

But on the feed breaking news, another mass shooting, they say this one shatters the record.

JUSTIN TORRES's first novel, *We the Animals*, a national bestseller, has been translated into fifteen languages and was recently adapted into a feature film. He lives in Los Angeles, where he is Assistant Professor of English at UCLA.

Don't Despair

When I was a child growing up in middle Georgia, I thought all white men were like Donald Trump. They too seemed petulant and spoiled, unhappy with everything they were not the center of, brutal toward the feelings of those beneath them and comfortable causing others to act out of hate. How did we survive this?

I think of my father, a poor sharecropper with eight children, so desperate for change in a system that left his family in danger of starving that he walked to the polling place, a tiny, white-owned store in the middle of nowhere, to cast the first vote by a black person in the county. Three white men holding shotguns sat watching him, for niggers were not supposed to vote and they were there to enforce this common law. My father voted for Roosevelt and a New Deal he hoped would also apply to black people.

I come from a line of folks who chose to live or die on their feet. My four-times-great-grandmother was forced to walk chained from a slave ship in Virginia, and carried two small children that probably weren't hers all the way to middle Georgia. There she was forced to work for strange, pale people who could only have appeared to be demons to her. She was given as a wedding gift to a young married couple when she was advanced in age; what the story of this event was is a mystery to this day. All we know is that she lived to bury all these people and that it is she who is remembered.

My aunts and uncles learned trades, tailoring, bricklaying, masonry, house building, whatever was allowed for black people, and raised their children in homes of stability and even comfort, while the white world beyond their neighborhoods attempted to squeeze them into corners so tiny that to the majority of citizens of the cities they lived in, they did not even exist.

How to survive dictatorship. That is what much of the rest of the world has had to learn. Our country has imposed this condition on so many places and peoples around the globe it is naive to imagine we would avoid it. Besides, do Native Americans and African American descendants of enslaved people not realize they have never lived in anything but a dictatorship?

In this election we did not really have a healthy choice, as is said in a commercial for something I vaguely remember. Or, as a friend puts it: "The choice was between disaster and catastrophe." If this puzzles you, here is the next step of my counsel: Study. Really attempt to understand the people you are voting for. What are they doing when they're not smiling at you in anticipation of your vote? Study hard, deeply, before the internet is closed, before books are disappeared. Know your history and the ways it has been kept secret from you. Understand how politicians you vote for understand your history better than you do, which helps them manipulate your generations. It is our ignorance that keeps us hoping somebody we elect will do all the work while we drive off to the mall. Forget this behavior as if it were a dream. It was. In some way, many of us will find, perhaps to our astonishment, that we have not really lived until this moment.

Our surprise, our shock, our anger—all of it points to how fast asleep we were.

This is not a lament. It is counsel. It is saying: we can awaken completely. The best sign of which will be how we treat every being who crosses our path. For real change is personal. The change within ourselves expressed in our willingness to hear, and have patience with, the other. Together we move forward. Anger, the pointing of fingers, the wishing that everyone had done exactly as you did, none of that will help relieve our pain. We are here now. In this scary, and to some quite new and never-imagined place. What do we do with our fear?

Do we turn on others, or toward others? Do we share our awakening, or only our despair?

The choice is ours.

• • •

ALICE WALKER is an internationally celebrated writer, poet, and activist whose books include seven novels, four collections of short stories, four children's books, and volumes of essays and poetry. She won the Pulitzer Prize in Fiction in 1983 and the National Book Award.

Her work has been translated into more than two dozen languages, and her books have sold more than fifteen million copies. Along with the Pulitzer Prize and the National Book Award, Walker, in 2006, was honored as one of the inaugural inductees into the California Hall of Fame.

Her upcoming nonfiction work, *Gathering Blossoms Under Fire: The Journals of Alice Walker*, will be a book of lasting significance—tracing her development as an artist, human rights activist, and intellectual.

EDMUND WHITE

Learning American Values

He had grown up in Rome as a sort of prince, not titled but rich, handsome and charming, with a lively personality, a fast car, beautiful clothes and the best hands in Italy—lean, articulated, muscled, neither too big nor too small and dusted with dark hairs that turned golden at the tips. If deer had hands they would have resembled his, so strong and elegant were they, undeniably but not oppressively male. He lived in a palazzo.

He was called Bobby Fitzjames and yes, he was American, but that was just a technicality since, as his parents discovered when he turned eighteen, his visiting American godparents revealed he couldn't speak English. Or not very well, though his accent was perfect—casual, slangy, a bit nasal. It was just that he didn't know many English words. His mother was rich, the daughter of the president of a major American corporation who'd left her a portfolio bristling with stocks. His father was penniless and an "artist," though no one could have named his exact art.

Bobby was the complete Roman who slurred his words like a greengrocer on the Campo de' Fiori, who wore his well-tailored dark jackets over his shoulders, who knew you should kiss a lady's hand only in private and never touch it with your lips. He didn't hesitate to park his car on the sidewalk, he didn't know how to swim but he could ride a horse, and he seldom read a book though he could work Proust's name and Elsa Morante's convincingly into a conversation with an elder statesman. He drank but had never been drunk, he ate pasta at lunch and at dinner but seldom gained a gram, women were more likely to seduce him than vice versa and he'd played an extra just for fun in an Italian crime thriller.

Sure, he'd spent the summers of his eighth and ninth years near Blue Hill, Maine, in his mother's family's compound, and at that time he was fluent in American boy talk. After all, he'd played with his Murphy cousins day and night (his mother was a Cleveland Murphy). But soon after that his parents had become so Europeanized and his aunt had been accused of murdering her husband; his parents had decided it was "easier" to go to their villa on Stromboli and Bobby, apparently, had soon forgotten his English. He even pronounced his own name with the dark Italian *o* as in *monster* not *hobby*.

His father was especially shocked about Bobby's lack of English, was embarrassed by it since he thought it reflected badly on him and showed he'd neglected his son. Bobby's mother, who was half-Italian (her mother), was the real Italophile and was secretly proud of his language deficiency, since she pretended to grope for words in English and always spoke to him in Italian (though he begged her not to talk around his school friends with her weird accent; he seldom brought anyone home).

He was enrolled at Brown, full of Eurotrash, true, but at least English was the campus language and the Europeans were more likely to be French or Greek than Italian and they spoke airport English to each other. His father chose Brown because he'd gone there when it was decidedly less chic and all male. Bobby wasn't a good student but his father got him in by funding an Olympic-sized pool anonymously, permitting the school to sell naming rights to someone else. The father feared naming the pool would embarrass Bobby. Brown, unlike Bobby, wasn't very well endowed and would admit rich but dim students if their parents were generous.

When Bobby arrived on campus at the beginning of September he was shocked by how hot it still was outside; he'd never known anything like it. He was impressed by the large squirrels bounding about. He thought it was strange the houses were built of wood (fire hazard) and had no walls between their lawns and he found the food served in the cafeteria nearly inedible. Soon he discovered a little Italian restaurant with a fake brick facade and, inside, watery paintings of Naples and Vesuvius behind niches filled with white plastic busts of Roman emperors. That's where he ate lunch and dinner, though he disliked the large portions and the inevitable sides of spaghetti. They also had the curious custom of serving a lemon peel with espresso. And the old unshaved waiter was friendly but could speak only Neapolitan.

The first few days Bobby was unbearably lonely. He was used to going out every night with a "fine group" of ten or twenty to one of the restaurants near the Pantheon. In Rome he spent the afternoons on the phone putting together that evening's group. He liked going everywhere *en bande* because that meant they could play musical chairs and you were never trapped with a bore. He was also used to cracking jokes and making funny sound effects that kept everyone amused. Here, in America, he was afraid to leave his room, and his chubby roommate, George Thomas from Alabama, slept all the time and smelled of Clearasil.

Then one day he heard two students speaking Italian and he jumped in with "*Come mai!*" ("How can that be?") and they lit up, too, and soon they were fast friends and he was driving them around in his vintage Cinquecento. They were both from Bergamo and knew Roman kids he knew. It was such a relief to speak his own language! They dressed well and didn't wear jeans or have fat asses.

He invited them to his Italian restaurant, which he described as "kitsch," and they brought along an extra girl for him, though they didn't say that. The girl, Rebecca, was very short but had big breasts and she could sort of speak Italian since she was "majoring" in Italian but "minoring" in something else, something to do with women, and had spent a summer in Perugia. She was fearless about speaking Tuscan and always smiled her way broadly through her linguistic faults and hesitations. They admired her for that.

She was a little too sure of herself and had learned almost to shout "*Dai!*" or "*Dai*, Bobby," which meant something like "Get off it" in English, as she explained. She said it so often that American customers looked at her with a queasy grin as if she might actually be homicidal.

When they were alone, just to be nice he offered to get them a hotel room (he couldn't take her to his dorm since George was sure to be there asleep).

"A hotel room?" she said in English. "What for?"

He stretched and said with a smile, "I feel like a little blow job."

She said, "How horrible! I don't feel safe with you."

"Not safe? What do you mean?"

"I thought we were friends."

"A blow job"—*un pompino*—"is very friendly, isn't it?"

"But I haven't agreed to that. We haven't discussed it. I have lots of issues with nonconsensual sex."

Bobby (crushed): "I thought you'd like it."

He'd imagined he was doing Rebecca a favor with her big butt under a dark skirt and her beginner's Italian and the way she shouted "*Dai!*" When he didn't want to fuck a girl but wanted to be generous with his body, he'd let her suck him off while he watched porno on his phone.

Since he didn't know many Italian speakers, he invited Rebecca out again in spite of her mysterious scruples. She suggested a Thai place on I-95 but he couldn't eat such spicy food and they ended up returning to his favorite Italian restaurant. Unfortunately, they started talking politics. "I don't see what's so bad with Trump. Berlusconi is no better and lots of my Roman friends have dads who wear ankle monitors." He had to mime *ankle monitor* since neither knew it in the other language.

"But aren't your parents liberal? Everyone at Brown is liberal. I mean, sure, they might own some iffy stocks that exploit Asian workers, but basically they're liberal."

Bobby wasn't sure what *liberale* meant, but wasn't that the neofascist, pro-Catholic party that used to be led by Gianfranco Fini? They had studied that in high school. "I don't think the liberals exist anymore, but yes, my parents are liberal, they're very Catholic and had an audience with the German pope."

Now it was Rebecca's turn to look confused. She shrugged and screamed, "*Dai*, Bobby, how can you say Trump is okay? He's anti-gay, at least I think he's anti-gay, and he only pretends to be religious but knows nothing about the Bible and he's surrounded by Wall Street crooks."

Bobby couldn't grasp her point. He wasn't exactly anti-gay and he'd even fooled around with a handsome swimming star in Puglia, a guy, but they had both been discreet; no reason to emphasize your temporary vices. And didn't everyone *pretend* to be religious and observe only their Easter duties? Like everyone at Brown pretended to be bisexual? He wasn't sure what *crook* meant in English (they seemed to have settled down in English) but Wall Street, that was good, wasn't it? Rich guys? Big shots? "So what if he's anti-gay? I'm not gay."

"You're not very sensitive. I mean about these sensitive issues."

He put his beautiful hands on the table, as if they were all aces. Surely they were sensitive. They usually won any argument. He smiled. "How about that hotel room? Have you changed your mind?"

"*Dai*, no means no! I'm afraid of sex if the guy is aggressive. I don't feel safe with you."

"We could have real sex, not just a blow job, if you want." He didn't know how to be more accommodating.

"But you're a big guy. You might rape me. I'm very afraid," and she rattled around with a pill box and swallowed three pink pills.

"You like to get high, I see. I have some good marijuana."

"I am not getting *high*, as you put it. These are *prescription meds*. I need them to stay sane. Several of my friends are on mood stabilizers. Some have OD'd. One is in rehab. I'm seeing a therapist. I'm afraid of you."

"But why exactly?" He had never frightened anyone before; he couldn't help preening over it slightly.

"What if you wanted to rape me? You're a big man—two hundred pounds?"

He couldn't convert that into kilos and just shrugged.

Over saltimbocca at their kitsch restaurant, he asked politely, "Are you interested in real politics, like equal pay for equal work or no more nukes, or just these lifestyle . . ."—he trotted out his new word—"issues?"

"What do you mean?"

"Like Ms. for Miss, things like that, marijuana freedom?"

"But those are the real issues of our day. By the way, this veal tastes great. I used to be a gluten-free vegan till last week, but I felt I needed my strength to fend off men here on campus."

"Are you interested in emigrants drowning or things like the husband's turn to do the dishes?"

"Both! I'm concerned by all of it."

"Babies drowning off Lampedusa the same as Ms. or Miss?" He was genuinely puzzled.

They argued right through the panna cotta, then he drove her home in silence. As she got out she pecked him on the cheek and said, "That's not a come-on but just out of friendship." He wondered why they never split the bill if she was so friendly.

The next time they got together she told him about her "work." "For my senior thesis I'm looking at body modifications."

"Tattoos? How about when you get older and they start to sag?"

"No, silly, like gold bars in tits, penis extenders, chastity cages, clitoris modifiers, castration—"

"Ouch!" he said. "You've actually castrated men?"

"I do not participate in the subject's genital choices; I just record them."

"Photos?"

"Would you like to see some?"

"Why not?"

Brown really was the home of freaks. Maybe he should have gone to Villanova, though he'd heard they had a black statue of Our Lady sitting beside a pile of aborted fetuses. Were all Americans crazy?

When he saw Camilla, the Italian girl, the next day on campus (he was heading to his course on the music of Bartók), he asked her to meet him in an hour for a coffee.

She was only ten minutes late. As soon as she sat down, she asked, "How's it going with Rebecca?"

He puffed his cheeks out and said, "Buh! She showed me some of her photos of clitoridectomies."

"I didn't know she was into African studies."

"It's for her minor in women's studies."

"Oh."

"She won't have sex because she says she's afraid of me."

"She just says that to get pills out of her shrink."

"I thought as much. *Mannaggia!* These Americans are crazy."

Camilla thought about it and said, "No, they just want to have an identity, which is a problem if you're a rich white girl like Rebecca. Everything over here is organized by identity politics."

"Rich?"

"Like you. Not a billionaire."

"But if she's rich why doesn't she like Trump?"

"It's not chic. It's like all those rich people in our grandparents' generation, the Brigate Rosse kidnapping bankers."

"Well, I want to be chic. Are only leftists chic?"

"Yes, but you can't want real social change. No one at Brown talks about class. They all pretend to be middle class. *Comunque*—anyway—most of them are very rich."

"If you're chic at Brown, what do you believe?"

"First and foremost, you're for transexuals' rights. No one actually knows one."

"Hermaphrodites?"

"No, men who've become women."

"My parents knew someone like that in London who married a lord and opened a restaurant."

"Then, you should like Native Americans."

"Native . . ."

"Indians." She held her hand to her mouth and made a battle whoop. "Whoo-whoo-whoo. No one knows any of them, either."

"Are blacks chic, too?"

"Very. But don't mention they're poor. You want to have a race analysis, not a class analysis."

"And all this stuff about gender?"

"Oh, you should study that next semester. It's impossible to understand it unless you've studied it. Like trigonometry. But it's essential. Tell Rebecca you're studying it and she might feel *safe* with you."

On their next date at Napoli, Bobby was determined to seduce Rebecca. Her odd resistance to him made her more desirable. He wouldn't even look at porn on his laptop as he fucked her. Was she very hairy, he wondered? He could always fantasize about Ginevra, the model he'd met on Capri.

"I've learned so much from you," Bobby said smoothly.

"Really? Like what?" She melted and smiled.

"You've taught me how sex must be consensual. Otherwise it's rape."

Her little smile reminded him of the Mona Lisa's. "What else?"

"How we are all androgynes. I had sex with a man in Puglia."

"Excellent! You know many people here at Brown identify as nonsexual?"

"I don't have an identity," Bobby said mournfully. "I'm American but Italian—I feel like a . . . a hollow man."

"Don't let people tell you that! That's outrageous! You're a very real, very dear man and I esteem you very much. I can see how you've been persecuted, as an Italo-American. Please don't think I'm denying your oppression."

Half an hour later they'd checked into the hotel. Rebecca had never realized the male organ—unmodified—could come in such a large size. She imagined few women could accommodate it, which must be a real problem for him. A deformity. She was determined not to say anything, to be accepting and to act as if nothing were abnormal.

EDMUND WHITE has written novels, short stories, biographies, memoirs, travel books, collections of reviews, plays—and five poems! He lives in New York with his husband, the writer Michael Carroll.

AMERICAN CIVIL LIBERTIES UNION

Anthony D. Romero
Executive Director

Dear Reader,

When I went to bed on the night of November 8, 2016, I knew I would be waking up to the fight of our lives. The election of Donald Trump as president of the United States presented an unprecedented threat to our rights and liberties. His administration's policies on immigration, voting, criminal justice, and LGBT and reproductive rights threaten to erode the freedoms that define much of what it means to be American.

As we prepared to challenge the administration's policies in the courts, millions came out to the streets to join the fight. Overnight, a new commitment to civic engagement was born. People joined women's marches across the country. They gathered en masse at the nation's airports when the president attempted to impose a Muslim ban. Among them were some of the finest writers and artists of our time. Their contributions and commitment to this struggle is displayed on these pages.

Literature and art have always framed our approach to the world. Stories can shape our attitudes toward race, class, gender, and identity. They offer us perspectives on the reality we experience, allow us into communities we don't know or understand, and force us to confront truths that we may not want to acknowledge. In a country that can seem like it's been divided into two separate worlds, each side unable to speak to or understand the other, stories have the power to bridge our divisions. Narrative has the power to broaden our appreciation of our shared identity as Americans.

America is unlike any other place on earth—a melding of people from the world over, a history of lofty ideals, and a commitment to realizing those ideals, even if it is through lurching progress, with intermittent setbacks and broken promises along the way. Progress comes only when we demand it and when we refuse to allow America's reality to fall short of its ideals. And I believe that as Americans, it is both our birthright and our responsibility to do so.

I am reminded of Arthur M. Schlesinger, Jr.'s book, *The Disuniting of America*, in which he observed: "What has held the American people together in the absence of a common ethnic origin has been precisely a common adherence to ideals of democracy and human rights that, too often transgressed in practice, forever goad us to narrow the gap between practice and principle."

At a time when the Trump administration is trying to redefine and limit what it means to be American, the artists and writers in this book are taking back that narrative. Through these stories, they reveal America's promise, failings, contradictions, and complexity. And they ask a question that has been central to the American experience for generations: How should we carry out the struggle to perfect this union?

Anthony D. Romero

Executive Director
American Civil Liberties Union

Acknowledgments

Occasionally, what begins as a simple idea to do something worthwhile can become big and messy and incredibly difficult. When David Falk and I had the idea for this book we were (and remain) altruistic, though the process of making it a reality was more than either of us imagined. As someone very smart once said, "It takes a village," and it did. There were innumerable obstacles and more than a few times when the struggles of working with so many people in such a short amount of time came close to overwhelming. What always saved us, what propelled us forward, was that something—some*one*—always stepped up to the plate and made it all worthwhile and meaningful once again.

We chose the anniversary of the Women's March as our publication date because it was, like this collection, a coming together of people, a way to say "No, we will not accept this!" Hundreds of marches took place across the country, and hundreds more marches bloomed around the world in support.

To see an ambitious literary and art project like this to completion—in an utterly unreasonable amount of time (a matter of months!)—took a tremendous group effort. What you now hold in your hands is the result of that hard work and creative energy, which would not have been possible without the help of so many people we'd like to thank, who willingly (eagerly even!) signed up for this Herculean task.

At Simon & Schuster, we wish to thank:

Susan Moldow and Tara Parsons, for signing off on the idea of the book when it was still just an idea. Thanks to David's assistant and publishing manager, Isabel DaSilva, for shepherding the great many piecemeal parts through and on to production, and meticulously keeping track. Thank you to Tamara Arellano, Laura Cherkas, and Josh Cohen for the breakneck yet ever wise copyediting. Thank you to Erich Hobbing for the elegant and thoughtful

369

interior design, and to Kathryn Barrett for her diligence. We're grateful for Mike Kwan and Anna Campbell, for masterfully guiding the book through the production process. To Lourdes Lopez, Emily Remes, and Elisa M. Rivlin, thank you for your wise counsel. Thanks to Amanda Mulholland and Julie Ficks, for keeping all the managing editorial trains running on time (and occasionally cracking the whip on us). Thank you, Paul Chong and Angela Hsiao, for (kindly) demanding planning. Thank you, Cherlynne Li, Daniel Rembert, and Ervin Serrano (with Jasper Johns!), for the timeless cover design and the numerous "final" iterations. Thanks to Shida Carr and Brian Belfiglio, for their keen and ardent publicity efforts. And very special thanks to the always creative and clever Meredith Vilarello and Kelsey Manning for helping this special book find its audience.

So many people joined in with suggestions and help, in particular: Noreen Tomassi, executive director of the Center for Fiction, and Elaina Richardson, President of Yaddo; Richard Shebairo, Eamon Dolan, Craig Popelars, and Jenna Johnson, who generously offered ways and means to contact various people. Many, many thanks to the unflagging and incredibly generous Heidi Pitlor. I would also like to thank Todd Shuster and Jane von Mehren, who not only offered suggestions and help whenever possible but firmly believed in this project.

Looking back on our early correspondence for this project, one of our very first brain-pickings was to Carla Gray. Much too soon after, the world lost a truly extraordinary evangelist of books, a tireless advocate of authors, and a dear friend of booksellers and publishing people across the country. Thank you, Carla.

Of course this could not have happened without the extraordinary people at the American Civil Liberties Union: beginning with Michele M. Moore, along with the ACLU's tireless leader, Anthony Romero, who despite his incredibly demanding schedule has been as smart and compassionate as his words and deeds, and Stacy Sullivan, Danielle Silber, and Eric Vieland, who took the time to hear out a couple of guys who wanted to use words and pictures to make a beautiful and enduring statement about what's good and necessary and must be preserved in our country, and then helped them clear the path.

ACKNOWLEDGMENTS

Naturally there would be no book without the many writers and artists who donated their time and talent, and for that we thank them and praise their work and their generosity of spirit.

To the many friends and family of David Falk and Jonathan Santlofer, who offered advice, comfort, and their shoulders in times of stress, we cannot thank you enough—you know who you are.

In the end, this book is a true partnership between David and myself. We worked together to make an idea into something real and tangible. It is what we believe and what all of us must do to move forward—work together for something better—and we hope the book conveys that message.

Permissions

VIET THANH NGUYEN is the author of *The Sympathizer*, which won the Pulitzer Prize for fiction in 2017, as well as *Nothing Ever Dies: Vietnam and the Memory of War*, shortlisted for the National Book Award and National Book Critics Circle Award in nonfiction. A recipient of Guggenheim and MacArthur Fellowships, he also wrote the short story collection *The Refugees* and edited the forthcoming collection *The Displaced: Refugee Writers on Refugee Lives*.

JONATHAN SANTLOFER was born in Manhattan, grew up on Long Island, and though he has lived in many places, both in the United States and abroad, he always comes back to New York City, one of the most culturally and racially diverse cities in the world.

Both sets of Jonathan's grandparents were immigrants. His father's parents fled Poland to escape the Nazis and were forever grateful for their lives in America. His mother's parents, also Eastern European immigrants, met in a New York City shirt factory, got married, and raised six children in a crowded Bronx railroad flat. They taught their children and grandchildren to be kind, caring, and inclusive and they never stopped believing in equality for everyone or gave up on the American dream.

Jonathan grew up wanting to be an artist, went to art school, undergrad and graduate, and spent the first half of his adult life as a fairly successful painter. When a gallery fire destroyed nearly ten years of his artwork he started writing. His first novel, *The Death Artist*, about a serial killer in the New York art world, was an international bestseller. Since then, he has written several novels.

He has also edited and contributed to many anthologies and has even illustrated a few.

Jonathan continues to divide his time between writing and art. His memoir, *The Widower's Notebook*, will be published by Penguin Books in July 2018, and he is at work on a new novel.

Let America be America again.
Let it be the dream it used to be.
—*Langston Hughes*

Congress OF THE

begun and held at the

Wednesday the fourth of March, one

THE Conventions of a number of the State

or abuse of its powers, that further declaratory and restrictive clauses should be added: And as ex

RESOLVED by the Senate and

concurring, that the following Articles be proposed to the Legislatures of the several States, as amend

said Legislatures, to be valid to all intents and purposes, as part of the said Constitution; viz.

ARTICLES in addition to, and Ame

of the several States, pursuant to the fifth Article of the original Constitution.

Article the first..... After the first enumeration required by the first Article of the Constitution, there s

which, the proportion shall be so regulated by Congress, that there shall be n

until the number of Representatives shall amount to two hundred, after which

nor more than one Representative for every fifty thousand persons.

Article the second... No law, varying the compensation for the services of the Senators and Representat

Article the third..... Congress shall make no law respecting an establishment of religion, or prohibiting

assemble, and to petition the Government for a redress of grievances.

Article the fourth.. A well regulated militia, being necessary to the security of a free State, the

Article the fifth....... No Soldier shall, in time of peace be quartered in any house, without the consent